ALSO BY LEAH STEWART

Body of a Girl
The Myth of You and Me
Husband and Wife

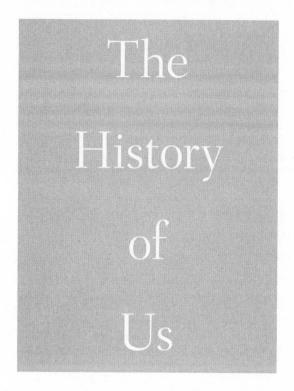

The History of Us

LEAH STEWART

A Touchstone Book

Published by Simon & Schuster

New York London Toronto Sydney New Delhi

★ Touchstone
A Division of Simon & Schuster, Inc.
1230 Avenue of the Americas
New York, NY 10020

First Touchstone hardcover edition January 2013

TOUCHSTONE and colophon are registered trademarks of Simon & Schuster, Inc.

For information about special discounts for bulk purchases, please contact Simon & Schuster Special Sales at 1-866-506-1949 or business@simonandschuster.com.

The Simon & Schuster Speakers Bureau can bring authors to your live event. For more information or to book an event contact the Simon & Schuster Speakers Bureau at 1-866-248-3049 or visit our website at www.simonspeakers.com.

Designed by Joy O'Meara
Map of Cincinnati by Alice Pixley Young

Manufactured in the United States of America

10 9 8 7 6 5 4 3 2 1

Library of Congress Cataloging-in-Publication Data

Stewart, Leah, 1973—
The history of us / Leah Stewart.
p. cm.
"A Touchstone book."
1. Brothers and sisters—Fiction. 2. Aunts—Fiction. 3. Adult children—Family relationships—Fiction. 4. Domestic fiction. I. Title.
PS3569.T465258W47 2013
813'.54—dc23
2012003018

ISBN 978-1-4516-7262-6
ISBN 978-1-4516-7264-0 (ebook)

For Eliza and Simon

The City is, indeed, justly styled the fair Queen of the West: distinguished for order, enterprise, public spirit, and liberality, she stands the wonder of an admiring world.

—B. Cooke, in the *Inquisitor and Cincinnati Advertiser*, May 4, 1819

"Why has he not done more?" said Dorothea, interested now in all who had slipped below their own intention.

—George Eliot, *Middlemarch*

Then & There

1993

Eloise Hempel was running late. She was forever running late, addicted to the last-minute arrival, the under-the-wire delivery, the thrill of urgency. That morning, unable to find a parking spot less than half a mile away, she'd jogged most of the way to campus in her painful high heels, slowing as her building came into sight in hopes that her breathing would normalize, the sweat at her hairline somehow recede, before she took her place at the front of the classroom. She was the professor. For two months now, she'd been the professor, and still she found it hard to believe that anybody believed that. Couldn't they see, these shiny young people who filled her classroom, how nervous she was? Couldn't they hear her heart's demented flutter? Hadn't they noticed the time she misspelled *hegemony* on the board? Didn't they think twenty-eight was ridiculously young to be teaching them anything?

No, because she was the professor, the one imbued with the mysterious authority of knowledge, the power to humiliate the students whispering in the back row. As she climbed the stairs inside her building students broke around her like water around a rock. Or maybe they were fish, spawning fish in casual but expensive clothes, and she was . . . what? She was the one trying to look older in a black blazer and a bun. Saying the word *professor* to herself made her smile in a way that people noticed, made them ask, "What are you thinking about?" and when that happened she had to concoct something amusing, something profound, because "I'm a professor at Harvard" would sound either arrogant or childish, depending on her audience.

She was hustling past the History Department office, her classroom visible, when she heard someone calling her name. She took a step back to stick her head inside the office door. Red-haired Kelly at the front desk was holding the phone, her hand over the mouthpiece. "This is actually for you," she said. "I was just about to transfer the call when I saw you go by."

Eloise hesitated, glancing at the clock on the wall behind Kelly's head. Only two minutes left before class.

"I think it's family-related," Kelly said, and Eloise sighed and approached with her hand out, prepared to tell her mother that not only could she not talk now but she had to stop calling her at school, for God's sake. Eloise lived nearly nine hundred miles away and couldn't help her mother with her grandchildren, who were staying with her while their parents were on an anniversary trip to Hawaii. It was no surprise that her mother, who was best suited to life in a sensory deprivation chamber, couldn't handle the three kids, even for a few days. But what did she expect Eloise to do about it?

She took the phone and flashed a pained smile at Kelly, who lifted the phone cord over her computer, adding length to Eloise's leash. "Mom," Eloise said, skipping *hello*, "I've got two minutes."

She rolled her eyes at Kelly. For some reason Kelly shook her head.

"Hi, Aunt Eloise," a child's voice said.

Surprised, and embarrassed by her mistake, Eloise raised her eyebrows at Kelly, who shrugged and then made a point of looking at her computer screen. "Theo?" Eloise asked. Theo—Theodora—was her sister Rachel's oldest child.

"It's me," the girl said. "Francine asked me to call you." Her voice was oddly flat.

Eloise frowned. It still irritated her that her mother had her grandchildren address her by her first name. Of course she didn't want to be a grandmother; she'd barely wanted to be a mother. She was a woman for whom the word *overwhelmed* was equivalent to *abracadabra*. She said it, then she disappeared. "Why'd she have you call?" Eloise asked. "Not that I'm not happy to talk to you." Theo was a remarkably adult eleven-year-old, but still it was a bit much to delegate the responsibility of complaining about the children to the children. Come on, Mom, Eloise thought. Keep it together for once in your life.

"My parents," Theo said.

Eloise turned away from Kelly, hunching into the phone. Something in the child's voice made her feel a need for privacy. "Your parents?"

"My parents," Theo said again.

Eloise heard her swallow. "Theo?" she asked.

"I'm sorry," Theo said. "I'm trying not to cry."

"Why?"

"Francine's in bed. Somebody has to look after Josh and Claire."

"Theo, please," Eloise said. "Tell me what's happened." Or don't, she thought. Please don't. The whole world had gone quiet. Her students were in her classroom. They waited in neat rows for her to arrive.

"My . . ." Theo abandoned the phrase. She tried again. "They were in a crash. They were in a helicopter. It was a helicopter tour, and it crashed. It crashed into a cliff."

In Eloise's mind, a helicopter bounced off a cliff and kept on whirring. "Are they all right?"

"Aunt Eloise!" Theo's voice was full of pained impatience. "They crashed into a cliff!"

The girl was trying not to say they were dead, that her parents were dead. Eloise understood that. But the fact that they were dead, that her sister, her sister—oh, Rachel! That she couldn't understand. "What do you mean?" she asked.

Theo took a breath. "Francine wants you to come home," she said.

Her sister was dead. No, no, no. Eloise couldn't think about that. She would think about that later. Here was the thing to think about now: her mother, her selfish, helpless mother, and the burden she'd placed on this child. "How could she, Theo?" Eloise asked. "How could she make you be the one to call?"

Theo didn't seem to understand the question. "Somebody had to," she said.

Eloise closed her eyes. She took a deep breath. She gripped the phone hard. "All right, Theo," she said. "Thank you for letting me know. I'll be home as soon as I can get there."

"Thanks, Aunt Eloise," Theo said. Her voice shook just a little as she said goodbye.

Eloise hung up the phone. She tried to smile in the face of

Kelly's curiosity like nothing was wrong. "Family stuff," she said. Then she went to class. Her feet just took her there. She walked in and said, "Sorry I'm late," as usual, and she arranged her books on the desk at the front of the room and her notes on the podium, and then she smiled at them, her students, and said, "So." They waited for her to begin. What was she supposed to talk about? Their faces were blinding. She dropped her gaze to the podium and noticed with detachment the way her hands gripped it, as if the room was shaking. How odd—her hands were beginning to recede. Were her arms getting longer?

"Professor Hempel?" someone said, and she looked up, startled to be called by that name.

Rachel had always been good in a crisis. Rachel had always taken care of her. Rachel would not have let her go to class. Rachel would not have chosen an eleven-year-old child to break the news, forcing Eloise to behave in this calm and unnatural way. Rachel would have let her go to pieces. Rachel would have expected her to. Instead Eloise taught her class, if not particularly well, and then when she got home she called the airline and booked a ticket for the last flight out that day, and then she packed. How long to pack for? She had no idea, so she took her biggest suitcase and stuffed it full. Then she made more calls—explaining, canceling classes. She used the phrase *family emergency*. All the while she watched herself with a bewildered combination of admiration and fear. She'd been possessed. Some other self controlled the movements of her body, the words that came out of her mouth, while her actual self trembled in a small and darkened corner of her mind. "You need to call a cab," she said out loud to herself, and then she went to the phone and dialed.

Cincinnati sprang itself on you all at once. Eloise forgot that, in between trips home. As you headed up the interstate from the airport in Kentucky, the view was nothing but hills, and then you came around a bend and—ta da! There it was, place of your birth, past-its-prime Rust Belt queen of the Lower Midwest, with a skyline and everything, just like an actual city. And then the house—for a while it had looked smaller than she remembered, but now, coming straight from her tiny Cambridge apartment, she saw it as huge. Gargantuan. Obscene. She stood on the sidewalk with her bag for a few minutes after the cab pulled away, staring at the house, *her* house, feeling an old, familiar urge to flee. Her father was dead. Her mother was self-involved, self-justifying, selfish, any variation you could imagine of self, self, self. Her sister was the one she came home for. Her sister who'd married young, had children, bought her own house in her hometown. Her sister's firm embrace, that shared look of amused recognition when their mother announced, after half an hour with the children, that she needed a drink. Her sister's calm and soothing voice, her sister's understanding and reassurance, her sister's love of exotic skin products, her one real indulgence, the jars and bottles arrayed in her bathroom, the way she'd smooth cool, thick, sweetly scented cream over the circles under Eloise's eyes. *There. That will fix everything.*

Eloise still had a key. Her rolling suitcase rattled over the front walk. She yanked it up the steps, bump, bump, bump, as reluctant as she was. The front door was ornate and beautiful and totally useless for keeping out the cold. Her mother talked every winter about *having something done* and then forgot her plans as soon as it was warm. Inside it was so quiet, Eloise closed the door as gently as she could, trying not to disturb. All the lights were off, all the blinds down. She started to call out, then thought better of it. She stood for what felt like a long time in the entryway, gazing up the grand staircase into the dimness of the second floor.

Even after all these years living elsewhere she knew where to step so the stairs wouldn't creak. Her mother's door was closed. Eloise knocked, heard a rustling from inside, and opened the door. Her mother lay on the bed, on her back, an arm thrown over her eyes though the room was dark. "Mom?" Eloise said from the doorway.

The arm came slowly away. Her mother blinked at her. "Eloise?"

"I'm here."

"Oh, thank God," her mother said. She didn't sit up. "Thank God." She pressed both her hands to her face. "The children need you."

"They need you, too," Eloise said, but her mother didn't respond. Eloise could sense, trembling just on the edge of the moment, how good a tearful rage would feel. But none of this was her mother's fault, was it? For once her mother had good cause to come undone. "Where are they?" Eloise asked.

"They're upstairs. I don't know what they're doing. They pretty much stay up there all the time."

"Even Claire?"

"She should be sleeping," Francine said. "Theo said she'd put her down."

Eloise said nothing.

"What?" her mother said. "She knows the routine. I don't. I don't know the routine."

Eloise sighed. "I'll go see them." She moved to leave, her hand still on the doorknob.

"Why did she leave her children with me anyway?" Francine asked, her voice full of fretful complaint.

"She thought you would like it," Eloise said. "She thought you'd be insulted if they went to Danny's sister every time."

"Oh," Francine said, and then she began to cry.

Eloise listened to her mother's weeping for a moment, wondering with detachment if the sound of it would make her cry. Then she closed the door.

Theo met her at the top of the stairs, her finger to her lips. Claire was in her arms, abandoned to sleep, her baby cheek plumping against Theo's bony shoulder, her lips impossibly pink. At eleven, Theo was just over five feet, possibly as tall as she would ever get, certainly tall enough to be a grown woman holding a two-year-old. And yet with the weight of the sleeping child in her arms she looked so small. Eloise reached out automatically to take the baby. She wanted to hold that warm, heavy body, to let that plump cheek rest on her shoulder, to feel weighted by her, like a house given sandbags in a hurricane. But Theo stepped back and shook her head. "I'll put her down," she mouthed and then slipped through the half-open door into a darkened bedroom. Eloise just stood there and waited, like Theo was the one in charge. After a moment the girl emerged empty-handed and pulled the door gently closed. "Josh is asleep, too," she whispered. She beckoned Eloise into an unused guest bedroom and carefully shut that door behind them. It was dark in here as well. Neither of them moved to turn on the light. Eloise reached out to hug Theo, but the child was already turning away, climbing onto one of the high twin beds, where she sat with her legs dangling, looking at her aunt with an air of patient expectation.

Theo was bright and capable, but also prone to dreaminess, or moodiness, depending on who was doing the describing. *Thoughtful,* Eloise would have said. *Interior.* The changeling, Rachel had called her, because Theo was so unlike her easygoing, one-day-at-a-time parents. She was always a little bit mystical, always only half there. Eloise identified with her, thought of this child as more *hers* than the sweet, obedient Josh or the big-eyed Claire with her solemn, unnerving appraisals. Eloise sat beside her on the bed, not touching her. Something about Theo's bearing seemed to request distance. "How are Josh and Claire?" Eloise asked, because it seemed easier than asking how Theo herself was.

"Josh is having a hard time," Theo said. "He can't stop crying, except when he's asleep. Claire doesn't really understand. She's lucky." She moved her eyes to her own lap. "Have you cried?"

Eloise bit her lip. "No."

"Me neither." Theo frowned, and the lines that appeared in her forehead seemed too deep for a child her age. After a moment she said, "Is there something wrong with us?"

"I don't know," Eloise said. In the silence that followed she had a sharp, painful vision of Rachel jumping on this very bed, singing, "You can't catch me! You can't catch me!" while Eloise stood on the ground, in tears, watching her sister bounce higher and higher.

"What will happen now?" Theo asked.

I don't know, Eloise wanted to say again, but perhaps she should be sparing the child such honesty. "We'll have some kind of funeral."

"I mean after that," Theo said. "Will we go back to our house? Will we live here with Francine?"

"Oh," Eloise said. How was it possible that this question had failed to occur to her? "What did Francine say?"

Theo shook her head. "I haven't asked her."

"Right," Eloise said. She stared at the wall, on which there was a framed painting of a sailboat she seemed somehow to have never noticed before. What would happen now? Danny's sister had three children of her own. His parents lived in a one-bedroom condo. Her mother was the logical choice for guardian, except for the fact of her personality, and now that Eloise thought about it, Rachel had mentioned, just last year, that she and Danny had finally made a will. "You're leaving the children to me, right?" Eloise had asked, half-joking, and Rachel had said, "Actually, yes. Is that okay?"

"Of course," Eloise had said. "Absolutely. But it's not like we'll ever have to worry about it."

"Let's hope not," Rachel had said.

"You know," Eloise said now, "I think I'm your guardian."

Theo let out a breath. "Oh, good," she said.

"But what should we do?" Eloise asked. Theo cocked her head, the considering expression on her face so adult it was impossible not to talk to her like she was one. "What do you want to do? You could come back to Boston with me. I'll have to get a new place. Mine's too small. And then we'll have to figure out school. I don't know anything about that. What time does school end for the day? I wonder. Sometimes I'm at work late. Do you want to come back with me? What about your friends?"

"I think maybe we should stay here," Theo said. "For now anyway. So everything doesn't change at once."

"So you'll stay here," Eloise said. "For now anyway. Maybe just for a while. With Francine. But I wonder if she can handle that."

"She doesn't have to," Theo said. "I'll help. I can take care of myself. I can take care of Josh and Claire."

"I just started at Harvard," Eloise said. "I can't get time off yet, I don't think."

Theo nodded as though such concerns were commonplace to her.

"I really like my job," Eloise said. "I was lucky to get it."

"Aunt Eloise," Theo said. "I'm not asking you to move back here."

Of course she wasn't. But that was the logical choice, wasn't it? The big house, the schools they already attended, their extra-curricular activities, their relatives, their friends. If Eloise took them back to Boston, she would be all they had. And she wasn't nearly enough. Eloise took a ragged breath. "I want my sister," she said.

"I know," Theo said. Her mouth was trembling.

Eloise tried to say something else, but the sorrow that seized her overrode her ability to speak. She sobbed like a heartbroken child, only dimly aware of the agonized sounds she made. Theo's arms went around her neck. Theo was almost as tall as she was, but Eloise pulled the child into her lap, and then, as if Eloise's tears had given her permission, Theo, too, began to cry. They stayed like that a long time, locked in a grief nobody else could witness, because the two of them—now they were the responsible ones.

Part One

Here & Now

2010

1

The house was on Clifton Avenue near the intersection with Lafayette. It, and the houses around it, had been built by men of note and wealth in the nineteenth century, when Cincinnati, Queen of the West, City of the Seven Hills, was as grand as its nicknames, when it meant something to be a river town. From the street the lawn sloped up to the house, so that the eye rose to it and then kept rising, drawn upward by decorative bricks to the gable with the half-moon window, the two high chimneys on either side. To the guests arriving for a party on a bright evening in late June, the house gave the impression of turning its face up to meet the sun. Even the people who'd been there before were struck again by the old-fashioned loveliness of the place. The way the arches of the porte cochere conjured images of the elegant necks of horses, the skirts of ladies alighting from carriages. The way the columned, semicircular portico and the bay windows above it resembled the top tiers of a wedding cake. As they grew close they noted the wrought-iron grille on the front door, the leaded-glass windows, and then inside they marveled at the chandelier in the entryway, the elaborately carved woodwork, the tiles around the fireplace with their raised seashells, the walls of the living room, upholstered in a faded pink damask with a pattern in gold.

Standing in the living room with a sweating gin and tonic in her hand, Eloise accepted compliments on these marvels, answered questions or directed the asker to Theo, who knew much more about the house than she did, and tried to resist saying anything she was thinking. Like for instance that she took little pride in the house, which she'd done nothing to earn, unless having lived there as a child counted as a kind of work. She couldn't have afforded it even at Cincinnati prices, and certainly not in any city where she would actually have liked to live. She didn't say, either, that she hated that stupid fabric on the wall, that to her its Victorian qualities were stultifying rather than charming, and made her feel like she'd been squeezed into a corset and offered a fainting couch. That fabric would be long gone if the house were actually hers rather than just hers to maintain. She understood the desire to make a romance of history, to see the work of long-dead artisans as proof of humanity's capacity for beauty, as a graceful intrusion of the past upon the present, like a benevolent ghost drifting through the attic in a long white gown. You could touch the glinting gold thread and imagine the weaver who'd made it, the lady of the house who'd chosen it, the workers who'd tacked it to the walls and filled in cotton batting, the partygoers of a hundred and more years ago who'd gathered before it like you and your friends gathered now, and you could think of how the past and the present telescoped and yet stayed firmly apart, of how we imagine and yet fail to understand other lives in ways that are both beautiful and sad, of the awesome brevity of a human life. Or, if you were Eloise, you could look at the fabric, at the room, at the house and for that matter the city, and see reminder upon reminder of all that had been lost.

Eloise had lived in the house from birth to eighteen, and then again from twenty-eight to—when? There was still a blank for that answer, like the one left for the death year on the gravestone of a person still alive. She was forty-five now, and still there, complaining about the dust and the creaky floors and the way the cold blew through the rope windows, original to the house and, like the front door, both too beautiful and too expensive to replace. When the children were younger she used to joke that once she'd been a prisoner in the house, and now she was the warden. But in truth *prisoner* was still how she felt—not all the time, but on her bad days. Among the things Eloise didn't say was that as soon as she could get Francine to—finally, finally— sign the house over, she planned to put it on the market and start wishing hard.

"I can't imagine what it was like to grow up in a house like this," said Marisa Li-Silva, who was the girlfriend of Eloise's young colleague Noah Garcia, the one Eloise frequently worried would leave their department for a job on one of the coasts. He was standing there, too, reading the label on his local microbrew. He'd been to the house once before and was leaving the exclaiming to Marisa.

"I didn't really know any better," Eloise said.

"I mean, that chandelier!" Marisa said.

"I know," Eloise said. "It's sparkly."

"You must have had a point when you realized that this wasn't, you know, typical," Marisa said. She was very pretty, and dressed like she expected the paparazzi, and Eloise felt a two-pronged pang of sympathy: for Theo, because Eloise suspected she had a crush on Noah, and for herself, because Marisa lived in L.A. and might compel Noah to move back there.

"I guess," Eloise said. "I mean I had plenty of friends who didn't live in houses like this. Though this is an old city, by American standards, and so most of the houses are old. Hardwood floors, stained-glass windows, fireplaces, plaster walls. For newer houses you have to go to the suburbs. That's where you have to go if you want to be able to pull a nail out of your wall without leaving a two-inch hole."

"But this isn't just old, it's a mansion," Marisa said.

Noah glanced up from his beer to say, "Imagine what this place would cost in L.A."

Marisa said, without looking at him, "It's not like we could afford it here either," and Noah said, "We could afford a lot more here than we could in L.A."

"You know what I do remember?" Eloise said, as if stepping between them. "I remember seeing some old movie—something black and white, with the actress making a dramatic entrance down a grand staircase—and thinking, That looks like my house. I think that's what made me realize the house was a mansion. Not life but the movies. After that my sister and I dressed up and took turns being the beautiful lady on the stairs and being the admirer below."

"*Rebecca*," Marisa said.

"What?" Eloise asked.

"I bet it was *Rebecca*," Marisa said. "That's a big scene in that movie."

"Marisa knows everything about every movie ever," Noah said.

"Well, you work in Hollywood, right?" Eloise asked.

"I do," Marisa said. She hesitated and said nothing more, probably, Eloise deduced with a glance at Noah's resolutely neutral expression, because her job and the separation it required was a source of conflict between them. Eloise knew from comments Noah had made that he'd tried and failed to get Marisa to move to Cincinnati with him a year ago, when he'd taken the job at Wyett College, where Eloise was the chair of the History Department. The subject needed changing, because Eloise sympathized with Marisa but couldn't say so, because she wanted Marisa to lose this fight. If Noah moved to be with her it would leave Eloise's department without a specialist in Latin America and her with one less colleague who wasn't certifiably insane.

"Do you like that beer?" she asked Noah, and he said he did and asked where she'd gotten it, so, glad of the excuse, she called Josh's name and waved him over. Josh, her sweet-natured, reliable nephew, ever ready to deploy his endless resources of charm. He walked up wearing a smile. He said, "Hi, Josh Clarke," and shook their hands, and Eloise watched Noah and Marisa lift their heads to meet his eyes, wondering if she'd ever get used to how tall he was, when once upon a time he had been so small. She said, "Noah wants to know where you got the beer."

"Jungle Jim's," Josh said. "Have you been there?"

Noah shook his head.

"You have to go," Josh said. "It's this huge grocery store about a half hour north of us. But *grocery store* doesn't even begin to describe it. It's a grocery amusement park. It's an acre and a half of everything from Amish butter to candies from Thailand. They have this international section along one wall that's made to look like shops in different countries—England, Italy, France. They have every kind of beer you could possibly imagine, and lots you've probably never heard of. Plus animatronic animals."

Marisa looked at Noah. "How come you've never taken me there?"

Noah looked back in some surprise. "(A) You never want to go anywhere, and (B) I didn't realize it was so awesome," he said. He raised his beer to Josh. "Tell her more good things about Cincinnati," he said.

Josh laughed. "Well," he said. "We have a good ballet."

"Oh, right," Noah said. "Your sister."

"His sister?" Marisa asked.

"Claire," Eloise said. "She's a ballerina. She started her training with the academy here. She's actually about to leave for New York to dance in a company there. Her flight's on Monday."

"Wow," Marisa said.

"I know, right?" Noah said. "There are a lot of artists here."

"I meant, wow, she's leaving for New York on Monday," Marisa said. "Because that's where you want to go if you're a ballerina."

"I guess they do think of New York as the big time," Josh said, "but the company here is really good. One of the principal dancers is coming tonight. Claire's former teacher. Or maybe she's already here."

"I don't think so," Eloise said. "But we'll introduce you when she gets here. There's also the symphony, and a good regional theater, and opera in the summer. Art-house theaters. Good music venues. Lots of bands come through."

"You know the band the National?" Noah asked. "They're from here."

"That's right," Josh said.

"Have you been to Music Now?" Noah asked Josh. To Marisa he said, "That's the festival the National guitarist curates. I told you about it."

"I've been, but not to the last one," Josh said.

"It was awesome, man, totally awesome. Joanna Newsom is a fucking angel. What kind of music are you into?"

"Oh, mostly that kind of stuff," Josh said. He had reasons for changing the subject now, Eloise knew, but she wished she could have stopped him before he changed it back to Marisa's job. She was, Eloise remembered as soon as Marisa said it, the assistant to a film producer—and though she answered Josh's first few questions briefly and warily, with occasional glances at Noah, as soon as she got going on a script she'd just read it was all smooth sailing. The script had come in from a college friend of Anita—that was the producer-boss—and Anita had asked Marisa to read it and write a nice note, pretending to be her. Anita couldn't bear to be the one to crush her old friend's dreams, even if the note would be in her name, which was a point neither Eloise nor Josh understood but didn't press. Anyway the script had turned out to be good! And now Anita was letting Marisa make notes on it. She was going to let Marisa talk to the writer. Maybe, maybe this would be the first film Marisa actually had a hand in getting made.

"You didn't tell me any of this," Noah said. He was obviously a little aggrieved but working at not sounding like it.

"Well," Marisa said. "It just happened, you know." She gave Noah a quick look and then turned back to Josh and smiled. How sad, Eloise thought, to be afraid to share good news with your partner because he'd just take it as one more win for your side. Josh wore a worried expression. He hated tension, confrontation, bad feelings of any kind. Eloise could see that he wanted to rescue them all.

"Here's an idea," he said to Noah. "Maybe she can get Joanna Newsom to play on the soundtrack and you can meet her."

"That *is* an idea," Noah said.

Marisa laughed. "Don't even think it. I don't want to compete with an angel."

"You know you'd win," Noah said, putting his arm around her, and Josh turned to Eloise with a smile of complicit pleasure.

She smiled back, if a little weakly. This party was taking so much effort. Other people wore her out, because—as her friend Heather was fond of pointing out—she felt compelled to entertain them. Well, she was used to everybody looking at her when she talked, wasn't she? The older she got the clearer it became to her that she liked other people best when they were contained by the seats in her classroom. These days she had parties out of a sense of obligation more than an anticipation of pleasure. This particular party—a celebration of the house's one hundred and twentieth birthday—she hadn't wanted to have at all. It had been Theo's idea. "Why?" Eloise had said. "Houses don't have birthdays. People will think they have to bring gifts."

"For the house?" Theo asked. "What do you give a house?"

"Furnace," Eloise said. "Roof." She ticked off the items on her fingers. "Water heater. New wiring. Paint. New pipes."

"You're afraid the guests will show up with new pipes?"

"I hope they do," Eloise said. "We haven't done any plumbing in a while."

"It's not just a birthday party for the house," Theo said. "It's a going-away party for Claire, since she won't let us throw her one. We just won't tell her that."

Eloise still shook her head. "I think it's weird to throw a going-away party for a house."

"For *Claire*," Theo corrected. "The house isn't going anywhere, is it?" Eloise, startled to realize her slip of the tongue, agreed to the party rather than answer that question.

"Hey," Josh said now, spotting something past Eloise. "Isn't that Adelaide now?"

Eloise followed his gaze to see a dark-haired, long-necked woman being ushered inside by one of Eloise's friends from book club. "I think so," she said.

"Got to be," Josh said. "Look at her. That woman is definitely a ballet dancer."

"Will you go talk to her?" Eloise asked. "I'll see if I can find Claire."

Eloise moved through the crowd across the foyer to look into the dining room, where people gathered around the hors d'oeuvres laid out on the table. No Claire, but she did see Theo, talking to Josh's boss, Ben. He was looking through the photo album Theo had made when she was supposed to be working on her dissertation, filled with every picture of the house she could locate, arranged in her best guess at chronological order. Now she was pointing out photos and narrating like a tour guide. Theo, with her mobile, expressive features, her tendency to gesture expansively, was the sort of person whose appearance seems to change with her mood. Happy and animated, as she was now, she was lovely. "This is about the time my grandparents bought the house, in 1958. Some of the woodwork had been painted"— she said this with a shudder—"but they restored it to how it would have looked when it was built."

"When was it built?" Ben asked.

"Eighteen ninety," she said. "It's in the Colonial Revival style, although it has three stories instead of the usual two. Do you know how we came to call the floors of a building *stories*? Because of the murals on the different floors. So if you were on the third floor you were on the third story."

"That's a good fact," Ben said.

"I know," Theo said. "I like that one. It's good to know where things come from."

"Do you write about houses? Like, architectural history?"

"No," Theo said. "Not at all. I've just researched this house, and the city, too, because I'm interested. I could tell you where the oldest house is, or where there used to be water—"

"Where there used to be water?"

"Yeah, like in Northside—one of the streets has newer houses than the others, because that area was water. Or, Over-the-Rhine used to be separated from downtown by a canal. Did you know that? That's how it got that name, because German immigrants called the canal the Rhine. When they were taking the canal out, that's when they got the idea to build a subway. But of course they never finished it."

Listening to her niece, the pleasure in her voice as she imparted these facts, Eloise winced. She'd tried without success to break Theo of her fondness for their hometown. Theo had come back for graduate school four years before despite offers from more prestigious schools, and moved back into the room she shared with Claire as though she'd never left. She put an I LOVE CINCINNATI bumper sticker on her car and wore T-shirts that said MADE IN OHIO or showed photos of local landmarks under the words THIS IS WHERE I'M FROM. Local landmarks, plus a shot of police in riot gear and one of Pete Rose grabbing his balls

with a fuck-you expression on his face. "It's the complete picture," Theo had said in answer to whatever wry comment Eloise
had made. "Cincinnati's gritty."

In Cincinnati you could make a virtue of grittiness, take
pride in not living in some cleaner, wealthier, wussier city,
though that was a problematic stance if you lived in a house
like theirs. Even if it was a six-minute walk from a hot spot of
crime, even if a friend who lived two streets over once had to
dive under a car to avoid getting caught in cross fire. Did Theo's
civic pride extend to the high crime rate? The conservative
provinciality of the population, the intractable problems of the
urban poor, the low self-esteem? To identify so strongly with a
city like this—what did that say about you? In Cincinnati when
locals asked where you went to school they meant what high
school. In Cincinnati when locals met a newcomer they asked,
"Why'd you move *here*?" It was a dying city, no matter how Theo
winced and protested when Eloise used that term. One day the
electricity would blink off, the shops would close their doors,
the people would get in their cars and drive away. Abrupt as a
cardiac arrest.

A hand slipped into Eloise's and squeezed. She looked over
to see Heather, who released her hand before Eloise could pull
away. So careful of Eloise's desire for secrecy, even as it clearly
hurt and sometimes angered her, even as Eloise went on spending nights in Heather's bed and then introducing her as her
"friend." Eloise wanted to reach out and push Heather's dark
hair back behind her ear, smooth it where the humid weather
was starting to make it frizz, but she didn't. Heather wore the
necklace Eloise had bought her the week before at an art fair,
a sparkly glass pendant on a black cord. The gold in the glass

seemed to call forth gold in her brown eyes. "I really like how that looks on you," Eloise said.

"Thanks," Heather said, her fingers going to the pendant. "How are you doing?"

"I'm feeling guilty." Eloise pointed her chin at Theo. "She loves this house."

"I know, but she can't stay here forever whether you sell it or not."

Eloise sighed. She didn't know how to make Theo understand that the house was, like many family legacies, as much a burden as a gift. Francine might have hung on to ownership of the house even after she moved to Tennessee, but she'd handed over its up-keep as if she were breaking a curse, or passing it on. Theo would say the place was more gift than burden, but she wasn't the one who had to offer up a four-figure sum to Duke Energy every month. She could complain about the cold (because winters in Cincinnati were quite cold) or the heat (because summers in Cincinnati were quite hot) without immediately thinking of how much these vagaries of temperature would cost her. Cold winters *and* hot summers—this unfair combination was another of the grievances against Cincinnati on Eloise's very long list.

"She's twenty-eight years old," Eloise said. "Why does she have to be told to move out? Why doesn't she want to do it on her own? And Josh. He's been back a year. He's still not even talking about getting his own place." She looked at Heather. "I stunted them somehow."

"Don't start that again," Heather said. "You always encour-aged them. They're just broke. Times like this make you hesitate to spend money. And the house is really big."

"I hope someone won't hesitate to spend money on this place," Eloise said. "Or I'll never get rid of it."

"Have you talked to your mother?"

"Not yet. I thought I'd call once Claire is gone."

"You think she'll actually do it this time?"

"That's what she said, the last time I asked. She'd sign it over once Claire was grown." Eloise made a face. "But who the hell knows. She lives to torment me."

"You can just walk away," Heather said. "Move in with me. You know I won't charge you rent."

"But then I have no savings. I have nothing to show for everything I've put into this place." Eloise gave her a rueful smile. "I'm tiresome, I know. I repeat myself. Are you sure you want me in your house, saying the same things over and over?"

Heather pretended to consider. "Do I have to listen?"

"Some of the time," Eloise said. "But we can bargain. We can work that out." She looked back at Josh, checking on him, and saw him talking with apparent ease to Adelaide. "I have to go find Claire."

"She went upstairs a while ago with a couple of her friends."

Eloise nodded, took a step toward the kitchen, then stopped. "Heather," she said, "am I wrong to want to sell this place? Does it mean too much to them?"

"You're not wrong," Heather said. "They love the house, I know, but they don't pay the property taxes."

Eloise found Claire in the den on the second floor, talking to two of her friends. They'd been dance majors together at the performing arts high school, but while Claire went on to a career in dance the other two were going to college, and perhaps because of that they treated Claire as if she were a little bit of a celebrity. It sometimes bothered Eloise that people were so careful with Claire, as if she were fragile, as if she were so special as not to be quite real. True, she was lovely, with her fairy-child eyes, her long, long neck. She looked so delicate, so ethereal, and yet she was anything but.

"Claire, move your butt," Eloise said, startling the friends and making her niece smile. "Adelaide's here." Claire scrambled to her feet with less than her usual grace. She worshiped Adelaide. "She's in the foyer talking to Josh," Eloise called after Claire as she and her friends disappeared out the door. For a moment, Eloise lingered, reluctant to return to the fray. This room, repository for the television and the video games and the music in all its assorted formats from records to iPods, had been the playroom when she and Rachel were young, and then the TV room as they grew older, the place they spent much of their time, the more formal first floor being the domain of their mother. Eloise still felt like that part of the house didn't quite belong to her.

Why didn't she just move in with Heather, whether her mother gave her the house or not? Why was she dragging her feet? Maybe it was because she'd never imagined finally leaving this house only to move across town. But here was the truth: Eloise was forty-five and this was where she had a job and friends and a secret girlfriend and a house she might or might not be able to sell. This was, now and forever, where she was from.

In the first year or so after coming home for the children, and intermittently since, she'd lived with an intense awareness of elsewhere. In this land, which encompassed New York and Boston and other northeastern cities and towns, life went on at a higher volume, a more rapid pace. While she waited to cross the street, its people built bridges. Their sky was bright with city lights and philosophies. She had recurring dreams of being not just late but incapable of arriving—some party or meeting or class already under way while the minutes sped past on her clock and she stood stupefied at the bathroom mirror, unable to comprehend why she was still half-dressed, why she hadn't yet brushed her hair. Elsewhere—once upon a time she'd been able to go there by car or by plane. Now she needed a tornado.

2

When the party was finally over, Eloise went up to her room and lay down on top of her quilt with one arm flung in dramatic exhaustion over her eyes. She heaved an enormous sigh, and at that moment Theo came in, said, "That's how I feel, too," and lay down beside her. Then Claire, so silent on her dancer feet that Eloise didn't notice her until the bed shifted under her weight. At times like this, when the girls came to her like children, warm and sleepy, seeking contact, it was easy to forget how old they were. It was easy to forget not to call them "the children." At most she could get away with "the kids." Certainly they were still kids to her, even at twenty-eight and twenty-six and nineteen. They were still *her* kids, even if it had taken her years to stop flinching when people called them that, as if in claiming them as hers she was stealing from Rachel.

"That was too many people," Theo said.

"It was your idea," Eloise said, feeling amused, annoyed, and a little sad. Theo was so like her—throwing herself into maniacal organization of a party she hadn't actually enjoyed.

"So I don't get to complain?"

"Yes," Eloise said. "I believe that's in the contract."

"I had fun," Claire said.

"That's because you didn't have to think of things to talk about," Theo said. "You never have to think of things to talk about."

"I wouldn't say never," Claire said. "It's only because people have so many questions about ballet."

Eloise took her arm off her eyes to look at her niece. "What do they ask you?"

"They ask what my favorite ballet is, and if I've done *The Nutcracker*. They tell me what ballets they've seen. Usually *The Nutcracker*." Claire shrugged. "They ask if all the men are gay."

Eloise laughed. "Haven't they heard of Baryshnikov? Do women ask you that more, or men?"

"I don't know," Claire said. "I haven't paid attention."

From below they heard Josh's footsteps on the stairs, then silence. "Shhhh," Theo said, and she and Claire giggled childishly. "Where is everybody?" Josh called. "Why am I cleaning up by myself?"

"Up here!" Eloise shouted.

His footsteps resumed and Theo whispered, "Hide!" The girls giggled again.

"Now, children," Eloise said. "Be nice to your brother."

"We're always nice to our brother," Claire said, and it was true, they mostly were. Every so often two of the kids bonded in a way that excluded the third. Sometimes it was Theo who got left out, sometimes it was Josh, walking around with an aggrieved and mournful air. It was never Claire. Nor was she ever the one to instigate the excluding. She was the prize in a silent game of tug-of-war. For all Eloise could tell Claire didn't even notice.

Josh came in the room slowly, nodding as if to say *I see how it is.* He stood over the bed and crossed his arms. Gazing up at him, Theo said, "Man, you're tall."

"Dude," Claire said. "Dude, you're tall," and the girls giggled again.

Josh ignored them. "What do we have here?" he asked. "You guys snuggle like kittens in a basket while I pick up beer bottles?"

"We're tired," Theo said. "We're not as naturally charming as you. We've been working hard."

"Natural charm takes it out of you, too," Josh said.

"I wouldn't know," Eloise said. "My charm is entirely unnatural."

"You make it look easy, though," Theo said. "Every time I looked at you, you had a circle of people around you, hanging on your every word."

Eloise winced. "I talked too much," she said. "You guys are supposed to stop me from holding forth like that."

"People like to hear you talk," Josh said. "You're interesting."

Eloise wanted to ask, "Am I really interesting? Or do I just coast on having once been interesting?" But for God's sake, woman, spare the kids your self-pity. "Play something for us, would you?" she said to Josh.

"Oh, good idea," Theo said. "I haven't heard you play in ages."

"Such demanding women," Josh said.

"Come on, Joshy," Claire said, and the nickname she'd used in her baby years worked on him, the way they'd all known it would. He shrugged in that agreeable way of his that sometimes drove Eloise mad—*yes or no!* she wanted to scream—and sometimes, like now, made her want to squeeze and kiss him like she had when he was a child, tousle his curls, bring out his sweet and joyful smile. He left the room to get one of his guitars, and Eloise said, "I'm surprised he's willing to play."

"It's for Claire," Theo said.

"It's for all of us," Claire said, and Theo said, "No, it's not."

Josh returned, sat in the chair at the end of the bed, and began to tune the guitar. "What should I play?"

"A lullaby," Theo said and yawned.

"A lullaby," Josh repeated. He strummed, strummed again, staring at the ceiling. Then he sang, his voice low and mournful, "Phone rings in the middle of the night. My father yells, what you gonna do with your life?"

Eloise laughed. Josh had started playing this melancholy version of the song—which at one point had been the girls' favorite—years ago. He'd always loved taking familiar songs and changing the tone, making a sad song an upbeat jaunt, a happy song a dirge. Emotion for him was malleable, manageable, while for Claire it was a wave you rode, for Theo something you compartmentalized, analyzed, pretended you could control.

On the chorus they all sang. At the end of the song they clapped, but Josh wasn't finished. "We had a party and now we're tired. Oh, who is gonna clean up the house tonight? Oh, Theo dear, this party was your idea. You'd better go and pick up the beer. You'd better go and pick up the beer."

"Everybody better stop saying the party was my idea in that resentful way," Theo said. "The house will hear you and think you don't like her." She reached out to pat the wall. Eloise could remember her father doing the exact same thing, a million years ago. He'd loved the house like Theo did, told everybody who would listen how old it was, how sound its structure. "I love this house," Theo said, with a little too much feeling. *Oh, baby,* Eloise thought, out of sympathy and guilt, even as she wished—heartily wished—that Theo would stop saying she loved the house, and what's more would stop loving it. She reached down, circled her niece's wrist with her finger and thumb. It was warm and bony, and though Eloise couldn't have said what she meant by this, it felt much, much too small.

At her aunt's touch, Theo wanted to cry. She felt as though Eloise had known her thoughts and wanted to comfort her, but of course no one knew her thoughts, and no one could comfort her. No one had noticed her absence from the party the half hour she spent hiding in the guest room on the third floor, before she steeled herself to face the happy couple. She didn't want anyone to notice, her absence or anything else, but sometimes she wondered why she'd never taken Claire, at least, into her confidence, so that one person would understand the effort it took to hide her longing, and maybe help her admire herself for that effort, even as she hated herself for the feelings that made the effort necessary. Theo did not want to want what she wanted. Noah.

Fantastic! he'd written in the email saying he would come. *Marisa will be in town.*

Great! she'd written back. She'd considered adding a second exclamation point, to emphasize how very much she meant it, but decided in the end that enthusiasm too overt might reveal the extent of her disappointment.

Her disappointment was ridiculous and embarrassing. She knew damn well that Noah was devoted to his girlfriend, as he brought Marisa up practically every time Theo saw him, which, toward the end of the last school year, had been a little too often, as Theo had taken to dropping by his office on the pretext of looking for Eloise. She'd sworn off this habit sometime in April, after going by and finding his office door closed and locked. She hated how bereft this made her feel, how not seeing him when she'd hoped to see him ruined the rest of her day. Theo worked very hard to suppress her doomed romantic notions. She was successful enough in these efforts to have gained a reputation among her friends for a sharp-tongued, hilarious cynicism about love. Oh, she was tough. She was so tough that every time Noah spoke to her she had to fight a melting urge to giggle. Instead she would lean away, make wisecracks in a lower than usual voice. If only she smoked, those would be the perfect moments to light a cigarette. She was as smooth as a femme fatale, so cool she should have been filmed in black and white.

Noah, he was an excitable guy. The first time she met him, when Eloise had him over for a welcome dinner, he'd talked with such passion about the lifestyles of the ancient Americans that Theo had been as jazzed as you were after a good concert. He preached and she wanted to shout *Amen!* He made her want to clap and whoop, to give full rein to her enthusiasms. It made little sense to try to attract a guy like that with withdrawal and sarcasm, but she wasn't trying to attract him, not at all. He had a girlfriend. Theo simply liked being around him. Or rather she just wanted to be around him. She didn't exactly *like* it. Feeling jittery, and manic, and under pressure to utter the world's most interesting remark—those weren't things she liked. The whole thing was exhausting. She was an idiot.

Before the party she'd managed to focus on her to-do list rather than the fact that Noah would be coming, and that he was bringing his girlfriend. She threw herself into cleaning the house, because she'd told Eloise she would, and she had to buy wine and beer, because she'd taken that chore from Josh, and she had to make hors d'oeuvres, because she'd taken that one from Claire. She'd spent hours and hours on the photo album.

She needed distractions, and she also felt guilty because she'd been the one insisting on the party, which no one else wanted to have, and like anyone used to being thought of as the good one, the capable one, the responsible one, she preferred feeling overwhelmed and overworked to feeling guilty. And in the end had they had a good time? She hoped they had all had a good time.

"I saw you talking to Adelaide, Josh," she said. "You looked pretty happy."

"Oh yeah." Claire lifted herself up on her elbows to look at Josh. "What was going on there?"

"Wouldn't you like to know?"

"She is my teacher."

"Was your teacher," Eloise said. "Now she's very nearly your peer."

"She's miles beyond me," Claire said. Then, to Josh, "What were you talking about?"

"I was asking her about the ballet," Josh said.

Theo laughed. "Whether the men are gay?"

"Yes, Theo, because that's uppermost in my mind. No—stuff you've never told me, C, like how many pairs of pointe shoes each dancer goes through in a year."

"I never thought to tell you that," Claire said.

"Even if you had," Theo said, "I bet it's more interesting coming from Adelaide."

"Anything Adelaide says is interesting," Josh said. "Because she's a pretty girl who's not my sister. She could have said *blah blah blah* and I would have listened with my mouth hanging open."

"Maybe a little drool," Theo said.

"Because the ladies love drool," Josh said.

"Did you ask her out?"

"No. Maybe you could take care of that for me."

"Being such an expert at romance," Theo said.

"No one's an expert," Eloise said.

"None of us are winning any prizes there," Josh said.

"Well," Claire said. They all turned to look at her like a spotlight had clicked on above her head. Claire had had boyfriends. They'd all seen her starry-eyed, and then awash in grief, but these passions stormed hard and passed quickly. If she was involved with someone now, she'd given no indication of it, and that was a surprise to all three of them. It was often hard to say what Claire was thinking, but, unlike them, she never found it necessary to hide what she felt.

After a moment Eloise said, "Well, what?"

Claire smiled. "You should see your faces," she said.

"Are you seeing someone?" Theo asked.

"Someone in New York?" Eloise asked. They both tried to keep any trace of the hurt and surprise they felt out of their voices. Stop being so dramatic, they told themselves.

Claire's smile widened. "Don't you know all ballet dancers are gay?"

They all laughed, but they were still uneasy. It wasn't like Claire to joke in that fashion. She normally smiled indulgently as the rest of them teased and bantered and topped each other's sarcastic quips. They waited for her to say something more, but she didn't. As they watched she sat up and stretched. Was she aware of them watching her? Was that what made her move her arm just so? Theo suspected it, Josh didn't consider it, Eloise didn't care. Claire's loveliness was all that mattered. Her death-defying grace. "I'm going to go practice," she said.

The rest of them waited to speak again until she was gone. Then Theo said, "That was weird, right?"

Her brother nodded. She was relieved that he agreed. Lately he'd seemed determined to contradict nearly everything she said, especially if what she said was in any way negative. According to him, Eloise's friend Heather was not underfoot and presumptuous but *trying to help*. He had, at moments, struck her as either self-righteous or oblivious or both. Self-righteously oblivious. She'd expected him to dismiss any concern she might have about their sister, but she should have known better. He'd always been particularly attuned to Claire. They all had. "Should we ask her what's up?" Josh asked.

"I think we just did," Theo said.

"It's not like her to keep things from us," Eloise said. "Let's just assume . . ." Her voice trailed off. She wasn't sure what she wanted to assume. "She can't hear us, can she?"

"No," Theo said. "I'm sure she's lost in concentration, practicing in front of the mirror. You know, dedicating her life to its essential purpose."

"Ah," Eloise said. "Sounds nice."

"Doesn't it?" Theo said.

There was a moment of silence, in which none of them looked at the others, and then Josh stood. "I'm going to spy on Claire for a second," he said. "And then I'm going to bed."

"Good night," Eloise said, and Theo said it, too, but didn't move to go. These days Theo's essential purpose was, like Eloise's, the study of history. Specifically it was her dissertation, a study of historical concepts of distance. Focusing was hard, though, when she was so distracted by all the petty, minor stuff. How bad the job market was, and all the strange and faraway places her friends had ended up moving, those lucky enough to even get jobs. After her parents died, she was expected to be the good one. That had been easy. It had been a relief, in fact, to have such a pressing reason to keep herself in check, because like any child she'd had her outbursts of temper or unreasonable sorrow, and she hated to lose control, she really did. She hated how she felt afterward, the emotional hangover, the embarrassment and guilt. She needed to be good for Josh and Claire, for Francine, and for Eloise, who'd given up her whole life for them. Eloise had tried not to show any regret about that, but even at eleven Theo recognized how hard Eloise had to work at it. She'd see the look on her aunt's face, quickly hidden, whenever Harvard or Boston came up. The look on her face that spoke of everything she'd surrendered. Theo felt guilty enough at being the cause for the radical shift in her aunt's existence. She wouldn't add to her burden. Besides, she needed to focus on Josh, Josh, who had come completely undone.

How Josh had cried. It had been terrible to watch him. Even now the thought of it made Theo's eyes fill with tears. When their parents died Josh had been the one who fell apart, while Theo had soldiered on, and yet now Josh could talk about their parents with a distant, nostalgic fondness, while Theo had clung to the ache of their absence as if it were her best, her imaginary, friend. Her parents, who had been good parents, had become in Theo's memory ideal ones. She loved Eloise and was grateful to her. But she'd never found anything that could replace what she'd lost in them.

"Do you ever wonder what would have happened . . ." Theo stopped and looked at Eloise. She couldn't say what she'd been about to say. But she had to say something. Eloise was waiting for her to speak. "Do you ever wonder what would have happened if Claire hadn't come to my dance class and the teacher hadn't seen her?"

"You mean, would she have become a dancer?"

Theo nodded. "We knew about Josh because he could play piano by ear. But what if we hadn't had a piano, and he'd never come across one? Would that talent have found another way to emerge?"

Eloise considered the question. "It's strange to imagine being made for something and not knowing it."

"Right. Like, what if you could have been a great painter, but no one ever gave you a brush?"

"That's a fascinating idea. Do you think you'd live your whole life knowing something was missing?"

"I don't know. Now I'm trying to think if I have that feeling."

"Hmmm," Eloise said. "That's a dangerous pursuit."

"What if you'd been a natural filmmaker born before the invention of film?"

"You would have been a painter, I bet. Or a writer, depending on the nature of your gifts."

"Maybe," Theo said.

"You know, I've never asked what made you start taking ballet."

Theo shrugged. "Mom wanted me to. She said I was too much of a mind person and I needed to do something with my body."

"You were only five!"

"I know. But she said all I wanted to do was read and whisper with my toys and be alone."

"That's what I was like." Eloise laughed. Then, struck, she said, "Oh. I see. She didn't want you to be like me."

"Well, she didn't have much luck with that, did she?" They both laughed, but neither one of them felt very amused. Theo missed her mother, and feared she'd have been a disappointment to her, and wondered why those feelings withdrew but refused to go away entirely. And Eloise—she felt tears pricking behind her eyes. She remembered being five years old, tossed out of Rachel's room when she'd wanted to play with Rachel's dolls. The door had slammed in her face, her big sister screaming, "I don't want you! Go away!"

This was not the sort of thing she wanted to remember. Instead: Christmas break her junior year of high school, the party Rachel took her to. They'd gone out during a winter storm warning, because their parents weren't the sort to stop them, and then while the world outside whitened and froze, Eloise got drunk and stoned and made out with a twenty-two-year-old reject who drove a Camaro. "He drives a *Camaro*," Rachel kept saying as she dragged Eloise out to the car.

The roads were so slick they could feel the tires slipping beneath them, barely catching the pavement. "We're going to die," Eloise said and started laughing. "And my last kiss was with a guy who drives a Camaro!"

Rachel ignored her, hands gripping the wheel, eyes fixed on the road. What was that she was whispering under her breath? "I'm going to get you home, I'm going to get you home, I'm going to get you home."

Five miles an hour, slipping and sliding the whole time. And when at last the car was parked in their driveway, Rachel turned to her, wearing a smile of triumphant relief. "I got you home," she said.

3

Josh did not, after all, look in on Claire. She deserved her privacy, even if she used it to hide something from the rest of them, and maybe she wasn't doing that anyway. Plus there were occasions when, seeing the intense and certain focus with which Claire practiced, he doubted his own choices. For the most part he managed to exist in a doubt-free zone. For him to second-guess even one decision he'd made was dangerous. Doubts could so easily multiply.

A month or so after his return to Cincinnati, when the relief he'd first felt at being home had begun to fade and he hadn't yet gotten a job, he'd begun to wake in the night with a new song in his head. He'd imagine playing it aloud, then imagine never playing it. His heartbeat and his breathing would quicken, as though in a race with one another, and he couldn't slow them, couldn't stop the waves of adrenaline that flooded through him, couldn't tamp down the frantic desperation. He told himself he never had to play a song again, but that didn't help. He told himself he could play anytime he wanted, but that, too, didn't help. The music itself panicked him, the fact that no matter what he did it was still in his head, building to the chorus, insisting on passion, when what he wanted was peace. The next day he'd be drained and nauseous, as after a stomach flu, and Sabrina would be on his mind. He'd hear the scorn in her voice as she said, "What do you think, you're a *rock star*?" and he'd insist that no, he didn't think that at all. He'd come back to Cincinnati to prove he didn't think that.

He stayed away from doubt as a preventative against nights like that. He'd told Eloise, once, about the heartbeat and the rapid breathing, and she'd said, "Oh, honey, you had a panic attack."

"No, I didn't," he said. "My heart just beat fast. I probably drank too much coffee." Eloise gave him a look so full of love and pity that it was almost unbearable. After that he never mentioned these experiences again. To make it through your days intact, it was important not to name certain things. Not a panic attack but a caffeinated heart. Not anger but exasperation. Not regret but nostalgia. Not grief, not self-loathing, not the conviction that you were a weak-minded fool so desperate for love that you'd handed your whole life over to get it. Certainly none of that.

His room was still a shrine to everything he'd left behind, the guitars that lined the walls, the framed posters Eloise had begun hanging not long after the band started playing gigs. On the top shelf of the closet, there were even more posters, rolled into neat cylinders and held with rubber bands. He no longer wanted to live with these things, but to get rid of them would be to face the fact that he needed to get rid of them. He preferred to go on telling himself he wasn't affected by these reminders, that he had no feelings about them that couldn't be expressed by a casual shrug. Those guitars—he'd bought every one with such a giddy sense of entitled pleasure. The year the band made money he'd hired an accountant who advised him to invest in tax write-offs. Thus his personal museum of expensive instruments, all purchased not just because he wanted them—God, how he'd wanted them— but in the service of fiscal responsibility.

The one he held right now had been the last he'd bought, so expensive he'd practically had to hold his breath and close his eyes when he handed over the credit card. He went to replace it on its waiting stand, which, without the guitar that had sat on it untouched for the last six months, looked empty-armed and sad. Without making a conscious decision, he held on to the guitar instead. He sat on his bed with it and strummed idly. As if to hide from himself what he was doing, he turned his thoughts to the party. Had he had fun? Sure, he'd had fun.

He'd anticipated a good time, at least a mild one. He'd never dreaded social occasions like Theo and Eloise, who dreaded even social occasions they'd instigated, though for a while after moving home he'd found himself wanting to avoid them. The questions about what had happened with the band, why he was home, what he planned to do next. The confused and sometimes disappointed expressions his vague and ambivalent answers provoked. Given the way people like Marisa behaved as though there was a hierarchy of places to live, and you got into L.A. or New York or Boston the way you got into Harvard or Yale, you'd think they'd have just assumed coming back to Cincinnati was tantamount to saying he no longer had any ambitions. Most of these conversations had already been dispatched over the past year, and had grown easier since he'd gone to work for Ben, a high school friend whose company made apps for mobile devices. So now, unless he met a stranger who knew his history, he no longer had to dread his own limp explanations.

With Noah, for instance, Josh could talk music, and never get a glimmer that the guy had any inkling of the stake Josh had once had in the subject. He'd actually felt a hurt surprise that Eloise had never told Noah about the band, but he'd vanquished the feeling by reminding himself he was glad Noah didn't know. He was spared the awkwardness of the moment when it became clear that this avid music fan—this guy who read Pitchfork like it was his daily devotional and drove an hour and a half to Indianapolis to see an obscure band—had never heard of Josh, or Blind Robots. Or that he had heard of them but didn't like them. Or that he'd loved them, and couldn't quite forgive Josh for bringing an abrupt halt to their career. It was freeing, instead, to talk, as they had after Claire interrupted his conversation with Adelaide, about the latest album from the National and how their live show compared to their recorded sound.

Adelaide. She'd been a challenging one. He'd done okay with her, though. He had a special skill with difficult or quiet people, because of his persistent interest in them. If he was aware of the effect of this interest, did that mean he was insincere? He'd asked himself this question many times and never arrived at a clear answer, so once again he set it aside. He had a lot of faith in the idea that he was a good guy. People were always telling him so, though these days not with the admiration he'd heard in their voices when he'd been semifamous and therefore could have claimed his right to assholery. On tour you started to believe most of the world was comprised of drunk idiots who irrationally loved or irrationally hated your band. It was easy to acquire both superiority and bitterness. He was glad he'd stayed a good guy in the face of temptation to be otherwise. These days it was the main thing he had going for him.

When he'd gone to greet Adelaide, he'd found her still standing near the front door, as if she wanted to have her escape route clear. Claire had really, really wanted her to come to the party. Adelaide had been Claire's teacher in the local company's summer program for three years, and the person who finally persuaded her to audition elsewhere, outside of Ohio. Josh had never seen Claire so eager to impress someone. Claire had been taken with Adelaide from the beginning, but her admiration for her had reached a fever pitch this year, after she saw Adelaide dance the lead in *Swan Lake*. Claire couldn't stop talking about Adelaide's "quality of movement," which was a phrase Josh liked, even if he wasn't sure exactly what it meant.

Adelaide looked stricken when he spoke to her, but maybe that was just the effect of her big eyes in her small face. She said that it was nice to meet him like it was her name, rank, and serial number, and then clamped her mouth shut. She glanced at him once and then looked away. Where others might assume arrogance or lack of interest, he assumed shyness and dove in. "So tell me something I don't know about the ballet," he said.

Adelaide stiffened. "Something you don't know," she repeated.

"There's probably a lot I don't know," Josh said. "Even though my sister's a dancer."

"Probably," Adelaide said.

Josh arranged his face into an expression of pleasant expectation and went on waiting for her to talk. After a moment Adelaide shifted a little from her dancer's stance, dropped her hands from her hips, surrendered just a bit. "What kind of something do you want to know?"

"Something that will prove to my friends I met a professional ballet dancer," he said. "Something only you would know."

"Why not ask Claire?"

"Oh, she's my sister." He smiled. "You don't talk to your sister."

Adelaide smiled back, and then let the smile fade, as though uncertain about whether he was kidding. "Something you don't know," she said again. She considered the question, and while she did he studied her appearance in a way he didn't study Claire's, because she was his sister, because he saw her all the time. He was struck by how small this woman was. Or *small* wasn't really the word, because she was at least five foot eight. *Skinny* didn't work either, the way it suggested scrawniness and pigtails, or anorexia. *Slender,* that was it. Small-breasted, long-necked, long-fingered. Was it the slenderness of her arms that made her hands seem outsize? Josh had an urge to hold his palm against hers to compare.

Finally she said, "Every season we go through a hundred pairs of pointe shoes."

"The whole company?"

She shook her head. "Each of us."

"You're kidding."

She shook her head again. "I'm in charge of the shoe ordering."

"What's it like having those on, anyway?"

"It's . . . Well, we joke that dancers must be masochists."

"That bad?"

"A little bit. There are days when by four o'clock I want to scream. All I want to do in the world is take those shoes off. You're watching the clock. Ten more minutes, nine more minutes."

"You're making my feet hurt just talking about it," Josh said. "Is it like that all the time?"

"No. And not when you're performing. You don't think about your feet at all then. You get onstage, and life comes alive." All of

her shyness, if that's what it had been, was gone. She had a glow-
ing look of conviction on her face.

Josh understood. He understood profoundly, and he both
wanted to tell her this and to flee, because something seemed
momentarily to be wrong with him. There was a glitch in the system. His social easiness was gone. *Life comes alive.* Was he about
to touch her? Was he about to say the wrong thing? "Oh, shit," he
said. "Nobody offered you a drink."

"Oh." She blinked. "Hey, you're right."

"What would you like? My skills are limited but I can do a gin
and tonic."

"That sounds good," she said. She smiled at him in a way he
recognized, a way that said she found herself inclining toward
him. This, too, made him feel torn between embracing her and
hitting the road. "Be right back," he said.

He passed Theo on his way to fix the drink, and caught her
looking at Noah and Marisa with a funny expression on her face.
"You okay?" he asked.

She ignored the question, lifting her chin in the direction of
Adelaide. "You going to ask her out?"

"What?"

"You have that look about you," she said.

"Oh yeah? What's that look?"

She made an exaggerated expression of interest, leaning in
close. He couldn't tell whether she was being hostile or just trying to tease him, but either way it pissed him off. "I'm not going
to ask her out," he said in lieu of *fuck off,* and then he brushed
past his sister in the direction of the bar.

Theo hadn't been entirely wrong, though. Maybe he'd like to
ask Adelaide out, he thought now, alone in his room, but he'd had

to work a little too hard with her, in a way that reminded him of Sabrina. He'd told himself his next girlfriend wouldn't make him work quite so hard, though he had to admit the last couple girls he'd dated had been so easygoing he'd found himself bored. Theo liked to imagine that his romantic life started and stopped with Sabrina. In fact, there had been girls before and after. Hell, he'd been in a band. And why, having argued so relentlessly in favor of his breakup with Sabrina, did Theo want to give him a hard time about considering someone new? Theo had always been such a good big sister, supportive and protective and reliable. Despite the depths of his resentment of the way she'd behaved about Sabrina, part of him understood she'd acted out of love. So he was baffled and stung by her recent prickliness. Ever since he'd quit the band, she seemed disappointed in him, disappointed by everything about him. Lots of people disapproved, but she was the only person whose opinion mattered enough to make him feel like a failure. He found himself retreating behind a wall when he was with her, which was not unlike how he'd felt with Sabrina toward the end. He tried to keep all of this out of his tone, to answer in the light, bantering way that was their usual style, because his approach to conflict was to behave like everything was fine in the hopes that it eventually would be. *Like pretending you're asleep until you are,* Theo had said to him, in one of her many speeches about his relationship with Sabrina.

He registered the notes he was playing on the guitar and stopped. The last few days he'd had a riff on repeat in his head. He'd done his best to ignore it, this nascent song, but now he was playing it aloud. The part of his brain that wrote songs refused to get the memo about quitting from the rest of him.

The door to his room swung slowly open and he saw Theo

there, hands in her pockets, nudging the door with her foot. "Heard you playing," she said.

"Yeah." He stood and crossed the room, put the guitar back in the stand, where it belonged.

"Sounded good," Theo said.

"Thanks." He didn't want to be so guarded, so brusque, so braced for argument. To counteract his tone he turned to his big sister and smiled.

But she was frowning. "Do you think we should be worried about Claire?"

"I don't know, T," he said. "You're basing an awful lot on one weird moment."

Now she flashed her smile. "I overthink things," she said.

"That you do."

She nodded. "It's hard to wrap my mind around the fact that she's leaving," she said.

"I know," he said.

"What about you?"

"What about me?"

"Do you think you'll stay here?"

"I don't know." Josh frowned. "I don't think any decision has to be made."

"No, I guess not," she said. "It's different for me. I'll have to go somewhere else, if I want to get a job. In fact everyone wants me to send out applications in the fall. The dissertation would be done by the time I started somewhere. At least I hope it would."

"So are you going to do that?"

"Eloise thinks I should." She drew a half circle on the floor with her toes. "One of my friends is about to start at the University of North Dakota."

"That's far," Josh said.

"It's really far," she said. She seemed about to say something else, then didn't.

"The party was fun," Josh offered.

She nodded again. "Yeah," she said slowly. "I'm glad."

"Good job with it."

"Oh, thanks. Thanks for helping."

"I didn't really do much."

"You talked to people," she said, and he wondered why she sounded so unhappy. He thought about asking. If she had been anyone else, he knew he would have asked. "Anyway," she said. "Good night." And then she backed away, and pulled the door until it shut.

4

In the car on the way to the airport three days later, Josh and Theo fought about what to do once they got there. Claire sat in the front seat, and she and Eloise both kept their eyes on the road ahead while in the backseat the other two squabbled like children. "She doesn't have a lot of time before her flight," Theo said. "It'll be faster to just drop her at the curb."

"We should park and go in," Josh said. "This isn't just any other trip."

"It's not like we can go with her to the gate," Theo said.

"I miss going with people to the gate," Eloise said. "Picking people up at the gate. It was much nicer that way." No one responded.

"But we can go with her to security, and say goodbye where you can actually hug," Josh said. "If we're not going to do that, why did we all come?"

"To see her off," Theo said.

"Right," he said. "Dumping her at the curb like a piece of luggage isn't seeing her off."

"I didn't say anything about *dumping* her," Theo said. "That was your word."

"But it was your idea."

Theo folded her arms and blew out air. "Fine," she said. "We'll do it your way."

"Great," Josh said. "That makes a nice change."

"What is that supposed to mean?"

"Oh, just shut up," Eloise said. She glanced at Claire, whose expression was pained. "Shut up, both of you." They did, thank God, because Eloise was on the verge of threatening to ground them. When she wanted them to be children again, this was not what she meant. She glanced at Claire again, testing her own feeling of calm acceptance. She'd expected to feel sadder when Claire left. And maybe she still would, maybe she'd collapse in tears outside airport security. But maybe she wouldn't, because it was right for Claire to go. Of all the kids she'd always been on the clearest path.

Eloise had done one sentimental thing this morning, and that was to pull from the top shelf of her closet the small, ornate mirror she kept up there. The mirror had been her mother's, but unlike most of her mother's things she'd kept it. She'd not only kept it but laid it carefully in a high back corner, where it would never be disturbed. This was because of the handprint three-year-old Claire had left on it, white and a little smudged, souvenir of a day when she'd insisted on applying her own sunscreen and had gotten it everywhere. Eloise had yelled at her. She'd been furious. They'd been late for swim lessons, and this was early in Eloise's mothering years, when getting all three children out the door often seemed like an insurmountable task. Not only had Claire coated her hands and face and some of the floor with a gloppy layer of sunscreen but she'd run away from Eloise when she tried to catch her to clean it up. She'd scrambled up the stairs, leav-

ing a white trail all the way to the third floor, where she'd found this mirror and put her hand on it. Eloise had finally caught her gazing with intense concentration at her own face, and when she scooped her up and away Claire fought her, screaming, "I want to see it! I want to see it!" Two or three years later Eloise had gone to take the mirror down and found the handprint. In all that time no one had cleaned it. Well, who would have? Every day Eloise fought a rising tide of papers and pencils and clothes and toys on the first two floors. She could barely summon the energy to get up the stairs to the third. But the handprint didn't make her feel guilt at this negligence. She felt—well, what had she felt? By then Claire was five or six. Still little, yes, but not this little. Eloise felt awed, that was it. Awed and moved by this evidence from an earlier age, like an explorer discovering drawings in a cave. She'd put the mirror away, but it was the handprint she'd wanted to keep.

"I want to see it!" Claire had cried. What had the *it* been? The sunscreen? The mirror? Or just her own image? Certainly Claire had spent a large portion of her life staring at herself in the mirror, evaluating what was right, correcting what was wrong. But Eloise didn't think of Claire as vain. Or rather, she saw vanity as a dancer's necessary attribute. "I'll miss you, Claire." She said it quietly, for some reason not wanting the two in the back to hear her.

Claire looked so unhappy. Really, wasn't she excited at all? "I'll miss you, too," she said. Then she nearly whispered, "I love you. You've been a good mom."

"Oh," Eloise said, and suddenly her calm was gone, replaced by barely held-back tears. She didn't think any of them had ever used the word *mom* or *mother* or another one like it to describe

her or anything she did. "Thank you," she said. She wondered what Rachel would think. She hoped Theo and Josh hadn't heard.

Theo had heard, though, and was absorbing not just what Claire had said but her own hurt and angry reaction. She shouldn't blame Claire for thinking of Eloise as her mother. Claire remembered nothing of their parents, or their deaths. It still amazed Theo that they'd all lived through a life-changing event only three of them recalled. In Claire's world her parents' death had essentially never happened, which left Theo both envious and glad. Claire didn't know what she'd lost. She didn't share Theo and Josh's memory—passed back and forth so often they no longer knew who'd originated it—of the warmth of their mother's skin when she came in from working in the garden, the way all summer her nails had dirt under them because she gardened in old, frayed gloves with holes in the fingertips, the way she wore her headphones outside while she weeded and from time to time sang along to the music so loudly she must have forgotten she was the only one who could hear it. How delighted their mother had been each year when the first emergent fruits and vegetables appeared, as if the plants had done a magic trick. She'd drag Theo away from whatever book she was reading and insist she marvel at the world. Eloise was not that kind of mother. She was the kind who looked up distractedly from her computer when you asked her for help with your homework and said, "Oh. Can't you figure that out by yourself?"

At the airport Eloise dropped the three siblings off and went to park the car. Josh hefted Claire's duffel bag through the automatic doors while Theo and Claire followed. Theo wanted to hook her arm through Claire's, but something made her hesitate, even slow her pace, so that she fell a little behind her sister. Claire was really exaggerating her dancer walk, Theo noticed. Usually she did that only with her dancer friends, all of whom dressed in the same tunic-and-leggings style and walked with their feet turned out, their legs leaping one at a time to the front. *Look at us,* that walk said. *We know who we are. We know you admire what we do.*

Look at her baby sister: so secure, so sure-footed. Theo envied Claire her passion for dancing. She envied Claire all her passions. Claire was in so many ways so much more practical than Theo. Or if *practical* wasn't the word, with her ballet-dancing ambitions, maybe grounded, or reasonable, or focused. And yet Claire's life was the one with the all-consuming romances, the one with the overwhelming griefs. "You feel what you feel," she'd said once. "And then you get over it." In her voice had been the verbal shrug with which she often answered Theo's questions about her nature, about how she lived her life.

Without glancing back Josh went ahead to the line for automated check-in. Theo followed Claire over to the display of arrivals and departures, and they both confirmed that her flight was still on time. Then Claire turned, gave her an uncertain smile, and went on standing there. "Don't you need to go with Josh?" Theo asked.

Claire shook her head. "He can check me in," she said. "I used his credit card to charge the flight."

"Oh," Theo said.

"I don't have one," Claire said.

"We should have gotten you one before you left," Theo said.

Claire shrugged. "I can take care of it."

"Right," Theo said and tried to sound like she meant it. It was hard to imagine Claire taking care of practical matters, without her or Eloise to guide her. That morning she'd repacked Claire's bag, which had been a chaos of balled-up T-shirts, single socks, hair elastics thrown in loose, and not nearly enough pairs of leggings for a girl who wore them almost every day and would for the first time have to do her own laundry. Theo sighed. "I'll miss you," she said.

Claire frowned a little, as though this were an accusation. "You'll still have Josh."

"Not really," Theo said. "He's always mad at me. I can't say anything without him getting his back up."

"That's because he thinks you're disappointed in him for giving up his music."

"Really?"

Claire nodded. She was watching Theo with a weird intensity. "Are you?" she asked.

Theo looked past her, up at the screen and its long, long list of where people went, and where they came back from. "Am I? I guess maybe. I guess so."

"But why?"

"It was his *purpose*. I feel like he sacrificed his purpose in life to that fucked-up relationship. He just quit. You don't just quit. How could you even think about quitting?" Theo shook her head. "I guess I understand why he came back here, but I don't understand why he stayed. He should be in a bigger city. He should be leading a bigger life."

"But you came back here. You could have gone somewhere else for graduate school."

"As Eloise is so fond of pointing out," Theo said with a rueful smile. "And the chances that I'll get a job here are slim. The chances that I'll get a job at all are slim, but if I do I won't be able to stay."

"Do you wish you could stay?"

Theo shrugged. "Eloise would kill me."

"Eloise wants us all to go," Claire said. "Everybody wants me to go."

"But not because we don't want you with us."

"Because you want me to be all I can be."

"It's not our fault you're a star."

"Maybe I'm not a star," Claire said, looking at the floor. "Maybe I'm a member of the corps and always will be, and I could be just as happy doing that here as anywhere else."

"Maybe," Theo said. She reached out to smooth her sister's already smooth hair. "But I doubt it. You should be where the action is."

"There's action here," Claire said.

Theo frowned. "Claire, what are you getting at?"

"Nothing." She bit her lip and released it. "Nothing. Just . . . don't be too hard on Josh."

"I'm not. He just thinks I am."

Josh was headed back to them now, Claire's boarding pass in his hand, just as Eloise came through the doors. They gathered in a circle, the four of them, their makeshift family. And then Theo, who couldn't bear her own sadness any longer, said, "Let's get this over with."

Obediently her family fell in step, trudging toward security. But a few feet from the end of the line Claire hesitated. She turned to Eloise and said, "Do you remember those bedtime stories you used to tell me?"

"Huh?" Eloise said. "Oh—about Elsewhere?"

Claire nodded. "Where anything you imagine comes true."

"Some prince was always rushing up to ask you to dance."

"I used to say, 'Where is Elsewhere?' And you'd say, 'As far as you can get from here.'"

"I don't remember that," Eloise said. "But I don't dispute you."

Claire dove, suddenly, into Eloise's arms, but almost as soon as Eloise tightened them around her, Claire pulled away. She turned—she pirouetted—and joined the line of travelers. This time she didn't look back, but they stood there anyway, watching until they couldn't see her anymore, watching an extra few minutes, as though she might change her mind.

"Well, that's that," Eloise said finally. Theo and Josh made noises of assent, all of them doing their best to affirm that it was good Claire was gone. They'd all worked for this—the endless chauffeuring, the hours of waiting in the lobby of the ballet academy. The thousands of dollars that had gone into classes and summer programs, fund-raisers and season tickets, uniforms and shoes and pair after pair of tights. The performances, the bouquets, the bobby pins, the trouble both Eloise and Theo had taken to learn how to make a proper bun, the bloody Band-Aids on the bathroom floor (Theo yelling, "Claire, that's disgusting! Throw them away!"). The encouragement, the praise, the stinging in their palms after all that applause. They'd all wanted her to go. But now each of them had an unnerving, weightless feeling, like they'd never realized before that they were balloons, and that Claire—Claire with her need for them, her exacting schedule, her purposeful and organized life—had anchored them to the ground. They could have comforted one another, if any of them had been brave enough to utter this nonsense aloud.

5

Josh was on the office phone with potential clients when his cell rang. He picked it up, saw Claire's number on the screen, and nearly succumbed to a powerful urge to hang up on the clients and answer her call. He'd been playing phone tag with her in the week since she'd left, and he wanted to know how she was. But more than that he wanted to get off this call. There were times in the course of fulfilling his duties when he became afflicted with an impostor's anxiety. He saw clearly that he got away with not really knowing what he was doing via the skillful deployment of jokes and personal charm. But when the charm didn't work—and when he was on speakerphone, with no idea how many people were listening on the other end and no ability to gauge their responses, it was really fucking hard to make it work—he was left spouting stock corporate phrases, checking his crib sheet for lines about Ben's development philosophy. He grew painfully aware of how often he used the word *approach,* or said he *looked forward* to future interactions, or referred to the listeners' content as *beautiful.* He felt like a salesman, like a bullshitter, and he hated feeling like that. The people today had made an appointment, asked him to call. You'd think they could have made an eensy bit more effort, could have laughed at at least one of his jokes. Instead they were mostly silent. He pictured a roomful of people rolling their eyes at one another, mouthing, "What an idiot."

"Excuse me one moment," he said. He pressed the Hold button carefully. His cell had stopped ringing. He pushed back from his desk, gripping the edge, dropped his head between his arms, and hyperventilated. He shouldn't be here. He shouldn't be doing this. Then what should he be doing? His mind obediently offered up a memory of the stage, the guitar strap on his shoulder, the sweat-soaked shirt clinging to his back, the crowd just handing him love: the energy, the adrenaline, the purity of doing only this, caring only about this. *Life comes alive.* That was all gone now. His only option was to finish this call.

When it was over, he put his cell and his keys in his pockets, called out to the office at large that he'd be right back without making eye contact with anyone who might ask to come with him, and went outside. He took long, purposeful strides toward the coffee shop, like any businessman out for a casual stroll. He'd forgotten Claire's call until the phone in his pocket rang, at which point he remembered it, and took the phone out to see that it was her again. "How's New York?" he asked. "Because I might be looking to run away."

"Really?" She sounded worried, so he hastened to say, "No, not really. I just had a rough time with my last call."

"Well, I have a present for you," she said. "Are you free tonight?"

"Why?" he asked. "You're not here, are you?"

"What? No. Of course not. But I got you tickets to a modern dance performance tonight."

"You did?" He groaned inwardly. He wasn't a huge fan of dance, modern or otherwise. He'd spent much of his life in the pop-culture trenches, but he'd mostly given high culture a pass. If it hadn't been for Claire's performances he'd never have gone to the ballet. He wanted the music to have words. He wanted the dancers to stop gesturing so dramatically. He could have watched more readily if it had been all leaps and spins, but as it was his attention wandered. "How come?"

"Because Adelaide's in it."

He could hear her mischievous smile through the phone. "Is that right," he said. "And why would that matter?"

"Oh," she said. "I just thought you might be interested in her quality of movement."

"I thought she was a ballet dancer."

"She is. But when the company's off for the summer sometimes the dancers do other stuff. Her piece is probably a contemporary ballet. She's so good, Josh. I think you'll enjoy seeing her."

"And that's your only motivation?"

"That's it."

"If I go, you won't be waiting to hear if I talked to her?"

"I won't ask. I won't even ask you how it was. You don't have to explain yourself to me."

There was a little too much emotion in her tone. "Everything okay?" he asked.

"Everything is good," she said. "I wish I could tell you about it."

"Why can't you?"

"You know what I thought about today for some reason?" she said, not answering his question. "How you used to take me on the carousel at the zoo."

When she said that Josh could remember it, too, her hand in

his as she tugged him toward the animal she wanted to ride, his hands on her waist as he lifted her, her little kicking legs, her serious, intense expression as she held on tight and waited for the ride to start. "You always wanted to ride the zebras."

"Zebras are cool. They have an excellent sense of style. But I guess you know that."

"Claire," he said. "You are weird."

"No, seriously," she said. "When you lived in Chicago all you ever wore was black and white."

"That's totally untrue. I had at least one red T-shirt."

"Well, I picture you in black and white." She laughed. "Like a zebra."

"Or a Pilgrim."

"Like a zebra in a Pilgrim hat."

"This conversation has taken a strange turn," he said. "Are you in a surreal mood?"

"Kind of," she said. "Yes. Kind of all the time."

"Sometimes it's like that after a big move. Like, whose life is this?" She made a noncommittal sound in response, and he waited for something more. Theo was right—there was something Claire wasn't telling them. "Hello out there?" he said.

"I have to go," she said. "Two tickets at Will Call under your name. Give Adelaide a kiss for me."

"Yeah, sure."

"Did I say a kiss?" she asked, mischievously. "I just meant tell her hello."

He didn't even consider inviting Theo to the performance, and though he did think of Eloise, taking his aunt would mean Theo knew he was going. He didn't want to invite commentary. He felt self-conscious enough already. Ben's wife was hugely pregnant and didn't like her husband going out at night, so Josh called Noah, who'd said at the party that he wanted to hang out sometime, and who agreed to go on the condition that beforehand they go to Grammer's, Noah's favorite bar, the virtues of which occupied much of their preshow conversation. Before they went inside, Noah made Josh pause to admire the huge, lit-up leaded-glass window—imported from Germany in 1911, Noah said—and Josh realized how strongly the other man reminded him of Theo. It took him a few minutes to shake off the association, to relax in Noah's company again. And, then, at the theater, almost as soon as they were settled in their seats, Noah unsettled him a second time.

"I have a confession to make," he said. "I've been debating whether to tell you, but what the hell." He smiled. "I know who you are."

"Well, I hope so," Josh said, though of course he knew exactly what Noah meant. "We've been hanging out all night."

Noah, rightly, ignored this. "You were in Blind Robots! Man, I loved that band."

"Yup," Josh said.

"You guys were awesome!"

"Thanks," he said. He was flattered. He would have admitted, under interrogation, that he enjoyed being recognized. But he didn't want to rehash old triumphs tonight. Or maybe he did. The day at work had left him feeling decidedly unawesome. He might benefit from a little ego boost.

"Can I ask you something?"

Josh braced himself and said a wary okay.

"What made you quit?"

Josh shrugged. "You know."

Noah shook his head. "I really don't. I really, really don't."

Josh trotted out his usual explanation, listening to himself inflect the words as though they'd just occurred to him, as though he hadn't arranged them in just this way a million times before. "We got to a certain level," he said, "and we weren't going to go any higher. I mean, we came close. We had the meetings with the majors and we made a video that would air at, like, two in the morning. But at some point I realized that was going to be it. And there was nothing wrong with that. We had a good thing going. It was just, to maintain it, I had to spend most of my life in vans and bars. For the other guys it was worth it, but for me after a while it just wasn't. You either want to be in a band more than anything else, or you don't."

"You think you would've stuck with it if you'd hit that next level?"

"I mean, maybe. Because we might've toured less. We might've gotten more songs in movies and commercials. We might've had more money, and not had to live with each other anymore. They're all still working musicians, you know. The other guys."

"Yeah, I read that," Noah said.

"They were not super psyched when I quit," Josh said. He looked at the black, empty stage in front of them and said to it, "An understatement."

"I have an aesthetic theory to explain why you never got bigger. Do you want to hear it?"

"I don't know. Do I?"

"Don't worry, it's not bad. When you're trying to figure out why, say, lots of people like *Avatar*, and a much smaller number of people like *Bottle Rocket,* you have to look at the emotional delivery system. Because it's all about that."

"The emotional delivery system."

"Right. Because all art is about emotion, right? I mean, not that it doesn't have an intellectual component, but in essence, at *base,* it's about emotion. Some people just like their emotion delivered straight up. I'd say most people. So that's why they like James Cameron films. But a smaller number of people, because of personality or training or both, need there to be something smart about the way the emotion is delivered, or they can't feel it. Sometimes that's irony or self-awareness or just quirkiness. Like Wes Anderson films. Those movies are actually really emotional, but there's this quirkiness and this irony, and if you're somebody who needs those things first, so you can let your guard down and allow yourself to feel, then you're going to love those movies." Noah looked around the theater, as if searching for the raised hand of someone who agreed with him.

Josh waited, still feeling wary. Was he about to be cheerfully offered unsolicited criticism? He'd never understood why people did that, or why they took for granted your polite response. What if he walked up to a stranger in a bar and said, "That shirt's a nice color but it makes you look fat"? Would he expect the person to thank him?

"Your music is really emotional and earnest but also ironic and smart," Noah said. "Some people don't see the sincerity because of the irony, and some people don't see the intelligence because of the sincerity. The people who loved you really, really loved you—because you gave them exactly the right emotional delivery system for their natures. But you were never going to get mainstream."

"So we were doomed from the start."

"No, man, no. You guys were *awesome*. You just were what you were, you know? I was one of the people who really, really loved you. I saw you guys play, like, ten or eleven times."

Noah's confidence and ease were impressive. In Josh's experience most people couldn't make a declaration like that without self-consciousness or excessive excitement, or this shyly hopeful quality, like they'd just proposed to him. But Noah didn't seem to feel that his onetime fanboy status put them on different planes. It was Josh, instead, who felt self-conscious. He made a show of opening his program. "Let's see what we've got here," he said and hunted for Adelaide's name. Her piece was in the second half of the program. The lights began to dim, the warning bell chimed, and he sighed and settled in, slouching lower in his seat so the people behind him could see.

Onstage five men threw five women in the air in perfect sync and Josh caught himself wondering if Adelaide was dating, or had dated, or wanted to date one of the male dancers. They were some very fit men. He hadn't said to himself that he planned to look for Adelaide after the show, but now he realized that he had, nevertheless, been planning to, and felt nervous about the prospect. But he didn't have to talk to her, he reminded himself. Not if he didn't want to. Not if he was happy with his life as it was now—steady, consistent. It had been a relief, when he quit music, to stop living like a gambler, riding waves of giddiness and disappointment. But, man. He hadn't felt something big in a long, long time. Despite himself, he hoped that when Adelaide came onstage she would mesmerize him. He hoped that she would stop his heart.

For the rest of the first half Josh managed to focus on the

dancing, though he wasn't entirely sure what he was supposed to focus on. Was he meant to be piecing together the story? Or admiring the length and flexibility of the dancers' legs? When you started using words like *length* and *flexibility*, it seemed like you were being pervy, but you weren't supposed to be pervy at a dance performance, you were supposed to be aesthetically high-minded, verging on philosophical. Right? Or maybe he was overintellectualizing, and you were just supposed to feel something—the kind of emotional transport he was used to getting from music. He needed some training for watching dance. At Claire's performances he'd always kept his eyes on her when she was onstage, tuned out when she wasn't. At intermission, as he and Noah downed beers in the lobby, he noticed that some of the other people had bouquets with them. Damn. He should have brought a bouquet. Next time. If there was a next time. How much longer, anyway, until Adelaide's turn? Why was he so anxious and scattered? What was wrong with him?

And then, at last, Adelaide. She was just as lovely as he remembered, maybe more, at this oblivious distance, with her limbs so beautifully displayed. She was alone onstage with one of the dastardly men. They were clearly meant to be a couple in some distress, as couples often are. They stalked each other, sprang together, sprang away. Her body expressed both yearning and confusion. The end of the piece was a rapid pow-pow-pow of ecstatic spins and lifts that made him think of the finale of a fireworks display. Then the male dancer set her down and she pulled herself up straight. They faced each other like fighters, and then turned their backs and did their stalking dancer walk off opposite ends of the stage.

Josh unfolded, slowly, in a daze, clapping vigorously as he got to his feet, barely aware of Noah standing beside him. He could hear his own heartbeat as she took her bows. He'd found her attractive before, but now she was definitively beautiful—she was a necklace in a window, a sparkly ornament on the Christmas tree. She caught the light.

Before and after Sabrina, love and sex had been easy—too easy—to come by. That was how it was when you were in a relatively successful band. He'd been a singer, a guitar player—the guy pouring his heart out at the front of the stage. Most girls he met already thought they were in love. It was only a matter of whether he felt like loving them back. And then right after he quit music his history seemed to exponentially multiply whatever his natural attractions might be. The first woman he dated at all seriously loved tales of his glory days—How he had a hit in France! How he met the guys in Phoenix! But then she started to want those days to return. She didn't say so, not at first. She introduced him to friends and family without a word about his current job. "Josh was in Blind Robots," she'd say. "You know, the band. He toured with Spoon! He had his picture in *Rolling Stone!*" People's eyes brightened at this news. He took a guilty pleasure in this. It was like having a ticket to a sold-out show, or better yet, a backstage pass. People let you in. They took for granted you were special, particular, worthy of their attention. But he really wasn't, not anymore.

After a month or so she started to ask, "Do you ever think about going back to it?" It was exciting to date a former almost rock star, but in the end that was just a gateway drug, and the more she thought and talked about his past the more she wanted it to be her present. Then she could go on tour with him and meet the guys in Phoenix herself. Then she could take a special pride in dating Josh without ever needing to explain why she had the right to do so. Then she'd never feel deflated by the people who failed to be impressed, who asked, "Why haven't I heard of you?" and took obvious pleasure in the notion that under their strict standard of accomplishment he could still be dismissed.

Josh had stopped calling her six or seven months ago, and hadn't been out with a woman since. He was done with music, with the currency it gave him. There was both novelty and excitement in being the one in the audience tonight, handing up his heart to the one onstage, hoping, hoping to be chosen. What he'd been drawn to, meeting Adelaide, was her passionate ambition, or ambitious passion. He liked her for that. It was the thing he'd lost, or surrendered, the thing he tried to stop himself from wanting back.

Outside in the lobby Noah said, "So, are we going to hang out and see if she emerges?"

"What?" Josh asked.

"The dancer. Your sister's teacher. Adelaide? That's why we're here, right?"

"I guess it is," Josh said.

"Good with me," Noah said. "Let me just hit the head and see if I can get another drink. I'll find you back here?"

Josh told himself he didn't feel awkward, leaning against the wall, waiting, surveying the room. If there was anything he had gained from his time as one of the nearly famous, it was an ability to stand alone in a crowd and feel self-contained rather than exposed, an assumption that eventually someone would want to talk to him. Except—that wasn't true here, was it? He'd believed for some time that he no longer traded on his sort-of fame, but almost everyone of his acquaintance knew about it. He hadn't realized that that was a kind of armor before having to stand here now, entirely without it. The dancers began to appear, approaching the lingerers with the hesitant air of deer in a garden. He understood—they were comfortable performing, but performing made people want something from them offstage, and they weren't always sure what it was or how to give it, because offstage they were just themselves. And now people began to swarm them, offering the same compliments over and over—and the dancers wanted those compliments, they *needed* them—but still there was an endlessness to nodding and smiling and saying, "Thank you, thank you," and beginning to feel the need for a transition to another topic, but not knowing how to bring one about.

Adelaide was one of the last dancers to emerge. It was startling to see her in street clothes again, the stage makeup suddenly garish, so that she looked at once normal and strange. She wore a red sundress and very high heels, her long hair released from its bun. He really didn't like how nervous he felt. Maybe he could walk up, remind her who he was, and then immediately say something about missing the postshow high, and then she'd ask what kind of performer he'd been, and he could tell her, and everything would be as it always had been. Same as it ever was. Except if that was what it took to get her attention he didn't want it. Except he did want it, and maybe he didn't care how he got it. No, he should stick to his resolution. Besides, what if he tried that and it didn't work? It wasn't like with Sabrina, when he could then invite her to a show. His failure to impress Adelaide would be a crater in his psychic landscape. This was just so hard, walking up to a woman without any idea what she thought of him. He really wished he'd thought to bring a bouquet.

He saw Noah, then, coming his way with two beers in hand. He watched as Noah spotted Adelaide, then looked his way, eyebrows raised. Josh shook his head. Noah made an oh-come-on face, reached him, handed him the beer, and said, "Follow my lead."

Feeling simultaneously trapped and grateful, Josh followed Noah up to Adelaide, who turned to look at them without apparent recognition. Still abuzz with adrenaline, she smiled at them anyway. "Adelaide, right?" Noah said. "I'm Noah. We met briefly at Eloise Hempel's house."

"Yes, right," she said. "Hello."

"And you probably remember Josh, her nephew," Noah said. "Claire's brother."

"Of course." She looked around. "Is Claire home?"

"No," Josh said. "She's in New York. She got us the tickets, though."

"You two came by yourselves?" she asked, pointing at them, and when they nodded she looked impressed. "I've always found it hard to get men around here to come to performances. Even the ones I've dated."

Dated, she said, not *dating.* "You were great tonight," Josh said. "You looked fantastic."

"Thank you," she said, smiling.

"You were terrific," Noah said.

"Thank you," she said again.

"I don't know much about dance," Noah went on. "But I thought your piece was the most expressive."

"Thank you." Now her smile was growing a little fixed, and Josh had a desperate need to say something to which she wouldn't have to answer *thank you.*

"How did you feel?" he asked.

She looked at him. "How did I feel?" she repeated.

"Onstage," he said. "You felt good?"

"I felt . . ." She shook her head. "I felt amazing."

He smiled. "You weren't thinking about how much your feet hurt?"

"You remember that? No, no, not thinking about that at all. Though it's good to get the shoes off."

All three of them looked down at her feet. "Because those ten-inch stilettos must be a lot more comfortable," Josh said.

She laughed. "They are. You'd be surprised."

"So," he said. "Did we compliment you right? What should you say to a dancer? What do you guys say to each other?"

"We say 'congratulations.' We say 'beautiful job.' We hug."

"You hug," he repeated.

"We say 'congratulations,'" she said again, sounding wary.

"We should have brought a bouquet," he said.

"Oh no," she said. "If everybody brought bouquets we'd have way too many bouquets."

Over Adelaide's shoulder Josh saw an older woman approaching, her eyes glued to Adelaide. Just before she reached them, he leaned in and said, "Can I call you?"

Adelaide glanced at the woman, now standing inches away, and nodded. "Here," Noah said, handing Josh a pen. While the woman waited, beaming, to congratulate Adelaide, she wrote her number on his program, both of them brisk and business-like. She handed him the program without looking at him, and then disappeared into the woman's arms. Josh listened for a moment to Adelaide being told she was beautiful, she was fabulous, she'd been the best one out there. Then he and Noah walked

away, and pushed out the glass doors into the hot, humid downtown.

"Well done," Noah said, but Josh wasn't so sure. He had no
idea if she'd given him her number because she was interested,
or because the woman bearing down on them had left her no
time to think. She'd seemed a little guarded, a little suspicious
of him, and he thought back to the days when girls came up to
him after shows, and how he sometimes wondered what they
would say if he asked just what it was about him that they liked.
He remembered those early days with Sabrina, when everything
had been so good, so charged with pleasure, and how he'd wondered what would happen when the novelty of dating a musician wore off, if they'd be left staring at each other blankly, with
nothing to talk about once *rock star* fell away and left her alone
with Josh.

As if Noah could read his mind, he said, "I bet it's been a
while since you had to make the first move."

Josh shot him a look. "Are you picturing groupies?"

Noah laughed. "Not groupies, exactly. Just hipster girls in
cute outfits."

"I guess there were a few of those," Josh said. He was walking, without thinking about it, toward Fountain Square, where
a very loud band was playing, and Noah walked alongside him.
Neither of them spoke again until they reached the square,
where teenagers danced with ecstatic violence between the stage
and the hundred-and-forty-year-old fountain that gave the square
its name, bronze and majestically tall and flowing with water that
was totally inaudible beneath the raucous music.

"These guys suck," Noah yelled at Josh, who nodded. Then
Noah said, "You know what I keep thinking? Why don't you re-

cord a solo album, just you, Justin Vernon–style? I bet a lot of people would be psyched to hear it."

"I don't know," Josh said. "Where would I do that?"

"Your house, of course," Noah said. "The acoustics are awesome. Man, the first time I walked in that place I thought, This would make a perfect studio."

Josh looked at Noah. "My house," he said.

Noah grinned. "And if you feel like making my dreams come true, I play a mean piano."

Josh looked away from Noah and back to the fountain, the metal woman atop it, shimmering in the artificial light, her arms outstretched and water pouring from her hands onto the creatures below. What was she thinking up there, way above the crowd? "My house," Josh said again. "I never thought of that."

6

Eloise could tell, when Heather called to invite her to lunch, that Heather had in mind a serious talk, probably about the house. Eloise wanted out of the house. Eloise wanted to be unburdened. No one knew that better than Heather. But Eloise wasn't unburdening herself on Heather's timetable, even though she'd promised—so long ago she didn't exactly remember promising, though she'd been reminded of it often enough—that once Claire moved out she'd force the issue of ownership with Francine. She'd insist on knowing whether her mother was ever going to sign the place over, as *she* had long ago promised. And then, one way or another, Eloise would be rid of it—that gorgeous monstrosity, with its ten-thousand-dollar box-gutter repairs, its room upon rooms, dusty and waiting, impossible to keep clean. Rid of it, she'd move in with Heather, and everyone would know about them. That was the prize. That was the brass ring, the golden egg, the finish line. So why—Heather undoubtedly wanted to know—wasn't Eloise sprinting toward it?

Eloise arrived at the sandwich shop in Northside feeling braced and wary, but when she walked in and saw Heather already in line at the counter, for a moment she forgot her wariness and just studied her. Her dark hair was pulled back into one of those stylishly messy buns Eloise could never achieve, her compact body both muscular and curvy. Heather was a devotee of Pilates. She had a truly enviable behind. Heather laughed at Eloise for using the word *behind,* but Eloise, though not usually prudish, did like elegance, and neither the humorous word *butt* nor the crass word *ass* captured the lovely curve of Heather's backside. Heather claimed that if Eloise would exercise with her she, too, would possess such an attribute, but Eloise didn't believe it. In Eloise's mind Heather was much younger than she, though in fact the difference between them was only six years. "Once I turn forty, you're going to have to stop talking about how young I am," Heather had said the other day.

"Only until I'm fifty and you're still in your forties," Eloise had said. "Then I can start it up again." From the way Heather had smiled, Eloise could tell that the implication they'd still be together in five years had gratified her. More and more lately, Heather wanted some kind of public confirmation of commitment, which so far Eloise had been unable to provide.

As she watched Heather checked the time on her cell phone, then glanced back at the door and spotted Eloise, who walked up to join her. "What were you doing back there?" Heather asked.

"Checking you out," Eloise said.

Heather grinned and leaned over to kiss her, but Eloise moved her head so that the kiss hit the corner of her mouth. The place was crowded, and for all Eloise knew there was a former student in here, or a friend of one of the kids. Heather was not Eloise's first girlfriend. There had been one woman before her, a brief and passionate fling that had taken Eloise completely by surprise. She and Heather had met about six months after it ended, when a grad school friend of Eloise's came to town to do research on the birthing center where Heather worked as a midwife. When Eloise met Heather she'd recognized the other woman's interest for what it was. Even if she hadn't, Heather wasn't one to leave her intentions unclear. "Do you date women?" she'd asked, and Eloise had said, "I'd date you." Heather had been delighted, her face breaking into a broad grin that somehow managed to be both friendly and full of desire. Eloise had later regretted her own frankness, not because of what it had led to but because she'd given Heather the impression that she was open and forthright about her romantic life. She'd proceeded to be anything but.

"Relax, sweetie," Heather said now. "It's Northside." Heather only called her sweetie when she was put out with her. Lately Eloise was getting called sweetie a lot.

"Is it Northside?" Eloise asked. "Is that where we are?" Eloise liked the neighborhood—gay-friendly and overrun with academics and artists and relatively diverse. The population was largely a mix of middle-class white and poor black people, everybody united in voting Democrat. On the business strip were stylishly funky restaurants and tattoo parlors and a yoga studio and the Gay & Lesbian Alliance. The convenience store near Heather's house sold microbrew six-packs and XXXL white T-shirts. Though the different populations passed each other on the street more than they mingled in the establishments, every year there were events with a palpable community spirit. At Halloween the residents sat on their porches handing out candy, elaborate cotton spiderwebs and dismembered baby dolls decorating the houses, the sidewalks a crush of princesses and superheroes. On the Fourth of July they turned out for the parade, sitting on the sidewalk to cheer not only the standard marching bands but the twenty-somethings dressed in Victorian wigs and elaborate costumes, the plumbers' floats featuring giant toilet bowls and plungers, the drag queens on stilts, the Lawn Chair Ladies, who danced with their titular lawn chairs, and the Men's Drill Team, who danced with their toy drills. This was where Eloise would have chosen to live if she hadn't been saddled with her parents' house. Still she'd built up some resistance to the place as a result of Heather's living-together campaign, and she was a little annoyed at the inevitability of Heather's suggestions that they meet there.

As was so often the case, Heather ignored her sarcasm. "What are you going to eat?"

Eloise started to name the sandwich she always ordered, and then stopped. "You pick something for me," she said.

"You don't have a preference?"

"It's a trust exercise," she said. "My adventure for the day. I'll go claim a table." She felt Heather watching her as she walked down the long, narrow hall toward the back of the restaurant. Three years together and still she felt Heather's desire, her persistent longing. While she hated that it hurt Heather that she kept their relationship from the kids, that she hadn't yet moved in with her, she wondered from time to time if there wasn't some advantage to postponing the moment when Heather got what she wanted. Of course there was the danger of postponing it so long that Heather's frustration overrode her desire. But why was Eloise thinking this way? She hadn't made any of her choices in an effort to manipulate Heather. She'd just been thinking about what was best for the kids. Sometimes it seemed like that was all she thought about.

"So what did you get me?" she asked when Heather joined her at the table.

"The Yeehaw Barbecue."

"I've never had that."

"You'll like it. I know you will."

Eloise smiled at her. "I'm glad you suggested this. I was having a crappy day."

"The book?"

Eloise nodded. Eloise's first book, about the history of marriage, had been published when she was only twenty-seven, and made her a star in the field. Unlike most first books by historians, Eloise's was not a hairsplitting examination of a small subsubject—divorce in 1950s Mississippi, say—but a book lauded for its ability to be both general and enormously detailed, its ability to appeal to both experts and undergrads. On the strength of it she'd been hired at Harvard. A few times, when a famous marriage went awry or divorce statistics were released, she was interviewed on morning talk shows. She could very easily picture the words *prominent historian* beside her name in *The New York Times*. Now, seventeen years later, she was a department chair at a small school with only a few more articles to her name and fifty-seven bureaucratic emails to answer. She'd taught at a midrung school without producing a second book for so long that her chances at ever moving to a better school were minuscule. She was trying to write a second book now, about location and identity, even though she'd have better luck publishing something else on her original topic. But what did she care, anymore, about marriage? Unless a number of things changed, that particular event was never going to happen to her. "I was just starting to write," she said, "when Noah came by."

"What did he want?"

"Oh, he was having a crisis of confidence and he wanted a pep talk. He's doubting the whole research-and-writing process, feeling like it's presumptuous to guess what people felt or thought a hundred and fifty years ago. He said what you're writing is a historical artifact that may be more useful for understanding your own moment than the moment before you, because you probably, in his words, fucking got it all wrong. He feels dishonest." She smiled. "*Super* dishonest."

"Do you ever feel like that?"

"I don't know. Not exactly. Maybe I worried about that in the past, but all I could think today was that he seemed so young, like I had Holden Caulfield in my office complaining about the world being full of phonies. I didn't say that, of course. I said it was natural to have doubts, he had to trust himself, I knew a good person at Duke University Press to pass his manuscript to." She spun the saltshaker around on the table. "I did my whole mommy-slash-coach thing. But then I was totally derailed from my own work. I started watching videos of flash mobs."

Heather laughed. "You need to go to rehab for those."

"But first I'd have to admit I have a problem," Eloise said. She had lately developed a bit of an addiction to YouTube. She watched staged public outbreaks of dance and cried. She sat in her office with the door closed, smiling and weeping, while Belgians danced in a train station to "Do-Re-Mi," Austenites zombie-stomped to "Thriller," or Cincinnatians shimmied in the rain. What was it about these events that created this particular sensation of overwrought pleasure? The communion of the dancers, the gentle conspiracy. The expressions of the baffled witnesses, whose faces morphed from openmouthed surprise to childlike delight. The pure satisfaction of watching multiple bodies move as one through time. Because there was no reason for the dance! No tickets sold, no careers at stake. No reason beyond the aesthetic. It was a purposeless, beautiful thing.

"Did I tell you Josh and Noah have been hanging out?" Eloise said. "I'm glad. Noah needs more friends here. I don't want him to leave."

"Okay, but I think you're worrying a little too much about Noah. I feel like he enters into every conversation we have."

"Really?"

"Since Claire left anyway. If we're not talking about whether Josh is stuck because he hasn't really dealt with what happened with Sabrina, or whether Theo will ever live up to her potential, we're talking about Noah."

Eloise spun the saltshaker again. "It hasn't been that long since Claire left."

"So?"

"So I feel like you're like, Claire's gone! Forget the kids! Change your whole life!"

Heather sighed. "But that's what you said you were going to do."

"I know," Eloise said.

"I assumed you meant it."

"I did," Eloise said. "I'm still bracing myself for the necessary conversations."

"With the kids?"

"Yes, of course, because basically I'm kicking them out of the house. But I think I'm dreading the call to Francine even more. You know how I hate going to her as a supplicant."

"So don't," Heather said. "Let her deal with the house for once. Just move in with me."

"But then . . ."

"I know, I know, I know." Heather waved her hands in the air. "Stop telling me about the money."

"Do you know how hard it's been to make it on my salary with three kids and that house? I have no savings at all."

"I know that, Eloise," Heather said. "But I also know you always have some reason."

"Money is a pretty damn good reason," Eloise said. "I don't want to be dependent on you."

"No," Heather said. "You'd rather have other people dependent on you."

"What is that supposed to mean?"

"You're so used to taking care of people you don't know how to stop doing it. I mean, if you were trying to write, why did you let Noah in? Why didn't you tell him to come back later?"

Eloise frowned. That had never even occurred to her, and it should have occurred to her, dammit. It would have certainly occurred to an earlier incarnation of Eloise. Somewhere along the way she'd lost the necessary selfishness to be a real scholar. "Maybe I just don't want to write the stupid thing," she said.

"I know this will make you mad," Heather said, "but you don't have to write it."

"I have to write *something*."

"Why?"

"Because I have to," Eloise said. "But I have no idea what I want to say about location and identity. It seems like I conceived of this topic as some kind of excuse for living here."

"You don't need an excuse."

"You know what I mean. A lot of people see it as a kind of failure to stay in the place where you're from, especially if you're from the Midwest. Like ambition is geographic." Heather didn't answer. Eloise watched her deciding not to speak and, impatient, spoke for her. "You're going to say I'm the one who sees it that way."

"I wasn't going to say that."

"You wanted to."

Heather shrugged. "Why say it again?"

"If I give up on this book, what excuse will I have to bore you with this topic?"

"None," Heather said emphatically.

"Better keep at it then," Eloise said. Their food arrived, and for a few silent minutes they busied themselves with eating it. Then Eloise said, "What about this? And just hear me out. What if instead of me moving in with you, we both just moved away from here?"

Heather practically flinched, but once she washed down the bite she was chewing and spoke, her face and voice were calm. "Where would we go?"

"Boston?" Eloise said.

"You just said money was important," Heather said. "What would we do for money?"

"We'd have to get jobs. I don't know. Maybe I could pick up a class or two. They need midwives everywhere, right?"

"Sure," Heather said. "But they probably have plenty there already. And I have a practice here. You have a job. We have friends. The cost of living is probably twice as high in Boston as it is here. I own a house, and I'd take a loss if I sold right now."

Eloise sighed.

"You know I love you," Heather said. "If moving to Boston was what it took to be with you, I'd do it. But, Eloise, you won't even tell your kids about us. You can't bring yourself to move one neighborhood over. It seems extreme to go from that to moving halfway across the country."

"I didn't really mean it."

"But I think you kind of do mean it," Heather said. "I think you've had in your head all these years that once the kids were grown your life could go back to what it was, and you're afraid that once you really commit to me it never will."

"My life can never go back to what it was," Eloise said.

"Yeah, but is that what you're wishing for? If you could snap your fingers, would you rather have that than me?"

Before Eloise could think about it, she leaned across the table and kissed Heather full on the mouth. Then she fell back in her chair, glancing around to see if anyone had noticed. Heather watched her with an amused and rueful expression. "That would have been a bolder statement if I hadn't gotten nervous after," Eloise said.

"Close enough," Heather said.

"I'm going to tell the kids," Eloise said, and not for the first time.

"I hope you do," Heather said. "They're grown-ups. It's been seventeen years."

"What does that mean?"

"Their parents left them. They didn't want to but they did. And you have to stop feeling like you failed them by not being the person their mother would have been. You have to stop trying to make up for their parents dying by refusing to live your own life."

"There's no way to make up for their parents dying."

"I know, honey. That's why you have to stop trying."

"I know you want me to be different," Eloise said.

"All I want," Heather said, "is for you to embrace the life you're living, and stop wishing it was something else."

Eloise smiled, though without the effort she was making she might have cried. "That's a lot to want," she said.

"If you can't do this for me, Eloise . . ." Heather shook her head. "I just don't know."

"You don't know what?"

Heather pressed her lips together and shook her head again. Eloise saw tears in Heather's eyes and felt alarm. She counted on Heather's perseverance. She had the freedom to be wishy-washy only because Heather was sure. "Don't talk like that," Eloise said. "I surrender. Just tell me what you want me to do."

7

Waking from an unintentional nap, Theo opened her eyes to the crack in the ceiling that had greeted her since she was eleven and moved into this room. She had a fondness for that crack, which looked to her like a rabbit. Unlike her aunt, Theo liked the fact of the house's age, and the evidence of it: the crack in the ceiling, the creaky floorboards, the stained glass, the panel in the front hall with buttons for calling the servants, the cushioned window seats on either side of the front door, where ladies could sit and wait for their carriages to arrive. She'd always loved the house, even when it had been her grandparents' house and not hers. In a room on the third floor Francine had kept old toys—artifacts not just from her children's childhood but from her own and even her parents'—and to Theo the door to that room had been as close as she came to the magical doors in her favorite books. So many mysteries, so much bewildering evidence of the childhoods of people who seemed impossibly old. The ancient rocking horse, the wooden dollhouse, the doll loved so long she was nearly bald—Theo wasn't sure where these things had gone, or when they'd disappeared.

At least in decor, the house looked nothing now like it had

when her grandparents owned it. Francine had favored a style appropriate to the era when the house was built, lots of spindly-legged tables and chests with carved crowns and animal feet. "Let's get rid of this junk," Eloise had said, nearly as soon as her mother headed south. They'd sold most of it, and used the proceeds to fund purchases of midcentury modern. Theo had never argued with Eloise's passion for disposal, but even these many years later she still regretted the elaborate vanity that had once been in her grandmother's room and the four-poster bed that had belonged to her mother. She would have liked to spend her girl-hood beneath the canopy of that four-poster, imagining the girls who might have slept in her room before her, wearing long white nightgowns and their hair in a braid. She had ended up a histo-rian, after all.

Instead she'd always slept in one of two sleek metal twin beds, and ever since she'd moved out of a crib, Claire had slept in the other. Claire had had her own room, but she'd always wanted to be with Theo. She'd wanted Theo to sing to her until she closed her eyes. She'd wanted Theo to comfort her after bad dreams in the middle of the night. Many mornings Theo woke to find Claire curled against her, her small, warm back pressed firmly against Theo's. Even when she was a teenager and Claire a child of six, seven, eight, Claire had clung to these rituals. Or Theo had. Sometimes, looking back, she wasn't sure which.

Theo missed her sister. She'd been having trouble working. She knew what she was feeling—aimless, depressed, adrift—but she failed to connect these feelings to Claire's absence. Like a lot of reliable people, Theo didn't realize how much she'd come to depend on being depended on. Growing up, she'd had Claire and Josh, of course, and though she'd often resented the expectations that she'd drive Josh to music lessons and Claire to the ballet, that she'd help them with their homework, that she'd be their therapist, those expectations had given purpose to her life. In college she'd been the still, calm center of a group of people experimenting with various versions of craziness—she was the designated driver, the one who gave tough-love advice, who heard late-night confessions of frightening drunkenness and weird sexual encounters with inappropriately older men. By the time she got to grad school, she'd lost some of her taste for crazy, exhausting friends, but still she had her professors and her classmates and her students, all of whom needed her energy and her attention and her best, most sincere effort, which she tried at all times to give. Now Claire was gone, Josh might as well be, and she had no one else's needs to give shape to her days.

She sat up, yawning, and resolved for the thousandth time to accomplish something with the remaining hours of the day. If she couldn't make progress on the dissertation, she could finally update her CV. She could send out emails asking for letters of recommendation. She could start writing a cover letter and a teaching philosophy. Sure, all that could be done. But first, she needed to make some coffee, and maybe rummage through the pantry after something sweet.

She walked into the kitchen, yawning hugely again, and heard Josh saying to Eloise, "I have a date tonight, but I'm not leaving for a while." They were leaning on the counter near the coffeepot, but it didn't look like anyone had made coffee, or had any intention of doing so.

"You have a date tonight?" Theo said. "With who?"

"Adelaide," Josh said stiffly, looking away.

"That's nice," Theo said, stung by his tone.

"What about you?" Eloise asked. "Do you have a few minutes right now?"

Theo hesitated, not because she didn't have a few minutes but because she didn't like the serious note in her aunt's voice. "I'm writing," she said, which maybe didn't express the facts but captured her intentions. "I just came down for coffee."

"I don't want to interrupt you," Eloise said. "We can talk later."

"Now's okay," Theo said. "I don't like suspense."

Eloise didn't respond to this, didn't make a joke or say there was nothing to worry about. She sat down at the kitchen table and waited for the other two to join her. Then she said, "I'm not sure how aware you two are of my arrangement with your grand-mother about the house." She paused as though waiting for them to jump in, but neither did. Theo had no idea what was in Josh's mind, but she was filled with a dread that kept her silent. "It was her idea that we sell your parents' house and move in here, and then of course she left for Sewanee. When she moved she prom-ised to sign this house over to me, but she's put that off over the years. A couple of years ago we agreed she'd do it once Claire was out of the house, and today she told me she was ready."

"Okay," Josh said, but warily, Theo noticed. He, too, must have sensed something bad coming.

"So," said Eloise, "why am I telling you this? Well, guys, the thing is, once Francine does finally make the house mine, I want to try to sell it."

"No," Theo said, before she could think. "You can't do that to us."

For a moment Eloise looked stunned, as though a student at the back of the class had risen to denounce her. But then her look of surprise slid toward anger. "I'm not doing anything *to you*," she said. "I'm hardly throwing you out today."

"No, you're throwing us out later," Theo said.

Josh looked at his sister. "It might take a while for the house to sell," he said.

"It might," Theo said. "Or it might not. Josh and I still live here."

Eloise made a visible effort at self-control. "But that's temporary," she said. "You're adults. You weren't going to live with me forever, and then I'll have this enormous house I may or may not be able to unload. Josh is right. It might take a while—it might take a year or two or more in this market—and I can't afford to wait much longer."

"Is that all the house is to you?" Theo asked. "Just something you have to unload?"

"Theo," Eloise said. "This is a very expensive house to maintain. I've put a great deal of money into it, and as a result I have almost nothing in the way of savings."

"What about the money from my parents' house? What about their life insurance?"

Eloise made an incredulous sound. "You think I kept that money for myself? It went into your college funds. It's where I got Claire's start-up money for New York."

"We shouldn't have spent it," Theo said. "We didn't have to go to such expensive schools."

Eloise stared at her. "That's a little beside the point now, isn't it?" she asked. "I'm sorry you're upset, I really am. My mother started out giving me money for the property taxes, and one year she paid for a new roof, but her house in Sewanee was expensive and her own savings were diminishing fast, so I couldn't expect more help from her. For two years I was just an adjunct, and even now I don't make a lot of money." She shook her head. "I don't know what else to say."

Theo rounded on Josh. "What do you think about this?"

He looked stricken. "What do I think?" he repeated.

"Is that such a hard question?" she said. "Do you even know?"

His expression hardened. "Fuck you, Theo," he said.

It was nice to know he had a backbone in there, if you looked for it hard enough, but why was Theo the only person he ever showed it to? She stood without a word, without another glance at her brother or her aunt, grabbed her bag from its place by the front door, and walked out of the house. Her house. *Her* house. She walked for several minutes without being aware of her surroundings, headed down Clifton to Ludlow, where the businesses were, the ice cream shop and the art-house theater and the New Age coffee shop that sold crystals and books about finding your inner Buddha. The stores had changed in the years since she'd been granted the right to walk down there by herself, but not all of them, not enough to make her feel the astonished discomfort of serious transformation. Theo had been twelve when Eloise first let her leave the house alone. She'd asked to go thinking Eloise would refuse, and she could still remember her nervous surprise when her aunt had said, "Sure, go ahead. I'll see you later," without even pausing to consider the question. Suddenly Theo's sense of herself as mature, nearly autonomous, had melted, and all she'd wanted was for Eloise to pull her into her lap like a child. But she'd asked for permission and been granted it, so she had no choice but to set out alone, frightened and free. Now she was more than twice as old, and still her family retained their power over her. The power to wound, to disappoint, to make her feel like a child, misjudged and abandoned, lost in the angry, sorrowful conviction that no one loved her, that she was alone in the world. She thought to call Claire, who would surely ratify her sense of betrayal, who would surely understand.

Except Claire didn't understand. She sounded distracted, preoccupied by New York City, by making it there, making it anywhere. She said, "I don't know, Theo. Her reasons do make sense."

"How can you say that? We're talking about the *house*."

"It's not like she wants to sell *you*."

"Yes, it is," Theo said, feeling both ridiculous and completely justified. "It's like she wants to sell our childhood."

"You didn't even live in that house until you were eleven."

Why did this statement of fact hit Theo like a slap? "I know that," she said, her voice trembling. "That's exactly the point."

"I don't understand."

"Of course you don't," Theo said and got off the phone before Claire could press her to explain. The house was a map of her memories. In this room, I cut my finger with a bagel knife so badly I had to get stitches. In this room, I made out with a boy. In this room, I said goodbye to my parents for the last time. In truth she could barely remember what had happened in what room. Had she said goodbye to her parents in the kitchen? In the living room? On the stairs? Had she yelled goodbye from her bedroom, too absorbed in a book to come downstairs? She didn't know. There was no one she could ask such a question. She had only the house to help her remember. If she lost it she'd be exiled from her history.

She'd reached the business district. A family emerged from Graeter's, licking ice cream cones. Theo turned away from their happy faces and called her grandmother. "It's Theo," she said.

"Hello, Theodora." Francine was the only person who ever called her that, out of perversity, Theo assumed, as she'd once overheard her grandmother say to Eloise that she still couldn't understand why Rachel had saddled her with that name. "It's like she wanted her to be from 1910," Francine had said, and Eloise had snapped back, "I like it," but there was no way to tell whether Eloise had meant that, or just instinctively contradicted her mother the way she always did. Theo's own perversity was to be jealous that she had no mother to contradict, no mother to drive her crazy, no real-life woman to diminish the ideal one in her head, the one who would have always made her feel better, always known exactly what she should do.

When Rachel had been alive she had been the dispenser of both justice and comfort. Few things had felt better to Theo than the moment she unburdened herself of a problem by telling her mother about it. Her mother, who would listen with her serious, sympathetic attention, pull her close, say, "Don't worry, little worrier, we'll figure it out." After she died, Theo had struggled to see Eloise in that role. Eloise had always been the fun aunt, the one who took her to movies she was a little too young for, who told her secrets of adulthood and then exacted promises that Theo wouldn't repeat them to her mother. It had seemed strange to go to Eloise as she had her mother, so mostly Theo had tried to solve her own problems. She tried to behave. The thought of Eloise, who had always made her feel so grown-up, reprimanding her like a child was intolerable. So Theo never gave her reason.

Then when she was sixteen she got drunk for the first time, and drove home in a state that she knew was less than sober. She woke a groggy Eloise in the middle of the night and tearfully confessed. "How much did you have?" Eloise said. She was sitting up in bed, wearing a Lucinda Williams T-shirt, her long reddish brown hair a crazy mess around her face, as though instead of sleeping she'd been standing in front of a wind machine.

Theo had collapsed on the end of the bed by Eloise's feet. Her nose was running, and she pressed it with the back of her hand. "Two beers," she said.

"Oh," Eloise said. And then, to Theo's surprise, she laughed. "Don't be so hard on yourself," she said. "I mean, absolutely if you felt drunk you shouldn't have driven. You should always call me to get you in a situation like that. You know I'll always come get you, right?"

Theo nodded, and then said, "I know," struck for the first time with the fear that by not calling she'd insulted her aunt, suggested she didn't trust Eloise with her secrets and mistakes.

"But two beers, for a sixteen year old . . . I mean, by that age I was an old hand with liquor and pot."

"Really?"

Eloise yawned as she nodded. "Your mom, too. I'm afraid we weren't always such good girls." She leaned forward across the bed and smoothed Theo's hair back from her face. "But I know I don't have to worry about you, honey," she said, her voice gentle, even sad. "You're just so heartbreakingly committed to doing the right thing."

Theo's relief at not being in trouble had been tempered with disappointment, though she hadn't really understood why. There was no one she could count on to stop her from doing things she shouldn't. There was no one to disappoint but herself, no one to rebel against. If Eloise had combined her consolation with remonstrance the way her mother would have, grounded her for a week, Theo would have felt better. Punishment would have allayed her guilt. All would have been right with the world. But Eloise was not, and never had been, her mother, and this latest incident was further proof of that. Her mother would never have sold the house.

"I was hoping to talk to you," Theo said to her grandmother, constrained by the formality the woman always inspired, the danger of hurting her sensitive feelings, of saying something that would make Francine retreat to brood over the offense. Eloise always said her mother was a woman who collected grievances like treasures. In this she wasn't wrong.

"Of course, honey," Francine said. "I'm glad you called. Is it about Eloise?"

Relieved that she didn't have to introduce the difficult subject, Theo answered in a rush. "She told us you're going to give her the house and that she wants to sell it, that she wants to put it on the market right away, even though Josh and I are still living there."

"I know, honey. I know."

"But how can you let her do that? It's your house."

Francine hesitated. "Well, yes, that's true, but your aunt has put a lot into the house. I haven't lived there in a long time."

"What about us?" Theo said. "We live there. I always assumed we'd keep it in the family, that someday . . ." She stopped, accustomed to repressing her daydreams of someday owning the house herself, raising her own children there, turning half the third floor into her library. But now wasn't the time to repress that. This was a battle. Now was the time to bring all her weapons out. "I imagined my own kids there," she said. "We have all this history in that house. How can we just let it go?"

"Oh, Theodora," Francine said, "do you really want to live there someday?"

"Yes," Theo said firmly. "Or if it doesn't work out for me, then I want it to go to Josh or Claire."

"Eloise tells me you kids won't stay in Cincinnati."

"Well, what does she know?" Anger flashed through Theo, the particular kind of indignant anger you feel when someone levels an accusation that might be true. "She has no idea what we'll end up doing. No idea at all. She only cares about what *she* wants me to do."

"And what does she want you to do?"

"She wants me to get a job at someplace like Harvard and never look back. She wants me to have the life she should have had. But I'm not her, Francine. I can't be her, and what's more I don't want to be."

"No, no, of course you don't," Francine said. "You have to live your own life, honey, and I don't want to do anything to hurt you, or your brother and sister. It's good to know you feel this way. I won't do anything rash, I promise. Let me just think about things."

"Thank you," Theo said.

"You're very welcome," Francine said. "I'm glad I could help."

After she hung up, Theo had a few moments of relief, when the bright street seemed a cheerful place, lively and welcoming. Then the guilt hit her. She heard again the pleasure in Francine's voice at Theo's outburst, at being appealed to, at the opportunity to put her judgmental daughter in the wrong. All those years ago, Theo had been the one to say, "I think we should stay here." Even now she remembered saying it, and not just because once, during the one huge fight Theo could remember ever having with her aunt, about her decision to come home for grad school, she'd said to Eloise, "If you hate it here so much, why did we stay?" and Eloise had said, "Because you wanted to." She had wanted to stay. Everything had hinged on her wanting to stay. Theo had been the cause for the radical shift in her aunt's existence, for the fact that Eloise's own academic career had been derailed. Now here she was trying to derail her again. The worst part was, she wasn't going to call Francine back and say she hadn't meant it. She *had* meant it. She was sorry, but not sorry enough. She felt so wretched with guilt and grief and a terrible gripping fear that soon the house really would be gone that she walked into the first bar she saw and proceeded to get very, very drunk.

Three vodka gimlets in, Theo could feel herself listing on her stool, but still she caught the bartender's eye and signaled for another one. The bartender obliged, and just as the drink landed in front of her a voice behind her said, "Hey. Professor Clarke?"

Theo turned on the barstool to see who had spoken, and only as she did so did she realize how very drunk she was. "Whoa," she said, in the general direction of a pinkish face surrounded by brownish hair. The face had a mouth, and the mouth smiled. Why was it smiling like that?

"Wes," the mouth said. "I'm Wes."

"Are you?" Theo asked. It was an attractive face. A very attractive face, now that her vision had cleared. Brown eyes, nicely shaped nose, generous mouth. Kind of a familiar face. "I'm not a professor yet," she said.

"But you were my teacher," he said.

"Oh," Theo said. "Oh, fuck."

"Why fuck?" He climbed onto the stool next to hers. "Was I that bad a student?"

"Were you that bad a student?" Repeating the student's question bought you time to think of an answer. A handy tip. Had she gotten that from Eloise?

"You gave me an A," he said. "My only A that quarter."

"Did you deserve it?" she asked, even though she knew who he was now, and she knew that he had. He'd been a good student, although at this moment the main thing she remembered about him was that he had a tattoo on his upper arm—some kind of circular design she'd seen poking out of the sleeves of his T-shirts and had assumed was some other culture's symbol for peace or deep thinking or a similar high-minded concept with which an idealistic college boy would want to decorate himself. She couldn't see the tattoo now, because he was wearing a long-sleeved tee, but she knew it was there. His shirt was the one with the wishful-thinking map of a Cincinnati subway. She had one too, in her collection of T-shirts that proclaimed her hometown pride. "I hate myself," she thought, and then realized she'd said it aloud.

"Why?" the guy—Wes—asked.

"I'm making an ass of myself in front of one of my students," she said.

"How so?"

She shrugged. "Being drunk."

"I'm drunk, too," he said.

"You are? Why are you drunk so early?"

"It was an accident. My friends wanted to play pool, and to play pool you have to go to a bar. What about you?"

She hesitated. What reason could she give? "All teachers are heavy drinkers," she said. "Our students drive us to it."

"Good thing I'm not your student anymore."

"I'm still sorry you're seeing me like this," she said. "I hate for the illusion to come crashing down all at once."

"What illusion?"

"That I'm wise and in control of myself and don't have a personal life."

He laughed. "Is that what you think people think? Or just what you want them to think?"

"Both, I guess. It's what I always thought of my teachers. I'm kind of an authority person."

"You're, like, a Fascist?"

"Authority, not authoritarian," she said, and then realized he was teasing. "Did that sound teachery?"

"Very," he said. "But explain."

"I've always had automatic respect for authority," she said. "If anything I have to fight the urge to do what I'm told. When necessary, you know. It was kind of a puzzlement to me to discover how many students aren't like that at all. I didn't realize I'd have to prove I deserved authority." She took a sip of her drink. "Maybe I *am* a Fascist."

He was looking at her with a funny expression.

"Are you about to agree with me? Are you going to say I was a Fascist as a teacher? I think you're supposed to contradict me now."

He said, "I had a huge crush on you."

"What? I'm sorry, what now?"

"I had a huge crush on you." He leaned back on his stool and spread his arms wide. "Huge."

She gaped at him. "No way."

"Wow, you are really surprised," he said.

"Yes! Yes, I am really surprised. You were, like, the boy all the girls in the class liked."

"Was I?"

"Oh, come on, you didn't notice that? They practically all swooned every time you answered a question."

"I only had eyes for you," he said and grinned. "I thought you guessed."

"Me? No, I had no idea." She leaned back and studied him. He'd cut his hair since he'd been in her class, when he'd worn it shaggy but not too long—a length that said, I'm cool and open-minded, but within reason. Over that hair—the sort of golden brown that had probably in childhood been blond—he'd frequently worn a purple knit cap, even in warm weather. Once, she'd asked him about this cap, and he'd told her reading Chekhov in his creative writing class had made him think about the importance of details in creating characters, so he was trying it on himself. This was both ridiculous and adorable and had caused her to be unable to look at him. "Huh. So the popular college boy finally had a crush on me, several years too late for it to matter."

"Hey," he said. He sounded genuinely injured.

"What? I'm sorry, what did I say?"

"That my crush didn't matter."

"Oh, I didn't mean your feelings were meaningless. I meant it was too late for me to do anything about it."

"About what?"

"About someone like you having a crush on me."

He grinned. "Why too late?"

She frowned. "Because I'm not in college anymore."

"But that's what I keep trying to tell you," he said. "Neither am I."

"Oh," she said. He had nicely muscled arms, defined but

not big, and the tightness of his T-shirts had always suggested a nicely muscled chest to match, and because she'd often noticed such details when she looked at him in class, she'd had yet another reason not to look at him. This noticing was not necessarily sexual or even personal—she similarly tried not to look at those female students who wore tight or low-cut shirts, especially the impressively breasted one whose nipples were often visible through her white tees. She wasn't supposed to be noticing their bodies. She was supposed to be educating their minds. Noticing their bodies was supposed to be the province of inappropriate male professors, and Theo had been mortified to discover that she registered those details—his biceps, his tattoo—at all.

Oops, she was totally checking him out. He caught her, too, following her gaze down to his own torso, then shooting her a grin. "I work out," he said.

She groaned and put her hand over her eyes. "What is wrong with me?"

"Nothing," he said. "It's totally legal to check me out. I'm not your student anymore. I'm not even an undergrad."

"This is such a weird conversation." She peeked at him through her fingers. "I was a lot more comfortable talking to you about history."

"Let's talk history then," he said. "Let's just talk."

She removed her hand from her face and looked at him. Oh, boy. He was awfully cute. "I can't remember anything about history," she said.

He laughed. "No, me neither."

"Now you're insulting me!" she said. "I didn't say anything memorable?"

"You're a good teacher," he said. "But the main thing I remember is the aforementioned huge crush."

"Oh yes," she said. "Right."

"I assume you're aware that I'm propositioning you," he said.

"You are? And what does your proposition entail?"

He glanced at her mouth, and he looked all overcome with desire, and he also looked quite adorably nervous. He wanted to kiss her, but it was hard to tell if he was going to. Theo leaned forward and put her hand on his thigh to stabilize herself, and maybe for other reasons, too. She frowned, blowing out air like a child imitating a horse. He waited. Maybe she would kiss him, just to see. She leaned in a little further, and a little further, and there they were: lips. Lips, and then—oh, hello!—tongue, and he was a good kisser, even in this awkward lean-to position where they couldn't really embrace without falling off their stools.

"Hmmm," she said, sitting back. She rubbed her lips together like she'd just put lipstick on.

"Did I pass?"

She smiled. "Yes," she said. "But there will be a final."

He lived in an apartment above the bar, which was awfully convenient. "Did you plan this?" she asked him as they walked up the stairs.

"Sure," he said. "But I didn't think it'd actually happen."

"No, I mean, did you rent this apartment in case you met girls at the bar?"

He laughed, looking through his keys for the right one. "No, but it is turning out to be convenient." He unlocked the door and, with a flourish, pushed it open.

The place felt very postcollege, and that gave Theo pause, but not as much pause as if she'd been sober. At least he had band posters on the walls and not beer and buxom girls. Theo took a leisurely stroll around the borders of the living room. Thrift-store couch that had seen some ill treatment by a cat. Huge TV. Lots of houseplants. The posters were for Band of Horses, Neko Case—"I love her," Theo said—Frightened Rabbit, Grizzly Bear. And, hey, Blind Robots. "No way," she said, pointing. "That's my brother's band. Was. Was my brother's band."

"Are you serious? They rocked, man. They were totally awe-some." He winced. "Did I just ruin this? Talking like that?"

She laughed, thinking of Noah and his fondness for superla-tives. "Apparently I like men who talk like that."

"Yeah? There's more where that came from." He was coming closer now. He had that going-to-kiss-you look. She felt like she was braced at the starting line, waiting for the gun to go off. "Uh-oh," she said.

To her surprise he stopped. "Uh-oh what?"

"I don't know," she said. "Did I say that out loud?"

"Did you not mean to?"

"You looked like you were about to kiss me."

"I *was* about to kiss you. Is that bad?"

"No, no, no. I'm for that. I'm pro that. Let's get to the kissing."

But he hesitated. Why was he hesitating? He'd apparently had a crush on her for ages, but ten minutes in close quarters and she'd already ruined it. She took a step toward him, wobbled a little, put a hand on his arm. He put his arm around her back, but gently, not with anything remotely resembling passion. Then he took his other hand and touched the side of her face. He slipped his palm around to the back of her head, and then, at last, he kissed her, but this, too, was gentle, and closemouthed, and brief. He pulled away, letting his hand slide down her arm until it grasped her hand. "Here's the thing," he said. "I think maybe you're too drunk."

"What?" Oh, shit, this was disappointing. But not over yet. "You're drunk, too."

"Yes, but I'm thinking now that you're drunker than I am. Really we should be the same level of drunk."

She pulled her hand from his. "So you've changed your mind."

"I didn't change my mind." He shook his head as if to emphasize this.

"But you won't . . ."

"I don't think so, no." He still had an arm around her back. His hand was warm through her shirt. "I'd like to, though."

She didn't know what to feel. "You certainly are honorable," she said.

"Would you rather I wasn't?"

She looked at him. "No," she said. "Yes." She walked around the couch and sat down on it. Against her will she remembered an afternoon in Noah's office, the last time she'd visited before her resolution not to stop by anymore. Somehow the conversation had drifted into how hard it was to maintain a long-distance relationship. He'd been leaning toward her, his voice low and pained, as he said, "I just don't know what will change things. I don't know if anything will." She thought of putting her hand on his shoulder. She could feel that if she did that, if she murmured a few words of encouragement or comfort, he might pull her into a hug, and then maybe as she lifted her face from his chest he would kiss her. Oh, God. She was on the verge of making that happen. She could see that future shimmering into being. But he had a girlfriend, and she wanted, always, to do the right thing. So she didn't touch him. She said, "I'm sure it'll work out," in a voice so loud and falsely bright that he looked startled, and then she made some excuse to go.

"I had a reason for getting drunk," she said now, in her best approximation of a conversational, casual voice. "I might lose my house."

"Oh, no." Wes came around the couch, too, and sat next to her, if a cushion's length away. "You can't make the mortgage?"

Theo laughed, startled by his misapprehension. "It's not my house like that," she said. "I don't own it. It's the family house, since the 1950s. But I live there. So it's my house that way."

"How will you lose it?"

"My aunt wants to sell it. She was waiting for my younger sister to leave, and now she's gone."

"Where did your sister go?"

"She went to New York," Theo said. "She's a ballet dancer. When I was a kid I wanted to be one, too. I danced until I was seventeen. But I didn't have her talent. I didn't have the body. I did, however, have the feet." She slipped off her shoe and pointed her toes to show him. "Do you see that? I still can't wear some shoes because I have such a high arch."

"I'm not sure what you mean."

"Look," she said, impatiently. She lifted her leg onto the couch and rounded the top of her foot, her exceptionally good foot, which even after all these years still remembered its perfect curve.

He traced the curve with his finger. "Pretty," he said.

"I don't know why my brother and I don't matter. My aunt thinks I need to move away, and my brother, too, and she wants to get rid of the house, like it's this old dog that shits all over the place and needs to be put to sleep."

"Your brother from Blind Robots? He's back here?"

"Yup. He lives down the hall from me." She wasn't sure how she felt about the interest in Wes's voice, the fact that Josh was the subject he'd chosen for a follow-up question. She pulled her foot away and put it back in her shoe. "He's not very exciting, I hate to tell you."

"He's not playing music anymore?"

"The other night I heard him playing his guitar, but no, not really," Theo said. "Enough about him. You want to know another secret? I'm not really writing my dissertation anymore."

"You're not?"

Theo shook her head elaborately. "I'm a fifth-year PhD, and I got a fellowship this year to work on the dissertation, because everyone thinks I'm so promising and I just needed this year to finish it. But you know what? I *have* finished it."

"Really? Well, why don't you—"

"What? Apply for jobs? Ha! You sound like"—she shook her head again—"everybody. You sound like everybody. I want to amend my last statement. I haven't finished it. I've written everything but the introduction. It's not that I can't finish what I start. It's that I can't start what I finished."

Wes considered her a moment. Then he said, "Do you want to tell me why?"

"I don't know why," she said. She leaned her head back, closing her eyes so tears wouldn't fall. "I guess I just don't want to leave."

"You can't get a job here?"

"Probably not. Schools don't like to hire the people they trained, even if there was an opening." Her eyes were still closed, and so it seemed like talking to herself when she said, "And I can't decide if it's okay that I want to stay, or if it means something is wrong with me."

"I'm not objective," he said, "but I don't think anything's wrong with you."

To her immense embarrassment, she was leaking tears. "How old are you, anyway?"

"I'm twenty-two." He said it like an apology.

"Why did I come up here?" she asked, in a voice that was peevish, and belligerent, and sad.

He put his hand on her shoulder, his fingers tickling the back of her neck. "I asked you to."

"Then why'd you let me make such an ass of myself?"

"Don't feel like that," he said. "I don't want you to feel like that."

"How do you want me to feel?"

"Happy."

She stared at him. Was he simpleminded? "Excuse me," she said. "I'm going to make a call."

She called Josh, who'd been so pissed at her before but now didn't even ask for an explanation, just said he'd be right there. Josh was the only person she could call who would come get her without asking questions, who would, for God's sake, be *nice*. She'd spent so much time protecting him from his own niceness that she sometimes forgot how much she herself had always relied on it. When she harangued him for always putting others first, she failed to think about the times he had done that for her. Once, exhorting him to break up with Sabrina, she had slammed her fist on the table right in front of him. "Jesus Christ, man," she'd said. "For your own *self-respect*." It had been so much easier to protect him when he was little. When she was nine and he was seven they'd had a snowball fight in the backyard with some neighbor-hood kids, including a boy named Chase, who was older than they were and bordered on being a bully. Breaking the rules of combat, Chase hit Josh in the face with a piece of ice. Josh's hands flew to his face, and when Theo pulled them away to see the damage, there was blood on his skin and on his gloves. Chase stood a few feet away tossing another ice ball from hand to hand, the look on his face a mixture of triumph and guilt. Theo ran at him in a fury, and he turned to flee, so that she tackled him from behind, slam-ming his face into the snow. She pummeled his puffy, snowsuited shoulders while he lay there, stunned, she thought later, by the shock of retaliation. What had eventually made her stop? She couldn't remember. She did remember Josh's face afterward, his sweet, blood-and-water-streaked face, wearing an expression of awe. He'd had crystals of snow in his eyelashes.

Now Josh got out of his double-parked car and came around with his fists at his sides, like he was there to protect her, like he was bracing for a fight. She saw his eyes go past her to Wes, who'd insisted on accompanying her outside but stayed back by the door while Theo made her slow and careful way to the car. "Hey, man," Josh said, in a way that was friendly but not really, and Wes said, "Hey." He put his hands in his pockets and leaned against the wall, but he didn't go back inside.

Josh came around the car to open the door for Theo, and as she stepped inside he asked, "Is that guy bothering you?" Theo nearly laughed at the question. It was so beautifully, typically male. The answer was yes, of course, but not for the reasons Josh might be imagining, so she shook her head.

"Thanks for coming to get me, Joshy," she said. "I'm too drunk to walk home alone."

He looked at her, surprised by the naked emotion in her voice. "Of course," he said. She leaned her head back against the seat and closed her eyes. She looked so sad, about the house, he assumed. He sympathized, he really did, and he might have said so earlier if she hadn't immediately jumped down his throat. He shut the door gently and then gave it a pat. His steps were slow as he made his way back around the car. That guy was gone. Whatever Theo said, her mood, this scene, must have something to do with him, and suddenly Josh wanted to find the guy and punch him in the face. Seeing Theo vulnerable was akin to being in free fall. He grabbed anger like a handhold and clung to it, stood there a moment squeezing his keys in his hand. He was seriously considering going inside, this twenty-six-year-old man who had never, in all his life, been in a fight. A rapping sound made him jump, and he turned to see Theo leaned over to frown at him out the driver's-side window. "What are you doing?" she said. He couldn't quite hear her, but he could read her lips, as well as her expression. His anger withdrew. Suddenly she seemed exactly like herself.

They drove back to the house in silence. Theo had returned to her position as soon as he got in the car: head back, eyes closed. He wanted to ask her what was wrong, but the idea made him nervous. It occurred to him that lately when he wondered why they couldn't seem to talk anymore, what he was wondering was why he couldn't talk to her. Had she ever come to him with her problems? He couldn't remember a time, but until things got really bad with Sabrina, he'd always gone to her with his. In a moment of familial telepathy, he, too, was visited by the memory of the time she clobbered the neighbor boy, whom Josh could picture although he couldn't remember the kid's name.

He'd been sitting in the snow, cold and wet and crying as blood streamed down his face, and Theo had been a superhero swooping to his rescue, the way she'd flown at that boy. He'd stopped crying immediately, filled, as he watched her pummel that kid, with the certainty that he was safe. He wondered if she remembered that moment with as much clarity as he did. He thought of asking her, but for no reason he could name, the silence between them seemed too hard to break.

8

When Theo called, Josh had been standing at the open door of Adelaide's apartment, having just arrived to pick her up for their first date. Adelaide was wearing a slim, pale dress and high heels, and her dark hair was down. Their reservation at a nice restaurant was in fifteen minutes' time. Even as he said, "Oh, sorry, hang on," and answered the phone, he wondered why he was doing it. Probably guilt over the last thing he'd said to Theo, before she'd walked out of the house and disappeared. He was surprised she'd call him after that, and the fact that she had gave him a presentiment that something was wrong. "Okay, this is really bad timing," he said after he hung up, "but I have to go pick up my sister. She's unbelievably drunk."

"It's so early," Adelaide said.

"I know. It's not like her, but she had a fight with my aunt this afternoon." He put the phone in his pocket slowly, deciding what to say. "Do you want to come with me?"

"Oh." Adelaide frowned. "I don't think so."

"Oh," he said in turn. "Right. Okay." He was flummoxed. "Well, we'll miss our reservation."

"How about this? You go get your sister and take care of her, and I'll order pizza. You can come back here with a bottle of wine."

"Really?"

She shrugged, then nodded, an ambivalent response if he'd ever seen one. "A first date at a fancy place is usually uncomfortable anyway," she said. "You know, the place makes you feel so formal. We can be relaxed here."

He hoped she was right. He felt anything but relaxed walking away from her door. He'd been tense all day, anticipating the date, and Eloise's timing in delivering her news hadn't helped. As soon as Eloise had withdrawn to her room, parting from him with a hug that suggested she thought he was on her side, he'd tried to put the whole thing aside to think about later. But the weird scene with Theo and that guy—that kid—brought back his dismay and confusion, and he began to feel that way too much was riding on this date, although what the "too much" was he couldn't be sure. By the time he took Theo home and got her upstairs with Advil and a glass of water and had her reassure him two or three times that she wasn't going to throw up, nearly an hour had elapsed, and he still had to stop and pick up wine. He got two bottles, not knowing whether Adelaide liked white or red. For an anxious, manic moment he considered getting more, because he didn't know if she liked Pinot Noir or Zinfandel, Sauvignon Blanc or Chardonnay. Driving back to Adelaide's he played the music loud to drown out his nerves. He pictured her sitting with a cold pizza, staring angrily at the clock. He hoped she'd waited a little while to order it.

There was no cold pizza, no angry stare, just Adelaide, still in her dress of ambiguous color, but now a few inches shorter, and wearing ankle athletic socks. She opened the door and stepped way back to let him in. "The pizza should be here soon," she said, closing it behind him. "How's your sister?"

"She's okay, I guess," he said. "She was really wasted."

"And that's unusual." She went ahead of him into the kitchen, and he followed. The apartment was kind of a boring, new-building place, the sort where everything would work but nothing had any special charm. He hoped this was no reflection of her personality.

"Yes, that's unusual," he said. He leaned against the counter and watched her reach up to retrieve wineglasses from a cabinet. "Really unusual. I'm sure it was the fight with my aunt, but the way she lost her temper was unusual, too. She's one of those people who prides herself on keeping it together. They both are."

"What were they fighting about?"

Josh found that he didn't want to answer this question. If he explained about the house, and Eloise's and Theo's positions on it, then Adelaide would probably ask about his, which had been complicated lately, truth be told, by Noah's suggestion that he could record a solo album there. Josh had been unable to stop himself from trying out the acoustics of various rooms. While he was making up his mind what to say, Adelaide was distracted by the insides of her wineglasses. She blew into them, then glanced at him as if to see if he'd noticed. "Maybe I should rinse these," she said.

"Why?" He grinned. "What's in them?"

"Just dust," she said. For some reason she was blushing. He felt much better himself, seeing that she was nervous, too. "I guess I don't entertain a lot."

"If you point me toward your corkscrew, I'll open a bottle. White or red?"

"Oh, either's fine," she said. She opened a drawer and made a little racket shifting everything in it around. "It's in here somewhere."

"If you don't find it I'll just use my teeth."

"Oh!" she said, missing his joke. "Here it is." She straightened with the corkscrew in her hand, triumphant, and thrust it, point forward, in his direction.

"Whoa." He jumped back, playacting that she'd been trying to attack him. And then wished he hadn't. She didn't seem amused. Her blush deepened. She looked like she wanted to flee the room. "Thanks." He took the corkscrew and opened both bottles without saying another word.

The doorbell rang then, and Adelaide said, "Pizza!" like she was saying, "We're saved!" Food and wine in front of them, they sat at the table and talked about food and wine.

"Have you been to Boca?" he asked her.

"Once." She pulled pepperoni off the slice on her plate, and he wondered why, if she didn't like pepperoni, she'd ordered it. "I don't get out much anymore."

"Really?"

"My life is kind of boring," she said.

"How is that possible?" he asked.

"All I do is dance."

"All day long? All night long? Like in *The Red Shoes*?"

She seemed, finally, to find something he'd said amusing. "I hope not. That girl dies."

"That's true. Don't dance until you die."

"I won't." Her mouth turned down. What had he said? Why was it wrong to ask her not to die? Take a deep breath, he told himself. You can do this. This is nothing you haven't done before.

"I admire your discipline," Josh said. "Now, me. I don't even exercise."

"Not at all?"

He grinned. "I'm supremely unathletic. And I'm a whiner, too. I get sweaty, I get tired, I want to quit."

"Really?"

"When I was in college one of my friends took me to her tae kwon do class. I had to go sit down in the corner and put my head between my knees. She was really embarrassed. She went around making sure everybody knew I was *not* her boyfriend." Adelaide laughed and he said, "In my defense, I'd gone out to dinner beforehand and had two beers. Also I wore jeans. Although come to think of it, telling you I went to tae kwon do drunk and wearing jeans might not be much of a defense."

"No, it is," she said. "You weren't a wimp, you were just—"

"A dumbass?"

"I didn't say *dumbass*."

"You were going to say *dumbass*. Weren't you? You were thinking dumbass."

"Oh," she said. "You don't know what I'm thinking."

"Well, that's true," he said, suddenly thoughtful. "That's definitely true."

He picked up his wineglass, and she picked up hers, and for a moment they drank in silence. Now what? Would she just wait for him to start talking again, ask her a question, tell another story? He knew he had a knack for filling silence, but even he got tired, sometimes, of talking. Usually he was good at finding out what was on people's minds. It was part of his drawing-people-out skill, asking them questions that led gradually, imperceptibly to the information he wanted. He'd been the one to figure out, year after year, what Eloise wanted for her birthday. He'd been the one to talk to the bass player when he fell into a sulk. He'd even been able to use this skill on Sabrina, ferreting out the reason for one of her moods even as she denied being moody. Why had he kept up this sleuthing, almost to the end of their relationship? The big reveal had always been the same: She was brooding over some inadequacy of his.

"What do you want to know?" Adelaide asked.

"About what?"

"About what I'm thinking." She narrowed her eyes in challenge. "I'll tell you one thing."

"Okay." He stalled a moment, feeling suddenly wary. Then his eyes lighted on her feet. "Why are you wearing athletic socks?"

"Oh." She twirled her glass by the stem, keeping her eyes on it. "You picked one I don't really want to answer."

"Should I try again?"

"No." She shot a look at him. "I'll answer. My shoes were hurting, but I like to wait awhile to let a man see my feet."

"Really?"

"But you've probably seen Claire's, right? So you might be the exception."

"I guess I've seen Claire's. I haven't really paid attention."

"Plus hers have gotten ten less years of use."

"Okay, I'm both curious and terrified. Are they, like, little monsters, your feet?"

"Kind of. They're so callused, it's like I'm always wearing shoes. I could walk down a hot street barefoot and not feel a thing. When I get a pedicure they always want to take the calluses off, and I have to stop them. Dancers need their calluses. But it's kind of gross."

"So I'll know you trust me when you let me see your feet."

She nodded, meeting his eyes. "In the meantime I'll let you ask me one more question. Because you didn't really ask what I was thinking."

What the hell, he thought, and asked what he actually wanted to know. "What do you think of me?"

"I think—" she said and hesitated. "You are really normal," she said.

He laughed. "You are really, really wrong," he said.

"Prove it," she said.

He pursed his lips, narrowed his eyes, made a show of considering. Now was the moment to tell her about the band. She'd asked! It wouldn't be an obvious play for her respect. But he wasn't going to tell her. He had the sense that doing so would be cheating, would give him an unfair advantage, and at the same time he had a contradictory but equally strong sense that there was a weird power in knowing this one thing she didn't know, that to tell her would be to give her power over him. So he shook his head. "You'll just have to find out," he said.

"Come on," she said. "Give me one thing. I can't stand the suspense."

"Let's see," he said. "So many to choose from." He grinned at her. "I lived in Chicago, during college and for years after. And I came back to Cincinnati. Voluntarily. For *no reason.*"

She laughed. "And that's not normal?"

He shook his head. "Not at all."

"Are you glad you came back?" she asked. "Do you ever want to be somewhere else?"

"Not anymore," he said. "I'm really comfortable here. It's a very livable city. Plus in Cincinnati you don't have to work too hard to be stylish."

Adelaide laughed. "That's true."

"Whenever I'm in L.A. or New York I feel broke and under-dressed," he said. "Everybody in those places is just trying so hard. It's exhausting."

She nodded, looking thoughtful.

"Why?" he asked. "Do you ever want to be somewhere else?"

"Sometimes," she said.

"Now?"

"No," she said, smiling. "Not now."

After that it seemed to Josh that the evening was going reasonably well. They sat on the couch with their wine and he interviewed her about her life before this moment. She was from Virginia. She'd started dancing at three. She kept insisting her life had been boring. Aside from the earlier talk about her feet, their exchanges were so entirely unphysical that he was surprised when she leaned over and kissed him. She kissed him fiercely, as though this passion had been anticipated, as though they'd spent the evening playing footsie under the table. He wasn't complaining. He wasn't thinking she should stop. After a moment he wasn't doing any thinking at all. He did notice, through everything that transpired afterward, that she kept her socks on.

Later, in her bed, she traced her fingers down the middle of his thigh. "I love this muscle," she said.

"Really? You have specific muscle preferences?"

"Absolutely," she said. "And don't make a dirty joke." She sighed and smiled at once. "The body is such a beautiful thing."

He kissed her for the sincerity in her voice. "You are a beautiful thing," he said.

"Thing?" she repeated.

"Oh, wait," he said. "This is real? You're not a blow-up doll?"

"I'd never be a blow-up doll," she said. "I'd be a tiny ballerina in a jewelry box."

He laughed. "I guess you would be," he said. He thought of other things to say—*You belong in a jewelry box,* for instance— and was both amused and horrified by his own sentimentality. Was this a symptom of lovesickness? When was the last time he'd succumbed to that disease? Not with Sabrina, not in that puppyish way, because he knew she would have hated it. High school, probably, and Jen Lovelace. Lovely Lovelace, he'd called her, in a note he'd left on her porch, under a single red rose. He'd nearly forgotten he was capable of such romantic idiocy.

Adelaide yawned. He watched her snuggle into the pillow. Her eyes were closed, her face relaxed, her hair a lovely, dark chaos against the white pillowcase, everything about her the opposite of the upright elegance she usually projected. "What would you be if you weren't a ballet dancer?" he asked, so quietly he wasn't sure she'd hear.

She opened her eyes. "You mean for real?"

He nodded.

"I am one," she said.

"But if you weren't."

She yawned again. "I wouldn't exist," she said.

That stung for some reason. She'd spoken so definitively, as though it should be obvious that her art was her vocation, her identity, her all. "I exist," he said.

"What do you mean?"

"I mean, I exist, and I'm nothing special." He heard the edge in his voice, the way the comment practically begged to be contradicted. He was sure she heard it, too, and he cringed.

"Oh, don't say that," she said. "When I said you were normal earlier, I hope you didn't think it was an insult. I'm happy you have a stable life and an office job. I've dated my fill of temperamental artist types. Plus I have to live with myself, and that's enough drama for anyone." She yawned again, stroked his arm, and then patted it, as if she were soothing him. "Normal is good."

Earlier, when he'd told her about his job, she'd asked, "So what do you do all day?"

"I think about where to go for lunch," he'd said.

"But that's just in the morning."

"In the afternoon I think about what to have for dinner."

She'd laughed, which was what he'd wanted, but she hadn't said, "No, really, tell me what you do," which was also, it occurred to him now, what he'd wanted. Maybe she really didn't care. Maybe she was one of those artists who imagined anyone with an office job must have a conventional, pedestrian mind to match his conventional and pedestrian life.

Maybe he did have a conventional, pedestrian mind. Not long ago he'd been trying his broken French on Parisian hipsters, smoking one of their pot-and-tobacco cigarettes in their apartment above a rock club, while girls milled in the street below with throats sore from screaming his name. Maybe even then some part of him had been longing for an office with a desk. Even the way he was thinking about that time was conventional and pedestrian—rock 'n' roll, cigarettes, girls. Why didn't he just picture himself in a black leather jacket, throwing his leg over a motorcycle? When he was in the band he'd supported himself with freelance Web design—that was how Ben had justified hiring him—and it was true he'd enjoyed those times when he spent the day in some office or another. He'd always found a certain novelty in getting up before ten, putting on professional clothes, making trips to the coffee cart. But back then he'd felt like a spy from Bohemia, traveling incognito, wearing his khaki disguise. Even after he started working in an office permanently, he'd felt like that for a while. When, and why, had that feeling gone away? Maybe learning that he was capable of making that transition would make Adelaide like him less instead of more. Instead of a stable, steady guy, she'd see him as a loser, a failure by his own design, a crass abandoner of dreams.

She was so warm next to him in the bed, her hand on his arm, her hair tickling his cheek when he turned to look at her, her legs pressed against his own. He'd been lonely, he realized. He'd been lonely even when he was with Sabrina, which meant he'd been lonely for years. He said, "I guess I'll be normal, then."

9

The email was there when Eloise turned on her computer in the morning. She came into the office as usual, put down her coffee, pressed the button on the back of the monitor, and then stacked papers on her desk while the computer sang itself awake. She opened her email, drumming her fingers on the keyboard tray as she waited for the in-box to load. All this was normal, and then there it was, this one unusual thing, a note from a woman who worked for the library downtown and had once been married to one of Eloise's colleagues.

> I'm sorry this is so last minute. Jason Bamber is speaking here tonight, and then we're taking him out to dinner, and when I picked him up from the airport we put together that you two know each other. I said I'd invite you to the talk, and he asked me to ask you if you would join us at dinner. I'm afraid we can't pay your way (strict budget rules these days!) but we'd love to have you there. Marianne.

Eloise took her hands off the keyboard and rolled her chair back from the desk. She sat with her hands braced on her thighs and read the email again. Jason Bamber. She couldn't go to a talk that night. Tonight was dinner party night at Heather's house. Once a month Heather and her friends gathered for an elaborate dinner, taking turns playing host, which meant spending hours in the kitchen preparing a feast for the others. At least once a week Heather could be counted on to ask what Eloise thought she should cook when it was her turn, and then in the month leading up to the dinner the frequency of these questions intensified, until Heather finally came to Eloise, the wild light of inspiration in her eyes, and announced what she'd decided on. Tonight it was Thai food, and Heather had spent days researching recipes as she planned the menu. She'd had to go to three stores to find lemongrass.

But, see, the thing was, they weren't really Eloise's friends. The other women. She liked them and everything, and certainly it was nice to have a social group where she and Heather were recognized as a couple, but they were really Heather's friends. They were all midwives, or mostly—two were nurses and one was a physical therapist—and when the conversation drifted, as it always did, toward work, the topics were dilation, and preterm labor, and unnecessary C-sections. About these things Eloise had nothing to say. Never given birth, never would. Never seen birth, probably never would. She'd been born, okay, but that wasn't much to contribute to the conversation. Sometimes after a while she picked up a magazine and flipped through it, but Heather was always put out with her after that, partly because Heather's ex, Suzanne, a member of the group, was always on the lookout for disharmony in their relationship, and was one of those people who would make a joke that managed to point out that disharmony to everyone else in the room. Doubtless Heather would have been equally bored during equivalent conversations at a party with Eloise's colleagues, but there was no way to prove this, since Eloise never took Heather to those parties, and so the comparison wasn't one she liked to evoke.

Jason Bamber. They'd gone to graduate school together in Chicago. He'd been a year behind Eloise in the program. Back then he'd been a nervous guy, and then at parties he'd drink too much, probably to calm those nerves, and start to exude jealousy and adoration, mostly at Eloise. When she'd found out her book was coming out, he'd said to her, "I don't know if I want to kiss you or be you." In the last few years, though, he himself had become a star in the field, thanks to the publication of his own much-heralded book, and now he taught at their alma mater.

She scooted back up to the desk and positioned her hands over the keyboard, her mind running along the tracks of polite regret. *Alas,* she wrote, but did that sound sarcastic? Marianne was a pathologically earnest woman who always suspected other people were being sarcastic at her expense but could never quite be sure. This was one of the reasons Eloise had failed to keep up with her after the divorce. She put her finger on the Delete key. One, two, three, four. She reached over and picked up the phone.

"What are you talking about?" Heather said. "Are you talking about tonight?"

"I'll come over afterward," Eloise said. "I'll still get to try all the food."

"You'll still get to try all the *food?*"

"If I'm not there, you guys can talk freely about all your work stuff. I won't be a drag on the conversation."

"No, you're not canceling on me, not tonight. That's bullshit."

Eloise wavered. She swayed from side to side in her chair. Then she said, "But I'm going to take Theo. I want to introduce her to him—I mean, Heather, this is a guy I actually know who's actually in a position to help her. She needs to meet people like him." This all made sense. This sounded like an idea she'd had all along.

A long, fraught silence. "Fine," Heather said. "I guess I'll see you after."

Eloise hung up, sorry she'd had to tell Heather, wishing the email had come on another day, any other day, when she could have just said she was working late. Or even better, said nothing at all. She didn't live with Heather, not yet, and so she didn't have to account to her for her whereabouts. The impulse to go, which was strong, had come with a slightly sickening, sneaky feeling, like she knew giving in to it was bad for her. Like she was rummaging for food in the dark, past-midnight kitchen, like a raccoon, like a furtive backyard animal. Jason was an emissary from the other life she could have had, and while she understood, of course, why Heather wanted her to let that life go, why that would make sense, she still wanted to look at him and see what she was missing.

Now it was time to magic the lie she'd told Heather into truth. In the week since she'd told the kids about the house, she and Theo had avoided one another, speaking when it couldn't be helped with a polite reserve. Theo's voice was formal and wary when Eloise got her on the phone. Eloise explained what she wanted, maintaining a bright, encouraging voice, and several times using the word *great*. Listening to herself, she wondered if she would always do the parent thing, the teacher thing, with Theo, and hide her own roiling feelings behind a mask of calm assurance. She could have said that this guy was someone who used to be below her on the career ladder and now he'd surpassed her by kind of a lot and she was both driven by curiosity and hampered by dread in thinking about seeing him. But since he knew she was here she didn't want to not go and have him imagine she was afraid to see him for the very reasons she actually was afraid to see him. She wanted to be as cool and breezy and comfortable with herself as she had been when she'd known him. Not just pretend to be. *Be.* She wanted Theo for moral support tonight and, now that you mention it, also on the issue of the house, but there seemed to be some law that she had to pretend support was nothing that she needed.

"Yeah, that sounds good," Theo said, but not like she really meant it. Because she was still angry? The thought of Theo being angry made Eloise angry, so she didn't ask. "Great," Eloise said again, and then told her niece what time she'd be home, what time they'd leave the house, and my God, it really was like they'd rewound twelve years, like they were headed to parent-teacher night at the high school.

Jason Bamber. Wow, that, too, had been a lot of years ago.

She was already running late when she knocked on Theo's closed bedroom door. This should not have been a surprise to her, and yet somehow it was. This was what Heather rolled her eyes about—not that Eloise was always late but that she always seemed baffled by her own inability to be on time. She *was* baffled. It wasn't an act. She wanted to be on time. She couldn't understand why it never happened. She knew, of course, that she'd always been late before, but that didn't stop her from hoping she could change.

"Yes?" Theo said.

Eloise pushed the door open. "You ready?"

Theo was sitting on the bed hugging a pink throw pillow in her lap, like a teenage girl who'd been dumped by her boyfriend. "I don't think I can go."

"What do you mean?"

"I think I should stay here and do work."

Theo's laptop was closed and on the floor. There were no papers or books on her bed, just Theo herself, who was, Eloise now registered, wearing pajamas. "You don't look all that busy."

"I know," Theo said. "But I should be."

"Theo, I told them I was bringing you. They'll be expecting you now. And this is a great opportunity for you, to meet him. He's somebody who could really help you. A letter from him would be—"

"I know, I know all that," Theo said.

"So come on. Let's go."

"I don't think I'm up to it."

"What do you mean?"

"I just don't think I can do it. I don't think I can talk to someone I don't know. I don't think I can make him like me. I'm not up to it. I'm sorry. It would be much better for me to try to work, because I'm just not up to anything social."

"Why not?" Eloise asked. "What's wrong?"

Theo shook her head like the reasons were beyond enumerating. Then she shrugged. Finally she said, "I miss Claire."

"Well, go see her."

"What?"

"Go visit her, Theo. It's not like she moved to another planet." Eloise thought, It's not like she died, and behind that thought came a flood of resentment at Theo's failure to appreciate all that she had.

"I guess not," Theo said. "I guess I could just go see her."

"It is possible for you to leave the city limits," Eloise said, against her better judgment, and Theo stiffened. Eloise made it worse. "It's also possible for you to leave the house."

"I'm aware of that," Theo said, her voice on a trembling edge. "You've made that quite clear. But I'm still not going."

"Do you not believe me when I say it would be good for you to meet him? Why can't you ever take my advice?"

Theo looked incredulous. "Maybe because you never give me any."

"What are you talking about?"

"You never give me any," Theo repeated slowly. "Not even when I ask."

"That's completely untrue. I give you advice all the time. I gave you advice about where to go to grad school, which of course you ignored."

"Okay, fine, you give me advice about my career. Everything else is up to me."

"Well, who should it be up to, Theo? You're twenty-eight years old."

"Now," Theo said.

"What?"

"I'm twenty-eight years old *now*."

"I don't know what that's supposed to mean," Eloise said. "And I don't have time to find out." She turned to go, but she still heard Theo say, in a soft but audible voice, "Of course you don't." She left angry—and not just angry but hurt. She was trying to help Theo with her career in a way that anyone else in her niece's position would have been grateful for, and all she got back was attitude, and this accusation that she—what? Trusted her niece? Failed to nag her enough? For four years of Theo's adulthood Eloise had let her live in this house rent-free, knowing the smallness of a grad student's stipend. In return Theo had tidied and cooked and done laundry and occasionally paid for groceries. In Eloise's opinion this was a pretty good deal for Theo. Where was the appreciation for that? Why, instead of thinking about all she owed her aunt, was Theo so certain that her aunt owed her a house? Because, these days in America, not until children have children of their own do they feel any gratitude to the people who raised them.

In the car Eloise gripped the steering wheel with both hands and took deep breaths. She punched buttons on the radio until she found a passionate song of the late 1980s—"In Your Eyes" by Peter Gabriel—and she sang along loudly and tried to lose herself in the music and forget her anger and her nerves.

Once Jason had called her breasts the twin towers of beauty and justice, and in his eyes was the puppyish longing of men who feel overborne and helpless in the face of their attraction to women. "I would make love to your breasts," he said, "if they were not attached to a woman." He was too ridiculous to inspire outrage, or much beyond a kind of annoyed bemusement. "But they'd just be two globs of fat in your hands," she replied.

Now she wondered if he'd even recognize her, though of course she knew he remembered her from Marianne's email. She fought hard to keep her expectations low, hating not just that familiar disappointment but the feeling that her own overblown hopes had paved the way for that disappointment to arrive. It was like having a hangover, the sickness made worse by being self-induced. Eloise had once been full of insouciant expectations, but that state of being was now as foreign and distant from her experience as the lives of people in faraway lands, as everything else about elsewhere.

He recognized her. She'd heard applause as she hustled toward the lecture room door and had slipped inside in time to see him making his way to the podium. Now he said his thank-yous while she made her way into the latecomer's seat—seven seats in, third row from the back. "Excuse me," she was whispering when his voice from the front of the room struck her consciousness, because he had just said her name. What he had said was, "I'd like to dedicate this talk to Eloise Hempel." When her head shot up to look at him, he flashed her a smile and added, "She's always been an inspiration to me."

What was his talk about? She had no idea. She sat in her seat and pretended to herself that she was paying attention, while her mind worked furiously at the question of what the hell that—his dedication—had been. Surely it was only her own insecurity—her own humiliated convictions of failure—that made her think he'd done it to embarrass her, like a hot guy pretending the ugly girl was his date. Because why would he do that? She'd never done anything to inspire such treatment, or if she had she couldn't remember what it was. Maybe he'd done it to impress her, because the desire to impress her still lingered from all those years ago. Maybe he'd wanted her to rush up to him after the talk, flushed and grateful. It seemed to be Heather's voice in her head saying, "There's also the possibility that he meant it." Yeah, okay, sure, there was that possibility, too.

After the talk she hung back while Jason received well-wishers, and then saw Marianne, similarly hanging back, as people do when they know they'll have plenty of time with the anointed one later. She made her way over to Marianne and said hello. "That dedication was so sweet!" Marianne said, and Eloise smiled and agreed that it was. "Where's your niece?" Marianne asked.

Eloise explained. "It's good to know she has the scholar's necessary selfishness!" she said brightly. Marianne smiled nervously and looked away. She didn't like to participate in criticism of others, even others she didn't know, and Eloise could tell Marianne wasn't sure whether Eloise had been criticizing Theo or not. Eloise wasn't even sure. She thought of another reason she wished Theo had come—so that when Jason asked her what she'd been up to for the last seventeen years, she would have had living proof of what that had been.

The last praise offered, the last questions asked, Jason walked toward them up the aisle. He had his notes clenched under one arm and both hands in his pockets, and so looked like a tense person trying to appear relaxed. "That was wonderful!" Marianne said, and Jason thanked her with a sincerity equal to hers, and then he turned and grinned at Eloise. "Hi," he said.

"Hi," she said. She was aware that she was supposed to note how much older he looked, or didn't look, but instead what she saw was that he looked happy to see her. He looked like he didn't care where she taught or what she'd published. He just looked like he was glad to see her face.

"Thanks for coming," he said.

"Thanks for that dedication."

"That was so sweet," Marianne said again.

"It was an impulse," he said. "When I saw you come in."

Eloise nodded. They'd never slept together. They'd never even been on a date. She'd been aware that he was attracted to

"I know," he said, lighting a cigarette. "I was a late bloomer. I don't know if you noticed at the time, but in grad school I was pretty much going through puberty."

Eloise laughed. "I noticed."

"I'm sorry for being such an idiot."

Eloise shrugged. "You weren't so bad."

"You know," he said, "I realize I'm literally blowing smoke here, but I meant all that stuff I said about your work and the impact it's had on me. What are you working on now?"

"It's about location and identity," she said.

"Sounds interesting. You should send it to me when you're done."

"Okay," she said.

There was a silence, then Jason asked, "Do you ever think about leaving here?"

"Only all the time," she said.

"If you got another book out you could do it," he said.

"Do you think so? It's been so long since the first one."

"Yeah, but that was a significant book. That means something. Especially if you paired it with something new."

Eloise looked out at Fountain Square, where an enormous TV screen was showing a Reds game. "You think so?"

"I think so. Let me ask you—would you ever consider something besides teaching?"

"It would depend on the something."

"I'm starting a journal out of my department. I have funding, but I don't yet have a staff. I'll need an editor, and I'm standing here thinking you'd be great. Is that something you'd consider?"

"I don't know," Eloise said. "I mean, I might enjoy the work. But there'd be complications to leaving here."

her, but it had never seemed very serious, because his com
had been so dumb they'd seemed like jokes. They'd been
banter partners, but all that sexual innuendo had just bou
off her like darts bounce off the edge of the board. So wh
she have this nervous energy, and why was she getting a ne
energy from him? Like they had a mutual past, lingering m
ries of a torrid affair.

"Shall we?" Marianne asked, and for a moment Eloise ha
idea what she meant.

All through dinner at a crowded downtown restaurant
frisson of excitement persisted, despite the presence of N
anne, one of Marianne's less interesting colleagues, and ano
younger one with holes in her eyebrows where piercings
been removed. Jason kept meeting Eloise's eye, and she'd
his gaze a beat too long, and then turn away as flushed as if
touched her under the table. He kept talking about her wor
how she'd inspired him in graduate school, how much he
mired her book, and the articles she'd published since, which
was impressed he'd even read. He said he was a hack compa
to her—that he could make an argument, he could do resear
sure, but Eloise had a gift for understanding and expression t
was, well, it was beautiful.

"I am pretty amazing," Eloise said.

"You are!" Marianne said, and Eloise laughed, because M
anne meant it, and Jason seemed to mean it, and the forme
pierced young woman had known who she was, and at this n
ment Eloise felt pretty amazing. She felt really damn good.

After dinner Eloise went outside with Jason, who said w
some embarrassment that he'd become a smoker since gradu
school. "You started smoking in your late twenties?" she said.

"Well, we can talk about it. We'll stay in touch." He dropped his cigarette on the ground and spent a long time rubbing it out. "I want to say something else, but I don't want you to think what I say means I didn't mean what I already said."

Eloise laughed. "I think I followed that," she said.

"I think we should leave together," he said.

"Cincinnati?" she asked, though of course she knew what he meant.

What was she thinking, saying yes? She stood there waiting while he offered Marianne and her people his goodbyes and thanks, and she could see by their expressions they knew exactly what was going on. She got in her car with the blood high in her face, and then when he got in, too, the click of his seat belt sounded so final, as if there was a contract in the shutting of his door. They both watched in the rearview mirror as Marianne's car pulled away, taillights bright against the night. And then he reached over and touched her hair. He ran his thumb down the side of her face. She undid her seat belt, and then undid his, and for a few breathless minutes they made out like teenagers in the car.

She drove him to his hotel with his hand on her inner thigh. She gave the keys to the valet, and held his hand as they walked into the lobby. In the elevator with an elderly couple, she pressed her leg against his and vibrated with anticipation. And then, just as the lights flashed green on his door and he yanked out his key card with a flourish, her phone rang. It was Heather. "Oh, fuck me," she said, staring at that name on the screen. "It's like she knew."

He was standing there in his open doorway, waiting for her to come inside. "It's like who knew what?" he said.

"I'm so sorry," she said. "I have to go."

"What? Really? Why?"

"I have this life here," she said. "I really do."

He frowned. "Well, of course," he said.

Eloise was nearly to Heather's house when her phone rang again, and though she lectured the kids about using the phone while driving she fished hers out of her bag and checked the screen. She was still in a fraught state of guilty desire and she thought maybe it was Heather, calling to accuse her, or Jason, calling to persuade her back. But instead it was Francine. Eloise let out a breath of exasperation and relief, thought, Oh hell, and answered. "I called the house but you weren't there," her mother said, "so I talked to the kids."

"Okay," Eloise said, already impatient.

"They want the house, too," Francine said. "So I can't sign it over to you."

They want the house? For a beat or two Eloise couldn't imagine what her mother was talking about. Who were *they*? "Theo and Josh?" she said slowly.

"Yes, honey," her mother said. "Those kids. What other kids are there?"

Eloise still couldn't quite make sense of things. "Theo and Josh want the house? What would they do with the house? Theo's not even going to stay in Cincinnati, and hopefully Josh won't either."

"Well, Theo's the one who asked me to stop you from selling it, so maybe the two of you should talk."

Eloise said slowly, "Theo asked you to . . ." She frowned at her face in the rearview mirror, and it looked back with angry puzzlement.

"At any rate, I've come up with what I think is a fair way to decide. I'm going to hold on to the house for now and see who needs it most. Unless there's some other pressing reason, I'll probably give it to whoever gets married first."

Married? She and Heather could never get married, not in Ohio anyway. "Wait a minute, wait a minute," Eloise said. "You told me you were going to sign it over to me."

"Yes, but that was before I understood the kids' position. I can hardly give it to you to sell knowing how they feel, can I?"

"I don't make all my decisions based on how they feel," Eloise said. Her mother laughed, and Eloise, taken aback, inadvertently said, "Do I?" She never liked to give her mother an opening—not just to criticize or tease but even to express love or sympathy. She never liked to give her mother an opening of any kind.

"Eloise, sweetheart, that's a subject for another day," Francine said. "I just wanted to let you know I've set this up."

"Set it up? Like a legal arrangement? Or, no, more like a competition." Eloise could feel her anger growing. "You should pitch it as a reality show. Matriarch pulls the strings while relatives race to the altar to win the family house."

"It's not a competition," Francine said, managing to sound wounded. "Getting married is just a good measure of whether people are ready to settle down in life."

Was this Francine's elaborate way of getting at Eloise for being, as far as she knew, single? What was Eloise if not settled down? "That's bullshit," Eloise said.

"Is it?" Francine said. "Look at history."

"Are you kidding?" Eloise asked. "Are you *kidding* me? *I wrote a book*—Never mind. You've got to be kidding about this whole thing, right? No one's even close to getting married. This is just yet another way to avoid keeping your promise. If you didn't want to give me the house, Mom, why the hell did you ever tell me that you would?"

"Don't be selfish, Eloise. I'm trying to think of everyone here. I'm trying to see the big picture."

"The big picture is that I need the house now and they don't. If you're assessing based on need, my need is greater."

"Your financial need, maybe," Francine said. "But there are all sorts of need."

Two blocks from Heather's house, Eloise pulled the car over to the curb and stopped. She closed her eyes. "Why are you doing this to me?"

"This is not just about you. I'm thinking of those children. When Theo called, she was practically in hysterics. She begged me not to let you do it. I don't think you've really considered how much that house means to her. It was what gave her a sense of security after she lost her parents."

"It was the house that did that, huh?" Eloise said. "I don't suppose it had anything to do with me."

"You did your best," Francine said, and the implication that her best clearly wasn't good enough hung in the air. Eloise had no idea why this should sting her like it did, when Francine's best was a damn sight less adequate than hers.

"You left me with them," Eloise said. "I gave up my life. You told me you were going to give me that house."

There was a pause before Francine spoke. "When you put it

like that," she said, "it sounds like you took them because you thought you were going to get paid."

Eloise pulled the phone from her ear and looked at the screen. She watched ten seconds of the call tick by, heard her mother's tinny voice say her name. Then she pressed End.

She called Jason Bamber's hotel and asked for his room.

"Hey," he said, "are you coming back?"

She hesitated. "I shouldn't," she said. "I can't. But, tell me, were you serious about that job?"

"You mean was I just trying to get into your pants?"

"Were you?"

"Well, obviously," he said. "But, no, I was serious. I think you'd be great. Are you saying you're interested?"

She didn't want to live anymore in her house, where there was water damage in the basement and enough cracks between the bricks that a multithousand-dollar tuck-pointing job couldn't be put off much longer, where there was an astonishingly un-grateful niece. She could live at Heather's, though, where, like tonight, there'd be music and laughter and wine. There'd be Heather waiting for her, waiting like she was right now. But. What was the but? The talk of dilation and meconium and the bloody show? Not those topics, not exactly, but the fact that the topics were always exactly the same. Here in Cincinnati her life returned and returned again to the same moments, and not just in repetition of the same meetings, the same classes, the same turn onto the same road, but in what defined her, what she thought about. Here every pain of childhood and family came back again and again, here she felt over and over the same god-damn things. This aspect of her life more than any other went on reminding her that the person she was now would be completely unrecognizable to the person she'd once been.

The person she'd once been had had Rachel. Rachel to make it better, to make it funny, to imitate their mother saying, "I'm thinking of those children," in a fluting voice, striking a pleased-with-herself pose. But now there was no eleven-year-old Rachel to choreograph elaborate dance routines in the playroom. No twenty-two-year-old Rachel insisting on reprising one of those routines, laughing, then serious, then laughing again. No Rachel—pregnant, three weeks away from Theo's arrival, hugging Eloise over her belly before Eloise went back to college, the baby moving between them and Rachel holding on a long time while the baby kneed and elbowed them both. Or maybe Eloise holding on a long time. Or both of them holding on. Sometimes Rachel's absence was all Eloise could see in that house. Signs of her everywhere. Her bedroom still the blue she'd painted it. Her voice emerging from Theo's mouth. The forsythia she'd planted going unpruned in the backyard. But never Rachel herself. Rachel would never stop being gone.

"Eloise?" Jason prompted. "Are you interested?"

"Yes," she said. "I guess I am."

10

Theo walked through the parking lot toward the Museum Center with the sun blazing in her eyes and her heart hammering in her throat. She was meeting Noah. She'd enticed him there under false pretenses, telling him she wanted his advice on the job search process, since he'd been through it so recently. He'd suggested a drink, but she'd panicked at the thought of something so overtly date-like and suggested they meet in the Cincinnati History Museum, which he should see if he never had. He'd agreed, amiable as ever, without any inkling of the real reason for her call. On the phone after she'd unveiled her plan for the house Francine had said, "Do you know what your prospects are?"

"Not exactly," Theo said. "I mean, I'm not sure."

"Well, you'd better start figuring it out."

The word *prospects* had made her think of Noah. That made no sense, of course, but there it was, and she'd ridden her illogical impulse all the way through calling him.

From childhood Theo had loved the model of the city in the Cincinnati History Museum, with its neighborhoods captured in different eras. She liked the fact that there were buildings she recognized in the 1940s downtown, the way the model illustrated the city's longevity. She showed her membership card to the nice old man at the door and made her way down the ramp that led into the body of the museum, passing models of hilly neighborhoods along one side. Noah was midway down the ramp, leaning over Mount Adams to watch the model streetcar climb an incline, signaling its rise with a tiny blinking light. He seemed engrossed, so she took the opportunity to look at him closely, something she normally didn't allow herself to do. Eye contact with him felt charged with significance to such a degree that she could barely meet his eye at all. Why did she like him so much? Any answer she thought of—his sense of humor, his rumpled good looks—seemed so banal as to be useless. It was incredibly frustrating to feel something so strongly and be unable to explain it. And if the feelings he engendered resulted largely in disappointment, guilt, and self-loathing—if she knew that—why was she nevertheless made so happy by the sight of his chaotic curls, his well-worn concert tee?

He turned and saw her before she could solve the problem. "Hey," he said. "This is cool. I can't believe I've never been here."

"I love the little streetcars," she said, joining him at the display. "I wish we still had the real ones."

"Well, there's that campaign to bring them back, right? Though not to Mount Adams, which is too bad. Imagine riding one up that hill."

"I know," she said. "The view is incredible."

"For some reason I thought Cincinnati would be flat." He started walking down the ramp toward the rest of the diorama, his eyes turned up to the model planes whirring in a circle above the model downtown.

"City of the Seven Hills," she said.

"I thought Midwest and pictured, like, Kansas or something. Wizard of Oz Kansas. Prairie lands and tornadoes."

Theo laughed. "In black and white."

"Exactly," he said. "The first time I drove up into that neighborhood that looks like San Francisco, it blew my mind."

"Columbia-Tusculum," Theo said. "I love those houses. I wish I lived in a purple house."

"Really?"

"Is that surprising?"

"You never wear purple," he said. "More like dark greens, or browns." He pointed at her shirt. "Or gray."

She looked down at herself and felt dismayed to see that he was right. She wore a denim skirt and a loose gray tank top. "I dress in camouflage," she said. Only then was she struck with the realization that he'd paid enough attention to her clothes to know what colors she chose. She felt a sudden need to look at the model and hurried ahead of him a few steps, to the edge of the miniature downtown.

"I know some of these buildings," Noah said.

"Don't you love that? My dentist's office has an old photo of downtown on the wall, and those two buildings are in it." She pointed. "And a ton of people on the streets, too, way more than you ever see downtown now unless there's a Reds game or a concert on Fountain Square. I stare at it every time I get my teeth cleaned. Where are all those people going? What are they doing?"

"Wouldn't you love to be a time-traveling mind reader?" Noah asked.

"My God, yes," Theo said.

"I love that Cincinnati is such an old city. For the U.S., I mean."

"Me, too," she said. "I like thinking about what came before in the parts of the city I know. You know? I like the idea of all the layers. New places don't have layers, just surfaces."

"You should go to Latin America," he said. "Try standing in a Mayan ruin if you want to feel some serious awe."

"I have to do that. Have you driven by the oldest house here? It's no Mayan ruin but it is from the late 1700s. It's near Columbia-Tusculum."

"You should take me on a tour," he said. "Show me the historical highlights."

"Definitely!" she said. "We have a great park system, too, you know. I bet you've never explored Alms Park, or maybe even Eden Park." He said nothing to that, and she worried she'd gone too far, been too open in her enthusiasm. And why had she brought up the freaking park system? That was a total non sequitur. She'd probably weirded him out, implying she wanted a romantic stroll under the trees.

After a moment Noah asked, "Would you live here? I mean if you got a job. Would you stay?"

"Yes." Theo sighed. "I *want* to live here."

"Really." He laughed. "I don't hear that a whole lot. But then I don't meet many people who are actually from here."

"A lot of my high school friends couldn't wait to get out."

"That's typical."

"Not if you live in New York, though, right? How many teenagers are, like, 'Get me the hell out of Manhattan?'"

"That's true," he said. "But with New York I sometimes think: Is it the place, or is it the idea of the place? Because the idea is great until you're paying a thousand dollars a month for a one-room apartment."

"It's both, don't you think? New York is one of those places that *is* an idea. Where people go to live out an idea. And then a lot of them are satisfied by the idea. Or I assume they are."

"You're absolutely right." He seemed excited now, waving his hand in expansive agreement. "L.A. is the same way."

"Well, yes and no," Theo said. "If you go there it's because you want to be in show business. So it's a much more specific idea."

"True." He sounded disappointed. "Maybe San Francisco is closer to what you mean."

"And Austin."

"Portland."

"Paris."

Noah laughed. "If we're leaving the country all bets are off."

"Where would you go?"

"Mexico City, baby." He smiled at her. "What about you?"

"I don't know." She looked around at tiny Cincinnati. "I really do like it here."

He stopped walking to look her full in the face. "Seriously, I like hearing that," he said. "Since I might end up staying, whether I want to or not." He sighed.

"The Midwest," she said. "It's like quicksand." He laughed a gratifying laugh.

They'd made their way past downtown and the headquarters of Procter & Gamble, and now they were standing before a model of Over-the-Rhine in the 1800s. The museum itself, built in what had once been the grand train station, was on the edge of this neighborhood, which abutted downtown. Now it was largely a poor black neighborhood with a huge vacancy rate, site of an ongoing debate about gentrification, with all its impossible questions about race and class and the value of historical buildings and the reasons for crime and what a city should be and who it was for. Music Hall, a gorgeous Victorian building that still hosted the symphony and the opera, had an enclosed bridge between it and a nearby parking garage, so, Theo had always assumed, suburban music lovers could avoid any encounter with the actual city. Theo could very easily work herself into anger at the people who lived on the edge of the city while still depending on it, yet feared and avoided it and resented any use of their tax dollars to improve it. But that wasn't the mood she wanted to be in, so she focused on the tiny nineteenth-century neighborhood of German immigrants, a riot of saloons and beer gardens, everybody stuffed with hops and sausages. Noah leaned in, too. "I wonder who built this," he said. "The detail is incredible. So intricate."

"I know," Theo said "I like to imagine someone working so hard to perfect something so small."

"I wish I could go to this place," he said, looking at the beer garden. "It looks like a rockin' good time."

"The whole neighborhood was a rockin' good time," she said. "You know how the ballet's right near here? It's built in the footprint of an old brewery. They store the costumes underground where the beer barrels used to be. The conditions are as perfect for the costumes as they were for the beer. Isn't that funny?"

"That's cool," he said. "If I say I'd take beer over the ballet, can we still be friends?"

She pretended to ponder this question. "Maybe," she said. "But you're on probation." She looked at the model again. "I just want to get in there and rearrange them like a kid, you know? See that lady there, in the yellow skirt? I'd hurry her up. She's forever missing the oompah band."

He nodded, grinning. "You don't want to miss the oompah band."

She laughed, and as she did she swayed toward him a little, and then caught herself and took a big step back. Did the odd look on his face mean he'd taken note of that? She couldn't read his expression but she imagined he was amused by her, that he could sense the adolescent flutterings of her heart.

"What's this way?" he asked, and then turned abruptly before she could answer, like a soldier on the march. She followed him to the vintage streetcar in the middle of the next room. At the door to the streetcar he turned and offered her his hand, and she took it automatically and stepped inside. He raised his hand a little as she moved, as though he was lifting her in, and absurd as it was—the step was no more than six inches off the ground—she felt like he *was* lifting her. She wanted to keep holding his hand, so she made herself let go so abruptly she practically snatched her own hand away. She walked to the front of the car and slid into a seat, and he slid into the one behind her. He sat with his back against the wall and looked up at the old advertisements above the windows: DELICIOUS COFFEE . . . EVERY TIME. She could still feel his hand on hers, but it struck her that the anxious desire he inspired was for his company more than his touch.

Her phone rang, vibrating her bag, and she reached for it automatically and glanced at the screen. It was Claire.

"Do you need to get that?" Noah asked.

"No," she said, though she'd been trying to reach her sister for three days, missing her, wanting escape, thinking that escape might be a visit to Claire in New York. She dropped the phone back in her bag. "It's my sister. We talk all the time." True enough, though increasingly less true.

"I envy you guys being so close," Noah said. "I don't have much in common with my sisters."

Theo wasn't quite listening, her mind still on Claire, who had been, in their recent conversations, even less forthcoming than usual with the details of her life. "No?"

"Not like you guys anyway."

"Do we have a lot in common?"

He feigned astonishment. Or maybe really felt it. "Do you have a lot in common? Are you kidding?"

"Well, I'm in history, Josh is a musician slash whatever he is now, Claire's a ballet dancer . . ."

"Arts and academia," he said. "Esoteric, low-paying, high-minded pursuits."

She laughed. "Maybe not high-minded."

"Plus, you and Josh have a very similar sense of humor."

"Mmmmm."

"You guys are lucky. Seriously."

Theo nodded, not meeting his eyes. Change the subject, she thought. Say something. The best she could come up with, looking around the streetcar: "Don't you feel like it's sixty years ago?"

"Except for the cell phone," he said. "But yes. I'm glad you called."

"You are?" she said and wanted to smack herself for the pleasure so obvious in her voice.

"I was sitting around feeling sorry for myself. This is a huge improvement."

"Were you trying to work?"

"No, I was thinking about Marisa."

Theo took a breath. "What about her?"

He shifted in his seat, looking out the windows as if at scenery. "She found a script that her boss wants her to work on. Like, if all goes well it could actually get made. She's so excited. This is what she's been working toward for years. I should be nothing but happy for her, right? But all I could think was, If this happens, she'll never move here. It just made me realize that some part of me has been waiting for her to give up on the whole film thing, and then I wonder if she's just waiting for me to give up on my own ambitions. Like we're playing a game of chicken, and even though that desire comes from wanting to be together, in the end what it means is neither of us is wishing the other well." He glanced at Theo. "That has to be bad, right?"

"It's . . ." She winced. "It's hard."

"It *is* hard," he said. "I don't know what to do. How do you decide whose career is more important?"

Theo shrugged. "I had a boyfriend when I was in my second year. We'd been dating maybe six months, and then we were out to dinner and suddenly he said, 'If I got a job, would you move for me?' I said it depended on the job, and whether I had an offer of my own, which he didn't really like hearing, so I asked him the same question, and he said, 'No.' Just no. Maybe because he was already pissed at me, I don't know. Either way, it seemed like he meant it."

"What happened?"

"We broke up," Theo said.

"Right then?"

"Yes," Theo said. She thought of the challenging way Eric had looked at her after he voiced that no. She'd had to call his bluff, and saying, "Then I don't think this will work out" was the only way she could think of to do it. She'd stuck to her guns even when he called her in tears a week later, even though she missed him. She couldn't get past the look on his face, how pleased, how satisfied he'd seemed to be able to tell her no. *I could live without you,* that look had said, so there was no recourse but to decide she could live without him, too.

"Wow. I can't decide whether to admire you or be a little scared."

"Both," she said, though *scared* was the last thing she wanted him to feel. Or maybe that wasn't true. Maybe it would be nice if she made him as nervous as he made her.

"I guess Marisa and I could have figured out earlier that our careers weren't compatible. But by the time we had to face that fact we were in too deep." He sighed, turning to look out the window again. "Sometimes I think it would be simpler to be single."

Theo looked at him. Suddenly she felt very tired. She wanted an end to all this pointless and exhausting emotion: the worry and resentment, the guilt, the desire and the anger and the fear, everything other people made her feel. Why, then, if she wanted peace, did her heart begin to beat so rapidly in her throat? Why did it speed her off a ledge, make her speak the next words out of her mouth? "If you were single," she said, "you could go out with me." She braced herself, feeling like she'd pulled a pin from a grenade, but as her heart rocketed on, it became clear there would be no explosion. Noah didn't move his gaze from the window. It was possible he hadn't heard her, mesmerized by the unchanging scenery, but Theo knew in her gut he was just pretending he hadn't. So it was to be an implosion, then.

"Why does Cincinnati have so many nicknames?" he asked. "Queen City. City of the Seven Hills."

Theo ordered herself to speak. "Don't forget the Paris of the United States."

"Paris," Noah repeated. He still wasn't looking at her. "I came home the other day and there was a potato chip bag on the sidewalk in front of my building, one of those oversize, extracalorie snack ones. So I went to pick it up, like the good citizen I am. It was weirdly heavy. And then I realized it was full of liquid. And then I realized that liquid was urine."

"That's disgusting," she said, with more than the necessary vehemence.

"Thank you, Cincinnati," he said. "I couldn't figure out if it was a prank, or if somebody just really had to pee and thought a bag made more sense than the bushes."

"I don't know why people do what they do," Theo said. "Although I propose all kinds of theories."

He said, almost under his breath, "I couldn't tell Marisa that story."

"Mmm," she said, because it was all she could manage. She felt shaky and uncertain. Why had he said that? As if he were inviting her to comment on Marisa's unsuitability. Maybe he really hadn't heard what she said. Or maybe, it occurred to her, he was telling her he had. Were those words his way of saying he was interested? Or of reminding her he had a girlfriend? Were they a way of making her feel nearly sick to her stomach with the weirdness of it all? Was she being encouraged, repelled, or just ignored?

And why—oh, God, why?—had she given rise to a moment when she had to feel like this? Awash in self-loathing at the pathetic exposure of all she should have kept hidden. People who keep their guard up, it suddenly struck her, are hiding a giant mess. "That could happen in Paris," she said. "Parisians have chip bags, don't they? They have urine."

He laughed as if the awkwardness in the air was entirely of her imagining, but their easy rhythm was gone. She wasn't wrong that his attempts at conversation seemed effortful after that, that he avoided meeting her eye. Their goodbye at the parking lot consisted of her saying, "Well," and then turning abruptly in the direction of her car. For someone who spent so much time priding herself on her resourcefulness and responsibility, she sure knew how to fuck things up. She needed to purge herself of what had just happened, find somebody to make her feel better about making an ass of herself. But who? She'd told no one about her crush, so she had no one instantly available as a sympathetic confidant.

She fished her cell phone out of her bag. Her fingers were trembling, and the memory returned, as it sometimes did, of how her hands had shaken as she dialed the phone to call Eloise after her parents died, trying first the home number and then the office, pressing each button firmly, one by one, carefully checking the numbers in her grandmother's address book. How the last thought she had before someone answered was, strangely, Be polite. Now she tried Claire, who'd so recently been available, but the phone rang and rang, then went to voicemail. Theo had been ready, at this desperate juncture, to confess the whole sad story to her sister, and now she felt thwarted, stoppered, uncomforted, bereft. She paged up and down through her list of contacts. "Wes," she saw at the bottom of the list, and for just a second couldn't remember who that was. "Oh, God," she said out loud when she realized. Oh, God, that night. She'd spent the whole next day in bed with a hangover made worse by worry and shock and embarrassment and shame. Had she really kissed a student in a public place? Had she really *cried*? Before Josh had arrived to pick her up Wes had taken her phone and programmed his number into it. "In case of emergencies," he'd said.

She pressed the Call button. He answered on the second ring. She might have hung up then, because he wouldn't recognize her number. There was a moment of possibility when he didn't yet know who she was. "It's Theo," she said.

"Hey," he said, the word long and drawn-out and undeniably pleased. "What's up?"

"I'm having a really bad day." She wasn't sure what she'd meant to say, but that was not it. There was no reason to think he would care. How pathetic that she was calling a near stranger—a former student!—for comfort. "I'm sorry," she said. "I don't know why I'm telling you that."

"Don't be sorry. Maybe you think I can make it better. Which would be, you know, flattering."

Man, this guy. What was it about him that pushed the button for tears? She swallowed hard. "You know how to look at things," she managed to say.

He talked her into meeting him for an early dinner, which, he insisted, would be his treat. He wanted to pick her up, too, but she wouldn't let him. She was only ready to rely on him so far. He chose a funky but expensive restaurant in Northside that had a menu of elaborate cocktails and a reputation for fantastic french fries. As the hostess led her to a table in the back, Theo could see him there, frowning at the menu, and she hoped he wasn't regretting insisting that he'd pay. He'd dressed up for her. She caught herself—why for her? Maybe for himself. Maybe for the restaurant. Whatever his reasons, he looked nice in his purple button-down shirt. Purple! She wondered if he still had the cap. He looked up and saw her, and immediately got to his feet, sitting only when she did. "My goodness, the manners," she said as soon as the hostess left them.

He smiled. "If you'd let me pick you up I would have opened your car door."

She smiled back, but could think of no response.

"Did you just say *my goodness*?" he asked suddenly.

"I think so."

"Wow. So we're both old-fashioned."

"I've been known to say *Lordy, Lordy*," she said. "Maybe I'm not old-fashioned so much as elderly."

"It's all okay with me, as long as you lay off *gee whiz*."

She laughed. "You draw the line there? Can I say *gee* or is that verboten, too?"

"I draw the line at *gee* and everything that comes after."

"Noted," she said. They smiled at each other, and then entered a space where it was clear neither of them knew what to say next, both of them longing for the easy banter of moments before. Theo picked up her menu, but before she could open it he said, "I'm glad you called. I'm glad we're on a real date. This is more like I imagined it."

"I still find it hard to believe that you imagined it at all."

"Why?"

"What was sexy—or, if you prefer, romantic—about an American history survey?"

"It wasn't the subject. It was you. You were so excited to be talking about, like, nineteenth-century beauty standards. You made me feel interested even though on my own I wasn't. I always felt jazzed after your class. Inspired."

All of this sounded uncomfortably close to what she'd first liked about Noah. "And what if I'm boring when I'm not talking history?"

He grinned at her. "You weren't boring the other night."

Theo cringed. "Oh, don't bring that up."

"I don't know why you're so embarrassed," he said. "You were just drunk."

"Don't judge me based on that behavior."

"If I judged you, would I have asked you out?"

She fiddled with her silverware, straightening the already straight fork and spoon. "I can't really date you, you know."

"Why not?"

"You're my student."

"Were."

"Huh?"

"Were. Was. I was your student."

"Right. You're right. I don't know why I'm acting this way."

"What way?"

"Going on a date with you to tell you I can't date you. It's bizarre."

"I think I can explain it."

"Do I want you to?"

"You want to go on a date with me, but you feel like you shouldn't. So you let yourself do it but say that you can't, like somebody's watching you."

"Like who's watching me?"

"Whoever you think would disapprove."

She made a face. "Are you studying to be a psychiatrist?"

"Designer."

"Fashion?"

"Industrial. Like doorknobs and stuff. I'm getting a master's degree."

"It never occurred to me anyone had to design doorknobs."

"Someone has to design everything. This chair, this glass, this vase, this table."

This situation, she thought, without being quite sure what she meant.

"This table started with an idea," he said. "And then a drawing." He pushed back his chair to look under the table. "Somebody had to decide on the shape of the legs, and where they'd attach, and how to attach them. How big to make the tabletop. What material to use." He put his palms flat on the table and smiled at her. "I could tell you a lot about the pros and cons of different materials, if that was something you wanted to know."

"And that's what you learn in your classes?"

"Yup."

"So you are still a student."

"But not yours."

"And not in psychiatry."

"I'm sorry." He let out a breath. "Maybe you don't want to be analyzed. I think I'm still trying to impress you."

She looked at him. His honesty seemed to call for equivalent honesty. "I'm attracted to you," she said slowly. "I feel weird about being attracted to you because you were my student. But the main reason I'm hesitating is because I have a crush of my own. It's unrequited. But I still feel like I'm cheating on this imaginary relationship, being here with you." She smiled grimly. "I know that's stupid."

He shrugged, trying, she thought, to conceal disappointment. "You're loyal to your ideas."

She laughed. "I'm a doctoral student," she said. "I'm all about ideas."

"But you're attracted to me?"

She nodded, and then went ahead and said, "Yes."

"That's not an idea."

"Well. It could be."

He shook his head. "No—attraction, that's the farthest thing from an idea. That's an urge, an impulse, a force. It's subconscious, physical. You can't make everything cerebral."

"Oh really?" she said. "Watch me."

"Love can be an idea," he said.

"That's true."

"But attraction. We can work with that."

She was finding it increasingly difficult to believe she'd ever been this guy's teacher. She had a powerful urge to put her hands on him, swept away by a vision of herself unbuttoning his shirt to examine that meaningful tattoo. She wanted to touch his hand where it rested on the table but stopped herself, and then she wondered why she was stopping herself when all he'd done, again and again, was invite her to believe in his interest. So she stretched her hand across the table, slowly, as if she were participating in the joke, and then reached out a finger and touched one of his. He flipped his hand over and caught hers, running his thumb across her palm, which confirmed for her both his desire and her own. She exhaled, with the feeling that she'd been holding her breath too long. "Okay," she said.

He didn't ask what she meant. She was pretty sure he knew.

11

Josh was alone in the house. This almost never happened, especially in the summer with both Theo and Eloise off from school. Sometimes he got an evening to himself, but that was increasingly rare. Theo's two closest friends from her program had finished their degrees, gotten jobs, and left town, and she didn't seemed to have replaced them, so most of the time she was home. But tonight he was alone. Eloise had left a note that she wouldn't be home until late, and at the bottom Theo had written *I won't either.* She hadn't signed her name. That was what living with someone was: leaving a note and neglecting, or not needing, to sign your name.

Truth be told, he didn't really like to be alone. He wandered from room to room in the empty house, thinking about the party they'd had last month, all those people clustered where now there was no one. He couldn't call Adelaide—after two weeks and most nights spent together she'd gone out with her dancer friends, saying that if he came he'd be bored. As bored as this? He doubted it.

On the third floor he went into the room they'd always called the "art room," because Francine had kept collage materials and

canvases and yarn there, detritus of her various abandoned hob-
bies. This was where he stored his heavy equipment, the amps
and the microphones and the microphone stands. He'd claimed
to be finished with music, but even he had to admit that the
fact he'd kept this stuff gave the lie to the claim. He'd lugged all
this weight upstairs rather than put the things in the basement,
where they might get damp. He had a funny definition for *finished*. He pulled a mic stand into the center of the room, raised it
high, and clipped in the mic. Should he try recording something?
Despite his efforts to repress them, there were a number of songs
in his head. But at the thought of singing his throat closed. He
stood there for a second as though he was going to sing, back to
pretending to be a rock star in an empty room in his house, back
to some facsimile of youth.

He should get his own place. He should buy a couch. He
should get a cat. Eloise had let them keep their cat after their
parents died, even though she was so allergic she'd had to start
regular use of an asthma inhaler. When that cat died, she'd let
them get two kittens. For a time she'd denied them nothing.
She'd taken such good care of them. Who had taken care of her,
in her loss and grief? No one. He'd tried, on more than one occasion, to say something about this, express some sort of retrospec-
tive sympathy and gratitude. She never let him get very far. What
he could do for her now was take her side about the house, try
to reason with Theo, try to talk Francine into signing the place
over to Eloise. But he hadn't done any of that. He'd called Claire
a few days ago thinking maybe she'd galvanize him into taking
action. Maybe she'd suggest that between the two of them they
could persuade Francine to do the right thing. But when he
told Claire that the house would go to whoever married first or

needed it most, she'd just said, "Really," in a strange, considering tone that he did his best to ignore. If she wanted the house, too, if she was another potential antagonist, he'd just as soon not know about it.

The truth was that he had wondered what Francine would say if he told her he wanted the house for a studio. The truth was when Francine asked, "Do you want the house? Or is this just between Eloise and Theo?" he'd answered, "I want it." At that moment, despite everything he owed his aunt, he did want the house, he wanted it fiercely. It wasn't just Theo who had the right to that desire. But since then certainty had eluded him. His own desires were slippery and vague. He tried to pin one down so he could examine it, at last understand what he himself wanted, but it flicked away like a fish. He knew he wanted Adelaide, and that was about it. The thoughts about how he should marry her and get the house and turn it into a studio were jump-the-gun ridiculous.

The trouble was that the sense of freedom quitting music had given him was gone. He missed that feeling. He'd counted on it for a long time and wondered when and why it had disappeared. Times like this, he didn't know what to do with himself. When his phone rang, and he saw it was Noah, he felt an immense relief, as if Noah had called to save him from himself.

As he stood in the crowd waiting for a band to go on, Josh did not always think about his own days as a musician. He didn't always picture the odd back rooms where you waited, some of them small concrete-walled cells painted gray or army green, some of them spacious labyrinths with cozy chairs and riders laid out on counters in front of mirrors large enough to be featured in the dressing room of a Broadway star. It didn't usually feel strange to him—hadn't for six months or more—that he was out here instead of back there. Now he waited for Noah to come back from the bar with a growing embarrassment. As though everybody was thinking, Why is that loser just standing there? As though everybody here knew that he was no longer the person he was supposed to be. But he'd quit music to quit that version of himself. This *is* who you're supposed to be, he told himself. Just a guy who needs another beer.

He was relieved when Noah reappeared. Noah handed him a pint glass, then clinked his own against it. "Can I ask you something?" Noah asked.

"Sure," Josh said, braced for the criticism-as-question he sometimes got from fans, like "Do you know you used the same chord progression in two different songs?"

"Your sister. Theo," Noah said. "Is she kind of a jokester?"

"What do you mean?"

"She said something to me the other day—I wasn't sure whether to take her seriously or not."

Was Theo a jokester? From adolescence on, and before Sabrina, they'd communicated largely through affectionate banter, a mode they could still enter from time to time now, reminders of how natural and easy they used to be with each other. "She likes to joke around, definitely," he said. "But she can be serious. She can be intensely serious. I guess that doesn't really help you. Do you want to tell me what she said?"

"She said if I were single she could go out with me." Josh must have looked startled at this, because Noah said, "I shouldn't have told you that. That was weird."

"No, it's okay," Josh said. "I'm just absorbing the information."

So Theo had a thing for Noah. She had the hots for him. She was in love with him? None of those descriptions seemed the right one. This must be one reason why she'd been so moody and strange lately. Josh had always thought of his big sister as practical above all, so resolutely had she insisted on practicality from him during the Sabrina years, and this made it hard to imagine her caught in the grip of an unrequited longing. He would have imagined, if he'd thought about it at all, that even if she found Noah attractive she would have dismissed him immediately as a romantic prospect as soon as she discovered he had a girlfriend. At this news of her weakness, he felt a mixture of triumph and disappointment.

"I just couldn't tell if she was serious," Noah said. "So I think I handled it really badly."

"What did you do?"

"I pretty much pretended that I hadn't heard her."

Josh nodded slowly. "How should you have handled it? I mean, what do you wish you had said?"

"Good question."

"Do you . . . I mean, would you . . ."

Noah spread his arms, palms to the ceiling, in the universal symbol for *who knows?* "There's Marisa," he said. "But if there wasn't, I probably would. I mean, that's what I keep thinking, ever since Theo said that. That I would."

"But you couldn't have said that to her."

"No. Right? Because that would be like I was saying I would cheat. Or maybe it would have seemed I was being patronizing, you know, lying to not make her feel bad. I don't know. I just feel like an ass."

Josh nodded, then realized how that might seem. "I'm sympathizing with you," he said. "Not agreeing."

"I'm sorry to dump all this on you, man, especially about your own sister. I haven't had anybody else to tell."

"No, you haven't dumped anything. I'm surprised, that's all. I had no idea."

"Me neither." Noah frowned. "But you think she was serious?"

"I don't know. It doesn't sound like the kind of joke she'd make."

"Well, it doesn't matter anyway, right?"

It matters to her, Josh thought. And it seems to matter to you. But this was the moment to drop the subject, before they both grew uncomfortable and Noah began to feel stupid for bringing it up. Josh took a sip of his beer, waited a few beats for the conversation to dissipate. Then he said, "Can I ask you something now?"

"Yeah, man," Noah said. "Ask me anything."

"Do you feel like if you gave up your research you wouldn't exist?"

Noah looked surprised. All at once his jocular, easygoing social self fell away, and Josh thought he got a glimpse of what Noah must be like in the classroom: intense, often serious, maybe even a little stern. "That's a very pressing question," he said.

"How so?"

"Because of Marisa."

"She wants you to give up your research?"

Noah shook his head. "She wants me to move to New York or L.A. But I can't get a job in those places—I tried. She wants me to go on the market and try again, but I'm no more marketable now than I was a year ago. In fact, I'm marginally less, because

I haven't published anything in the meantime, I'm not shiny and new anymore, and they'd wonder why I was leaving my first job after only a year."

"So if you moved . . ."

"I'd have to get some other kind of job, probably teaching high school. But I love research. Research is what led me to teaching, because nowhere but academia are people interested in the things I'm interested in. But you think I'm going to teach the American Revolution all day in a high school and then come home and write about nineteenth-century Mexico? Nah, man. I'm going to be exhausted. I'm going to come home and watch TV."

"But you've thought about it anyway."

"Sure, I've thought about it." There was an edge to his voice, as if Josh had accused him of something. Did Noah feel defensive about considering abandoning his work? Or about the suggestion that he might not have considered it? "I love her, man. I want to marry her." He took a big swig of his beer. "Plus to tell you the truth I've been hating what I've been writing lately. And then I think, How can I look her in the eye and say this shit is worth it?"

Josh was ready to let the subject drop, feeling he'd trampled delicate ground. But after a moment Noah said, "I'd still *exist*. I'd still feel like myself. But I think I'd feel like a lesser version of myself, you know? Like, you remember *The Dark Crystal*? You remember what those little Muppet people looked like after the Skeksis drained their blood?"

"You'd be a pale Muppet person," Josh said.

"Exactly. That's what I'm afraid of."

Do you think I'm a pale Muppet person? That was what Josh wanted to ask. But that wasn't the kind of thing you asked, even if the conversation bordered on the confessional. Asking that was like wearing a big sign that said HI, I'M PATHETIC. Instead he said, "Adelaide said if she wasn't a ballet dancer she wouldn't exist."

"Wow. Well, I guess her whole life's been about that, right? Where are you with that, anyway?"

"Good, I think," Josh said, even though *good* wasn't an answer to *where?*

"I'm a little jealous. Being at the beginning, when things aren't so complicated." Noah sighed. "I feel like Marisa and I are in a standoff. Somebody's got to drop their guns. I'm seriously considering proposing."

Noah didn't seem to be considering the possibility that she might say no, or that a yes would make no difference. But Josh didn't point that out. Noah would encounter those possibilities soon enough without Josh's saying so. The band came on and they stood there and listened, bobbing their heads along, drinking their beers. Josh did not want to think about how bland these songs were, despite the self-consciously clever lyrics, really just the same chords over and over, and why in hell this band had been getting such good buzz. He did not want to watch the guitarist's hands and feel the way the strings pressed against your fingers, leaving calluses that were, after these many months, nearly gone. They were entertaining, man. They put on a good show. The singer had moves. They were fun, and that was what mattered. That was all he needed to think about.

He dropped Noah off and drove all the way home before he surrendered to the urge to contact Adelaide. It was too late to call, so he sat in the car and sent her a text: *You still up?*

She replied with gratifying immediacy. *Yes. Can't sleep. Come over?*

When he got there she threw her arms around him like he'd done something far more heroic than drive across town. "I'm going nuts," she said, releasing him. "Did you know I'm an insomniac?"

He shook his head. "I don't think you told me."

"All my life. It comes and goes, though." She took his hand and led him farther into the apartment. She seemed wired, wild-eyed. "I knew tonight would be bad as soon as I turned out the light. I was so sleepy, but my head hit the pillow and I startled awake, thinking about this one move I'm having trouble with. And when that happens, that's it. I'm through. It's over."

This was the longest she'd talked about herself without being asked. "And then do you get up?"

"Sometimes I do," she said. "Sometimes like tonight I just lie there and keep trying to sleep, which is stupid, the worst thing you can do. You'd think I'd have learned by now how stupid that is."

"Why? What happens?"

Her whole body shivered. "Well, I'm not distracting myself, so all I can do is think about how I can't sleep, or maybe about the thing that woke me up in the first place, which is usually whatever I'm working on. Usually some mistake I've made. Sometimes the music plays over and over in my head. Just a snippet, over and over, and I can't turn it off. After a while of that I panic, and the panic is worse than the sleep loss."

"Oh, yeah?" he said, as though he'd experienced nothing like that.

"Yeah, it's like it gives me a hangover. There must be some kind of hormone that gets released or something when you freak out. The whole next day I just feel headachy and tense and awful." She groaned. "I have rehearsal all day tomorrow. All day! And if I don't sleep I'm going to be disastrous."

"So what helps?"

"Music, sometimes. Really different music, that can stop whatever's playing in my head. TV, sometimes, if it's absorbing enough that I can turn off my mind. The trouble with getting up to watch TV, though, is that the place is dark and still and the TV sounds really loud when you turn it on, and it's just all so lonely. Knowing everyone else in the world is sleeping."

"I'll stay up with you," Josh said.

"You will?"

"Can we stay up lying down, though? I feel a need to be prone."

They got ready for bed—Josh had to brush his teeth with his finger, as it still seemed too early to suggest he leave a toothbrush there. And besides, he wanted her to be the one to suggest it. They got into bed at the same moment, lifting the covers and climbing in with a determinedly matter-of-fact air, as if in a scene from a movie about awkward adolescent sex. This was the first time they'd gotten into bed together like longtime couples did, with sleep the primary thought in their minds. Funny that it should seem more awkward to climb into a bed together for sleep than to tumble onto it for sex. He lay on his back, and after a moment she slid over to rest her head on his shoulder. She was so tense he could feel it, like a reverberating sound. He picked up a piece of her long hair, running his fingers through it until they snagged on a tangle. "Ouch," she said, but mildly.

"Sorry," he said. "Or is pain a good distraction?" She didn't answer right away and he felt instantly sick with nerves. He'd been joking, of course, but what if he'd sounded like he was proposing something kinky? Would she even ask if that's what he meant, or would she just never call him again? "That was a joke."

"Hey, I have a sense of humor," she said.

"I know," he said, although he didn't, really.

"You're always telling me what was a joke."

"Not because I think you don't have a sense of humor. Because I worry my joke was so not funny you wouldn't recognize it as one."

"You should wear socks on your jokes."

"Okay, I don't know if you're funny, but you definitely qualify as weird."

"You know what I mean," she said. He was struck by the confidence with which she said it. He did, more or less, know what she meant. She was linking his insecurity to her own.

"I still haven't seen your feet," he said. "The rest of you. *All* the rest of you. But not your feet."

"Now there's too much buildup," she said. "I shouldn't have told you. Now I'll be too self-conscious to ever show you. Or when I do you'll be unimpressed. Or you'll assume I'm exaggerating and then when you finally see them you'll pass out from the shock."

"Once I saw photos of a bound foot. My sister was writing a paper about China in high school, and she showed me."

"Just picture that then, and mine won't seem so bad." She snuggled deeper into his chest. He could feel her body relaxing and was pleased. She sighed. "I have nine hours of rehearsal tomorrow."

"Don't think about that."

"I can't stop."

"Okay, then, think about it without thinking about it. Tell me about your day. How does it go?"

"We start at nine-thirty with company class."

"What's that?"

"It's everybody working for an hour and a half with the ballet master and the director. It's a warm-up for the day."

"Is it all really formal? I picture the master yelling at you. *Master*. That's a scary word."

"It's rigorous," she said. "The vibe depends on who's running things. And there are plenty of breaks throughout the day when we just hang out and talk. Or show off, in the case of the guys."

"Show off?"

"Oh, they have a lot of testosterone," she said. "They've been teased about being dancers, so they have to be that much manlier. They have something to prove. Max and Carlos especially. They're always flying across the room during breaks, doing all their tricks, leaping and spinning. We call it 'testosterone time.'"

"Carlos—is that the guy you danced with when I saw you?"

"I get partnered with him a lot. We dance well together."

"Yeah, you do." Josh was thinking about the way the male dancer had held her with the length of her body pressed to his, and the uneasy feeling the memory gave him got worse when she said, "He's my ex-boyfriend."

"Oh, crap," he said. "That's bad news."

She laughed. "It was a bad breakup, but it was also a long time ago."

"How long of a long time?"

"It's been, let's see, it's been five years. Wow."

He didn't like that *wow*. He wanted it to have been ten years, and to seem like twenty. "And how long did you date before that?"

"Five years."

"That's a serious relationship."

"We were kids. We're just like old friends now."

"Now you're just really good friends. Really good half-naked friends rolling all over each other."

She laughed again, but he could feel the tension returning to her body. She'd probably had guys act jealous about this before. He needed to be less predictable. He needed to keep it light. "I hope you're not going to hold me to his standard. I can't possibly jump that high."

"Not a requirement," she said.

What was a requirement? Why was this girl with him at all? He felt an intense need to do something impressive. "So music helps you sleep?"

"Sometimes," she said.

"I could sing," he offered. Did he imagine that she sounded a little wary when she said okay? "Name a song you find relaxing."

"Um. There's a Simon and Garfunkel song. My parents used to play it. 'I am just a poor boy.'" She spoke the line rather than singing it, though she inflected the words as if she was singing. He assumed she must be self-conscious about her voice. She was so careful about what she revealed.

"'The Boxer,'" he said.

"'The Boxer,'" she repeated. "Okay. There was another one I liked, too. With the line 'all come to look for America.'"

"Okay. Which?"

"You know them both?"

"I know a lot of songs."

"You're like a jukebox."

"Exactly like one."

She laughed. "'The Boxer,' then."

He tried to sing it as a lullaby, sweet and soothing, although some of the lyrics—like "whores on Seventh Avenue"—challenged that interpretation.

"You have a really nice voice," she said when he was done.

"Hmmm," he said. "Is it helping?"

"Lots." He felt her yawn against his chest. "Will you do the other one?"

Toward the end of the song he forgot himself a little. He didn't just croon the ending but full-out sang it, emoting like mad: "Empty and aching and I . . . don't . . . know . . . *why* . . ."

"That was beautiful, Josh," she said. "You should be a singer."

He was pleased. He was gratified. "Thanks," he said. "But you're not sleeping."

"I wanted to listen," she said. "Were you ever in a band?"

He opened his mouth to tell her, and then he thought of Sabrina, and on the heels of that thought came the impulse to lie. "No," he said. "Never was."

"That's too bad," she said. "You should start one."

"Thanks," he said, "but I don't think I'm good enough for that."

She fell asleep, at last, not long afterward, and he lay awake and wondered why, exactly, he'd lied. Well, why tell her? So that she could be briefly impressed, and then begin to see him as a failure? The last thing on earth he wanted was to repeat history.

Josh met Sabrina when he took his friend's cat to the vet hospital in the middle of the night. The cat was staying with him for two weeks while his friend was away, and on the second day he'd come home to find the cat gone. It had been like a locked-room mystery until he'd realized the screen on one of the windows was torn. Two hours later he found the cat crouched in the courtyard under a fire escape, wearing a hunted expression.

She was a vet student. She'd been wearing blue scrubs, with her blond hair up in a ponytail. She'd seemed suspicious of him—he fought the urge to explain that he hadn't encouraged the cat to jump—but with the cat she was all soothing voice and gentle hands. "How old is she?" she asked.

"I don't know," Josh said. "She's not mine."

"You don't like cats?"

"No, that's not what I meant."

"You just said that so emphatically." She imitated him, putting her free hand up in the sign for stop. "'She's not mine!' Like you wouldn't want anyone thinking you had a cat."

"No. No! I love cats. I always had cats growing up."

"Mmmm," she said. She seemed to have lost interest in him entirely, her focus returned to the animal on the table.

"I can't have a pet these days," Josh said. "I'm always on tour."

She didn't respond. Either her concentration was so intense she hadn't heard him, or she'd decided to pretend he wasn't there. He was guessing the latter, and he felt unsteady, a landlubber on a rocking boat. She seemed to dislike him, and he wasn't accustomed to being disliked. She cooed at the cat, whispering that she was a good girl, that everything would be all right. Then suddenly she looked up, her fingers gently palpating the cat's belly. "On tour?" she said. "What does that mean? You're military?"

He laughed, and then saw she wasn't kidding. Clearly she wasn't clued in by what he considered pretty good rocker hair. "I'm in a band."

"Like a rock band?"

"Well, we're not straight-up rock, but, yeah, basically."

She straightened, keeping a soothing hand on the cat, who closed her eyes as if in exhausted relief at receiving care from someone competent to give it. "Are you any good?"

He blew out air. "No," he said. "We suck. We suck *and* we blow. Someone should really put a stop to us."

She didn't laugh. She eased the cat back into the carrier and closed the door. She said, "We should take X-rays, but I think your cat's front paws are broken."

Not my cat, he wanted to say. "So now what?"

She paused with her hand on the doorknob. "I'll have one of the techs come take her for X-rays, and then we'll see."

"Okay, thanks," he said, but she was already out the door. He paced the length of the room, trying to shake the unsettled feeling she'd given him. Honestly she'd managed to make him feel as if he'd personally thrown the goddamn cat out the window. He felt guilty about the whole situation, and craved an impartial jury to confirm for him that what had happened to the cat was not his fault. But all he had was the cat, and who knew what she thought? He stuck his fingers through the squares in the door of her cage, and she sniffed them, then rubbed the side of her face against them. "Poor, poor kitty," he said, and she mewed as if to say *no shit.*

The cat's paws were indeed broken. Sabrina—Dr. Wells, she was then—showed him the fracture lines on the X-ray, on each side a semicircle traced from toe to toe. "You could operate," she said. "But I'm not sure it's worthwhile."

"Especially not if I do it," he said.

She looked at him. They were standing awfully close, looking at those X-rays. He could smell her fruity shampoo. He could see the odd color of her eyes, green ringed by gray. "You keep trying to make me laugh," she said, in a tone that suggested there wasn't much hope of his succeeding.

"It's a reflex," he said.

"I won't take it personally, then." She took a step back and faced him. "Cats are amazing healers," she said. "Really what you want to do is make sure she doesn't jump."

"How do you keep a cat from jumping?"

"You could buy a rabbit run to keep her in or build a cage out of chicken wire."

Josh lived in a small apartment with a living room barely big enough for his coffee table. He had little money. He didn't want to buy a rabbit run or build a cage. She must have read this in his face, because she said, "Or you could just keep letting her injure herself," and her tone suggested he must have the morals of a serial killer. She bent over the cat again, murmuring more sweet nothings into her ear. Was that the moment? Was that the moment when he resolved to win her? In retrospect he thought so. It was the combination of her crisp, dismissive authority and her capacity for tenderness that attracted him to her. He saw how loving she could be, if he could just persuade her he was worthy. If people could be divided into cats and dogs, he was the latter, pliable and obvious in his affections. People who saw him as a rock star failed to realize it, but winning him over was no big deal. Sabrina, though, she was a cat, and not just any cat but the kind who hides beneath chairs and swipes at the ankles of passersby. A cat like that loves only one person. One person who has risked injury. One person who has tried really hard.

"Do you want to come see me play?" he asked. "I—we—have

a gig tomorrow night. I could put you on the guest list." He was all-in. If she said no to this, he had nothing left to bet.

She straightened up to look at him, and then for the first time she smiled. All at once she was the one who seemed excitable as a puppy. "Sure," she said. "Yeah, that sounds like fun."

He'd stopped getting nervous before gigs some time before, but goddamn was he nervous before this one. He sat in the dressing room jiggling his leg and ripping tiny pieces from the label on a bottle of water, rolling those tiny pieces into balls. "What's up?" asked the bass player, and Josh just shook his head, because the bass player was the kind of guy who'd give him endless shit if he explained. See, I met this girl, and I didn't even exactly like her, but for some reason I want her to like me, it's very important that she like me, and as stupid as it sounds I have to impress her. I can't talk myself out of it, and I know because I've tried.

The process of walking out onstage and strapping on his guitar and making sure everything was a go seemed even longer and more excruciating than usual. He always hated this part, where everybody watched and waited. He felt the audience's collective impatience, the collective desire for the band to be awesome, to give them something they could take home and keep, rushing toward him like a tidal wave. But tonight all he felt was that she was out there somewhere, watching, waiting, judging. He was about to take a test that he might fail. He didn't look for her, not that he could have found her if he tried. It was a big crowd, a sold-out show. Maybe that in itself would impress her.

He skipped his usual greeting to the audience, his usual joking around, and just launched right into the first song. He closed his eyes and sang like it was the last song, like he wasn't saving anything for the encore, and as always once the music was under way, he was fine, he knew what he did and who he was, and everything was as it should be. He was sweating under the lights and everything was fine.

His preshow nerves must have spiked the punch, because everybody in the band insisted with a wild-eyed conviction that they'd played one of their best ever shows. And the audience had been right there with them—he'd seen that looking out during the encore, the way they jumped and danced and pumped their fists in the air. What could be better than this? Was there anything in the world better than this?

"Hey, Josh," the club manager said to him. "The girl you put on the guest list is asking if she can come backstage."

"Oh." He was crouched down, putting his guitar in its case. "Yeah," he said. And then he listened as the footsteps retreated and others approached. He took a long time to settle the guitar, close the lid, snap the locks into place, so that he was still down there when she reached him, when she said, "Hi." That was all she said, but as he rose to meet her he absorbed the sweetness, the tenderness that had been in that *hi,* and when he met her eyes and saw the look on her face, the *admiration* on her face, he knew that what he wanted could be his, that the best thing in the world wasn't just to do what you loved but to be admired for it, by someone whose admiration you really, deeply wanted.

Her admiration hadn't lasted. The thing that first won her heart became the very thing she hated. There were other problems of course. Not long into the relationship she began to test him, trying to find his limits. The first Thanksgiving they were together she announced plans to drive to Philadelphia, where her parents lived, and said nothing about his accompanying her. When he asked if he could come, she said, "No, I really don't want you to meet my family," and she stuck to this until the day before she was to leave, when she suddenly begged him to come. He canceled the plans he'd made with his friends and went. He had a million of these stories, of the hurtful things she said and did, of the many times those things failed to make him leave. Once right after sex she said, "I've done stuff with other guys I'd never do with you. You're not the right type." When pressed about this "stuff" she refused to say what it was, leaving him to imagine scenes far more dangerous and erotic then anything she'd probably done. That was probably the point. But he couldn't be sure, so the torture worked anyway.

She was a troubled person, he could see that now. She was so full of self-loathing she wanted him to loathe her, too, and when she couldn't make him hate her she hated him instead. She didn't think she was worthy of his devotion, so she saw it as an unforgivable weakness in him. Or maybe, he could hear Theo saying, she's just a cruel bitch who tormented you for sport.

He thought he could see, now, with the distance of a year and three hundred miles, why he'd stayed with her. As the band's big break turned out to be more of a medium one, she'd shored up his confidence, and at some point she'd become the source of his confidence. So when she was cruel to him—and he could admit, now, that she'd been cruel—there was no cure for his misery but her affection.

And her affection had come at a price. Once, hoping for comfort, he'd made some self-pitying remark about their latest single's failure to move past college radio, and she'd said, "Well, what do you really expect? That you're going to be a *rock star*?" She managed to inject a bottomless contempt into the last two words.

"No," he said, defensively, in a state of confusion about what exactly he was defending against. He did want to be a rock star. In a way he was one. So why had he just said no? Because she made it sound like such a ridiculous, adolescent, self-aggrandizing thing to want.

This was around the time she began to complain about the band and everything that had to do with it. She didn't want him out late at night, gone on weekends, let alone for weeks at a time. "If you loved me you wouldn't be gone so much," she said. "I couldn't possibly marry a man like you," she said, and why oh why did this make him determined to prove her wrong? "You're not an adult," she said. "You're an overgrown kid playing with toys. What, are you going to be playing in a bar band when you're fifty?"

He was hardly in a bar band. Right? Right? Late at night, sweaty and weary in the flickering lights of some club, the floor sticky with spilled beer, he heard her words in his head. Once, in college, he'd tried cocaine, and for a while he'd been in love with his small version of the world, the dancing people, the cold, crisp beer, the raucous band. And then the drug had worn off, and he'd hated himself and everyone there. What a cavalcade of losers. What an array of what was wrong with America. He felt something akin to this now, after gigs, when the buzz of the music wore off, and he began to slide into a depression that he didn't recognize as such, with Sabrina's voice telling him his unhappiness was inevitable, and only what he deserved.

When he told the others he was quitting, the drummer threw his sticks at him. Josh made no effort to defend himself. Whatever anger they felt he certainly deserved, but nothing they could say would make him change his mind.

Only after all that was over, the last outstanding gig canceled, the last plea from the bass player turned down, did it really hit him what he'd done. He'd gotten a part-time job right away, but suddenly there was so much more time. He'd stretched time and stretched it, filling every minute with his single-minded passion, and now it sagged back, oversize and deflated. He began to play a lot of video games, and Sabrina, instead of seeming happier, grew more and more annoyed. "I thought you wanted me around more," he said.

"I wanted you around *more*," she said. "Not all the time."

This was two months after he'd quit. She began to upbraid him, and all of a sudden, to his amazement, he registered that he didn't care. She yelled, and he ignored her, playing the best Super Mario of his life. Once again she slammed out of the apartment. He finished his game, marveling over his own indifference, and then beginning to relish it. He put his controller down, stood up and looked around the apartment. The couch was orange, a color he never would have chosen. What the hell was he doing there? He seemed to have woken from a dream of absurd events and bizarre but urgent concerns. At the time it had all seemed so real.

What Theo couldn't understand was that he hadn't been capable of ending the relationship any sooner than he had. He'd been chasing victory, and only once he stopped caring whether he got it did it come, in the form of drunken late-night phone calls begging him to come back. But he couldn't make himself stop caring. He just, miraculously, had. After that he'd gone around for weeks in a bliss of nothingness.

Maybe he could have called the guys, when his love for Sabrina finally released him. He could have spent days or weeks apologizing, promising never, ever to abandon them again. But all of that would have required emotions, and, man, did this indifference feel good. He took it home with him from Chicago to Cincinnati, determined to cultivate it as long as he could. Eloise seemed glad to see him. Ben seemed delighted to hire him. Nobody troubled his calm waters but Theo. "How are you?" she asked, in that voice people use when they really want to know. They sat on the couch where they'd wrestled over the remote as teenagers, now polite adults, perched on the edges of the cushions with their hands folded on their knees.

"Great," he said.

"Really? I'm so glad." She did seem genuinely glad. Her gladness was annoying. "How long are you here for?"

He shrugged. "Indefinitely."

She cocked her head. "Eloise said you were just back for a while."

"Sure, if by *for a while* you mean forever."

"What about the band?"

"What do you mean? The band is over."

"But I thought maybe now that you and Sabrina . . . I thought you might start it up again."

"Why? What does Sabrina have to do with anything?"

"Well, I mean . . ." Theo hesitated. "I just thought—I thought you quit for her. Didn't you quit for her?"

"No," he said. "I was just done with it. I'd gone as far as I could." She didn't argue, but he could tell by her face that she knew he was lying. Why did her face have to be a mirror in which he saw his own regret and shame and confusion? It was so hard not to hate her for that.

12

"What about this?" Wes asked, putting one of Theo's fingers into his mouth.

"Yes, that's good," Theo said. "I hope you're taking notes."

He pulled that finger out. "I'm making a map," he said. He touched the next finger. "What about this one?"

"I think you'll find you get the same reaction with all of them." He didn't answer, his tongue busy curling around her finger. She closed her eyes and sighed. "Except the ring finger on my left hand," she said. "That one's kind of standoffish."

He released her hand, moving his mouth to the hollow of her collarbone. "Is that your way of saying you don't want to get married?"

"Ooh," she said, as his breath hit that spot and a shiver went through her. "I didn't even know about that one."

He kissed her there, then made his way up her neck. "Oh, I'll find them all."

"I bet you will," she said. She closed her eyes and waited. It was wonderful to surrender. Theo had forgotten that, or perhaps never known it.

"Do you know you didn't answer my question?" Wes asked.

"What question?" She was concentrating on the sensation of his teeth against her earlobe, weighing her response as if there were going to be a test. "That's good, too, but so far the collarbone is winning."

"About your ring finger."

"Huh?" she said, in feigned confusion. Despite her efforts not to comprehend, she knew exactly what he'd asked her. She just didn't know how to answer. Since Francine's announcement—the bizarre competition that she seemed to think solved everything—marriage had been on Theo's mind. Thoughts of who she might marry, if she could snap her fingers and have husband and house in one fell swoop, led to thoughts of Noah, which led to confusion about what exactly she was doing with Wes, and then circled back to the self-defeating nonsense of imagining how she could get the house, even though it was early August and she knew damn well that fall and a job search were fast approaching. Several times in the last couple weeks she'd sworn to herself that she wouldn't engage in a destructive competition for the house. She was depressed and exhausted by the tension, the way she and Eloise were avoiding one another, speaking only when necessary, with the razor-blade politeness of a couple sharing custody, or British people. But every time she gave in to the longing for peace and made the resolution to surrender, her indignation surged forth again, and she went back to thinking about how she could win. "So," she'd said to Josh that morning, joining him at the coffeepot, "are you going to get married?"

"What?" He reached up to get her a mug. "Oh, you mean Francine's race to the altar?"

Theo nodded.

"First prize, one enormous house," Josh said. "Lots of prop-

erty taxes." The coffeepot gurgled one last time and then subsided, and he poured them each a cup and added cream. He
knew exactly how she liked her coffee. Sometimes she felt like
they were strangers to each other, but that was just not true. And
if it was true—if it was true right now—whose fault was that?

"I'd get married if I had someone to marry," she said.

"You really want the house, don't you?" Josh said.

"You do, too."

"Why do you say that? I never said I wanted it."

"No," Theo said. "But I've noticed that you've also never said
you don't."

"I hate it when you act like you can read my mind," Josh said.
"You have no idea what I'm thinking."

"You're still not saying you don't want it."

"Why do you assume you should get it? Because you're the
oldest child? You're less likely to stay here than I am."

"How do you know? You don't know what I'm thinking either."

"Great," Josh said, picking up his coffee and turning to go.
"So let's just plan on a battle to the death, okay?"

I'd get married if I had someone to marry. Would she really?
What about her research and her teaching, both of which, despite her recent fretfulness, she really loved? How badly did she
want the house? What kind of desperate was she?

Wes had returned to his original line of questioning. "What
about this?" His tongue flicked the inside of her ear.

"You know, I've never liked that one," she said. "I had a boyfriend in high school who used to jam his tongue in my ear, and
it was disgusting. I couldn't see the difference between that and
a wet Willie."

"Okay," he said, pulling back.

"But wait," she said. "Now I'm thinking he just wasn't doing it right."

"And I'm doing it right?"

"You get an A," she said. She giggled. "You get lots of A's. All the A's at my disposal."

"That's a lot of A's."

"Now I'm all out. I'll have to restock."

"You can do that while I'm gone."

"While you're gone?" Her eyes flew open. Had that been panic in her voice?

"Didn't I tell you? I'm going home for three days to see my parents."

Of course he had parents. Of course. He wasn't just a character in her story, but she felt as surprised as if someone in a book had said "Enough" and walked off the page.

"Oh, don't go see your mommy," she said. "Stay with me."

"I have to go," he said, with a surprising sharpness in his voice. Then he softened, so quickly she thought maybe she'd imagined that tone. "I get the feeling you're going to miss me."

"Yes."

"Good."

"Indeed," she said. She thought of the great gift this year of free time had seemed to her at the beginning. Now she couldn't think how to fill three days. She'd always marveled at the calm with which characters in Jane Austen novels pursued their cloistered lives, filling up hours with visiting and stitchery, passing the time, just passing the time. Now it seemed to her she'd expended a lot of energy inventing purposes to disguise the fact that she was doing the same thing. That everyone was doing the same thing, just passing the time, blog posts and emails and Twitter feeds instead of stitchery and whist.

Wes moved to kiss her, but she was a little angry at him for being about to leave her alone with her thoughts. A rogue impulse made her say, "Oh, Mommy," in a voice that was breathy and childlike, just as his lips met hers.

He pulled back and looked at her a moment, as though trying to recognize her. Then he pushed himself to sitting. He stood. "Theo," he said, picking up his jeans. "I want to explain why that's not funny." He pulled the jeans on and stood with his hands on his hips. He was still shirtless. She still had an urge to misbehave. It was strange that she could see how wrong things were going and yet want to make them worse.

"You don't look very stern like that," she said, and he, unsmiling, worked himself into his T-shirt. She sat up, and pulled up the sheet. She wished now that she had not draped her clothes neatly on the chair across the room, as if this had been not a passionate rendezvous but a doctor's appointment.

Now his arms were folded across his chest, and she could still see most of his tattoo. She'd had plenty of opportunity to study it—it was all black, an intricate design that looked rather like a star, or like several stars arranged into one star, except instead of lines or triangles the stars were made of script that maybe was, or at least looked like, Arabic. She hadn't yet asked him what it meant, because she feared the answer would make her roll her eyes, or at least repress the urge to do so. He's a boy, she thought. An angry boy. "My mother's depressive," he said. "Two years ago she checked herself into a psychiatric hospital because she was afraid she might take her own life."

Take her own life—why did he use that phrase? So oddly formal, not just for the conversation but for him. She had time to think that before her sense of mischief vaporized, and she was left with nothing to protect her from feeling like the terrible, careless person she was.

"I go see her as often as I can," he said. "It's important that she see us—me and my brothers—as often as possible."

"Of course," Theo said. "I'm sorry. I didn't know."

"Of course you didn't know," he said. "What do you know about me? Do you know where I'm from? Do you know what my politics are? Whether I go to church? What my childhood was like? Do you know my last name?"

"Bryant," she said quickly, but the way she jumped on that answer only proved his larger point.

"Bet you wouldn't even know that if I hadn't taken your class," he said.

"I'm sorry I was insensitive," she said.

"I know you are." As she watched, his expression softened from anger into something that looked more like pain. "Do you know in all the time we've been doing this, you haven't asked me a single question about myself?"

"That can't be true. How can that be true?"

"Can you think of one?"

"Well, not right now. But that doesn't mean . . ."

"Look, I'm glad you want to have sex with me. I'm not complaining about that. But I feel like you're treating me like a distraction. Like a drug. And I want to be more than that to you."

"You think I'm using you?"

He shrugged. "Are you?"

She blinked. "I don't know how to answer that. I think you have to define your terms."

"Let me put it this way. When the fever burns off, will you want to go to the movies with me?"

"I don't see why not."

"You don't see why not," he repeated. He turned and sat heavily on the edge of the bed. "That's not really the answer I was looking for."

"Please don't be mad at me, Wes," she said.

He shook his head. "I'm not *mad*."

She moved to put her hands on his back, and then stopped. But she was allowed to touch him—that was the point and the meaning of this. What she thought of when she thought of him was the pleasure of contact. She was set to his frequency. She vibrated at his touch. "How many brothers do you have?" she asked.

"Two."

"Will they be there this weekend?" She realized as she spoke she didn't know where *there* was. Was that even possible? How could she not know where he was from?

"The middle one will be. He lives in Columbus. My oldest brother lives in Chicago. He could drive in, but it didn't sound like he was going to."

"You're the youngest?"

"That's right."

"What are their names?"

"Alex and Anders." He turned to look at her. "You can stop now."

"Anders," she said. "That's an unusual name."

"My mother was learning Swedish," he said. "It's a Swedish name."

"How'd you get to be Wesley?" she asked. "She was learning British English?"

But it was too soon to make a joke. Or maybe his mother was just off-limits. He said flatly, "It's her maiden name."

"So which one is older? Alex or Anders?"

"Anders is the oldest," he said. "He resents being born in her Swedish phase."

"What's he like?"

"He's . . ." He shook his head. "Really, you don't have to ask me all these questions."

"Can I ask you questions later?"

He took a moment to consider. "Sure. But you'll have to make an appointment with my secretary."

"That seems fair," she said.

"You worry a lot about what's fair, don't you? Anders does that, too. I think it's a firstborn thing. I don't worry so much about fair."

"What do you worry about?"

"Getting what I want," he said, but not like he thought such a thing was possible.

She took a breath and finally put her hand on his back. "I'm asking questions because I'm interested. I'm sorry I didn't ask before. I didn't mean to be . . ."

"I know. You can stop."

"But I really . . ."

"It's okay. Seriously."

It didn't seem okay. She'd had no idea he was capable of looking so resigned, so downcast. She felt like she'd broken him. She'd been handed a rubber ball and thrown it, and instead of bouncing it cracked. But it had looked like a rubber ball! Surely it wasn't her fault for failing to realize the truth. "Wes . . ."

"I really, really, really don't want to have a talk right now." He turned fully toward her, put his hands on either side of her face, and looked her in the eye. "Really."

"Okay," she said. "I believe you."

He pressed her cheeks together gently so that her lips pursed out and then he kissed them with a theatrical smack.

"Sexy," she said.

"I'll show you sexy," he said. "I'll show you enough sexy to last you for days."

She was relieved. She was annoyed. She was confused. Aroused. Uneasy. Lonely in advance. "Just enough for three days, right?" she said.

"That's all you'll need," he said.

Three days was too long. Without Wes, she couldn't ignore the rest of her life, which included self-loathing over how long she'd been ignoring it. The next morning she emailed her professors about letters of recommendation. That task accomplished, she still felt restless, adrift, unsatisfied. She called up the file labeled "intro. doc" and read over the first few paragraphs. They didn't seem so bad. She even had an idea for what might come next, though it dissipated halfway through her third sentence and left her staring at her computer screen, at a thought that went nowhere. She shook her head and put her fingers on the keyboard, looked alertly at the sentence as though she were going to finish it. But she wasn't going to finish it. Why should she? This whole project was futile and idiotic, writing some ridiculous, arcane book for a tiny group of people to read and criticize. Conceptions of distance among nineteenth-century immigrant midwesterners—who cared! Footnoting and footnoting so no one could call her out on any failures in her research. There was no good reason to have devoted her life to this. And yet, she had, dammit. This was all there was. If she couldn't finish this sentence, she didn't deserve to live.

"Shit," she said after a moment and slammed her laptop shut. The problem wasn't just the sentence. Maybe it was the environment—not just the room but the house, maybe even the neighborhood. She needed a radical change of scene. Cincinnatians swore by the distinctions between neighborhoods. It meant something to say whether someone was from the east or west side, Clifton or Cheviot or Hyde Park. Hyde Park—that's where she would go, to hide among the conservative and the monied. She'd be a visitor to a foreign country there.

In the car, to her great relief, she thought of an end to her sentence, and once settled in a coffee shop on Hyde Park Square, she typed that sentence and wrote a few more until she had an actual paragraph. She got up to get a refill on her coffee. She thought about this later. If I hadn't wanted a refill. If I hadn't happened to notice the poster on the front window. If I hadn't walked over for a closer look. If I hadn't glanced outside. Because when she did glance outside, she saw Claire.

She saw Claire, her gone-to-New-York sister. Claire, who'd been calling regularly and saying things were fine, that rehearsals were hard but things were fine, they shouldn't come see a performance yet, not until she had a bigger part. Not really wanting to talk about herself, Theo had noticed but hadn't worried much about because it wasn't as if Claire had ever been particularly chatty. That Claire, Theo's Claire, was standing across the street with her hands on her hips and her feet in fourth position, looking in the window of a boutique. But that wasn't possible, because Claire was in New York. And Claire didn't have that haircut. Claire's hair was long, and suitable for pulling back into a ballet bun. This girl's hair was in a jagged bob. It was cute, but it wasn't Claire. This must be a girl who looked like Claire. A girl who looked exactly like Claire and owned Claire's favorite dress, a pale blue sleeveless one belted at the waist. Not-Claire turned, and Theo instinctively stepped away from the window. She went back to the table for her phone, her heart careening, and when she found it she scrolled to her sister's name and pressed it to call her. Claire, she thought, and then returned to the window where she could see the girl, who was walking now, up the street away from Theo. Her mind hollowed out while she listened to the ringing of the phone. It rang twice and the girl didn't stop walking, but just as Theo's throat unclenched, the girl stopped and slipped her hand, with a dancer's graceful movements, into her bag. "Hey, T," her sister's voice said into her ear as the girl spoke into her own phone, and yet Theo stayed frozen in disbelief. "Theo?" Claire said again. "You there?"

Theo opened her mouth but made no sound.

"Theo?" The girl took the phone away from her ear, looked at it, put it back again.

"Claire?" Theo said.

"Hey," Claire said. "Where'd you go?"

"Where did I go?" Theo repeated. "I don't understand."

"I couldn't hear you for a second."

"Oh. Oh. Really?" Theo glanced around as if looking for company in her confusion. "I don't know. I've been here."

Across the street the girl—Claire, it was *Claire*—tilted her head. "Are you okay?"

"I guess so," Theo said. "I was wondering how you are."

"You sound really strange, Theo. Please tell me if something's wrong."

"No." Theo took a deep breath. "No, it's nothing like that. Really, everything's fine. I just . . . miss you. I miss you."

"I miss you, too, T," Claire said. She sounded like she meant it. Across the street she brought one foot up and rested it on her other leg. "Stork pose," the rest of them had always called it. She'd done it since she was a little girl. In someone so preternaturally self-contained, it was a rare visible sign of discomfort.

"I love you," Theo said.

"I love you, too," Claire said, and then, when Theo didn't speak again, she said, "You still there?"

"I'm here," Theo said. "You still there?"

Claire laughed. "Obviously," she said.

"Yes," Theo said. "Obviously." Claire brought her lifted leg around front and lifted it higher, looked down at her pointed toe. Was she aware of what she was doing? There was no way to tell. "I have to go," Theo said, and then there were goodbyes, and she hung up the phone. From her hiding place she watched as Claire replaced her phone in her bag, and then as soon as her sister moved Theo followed, trying to remember what she'd learned from Hollywood about tailing a suspect on foot. Stay on the other side of the street? Hang back, but how far? It was certainly too late for any kind of disguise. She hadn't come prepared. She was radically unprepared.

They didn't go far, certainly less than a mile. Crossing a tree-lined street Claire dug in her bag again—watch for cars! Theo thought—and this time she pulled out keys. She walked up a flight of concrete stairs that led to a house, and when she reached the door she unlocked it. The house looked ordinary, or at least ordinary for Cincinnati, where many houses were a hundred years old and three stories tall. This house didn't even have the flourishes of their house—no columns or stained-glass windows. It was a skinny white house with a brown front door. Ordinary. But how could it be? None of this was ordinary. Claire had closed the door behind her. After standing there for a long, uncertain moment, Theo climbed the stairs, too. They were steep. She stood panting at the front door, which was half window. She was going to rap on the glass, as soon as she caught her breath. In the meantime she cupped her hands around her eyes and peered through it.

The foyer was much smaller than in their house, just a space big enough for the door, the bottom of the staircase, the cabinet Theo recognized as being from IKEA. Claire's bag was on top of it. As Theo stared, looking for some explanatory detail, Claire suddenly appeared through one of the two doorways off the foyer. She didn't notice Theo, engaged in flipping through the mail in her hand. It was all so normal, and that normality was utterly unnerving. Theo might have been less surprised to see cages full of imprisoned girls. If there had been any sign that Claire didn't want to be where she was, that Theo could have handled. She could have charged in, demanded explanations, rescued or scolded or comforted, whatever it was that needed to be done. Her sister had unlocked the door of this house, gone inside, put down her bag, looked through the mail. What rescue or remonstrance or comfort could Theo offer against the ordinariness of that?

There was no doorbell, so Theo knocked—rap, rap, rap—on the front door's window. Claire looked up from the mail, and

Theo saw recognition dawn on her sister's face. Her expression morphed from surprise to worry to what? What did that look mean? Claire opened the door. "Hi, Theo," she said.

"Hi," Theo said. My God, this woman was a total stranger.

"How did you know?" the stranger asked.

"How did I know what?"

"Where to find me."

"I saw you. I saw you in Hyde Park Square. That's why I called. Then I followed you."

The woman's eyes welled up, and she was Claire again, and Theo was her big sister. That was who she was. Claire bit her bottom lip and released it. "I'm sorry," she said.

"Oh, Claire." Theo stepped inside, shut the door, and put her arms around her sister. "Claire bear, what is happening? Is it something awful? Are you sick? Are you pregnant? Are you a drug addict? What are you doing here?"

Claire shook her head against Theo's shoulder. "I'm not sick," she said. "I'm not pregnant. I'm not a drug addict." She stepped back, pressing a knuckle to each of her eyes and then her nose. She sniffed. "I'm fine. I just didn't go."

"You didn't go at all?"

"I went through security and waited awhile, and then I came back out and went home."

"You didn't go home. You came here." Theo walked into the living room, where everything from the couches to the silver picture frames seemed to be from Pottery Barn. "Where is here?"

"Do Eloise and Josh know?"

Theo shook her head.

"Can you wait to tell them?"

"Wait for what?"

"For me to do it."

"When will that be? Looks like we might all have waited forever if I hadn't spotted you. And I still don't know what exactly you plan to tell. Why are you here? What is going on?"

"I just wanted to give it time. To be sure. I knew how disappointed you'd all be."

"Give what time?"

Claire, already so upright, managed to find some more length in her spine. "I fell in love."

"Are you serious? With who? Someone at the ballet?"

"No, though I met him there. He was at a fund-raiser a few months ago. He's a donor."

"A donor? So he has money? How old is this guy?"

"He's forty-five."

"Forty-five? Are you kidding me? And this is his house? That's his car?"

"This is our house," Claire said. "It's a rental."

"Forty-five!" Theo said again. "What does he do?"

"He's a developer."

"Oh my God. A developer?"

Claire seemed amused. "Would you be less upset if he had a different job?"

"Well, Jesus, Claire. It's just bizarre. At least if he was a ballet master or something this would make more sense. You can't even claim to understand each other. You can't say this is about your respect for what he does."

"It's not bizarre," she said quietly. "I think you'd like him. He's very into local history."

"I feel sick," Theo said. "What about your life?"

"I'm living it."

"Here? With a forty-five-year-old rich guy? I mean, what do you do all day, sit around perfuming yourself like a concubine?"

"It's not like that. We fell in love. You have to understand that, okay? And I wasn't really sure that going to New York was the life I wanted, but none of you wanted to hear that so I didn't tell you."

"What are you talking about?"

"You're all so invested in me being a dancer."

"Because *you* were invested in it!"

"But I never chose it, don't you understand that? It's this all-consuming life. Your whole life is dance. But I never chose it. It just happened to me, and it was about to take over completely. So when Gary had to get his own place, I realized I didn't want to go to New York. I wanted to stay here with him."

"His own place?"

"He's married. He's separated. Now."

"You mean you were involved before . . . you mean he left his wife for you?"

Claire flushed, then tightened her jaw, looked Theo in the eye. She nodded.

"You're a mistress?"

"We're going to get married. I'm his fiancée."

What made Theo the angriest was the pride in Claire's voice as she said it. "The fuck you are," Theo said. She hated the challenging expression on Claire's face. She'd had no idea she could hate any look of Claire's this much. Without a word her sister raised her left hand with the back toward Theo. Sure enough, on her finger was a ring. A clichéd princess-cut diamond, of a pretty good size. Theo blanched. She took a step back like Claire had raised her hand to hit her, and something in Theo's face must have tapped Claire's reservoir of guilt, because her sister's expression softened.

"I'm so sorry I've upset you," Claire said. "I didn't do this right, I know. But this is how I had to do it."

Theo shook her head. "I just don't understand."

Claire grabbed her hand. "I know I might be making the biggest mistake of my life," she said. "But that's okay. Let that be my regret, not yours."

Theo tried not to reject this request without considering it. She really did. She withdrew her hand, but slowly. "Did you quit the company?"

Claire winced. "Not exactly. But I'm probably going to."

"I hope you told them something. I hope you didn't just not show up."

"No, of course not," Claire said, which Theo found hilarious. *Of course not.* "I said I had a family emergency."

"I hope you didn't kill one of us off."

Claire pressed her lips together, the color in her cheeks deepening.

"You did, didn't you? You killed one of us."

"No, I didn't! I said illness."

"Illness? What illness?"

Claire sighed. "I said my aunt had breast cancer."

"Oh, God, Claire. That's like wishing it on her."

"No, it's not! And I didn't say it was Eloise. I didn't specify."

"If she gets breast cancer you're going to feel like you gave it to her."

"Jesus, Theo. Are you hoping that will happen? Do you need that badly to say 'I told you so'?"

Was that what Claire really thought of her? Theo remembered her little sister at four, looking at her with her big, serious eyes. "When Aunt Eloise dies, will you be my mommy?" she'd asked.

"Did they know you had a dead mother?" Theo asked now. "Because you could have just told them your mother died and failed to mention the year. A dead mother's pretty bad. You might as well get some mileage out of it."

"Like you?"

"Excuse me?" Claire walked across the room but Theo followed. "I'm sorry, how do I get mileage out of it? I'd really like to know." Claire just shook her head. "Yeah, that's what I thought."

Theo was out the door and down the street in a panting, fast-walking rage. Her feet slapped the pavement. Her hands were fists. Her heart was furious and kept a pace that proved it. Goddamn that little bitch. And then, as that thought reverberated and she realized that never, ever would she have imagined she'd use those words about Claire, Theo knew she was about to cry. She ducked into an alley and jogged toward the back, where she propped herself on a brick wall and fought the tears. Though she told herself she was angry, not sad, her throat wouldn't stop its stupid lumping. Her eyes burned. Why couldn't her body do what she told it to? The body should be subject to the mind. In all things. In all things. In *all things,* goddammit. She said this aloud like a mantra until the crying lost its grip on her. Then she strolled out of the alley with an air of casual purpose and went back to the coffee shop. No one had stolen her laptop, so that was something to be thankful for. She still hadn't gotten that refill, and decided instead to try one of the complicated confections listed on the board. Why not a little caramel? Why not whole milk? While she waited for the steaming and the stirring to end she stood next to an empty table and flipped through the day-old copy of *The New York Times* sitting there. Isn't that interesting, she thought, without knowing quite what she was thinking it about.

Her drink was ready, so she accepted it with a smile and a thanks. She collected her things and went back outside. It was a pleasant day, really, not too hot. She took an unguarded sip of coffee and burned the hell out of her tongue, and that was just one thing too many. Before she knew it she'd thrown the cup to the ground. At her feet a milky brown splash sent out its runners in all directions. "Oh no," a voice said, and she realized an older woman was sitting at an outdoor table, watching her.

"I dropped it," Theo said.

"Too bad," the woman said. "Did you burn yourself?"

Theo shook her head without speaking, because to open her mouth would be to sob. She picked up the cup like a good girl and threw it in the trash. She started walking fast, then faster, until she was running, and when she finally reached her car, panting and sweaty, she leapt inside like a getaway artist, pulling out so fast she made the tires squeal.

13

You look happy," Eloise said when Josh walked into the kitchen after work, and Josh said, "I *am* happy." He loosened his tie, feeling not like a cliché of a businessman home from a good day's work at the office but like an actual businessman.

"How about I fix us a celebratory drink and you can tell me what there is to celebrate?" She stood on tiptoes to open the liquor cabinet, then stared up into it, hands on her hips. "It's good gin and tonic weather," she said.

"That sounds great," Josh said. He reached up past her to lift down the gin.

She turned with a smile. "I was just going to ask you to do that."

He tapped his temple with a finger. "Psychic," he said. He went to the fridge and hunted through the fruit drawer until, at the very back, he found a slightly dented lime. He grabbed a bottle of tonic and, on the way back to the counter, passed Eloise headed to the fridge with two glasses needing ice. His current mood made him take an exuberant pleasure in their teamwork. It was nice to understand another person, and to feel understood, even in this small and particular way.

Eloise mixed the drinks, handed him one glass and lifted the other. "Here's to—" She cocked her head and thought. "Whatever you haven't told me yet," she said.

"Here's to that," Josh said, and they clinked glasses and each took a healthy swallow. She'd made the drinks strong. "Wow," he said. "It's a gin and gin," and she laughed. After this, neither one of them was likely to be in any state to cook dinner. They should order pizza. He'd offer to pay. "Are you ready for this?" he said.

"Hang on," she said and took another sip. "Go."

"I got a really big client today."

"You did?"

"All by myself." He gestured at himself. "In my business suit."

Eloise laughed, then brought her hand up to the one holding her glass and lightly applauded. "Am I still allowed to say I'm proud of you?"

"By all means," Josh said, grinning. "Knock yourself out."

"I'm proud of you, then."

"Aw, thanks," he said and felt an actual blush heat his cheeks. Did you ever get over wanting praise from the person who raised you, wanting it on such a primal, childlike level you were embarrassed when you got it? Anyway, he was proud of himself, too. The successful meeting, with the CEO of a corporation Josh had actually heard of, had reminded him that he was good at a large part of his job—what his friend Ben, who'd hired him, called the "charm offensive." Most people he talked to worked for content providers that had approached the company, looking for help developing apps for mobile platforms, so they were already interested and receptive. He liked talking to them, liked making them laugh, liked listening to their problems and convincing them he was the one to solve them.

"It's nice to get good news," Eloise said.

"Uh-oh," Josh said. "Did you get some bad news?"

"No, no, no," she said. "I'm just dreading the start of the school year. I feel like the meetings are mating and dropping litters of other meetings. And I feel a little . . . stressed. A little under attack. In general."

Josh assumed she was talking about Francine, and Theo, and not knowing what would happen with the house. Did she want to talk about all that? She must, if she'd brought it up. But he didn't want to say anything that might seem critical of her, or otherwise commit himself, so what exactly did he want to say? He'd just opened his mouth to ask if she was upset about Theo's behavior when, as if on cue, he heard a car motor slowing outside. He listened, feeling his shoulders tense at even the idea of his sister. "I think Theo's home," he said.

Eloise made a no-comment face and poked at the ice in her drink.

The door slammed. Theo's footsteps in the hallway were loud. She came into the kitchen with an air of angry confusion, looked at them with suspicion and surprise, and then turned sharply around to disappear.

Josh and Eloise exchanged a glance. "I think she could use a gin and gin," Josh murmured, and Eloise nodded. "You know," he said, suddenly sure that he should renounce the house, ready to divorce himself from ill-tempered Theo and declare himself on Eloise's side, "I've been meaning to tell you—"

But Theo was back in the room, her hands in fists at her sides. "She asked me not to tell you, but I'm going to tell you," she announced.

"Tell us what?" Eloise asked. Her tone was mild. She seemed

more interested in calming Theo than in getting the information.

Theo pulled a chair out from the table, dragging it some distance from the two of them, and flopped down in it. She looked so miserable, like a good child in the principal's office, confronted with the inexplicability of her own bad behavior. Josh could tell she was upset, but until she started talking he thought that the problem would turn out to be something small. Somewhere along the line he'd decided that Theo made a big deal out of nothing. This had been a necessary defense mechanism in the Sabrina years, when to take her seriously would have been to end his relationship or hate himself or both. But if he'd stopped to review the sum total of his experience with his sister, he'd have had to face the conclusion that Theo did not, in fact, make a big deal out of nothing. If anything Theo made a small deal out of something, at least when the something concerned herself. When she had appendicitis in high school she carried around a bottle of Pepto-Bismol for two days, insisting that she just had a stomachache, until the morning she couldn't stand up straight, her body folded around the pain.

In the back of his head he knew all this, but when she'd told them everything she knew about Claire, he still said, "Come on, it can't be as bad as you're making it sound." Theo gave him a look of such incredulous scorn that he went one step farther. "So she doesn't want to be a dancer anymore," he said. "That's her choice."

"And you're not the least bit upset about the way she did it?" she asked. "It doesn't make you sick to imagine her waiting on the other side of security until we left the airport and then sneaking out? It doesn't bother you that for more than a month we've all thought she was in New York City, when actually she was a kept woman in Hyde Park? You don't care that she lied to us?"

Of course he cared. His stomach caved in, as though he himself were the disappointment. But he shrugged. "She's nineteen," he said. "She's in love, and right now that probably seems bigger than anything. Bigger than us."

"Did you know?" Theo asked him.

"Me? Of course not. Why would I know?"

"Maybe she thought you'd sympathize."

"Because I quit ballet and moved in with a sugar daddy?"

"Sugar daddy," Eloise repeated, as if she'd never heard the term before. It was the first thing she'd said since Theo began her story.

"What are we going to do?" Theo asked.

"This is so funny," Eloise said. "I feel like we're in a Jane Austen novel. A scandalous elopement."

Theo stared at her a moment, then turned back to Josh. "What about Adelaide? Can you maybe ask her what's going on?"

"What if she's offended that I want her to break Claire's confidence? Or what if she doesn't know anything and I'm the one who tells her?"

"Also we don't want Adelaide to know Claire's so unprofessional," Theo said, as though she hadn't been the one to suggest calling her. "They probably all talk to each other, those ballet dancers."

"I don't think so," Josh said. "You make them sound like spies."

"Well, what if she ends up wanting to audition for the company here? We don't want them knowing." Theo pointed at Josh. "Don't tell Adelaide."

"I was never going to. You were the one who—" He stopped himself, sighed. "I won't. I promise."

"But here's what you can ask her—what would happen if a dancer didn't show because of a family emergency and then wanted to come back? Would they let her? I don't think rehearsals were starting much before now. Would she have to audition again?"

Josh wanted to know how he was supposed to explain to Adelaide why he was asking. "Sure," he said, although he had no intention of complying.

"I guess you can't do that. Why the hell would you ask her that?"

"Right," he said, relieved. "Even I might have trouble making that plausible."

"So what can we do? What's our first step?" Theo asked. She looked from Josh to Eloise. "I think I should figure out whether the company would even take her back. That's number one. And what about her apartment? They must have replaced her with another roommate, right?"

"If this *were* a Jane Austen novel . . ." Eloise said, but she didn't finish the thought.

"They must have," Theo said. "It's New York. They can't do without the rent. So we'll have to find her another place. You know people in New York, right?" She looked at Josh.

"Sure," he said. "Yeah." Sure, yeah, he knew people in New York, lots of people he'd met at some drunken party or backstage or over the merch table at one of his gigs. No one he'd call to get his little sister an apartment.

"Okay." Theo nodded as if something had been settled. "How hard do you think it will be to convince her to go back? Or go in the first place, I guess. I don't know if I can do it. I kind of flipped out." To Josh's dismay her eyes filled. "I screwed up."

There was no resisting the sadness in her voice. "It's not your fault," he said. "*She* did this. It's not like it would be different if you'd stayed calm." Did he mean this? Maybe. He wasn't sure.

"She can't marry that man until he's divorced. How long does it take to get divorced here? How much time do we have?"

"I have no idea," Eloise said. She didn't offer to find out, though you'd think with her research on marriage laws she'd have known how to do so. Maybe it was shock, but Eloise was doing a pretty good job of appearing not to care, and that was agitating Theo, who, if Josh didn't step in, would feel compelled to care enough for all of them.

"Would you like me to go find that out?" he asked.

Theo shook her head. "I can do that. Could you go to talk to her? Things got so ugly between us. She might be more receptive to you now."

"Okay." Josh nodded. "Sure."

"Thank you," Theo said, with more gratitude than necessary. In the last several minutes he and Eloise must have left her feeling very alone. "I know you haven't always felt like . . . I mean, I know you . . ."

She was trying to say something about Sabrina. Whatever it was, he didn't want to hear it. "I'll call her right now," he said, getting up. As he headed for the door Theo called after him, "We've got to fix this."

It was hard for Josh to see how they could possibly do that. But he didn't argue with her. He took out his phone and made the call.

• • •

Claire met him after work the next day at the coffee shop in Hyde Park Square. She was reluctant to come into Clifton, Northside, or downtown, and by that reluctance he understood that she'd kept her doings a secret from her friends and her teachers at the ballet as much as from her family. He was standing near the counter, studying the menu board, when she came in, and when she saw him she rushed to him so quickly he barely had time to get his hands out of his pockets to embrace her. "Hey," he said into her hair, which was suddenly very short after a lifetime of being long.

Claire stepped back and gave him a grateful smile. Of course she wasn't just angry and imperiously withdrawn, the way Theo seemed to think. She'd been as upset as Theo by their encounter. She'd always wanted their big sister's approval. He and Claire had that in common. "Hey," she said.

"Until this moment I thought Theo was imagining things," he said. Then, because she looked so stricken, he added quickly, "I like your hair."

"Thanks," she said, one hand going to the nape of her neck. "I always had to keep it long before."

"I guess that's a benefit of quitting."

"I've always wanted short hair," she said, not sounding so sure that was true. "I went to the salon the next day."

Why? Josh wanted to ask. *So you couldn't change your mind?* "Well, it looks good," he said.

They ordered and waited for their drinks and found a table and all the while Josh tried to decide how he felt and couldn't. Theo seemed to have no such difficulty, so certain that Claire had made a terrible mistake. She was angry and hurt and sick with bewilderment. Josh for his part understood what Claire had done, and not just the parts that rhymed with his own history. He understood why she'd hidden her choices from them. He, too, would have liked the luxury of living alone for a while with the decisions he'd made.

Claire toyed with the sleeve on her coffee cup. "Are you mad at me, too?"

"No," he said. "I was surprised."

"I'm sorry," she said. "I wanted to tell you. But I felt like it would upset Theo and Eloise more if they found out you knew. And I didn't want them mad at you, too."

"Theo wondered if I knew," he said.

She grimaced. "I don't want to get you in trouble."

"Don't worry about that. You should come to me if you need me."

"Thank you, Joshy."

She looked so relieved, he wanted to give her more. "There's no law that just because you're good at something you have to keep doing it."

"I knew you'd be the one who understood," she said.

"I do," he said and then willed himself to mean it. If dancing had been a burden, shouldn't Claire look lighter? Shouldn't she look free? She looked to him like someone in mourning. She looked so terribly thin, without her art to explain her appearance.

"Will you help me with them? Will you talk to them for me, make them see?"

"Sure," he said, feeling a little sick, because that was the last thing he wanted to do.

Claire relaxed into her chair as if everything was settled. "I've been dying to talk to you about Adelaide!" she said. "I'm really glad you're dating her."

"Me, too," he said.

"I'm so curious what she's like up close. You know, behind her teacher-dancer persona."

"What do you mean?"

"Well, she's sort of cool and remote. You know. She seems very self-contained. Onstage even when she's surrounded by others you don't really feel like she needs anyone else."

"She's, well, she's . . ." he tried, but Claire's little speech had left him unable to formulate a thought. He gave her what he could tell was a weak smile. "I'm still figuring her out."

"We can double-date!" she said. Was she serious? The question must have shown on his face, because Claire laughed, and then looked solemn. "I mean, after a while," she said.

"Sure," he said again. Ask me anything! he thought. I'll say sure!

"But you should meet him now," she said. "I want you to meet Gary. Do you want to?"

Just to switch things up he said, "Okay."

The house was way too big for two people, three stories and spacious ones at that. Why rent such a big house for two people in the city's most expensive neighborhood? What did Claire do alone in these giant rooms all day? Josh moved around the living room, looking at the vacation shots in silver frames and the gray, velvety couches so he wouldn't have to look at Claire. "All this stuff is Gary's," she said, and Josh couldn't tell whether that was meant as praise of the guy or apology for him. The room looked like he'd set out to reproduce a catalog. "I'm sorry he's not home yet," she said. "I thought he'd be home."

"Where is he?"

"He works late. Or he might have gone to see his daughter."

"His daughter?"

"She's three. I haven't met her yet. We're waiting."

"Wow, Claire. You're going to be a stepmother?"

"I know, right?" She smiled. "It's crazy."

Yes, it really is, he wanted to say. "Where's the bathroom?"

She made a face. "It's on the second floor," she said. "Isn't that annoying?"

"Well, most of these old houses . . ." He trailed off, unsure he wanted to comfort her about her concubine house. *Concubine*— a word Theo had used. What was Theo's word doing in his head? "I'll be right back," he said.

He didn't really have to use the bathroom. He wanted a moment away from Claire's happy belief in his understanding, her relief at his support. And now that he was up here, he wanted to snoop. He took a quick glance in each of the rooms on the second floor. One was a study, furnished in the same inoffensive style as the living room. One had yellow walls and a bunch of IKEA boxes in it—of course, a room for the little girl. Best, for now, not to think about her, her future presence in Claire's life, the fact that Claire thought she was remotely ready for . . . Best not to think about that. Another room had a bed but little else. The guest bedroom, he assumed. And then the last was the master. The bed wasn't even made, the sheets and quilt not just disarranged but disarranged chaotically, and he stepped out quickly, feeling a little sick, and decided to look at the third floor. He crept up the stairs on the balls of his feet, trying not to make a sound.

The third floor was two large rooms divided by a door. In the second, smaller one were two standing full-length mirrors, between them a ballet barre. Josh ran his hand along the barre, watching himself in the mirror. If Claire didn't want to be a dancer anymore, what was this doing in the house? He wondered if Gary had set this up, trying to please her. He pictured Claire dancing in this little room and thought of Adelaide's tiny ballerina in a jewelry box. He hoped that wasn't what his sister was to Gary—an acquisition, a toy, a valuable object made more valuable by being hidden away.

He jumped at the sound of Claire's voice, distant and muffled but still unmistakably calling his name. He tried to be both quick and quiet on the stairs, and found her waiting at the bottom of the second flight. "There you are," she said. "He's just pulling up." She said it like Josh was expected to be awaiting the guy the moment he came inside, and perhaps this was why Josh felt like he was standing at attention in the entryway, anticipating inspection by the king.

Some king. Gary fell a couple inches short of Josh. He was impressively broad-shouldered—he looked like a swimmer—but balding fast, with a briefcase and a very white expanse of forehead. Who carried a briefcase still? Josh himself toted his stuff around in a messenger bag. Maybe a businessman in his midforties would feel self-conscious with a messenger bag, like he was trying too hard, which was exactly how Josh would have felt arriving at the office with a briefcase. I don't get it, was Josh's first thought, and his second, and also his third. Gary put the briefcase down to shake Josh's hand, looking him right in the eye, and for a moment Josh expected to be sold insurance, or real estate, or a car. But though the man had a salesman's grip and gaze, he lacked the easy, direct manner of one. In fact he sounded pained and awkward as he said how glad he was they'd finally met. Well, like a salesman, he was totally full of shit.

"Me, too," Josh said, and then, exerting himself in the face of Gary's silence and Claire's hopeful eyes, he said, "So, you're a developer."

"Yes," Gary said.

Josh had no follow-up. "I don't know much about that," he said. "Except what I've seen on *The Wire*. But that's not very pro-development, of course. I'm sure it's, you know, got a particular political . . . thing."

"What's *The Wire*?"

"Oh, it was a TV show," Josh said. "A really good TV show."

"Ah," Gary said. "The glass teat."

"Huh?" Josh said.

"TV."

"Gary doesn't like TV," Claire said. "Not even the good stuff."

"There is no good stuff," Gary said.

Claire rolled her eyes indulgently. "Everybody but you agrees there's good stuff. Even snobs liked *The Sopranos*."

"People just believe what they're told," Gary said. "Everything's advertising. Without advertising you probably couldn't even tell the difference between Pepsi and Coke."

"Sure I could," Claire said.

"Me, too," Josh said.

"If I blindfolded you and gave you a taste of each you think you could tell?"

Bring it on, Josh wanted to say, but he swallowed his irritation and held up his hands. "We just met," he said. "We'll get to the blindfolding later."

Gary checked his watch, as if to say this meeting was over. "Anyone want a drink?" he asked and then headed for the kitchen without waiting for an answer.

"Sorry, he was being obnoxious," Claire said. "I've noticed he does that when he's nervous. I'm still figuring him out, too." She smiled as if figuring out this self-important asshole were a delightful prospect. She seemed so young—not just nineteen but thirteen. Twelve. And Josh wanted to tell her what he knew: that love might look like a shore but turn out to be a desert island, where you roamed alone, talking to yourself, trying to crack open coconuts with your shoe. So thirsty you drank the salt water. So hungry you ate the sand.

He wanted to sail up in a boat and rescue her, and he had a sudden, painful understanding of all that Theo had felt about him. Once, Sabrina had said in front of Theo that she'd leave him as soon as she had enough money to pay for a place on her own. He'd insisted to Theo that Sabrina had been joking, growing angry when Theo didn't seem to believe it. He'd never considered how hard it must have been for his sister to see him treated that way. She must have wanted to knock Sabrina to the ground like she had that neighbor boy, rub Sabrina's face in the snow, take her baby brother home to wipe the blood away, set the world right again.

But Josh refused to make Theo's mistakes. He wouldn't judge. He wouldn't urge. He wouldn't harangue. He'd let Claire see for herself how wrong this was. He'd wait it out. Hadn't it been, in part, Theo's insistence on Sabrina's faults that had made him so determinedly blind to them?

"So," he called after Gary, "how about that drink?"

14

The first day of classes at Wyett College was a week away, and Eloise needed to write a new lecture and change the dates on her syllabus and have a meeting with the two older professors who were refusing to do committee work. She also needed to make a decision about the offer from Jason Bamber, who'd all but promised her the job. She wasn't doing any of that. She was leaning against her kitchen counter with a glass of wine in her hand and watching Heather mince garlic for bruschetta. Watching Heather cook was one of the pleasures of Eloise's life—the clean, brisk confidence of Heather's movements, the rhythmic tapping of the knife against the cutting board. But tonight even that simple joy was denied her.

Things were a mess. The house still wasn't hers. Theo would barely speak to her. Josh wore a constant crease line of worry in his forehead. Eloise hadn't told Heather about the job offer, even as she considered it, which was tantamount to lying. She had a confused sense that she needed something definitive to happen with the house before she could decide about Chicago, or even talk about it. If she could sell the house, she could move in with Heather and be content. But if she had to walk away with nothing, if her kids and her mother did that to her, she could endure her own anger and disappointment only if she could consign them and the house to a completed life, and start living a new one.

Old-country societies had it right when they said you owed something to the people who'd taken care of you. All the things they'd done for you should give them a say in your destiny. I labor for you, you labor for me. I house you, you house me. I choose the person you marry. I get something in return. But contemporary Western types had to go and decide children were not ours to keep and make use of, but rather a gift we offer the universe. Here you go, universe, here's a child I gave up my life for. Let her do what she wants. I'll just sit over here and die. In America people were surprised over and over when their years of effort were met with ingratitude, when their children drove around in brand-new cars failing to visit them in the moldering nursing home. But that was what happened if you didn't raise them to believe it was their duty to return the favors you'd done, remind them all the time of what they owed you.

For nearly a week after Claire's secret emerged, Eloise had waited to see if the girl would call. When she finally did, and Eloise answered, Claire said, "Aunt Eloise?" though none of the kids had used that title in years.

"Yes," Eloise said. "It's me."

"How are you?"

"Fine. How are you?"

"I'm so sorry you found out the way you did," Claire said. "I know I shouldn't have handled things like this."

"Okay," Eloise said.

"I thought maybe everybody could get used to the idea. With a little time."

"You have to live your life," she said. And because that was all she could think of to say she said it again.

"I want to come see you," Claire said. "Can I come see you?"

"Oh. Now?"

"Whenever," Claire said. "Whenever I can."

Eloise was in the kitchen, then, too, well into a bottle of wine. She looked around in a panic: dishes in the sink, newspapers strewn across the counter, a toppling stack of unsorted mail on the table. She couldn't have said why it mattered whether Claire saw the house messy after years of living blithely in the mess. She only knew that it did. "Let's do it in a few days," she said. "We'll have a family dinner."

"At home, you mean?" Claire said.

"Here, yes," Eloise said.

"There," Claire said. "Right. When?"

"Let's see," Eloise said. She walked over to the calendar and stared at it blindly. "How about Friday?"

"Okay," Claire said. "Friday."

"Great! We'll have a family dinner." She stressed the word *family,* and then just in case Claire still didn't get it, she said, "You, me, Josh, and Theo." *You, me, Josh, and Theo,* she repeated in her head. "Seven-thirty," she said, and then as fast as she could she got off the phone.

She had no idea what she was doing. She had no idea what to do. The feeling plunged her back into her early years with the kids, with Josh and especially with Theo, when she felt like the substitute teacher, making herself look foolish by failing to know the real teacher's method, fucking up the lesson plan. Growing up, Claire had been willful and defiant—prone to tantrums and claims that she didn't love Eloise anymore—but these rejections had been more affirming than Josh's agreeable acceptance or Theo's stunned obedience. What Eloise did really mattered to Claire. Claire was the only one who remembered nothing but Eloise. Claire was her child. Not the most like her—Theo was the most like her, because of genes, or happenstance. Claire was the one whose personality Eloise helped form. Claire was the only one whose mother Eloise really was.

Eloise had told Josh and Theo about the dinner, and she'd told Heather she was having it, but otherwise she'd been in a state of denial for the last several days, from the moment she hung up the phone. For God's sake, the last thing she wanted was a family dinner! She and Theo could barely look at each other; she had no idea how she wanted to behave with Claire, and less idea why she'd suggested they stage a false display of togetherness and normalcy. Why, why, why was she forever agreeing to things she had no desire to do? And not just agreeing but instigating. Once upon a time she'd been a person who just said no.

Now she swigged her wine, and made a face. "I don't want this," she said. "I want a martini." Heather stopped mincing and looked up. "Not just a regular martini. A huge martini. In one of those joke glasses."

"No liquor," Heather said. "In the mood you're in, wine is bad enough."

"But I want it," Eloise said. "It will change the mood I'm in." Heather ignored her, the way you might ignore the mulish, futile protests of a small child. She set the knife down so that she could pull Eloise's head forward and kiss the top of it, an offer of comfort that made Eloise's eyes fill with tears. "Don't be nice to me," she said.

"Okay," Heather said and gave Eloise's cheek a painless smack. Then she went back to mincing. Eloise hadn't asked Heather to come cook. Heather had just shown up, and seemed unsurprised to find Eloise in a state of sedated panic, a glass of wine in her hand, not a single thing done. Sometimes it drove Eloise insane, how much Heather seemed to know. Sometimes she wanted her quirks and failings to go unobserved. Sometimes Heather's air of businesslike amusement about those quirks and failings made Eloise want to up the ante. To be even later. To be even more dramatic. To just take the roof off the place. "Ugh," Eloise said, closing her eyes. "I hate myself."

"Well," Heather said. "That happens sometimes."

"I want my sister," Eloise said. Again the sounds of the knife stopped, and Eloise opened her eyes to find Heather looking at her with such openhearted sympathy she felt she'd collapse under the weight of it. My God, of course she wouldn't take that job. How could she even think about doing something that might mean leaving Heather behind?

"I love you," Heather said.

"I know," Eloise said. "Hey, here's an idea—let's move in to-gether."

"Really?" Heather's voice held a carefully controlled excite-ment.

If she said yes and then changed her mind, Heather wouldn't forgive her anytime soon. To say yes was a commitment. Heather had come over to cook for her, to cook a meal she wouldn't be eating, for people who had no idea how important she was. "Yes," Eloise said.

Heather smiled. "That makes me happy," she said.

Eloise laughed. "I'm glad."

Heather resumed mincing, a new energy now in the tap-tap-tap of the knife. "Oh, that makes me very happy," she said.

"Let's just do it now," Eloise said. "Forget this dinner. Let's get out of here."

"Maybe it won't be that bad," Heather said. She picked up the cutting board and used the knife to sweep the garlic into the bowl. She stirred, then dipped in a spoon to taste.

"You think?" Eloise said.

Heather turned, holding out a spoonful for Eloise to sample. "No," she said.

"It smells really good in here," Theo said, coming into the kitchen. Heather had taken her knives and gone home, leaving Eloise to wait, with increasing dread, for the children to appear. Theo was the first. She wore a skirt with a cute top Eloise recognized from the catalog of a rather expensive store. Theo looked like she'd actually taken the time to blow-dry her hair. So Eloise wasn't the only one treating this like a dinner party, one to which they'd invited some important and barely known guest. Eloise herself coveted the clothes from the store that had sold Theo her shirt, and sometimes went there and walked around looking at the clothes and touching them, but she hardly ever allowed herself to buy something. Theo was living here rent-free. Eloise hoped she'd bought that shirt on sale.

"I didn't do shit," Eloise said. "It was all Heather."

Theo cocked her head. "Heather? Is she eating with us?"

"Nope. She just came over to cook." Eloise studied the look of puzzlement on Theo's face, noticing that she took pleasure in her own failure to explain. Her anger at Theo over the house was a flavor added to every thought about her niece, every interaction they had.

"That was nice of her," Theo said.

"She's a nice person," Eloise said, bending to pull the last tray of Heather's brown sugar cookies from the oven.

"Yes, but that was *unusually* nice of her."

"She's a fucking nice person." Eloise said this with her back to Theo, and when she turned from the oven she found that her niece had left the room. The sight of the empty kitchen brought tears to her eyes, even though she knew she'd been behaving badly, acting like she wanted Theo gone. She ate a hot, crumbly cookie, chased it with another swig of wine, wiped her eyes on her sleeve, and picked up the platter of bruschetta to carry it into the dining room.

She found Josh at the bar making two vodka tonics. She placed the tray on the table—already set with the good china, which was also Heather's doing. "Where's Theo?" she asked.

"I think she's watching for Claire," he said. He sipped one of the drinks and made a face. "Though I doubt she'd admit that."

"Too strong?" Eloise asked.

"Not strong enough," he said.

"I'm kind of drunk."

He turned to appraise her, his expression falling somewhere between amusement and concern. "Really?"

"It was an accident."

He nodded. "I think I'm about to have a similar accident."

"I have no idea why I suggested this."

Josh shrugged. "You have to see her sometime."

"Maybe," Eloise said. "Maybe not. Heather made bruschetta."

"That was nice of her." Josh came over with one of the drinks and took a piece.

Eloise watched him take a bite. For some reason it was important to her that he comment on how good it was, and because he always seemed to sense what was important to her, he said, "This is delicious."

"She cooked the whole dinner."

"Wow." Josh studied her face, wearing a vertical crease in his forehead, like he knew *she cooked the whole dinner* was code for something. Was he going to ask what? "That was nice of her," he said again.

Theo appeared in the doorway. Her gaze bounced off Eloise and landed on Josh. She pointed with her chin at the drink sweating on the bar. "That mine?" He said it was, and she retrieved it. Her reluctance to look at her aunt filled Eloise with guilt. Eloise darted into the kitchen for her wineglass and then walked back toward the kids with it raised. "Cheers," she said.

"Cheers," they said in unison. The three of them clinked glasses, and then the doorbell rang. They all looked in the direction of the sound, and then at each other. "She rang the doorbell," Theo said. For a moment no one moved to answer it, and then Josh—of course, Josh—set his drink down and went.

Theo and Eloise stood side by side facing the door, clutching their drinks to their chests, their hips touching. "I'm sorry, Theo," Eloise whispered, and Theo said, "For what?"

Then Claire walked in the room. She'd cut her hair. Eloise had an absurd notion that her niece had become a flapper—bobbed her hair, taken up jazz—and that she herself was a 1920s matron shocked at the decline in today's youth. "Hi," Claire said.

"Hi," Theo said, and Eloise echoed her. The hesitancy visible in Claire was so strange, so startling. Her weight shifted as though she meant to approach and embrace them, and then she didn't. She checked herself. How odd to see her make a movement she hadn't intended. How odd to see her body betray her mind.

"Let's eat," Eloise said.

They never ate in the dining room except on holidays. Only then did they spoon food from serving dishes instead of straight from the pot. Only then did they use this china, which had belonged to Eloise's great-grandmother and was one of the few family heirlooms she'd kept, all fussy and floral and Victorian. But even on holidays they didn't sit around the table in near silence, asking each other politely to pass the salt. Eloise was determined not to be the parent, not to be the teacher, not to be the one who talked. And then she heard herself saying, "So." She had no follow-up.

After a moment, Claire said, "I guess I should say something."

"Okay, great," Eloise said, in the encouraging voice she used on students. Wow, she was losing track of what was going on here. She really was drunk.

"I'm really sorry," Claire said. "I'm sorry about how I did this. I'm sorry I let you all think I was gone."

Theo and Josh looked at the table. Not even Josh was going to say, "That's okay."

"I guess I was afraid of telling you. I was afraid of how you'd react. So I postponed it. I shouldn't have done it like that."

Eloise wanted to say that she shouldn't have done it at all, and she thought Theo probably wanted to say that, too. She waited for Claire to go on, but the girl just took a sip of her water. Was that really, truly, all she felt she needed to say? "So what are your plans now?" Eloise asked. "What about the company?"

"I finally called the company yesterday and told them I couldn't come," Claire said. "They're replacing me."

Eloise nodded. Her voice was surprisingly steady as she said, "So you're giving up dancing?"

"I think so. For now."

"And what will you do?" Why were Theo and Josh so silent? Why was it her job to interview the prodigal child?

"I'm not sure. I have to think about that." Claire moved her water glass around on the table, then looked up from it to meet Eloise's gaze. "Right now I'm planning the wedding."

"I see," Eloise said. "You're planning the wedding."

"I know you don't approve," Claire said. "And I know, Theo, that you don't approve either. But I love him. I know this is the right thing for me. I hope you'll get to know him. I hope you'll be in the wedding."

"Of course," Eloise said, without meaning it at all. None of this was happening, so what did it matter what she said?

Claire flashed her a relieved smile. "I even thought maybe we could get married here. In the yard. Like Mom and Dad."

Her voice faltered on *Mom and Dad*. Maybe from shame. Eloise thought it should be from shame. There was a silence, and after a moment Eloise realized they all expected her to fill it. "I don't know that the house will still be available, Claire," she said, in her best approximation of a neutral tone. "I am hoping to sell it."

"But I thought . . ." Claire shot a look at Josh. "I thought Francine said it would go to the first of us to get married."

"Well, sure, but—" Eloise stopped, understanding. "Oh," she said.

"Oh," Theo echoed, in an angrier tone, and Josh, barely audible, whispered, "Oh, no."

"You think she'll give you the house," Eloise said.

"I just . . . Yeah, I guess so." Claire shrugged. "Gary's wife will get their house, and he doesn't have the capital for a new one right now. We could use it." She looked at Theo. "You wanted it to stay in the family," she said. "I'm the only one even close to getting married, aren't I?"

Capital, Eloise thought. A Gary word.

Theo said, "I don't think you should be rewarded for this. You don't get to behave this way and then snatch the house out from under us."

Claire was flushing. "I haven't done anything to you."

"But if you take the house, you will have," Theo said.

"Why?" Josh said. "Because the house should obviously be yours? You're getting so righteous that Claire assumes she'll get it, but that's exactly what you've been doing."

From a long distance away Eloise watched the kids squabble over the property that should belong to her, as though none of them had even the slightest sense of responsibility toward her, even the slightest care about whether she would ever be able to retire, or what she might live on when she did. They're not even really my children, Eloise thought. The pain and sorrow that children visited upon their parents, anticipated generally and yet somehow never particularly, were the price for the joy of the homemade card addressed to Mommy, the pleasure of your eyes looking back from someone else's face. She hadn't had those things, not really, not exactly, but, more important, she hadn't sought them out. She hadn't asked for the joy, and so she didn't deserve the pain and sorrow. Imagine she had no investment in this house or who lived in it or whether it sold. Imagine Claire had never been anything to her but her niece. Imagine Rachel had called her, sobbing, on the phone, and Eloise could have sympathized from her apartment in Cambridge, sitting at her desk in her study, the shelves lined with her published books. Maybe Rachel would have asked her to talk to Claire, because Eloise would have been the cool aunt, the one the kids felt like they could talk to when their mother was being too much a mother, predictable and patronizing and not realizing that they were, like, adults now, and needed to make their own choices. That might have been the extent of Eloise's responsibility: to call Claire and say, "Your mother's really upset, Claire. Are you sure you've thought this through?" She would have cared—of course she would have cared—but she wouldn't have cared like *this*. She was not a mother, and yet the world insisted that she suffer like one.

These children are not mine, she thought. This fact, which at times had come with a pang of sorrow, now brought her comfort. She was just their aunt. If the world had turned as it should, she'd be nothing but a voice on the phone.

Eloise looked at them, noting her own state of puzzled de-tachment. It was as if they were not her flesh and blood but strangers claiming to know her. "Why do you want to live here, any of you?" she asked. "Why do any of you live here?"

"This is where we've always lived," Claire said.

"But you don't live here, Claire," Eloise said. "You're the only who doesn't."

"I just meant . . ." Claire said and then looked down at her plate.

"And you haven't always lived here. You moved here when your parents died. I'm the one who's always lived here, or almost always. It should be my house."

"But you want to sell it," Theo said.

Eloise looked at her. "That *is* what I want to do. Do none of you believe I should ever do what I want? Am I supposed to be the only one who thinks about how my actions affect everyone else?" She looked at Josh. "Aren't you doing what you want?" She looked at Theo. "Aren't you doing what you want?" She looked at Claire, though she didn't want to. "Aren't you?"

Claire's eyes were so solemn. They'd always had that quality, even when Claire was two years old, and thus she'd managed her entire life to give the false impression she was older than her years. She said, "You're not giving me a chance."

"A chance to do what?"

"To show you why this is right for me. You haven't even met him! You wouldn't even let me—"

"I don't want that man in my house," Eloise said, and as she spoke, she felt a cold rage overtake her. Claire was a favorite and favored student who'd turned out to be a plagiarist and still, inexplicably, wanted an A. Eloise rose, as if she were in the classroom, and said, "Do you really—is it even *possible* that you really—fail to understand what it says about that man that he left his wife and child to marry a nineteen-year-old girl?"

"He loves me."

"He wants to be the dominant one. He wants someone to look up to him. He wants you for your youth and beauty."

"Aunt Eloise," Claire said. "He loves me."

"Oh, Claire," she said. "Get a fucking clue."

"Please, can you just meet him? I'd like you to meet him."

"I don't want that man in my house," she said again. "At least as long as I pay the bills. Choices have consequences, Claire. What did you expect?"

"Not this," she said.

"Well, this is what you got," Eloise said and then stopped talking, because her throat was swollen with every cruel and hurtful thing she could think of to say. *You're not mine. I didn't want you. I never wanted you.* She couldn't say those things, so she smacked the table with her palm, over and over, until it stung. Then she straightened up and looked at them, her hand throbbing, and saw that they were frightened. Frightened and wide-eyed like children might have been. My God, she was so angry. She hadn't realized she was quite so angry. She frightened herself. Better to return to shuffling around like a weary old lady, avoiding eye contact, keeping her voice low, rather than unleash that anger again.

She dropped back into her chair. "The house is mine," she said, "until Francine does whatever fucked-up thing she's going to do. Everybody will have to move out. Everybody's on their own."

"Eventually, you mean?" Josh asked.

"Now," Eloise said. "I mean now." She could see by the set look on Theo's face that Theo hadn't needed this clarification, and by the confusion on Josh's face that he still needed more.

Theo stood, her chair threatening to fall before it righted itself. "Fine," she said. "I'll go pack." Moments later they heard her footsteps pounding up the stairs.

Claire slid her chair backward as if trying not to make a sound. She, too, left the room. Who knew what she felt? Who could ever tell what she actually felt, looking at that unaffected, upright spine? The front door opened and, quietly, closed.

Josh and Eloise sat at the table. Eloise looked at her palm, which was not scarlet and pulsing, as you might expect, but merely a faint pink. She'd never shown her hand to a palm reader. Would anyone have predicted this?

"Aunt Eloise," Josh said. His voice was cautious and sooth-ing, the voice you might use to talk to a wild animal, the voice, it struck her, he had probably used on Sabrina. "Should I go, too?"

She looked up at him. Her boy. Her boy who wasn't her boy. "I guess you might as well," she said.

It took a surprisingly short time for Theo and Josh to pack. Eloise didn't know precisely how long it took, because she went into her room and lay on her bed in the darkening evening and fell asleep. Before she fell asleep she thought of the day she came home, the day she heard the news of Rachel's death, and found her own mother lying on her own bed in this very room, utterly incapable of helping a soul.

She woke into an empty house. It was ten o'clock. She got up and walked from room to room. Theo had taken nearly ev-erything—her clothes, her books. Of course she had. If there was anything Theo couldn't bear, it was the idea that she might impose herself on someone who didn't want her, that she might presume. And Josh, of course, had left most of his things un-touched. Josh believed above all that trouble would blow over. As far as Eloise could tell he'd only packed an overnight bag. Where had they gone? she wondered. Funny that for more than a month she'd been wrong about where Claire was, and now Claire was the only one whose location Eloise could pinpoint.

Eloise walked through all the rooms, feeling a compulsion to check each one, as Claire had once made her check every closet for ghosts. They were free of people, and seemed surprised to see Eloise. There was a faint buzzing quality to their silence. All these years she'd been the one who wanted out of the house, and now she was the only one in it. She could have gone to spend the night at Heather's. She could have gone to Heather in a state of triumph, if an approximate one—no, she hadn't told the kids she and Heather were a couple yet, but she was one step closer to moving out of the house. So their dreams could finally come true. So they could remind each other to buy toilet paper and argue about where to set the thermostat.

She went back to her room. Her mother's room, as she kept for some reason thinking, though her mother hadn't lived there in years.

The first summer of her guardianship, after her mother had gone, Eloise decided to take the kids on vacation. The fall and winter had been a blur of grief and confusion. By the time she emerged from the fog it was far too late to try to get teaching for the spring. So she'd spent the rest of the school year rearranging the furniture, sending CVs into the void, trying to cope with Claire, and making halfhearted stabs at potty training. At times it felt like both her body and her mind were itchy and burning, like she had an internal case of hives. Finally, in July, she heard from the chair of the History Department at Wyett College, offering her three courses for fall. The news that a little money would soon be coming in seemed sufficient justification to travel. She told everybody the kids needed to get out of town, and for all she knew that was true.

She got a deal on a rental in Gloucester because it was in the woods, a few miles from the beach. "Long drive to Massachusetts," people said. "Do you have friends up there?" She said no, and then made no effort to help people through their resulting confusion. She hadn't really had time, those few months in Boston, to make friends. She'd been so focused on getting settled, running to Target for trash cans and towels, writing her syllabi, deciding whether to alphabetize the books in her office or arrange them by topic. She'd been getting her life in order in anticipation of actually living it. Sometimes she could feel that life pulsing beneath this one, as though it had gone on without her. She could see herself teaching her classes, counseling a student, having lunch with a colleague in Harvard Square. She could feel her hand on the railing as she climbed the stairs to her office, students swarming past her with their books and their bags and their single-minded purpose. *Get to class, get to class, get to class.* She remembered the satisfying clunk of her office door unlocking, the gorgeous, expensive rug she'd bought at a funky furniture store and later, in her haste the weekend she came back to pack, left behind.

She couldn't afford to take the kids to Boston for a whole week, and besides she would've spent the entire time searching for parking or schlepping them around the city on the T. The thought of that exhausted her. But in Gloucester they could run around and go to the beach, and one day they could even drive into the city. The kids would love the Children's Museum and the street performers in Harvard Square. They could get a taste of life in the Northeast. And she could—what? She could pretend.

The house was at the top of a long gravel drive that turned off a long gravel road. It had a huge yard surrounded by woods, and a swing set and jungle gym, and neighbor dogs who came over to play every morning. All the kids loved the dogs, but Claire in particular had to be dragged away from them, even to go to the beach. Eloise had vacationed with the kids before, but never without their parents, and in envisioning herself reading and relaxing while Claire played and Josh made up his little songs and

Theo read, she'd forgotten she'd still be doing all the planning
and the driving and the cooking and the cleaning and the moni-
toring of the heedless, newly defiant Claire. By the third morning
Eloise was in a terrible mood. Claire had been up four times in
the night, and Eloise was wrung out, wondering why the child
insisted on coming to wake her even though she was sharing a
room with Theo, wondering why she'd put herself through seventeen hours in the car and considerable expense to relocate her
duties to a house that wasn't even childproofed. Thank God for
Theo, who took seriously her big-sister duties. Theo was so endlessly responsible, Claire so endlessly exhausting. Eloise could
just assume Theo was with Claire, and that's why she didn't even
look up from her paper when she heard Claire say, "The doggies
are here!" That's why she registered only dimly the screen-door
slam. Five minutes later she looked up, struck by one of those
eerie, sudden parental alarms, when you register an unnatural
quiet in the house. "Kids?" she called, and from upstairs Theo
called, "Yeah?"

"Is Josh outside with Claire?" Eloise asked.

"No, he's in the shower," Theo said.

Eloise rose from her stool. She looked out the screen door at
the lawn, where there was no sign of Claire. "Hmmm," she said.

"Aunt Eloise?" Theo called. "Is Claire okay?"

Eloise heard both fear and recrimination in the child's voice
but couldn't spare the time to answer. She picked up her sandals
and carried them out onto the porch. Even with a wider view of
the yard she didn't see the little girl. She slipped on her sandals
and walked down the back steps without fastening them, so that
they flapped and wobbled on her feet. "Claire?" she called. She
heard nothing. "Claire?" She walked down to the place where the

gravel driveway split. To the right it led down a hill to the main road. To the left it became a trail into the woods. "Claire?" she called again. She bent to fasten her sandals, but she couldn't do it, it was taking too goddamn long. Finally she kicked them off and began to run, barefoot, her breasts bouncing beneath her pajama shirt. Which way to go? She had no idea which way to go. She ran toward the road, because her first vision was of Claire hit by a car: Claire ran out into the road, reckless and small, and there came the car, her body flying into the air. Eloise's mind rewound the vision and showed it to her again, and all the while she ran, screaming Claire's name and hearing nothing in return. At the road, no Claire in sight and another choice to make, but as Eloise swung wildly around, still calling for her niece, she realized there was an old woman on the porch of the house right by the road, clutching the railing, leaning forward, her face worried, surprisingly worried, because she didn't know them, didn't know Claire, but she must have known what was happening. She sensed a missing child. "She didn't come this way," she was saying. "I've been out here all morning. She didn't come this way."

Eloise nodded and then spun back into her run. Her feet slipped on the gravel. Her body threatened to fall, but she didn't let it. She leaned into the hill. She ran back the way she'd come. She was not aware of her feet on the gravel, the movement of her body, only the empty spaces ahead, the spaces that did not contain Claire. She barely registered Theo, standing at the intersection of trail and drive. "Where is she?" Theo called, as if Eloise could tell her, as if Eloise knew. "Stay here!" Eloise shouted and kept running. "Claire!" she screamed. "Claire!" She heard the hysteria in her voice. A calmer voice inside her head said she'd find her niece, that everything would be fine. This voice seemed to have nothing to do with her. Even the visions her mind was playing now—Claire falling from a cliff, Claire mauled by a bear, Claire snatched by a predatory passerby—seemed to have nothing to do with Eloise. She was a machine who existed entirely for running like this, for screaming that crucial name.

It would be hard, later, to describe how she'd felt. *Panicked, freaked out, scared.* Such inadequate words. She'd want to explain—but couldn't even try—that she had not been real, that nothing had been real. The trees, the path, the dappled light: they'd formed a magical tunnel. She'd been in a fairy tale. Not the pretty Disney kind, but a real fairy tale, the kind people told to explain why children disappeared.

Claire's voice broke the spell. Eloise heard it—her piping small-child voice—somewhere close by, around the curve up ahead. She wasn't answering Eloise. She wasn't calling out in fear or pain. She was talking to the dogs. "Hey, Belle," she said. "Hey, Belly girl," and then she laughed. She laughed. Like everything was normal.

Eloise slowed to a fast walk. The bad magic began to ebb away, though the world still seemed brighter and stranger than normal. Shiny. Her breathing was loud in her ears. She rounded the corner, and there was the object of her quest: a little girl. Just a little girl in a blue sundress, playing in a clearing with two dogs nearly as tall as she was, sunlight in her hair.

In the moments before Eloise picked up her niece—her baby girl—and hugged her and scolded her and hugged her again, she acknowledged a truth that had lurked for months in a cave of her mind: She had not wanted these children. She'd been angry at Rachel for leaving them to her. A hopeless, futile anger, which she'd been doing her best to hide behind her grief. She struggled to find joy and purpose in taking care of others, the way her sister always had. She wanted her job back, and her little apartment, and the satisfactions of her research, the time and energy to work. She was selfish and solitary, like her mother, and like her mother she wanted to be left alone.

And yet the prospect of being left alone had become the worst she could imagine, so she must never wish for it again, not after this glimpse of how bad it could be. She had not wanted these children, but now they were hers, and they must never, ever know she'd felt that way. She herself must pretend not to know it. She said Claire's name and ran, now, to scoop her up. She believed in magic. She believed that that thought would vanish forever the moment she felt the weight of the child in her arms.

Part
Two

Elsewhere

15

Somehow it seemed worse to call first. At least there was drama in the unexpected arrival at his door, a bag in hand. He might be alarmed or delighted, but either way there'd be some kind of flourish to the moment. Theo didn't say this to herself, but she was fairly certain he wouldn't say no, so that was another reason she didn't have to call. Of all the people she could think of he seemed the most likely to happily take her in.

In the seconds after she knocked at his door she suddenly, intensely regretted her decision to come. She felt like a hobo, with her portable belongings, knocking on a stranger's door in hopes of shelter and sustenance. This was pathetic—what had she been thinking? Before she could bolt Wes opened the door wide, and as he surveyed her standing there a broad smile broke across his face. "Are you moving in?" he asked.

She felt herself flush. "My aunt said we have to move out," she said. "But of course I don't expect you to . . ." She waved her hand, not quite sure what the gesture was supposed to mean.

He raised his eyebrows, still grinning. "You're moving in," he said.

"Just, you know, tonight, or—"

"Explain later," he said. "Come in, now." He reached out to put an arm around her waist, pulling her close. "Put your toothbrush in my bathroom," he said, and then he kissed her. She dropped her bag, awash in relief and gratitude, and put her arms around his neck. She stood there kissing him in the hall for a full thirty seconds before she remembered herself and pulled away.

"You don't mind?" she asked.

"Why would I mind?" He pushed a piece of hair off her forehead. "Who'd object to you for a roommate?"

Lots of people, she thought, though really she was thinking mostly of her aunt, and maybe of Noah, or Josh, or Claire. Wes picked up her bag. "I kind of have an urge to carry you over the threshold," he said. She laughed, but she sensed that he was partly serious, and hurried inside before he could put that idea into practice. What if he tried to pick her up and realized that she was heavier than he thought? And how was it that he could bring himself to say things like that with any degree of sincerity? How had he come to be okay with saying so openly what he wanted?

She circled the living room, looking at the posters like this was the first time she'd been here, and as she passed the one for Josh's band it occurred to her to wonder where her brother had gone, or if maybe Eloise had let him stay. Maybe this eviction notice had been only for her. She sighed and resumed her course, annoyed with herself for harboring, even nurturing, this sense of being personally under attack. *Nobody loves me, everybody hates me, think I'll go eat worms.* It wasn't as though she didn't recognize the feeling, but not since adolescence had she had it so consistently and for so long, and even then it had been tempered by the obvious devotion of her siblings, especially little Claire. Now she could hardly think of Claire without being shot through with frustration and hurt, and that was the problem, wasn't it, that was the reason for this conviction that no one cared for her, that no one needed her, that no one wanted her company or counsel. Because Claire didn't, and Claire was the one who always, always had.

Theo sensed Wes approaching rapidly from the side and turned just as he grabbed and lifted her, propelling them both through the door into the bedroom and onto the bed. "Whoof," she said, laughing and breathless. He rolled off her to lie on his back beside her. "So instead of carrying me you decided to tackle me?"

"Yes," he said. "That's my special way of welcoming you to my home."

Theo blew out air at the ceiling, which did not have a crack, which had puckered paint and a rather hideous light fixture. "I'm a sad case," she said. "Not just sleeping with a student but sponging off him."

"For the hundredth time, I'm not your student anymore." Wes rolled back over, holding his weight off her so that he could look her in the face. "Except," he said, "in the ways of love." And then he began to tickle her, finding the spot just under her ribs that no one had discovered since she was small and her parents were alive. She laughed helplessly, convulsing as she tried to evade his hands. "Stop, stop!" she cried. He did, and regarded her seriously for a moment. Then he moved down, lifted her shirt, and blew a raspberry on her stomach. She laughed again. He turned his face to the side, away from hers, and rested his cheek on her bare skin. She slid her fingers into his hair, feeling his head rise and fall on her stomach as she breathed. She felt like a child, like a safe and happy child. She remembered—like a room suddenly illuminated, like a camera flash—how that had felt.

Wes had a gift for making the world go away. For a week it didn't even occur to Theo to work. Life was eating and sleeping and having sex and starting a movie and then abandoning it to have sex. She was on vacation from herself. No thoughts of her family, of money, of the fact that she had no place to live, of the fact that she should be finishing her introduction or gathering her application materials. Would she even get a job if she applied? Who cared? She was in the here and now, after years of living in the future. She'd been struggling up a mountain, and here was a nice, wide plateau.

"I'd like to build a house right here," she said to Wes. They were lying in his bed. They were always lying in his bed.

"It would be a small house," he said.

"It would be a metaphorical house."

"Good," he said. "Because we only have metaphorical money."

She liked that he never seemed baffled or annoyed by the stranger things she said. The guy she'd dated in grad school—his favorite question had been "What are you talking about?" He'd called her weird so often she'd just shut that part of herself down. And that part of herself was shy to begin with. Hide it away too long, and it might never come back out. "How much metaphorical money?" she asked.

"A million dollars," he said.

"That's it?"

"Don't be greedy." He picked up her hand and studied the palm. "How much money do you need?"

She sighed. The question punctured her unreality, reminded

her too much of the actual world. "More," she said. "A million real dollars, that would be good. Several million."

"What would you do with it?"

"Buy my house," she said. "No, sorry, that's the real world. Buy the Bolshoi Ballet and make myself the prima ballerina. And perform nothing but *Swan Lake*."

"Did you really want to be a ballerina?"

"I don't know why I said *Swan Lake*," she said. "That's not actually my favorite ballet. That's Claire's favorite ballet."

"I guess she's on your mind."

Theo shook her head, as if that would dislodge Claire from it. "I don't want to think about her," she said. "Let's return to not thinking about her."

"Done," he said. "So what's your favorite ballet?"

"When I was little it was *The Nutcracker*. Now I usually prefer the contemporary stuff. I get a little bored with the storybook ones."

"Don't you like to see princesses get rescued from poverty and spinsterhood?"

"And evil stepmothers. Don't forget them."

"If you had an evil stepmother I'd rescue you from her."

"Well, you rescued me from my evil aunt," Theo said and then fought the guilty urge to explain that her aunt was, of course, not actually evil. "Do you have some kind of prince fantasy?"

"No, but I did want to be a fireman when I was a kid. I also wanted to be a superhero. That was a long-standing ambition."

"That's very traditionally male of you."

"Well, ballerina's not exactly breaking the mold."

"Damn it," she said. "I wish I'd wanted to be a fireman."

"Not too late."

"I don't want to, though." She sat up and rolled her shoulders so they cracked. "Maybe nobody should have given me the impression that it mattered what I wanted. They should have sent me to military school. Talked to me about duty. And necessity."

"I think those things come up whether you go to military school or not."

"The thing is, what used to look practical all of a sudden isn't. Like, law school. Remember when everybody thought law school guaranteed you a job? I should have gone to nursing school. Or, what's the other thing?"

"What other thing?"

"The other thing they keep saying where there are still jobs."

"I'm not sure that sentence was English," he said.

"I think you know more about duty and necessity than I do," she said.

He shrugged one shoulder. "Oh, I don't know. You mean because of my mom?"

"Can I ask you about that now?"

"You could have asked me about it before."

"I know. But I didn't want you to think I was asking about it because I thought you'd be mad if I didn't ask about it."

"First I would like a signed affidavit testifying to your reasons for asking."

"That might take some time. Can we get a continuance?"

"No. You have to state right now, for the record, why you're asking."

"I want to know more about you." She rolled her eyes up at the ceiling, smiling sheepishly. "Why does it embarrass me to say that?"

"It's scary to be sincere," he said.

"For me, anyway."

"For you, anyway." He grinned. "Except about history."

"So tell me. What's your mom like?"

"She's . . ." He looked up at the ceiling himself, thinking. "She's one of those people who's really bright but never quite figures out the right use for their brightness. You know? She started out wanting to be a playwright—young, like fifteen. She won a national competition and got one of her plays read by actual actors in New York. And then she quit doing that and decided to be a linguist sometime in college. There might have even been something else in between. I think there was."

"So far it's all language-related."

"Yeah, she has a real facility with language. She spent some time in Japan during college, and she's still fluent."

"And she speaks Swedish."

"That's right. She taught herself Swedish. I don't even know how many languages she speaks. French, Spanish, Japanese, Swedish. I'm forgetting something."

"English?"

He laughed. "Well, yes. But I'm forgetting some others, too." He shook his head. "She's really pretty amazing."

"So now she's a linguist?"

"No. My dad is. He teaches at OSU. They met in grad school, but she dropped out. She never finished her dissertation."

Theo shuddered. "Oh, dear," she said.

"I think she was kind of lost after that, because she almost immediately started having children, and she made a project of teaching us languages, but then once we went to school I don't think she knew what to do with her time. I'd come home from school and she'd be in her bedroom watching TV. She'd switch it to a kids' show and I'd sit with her and watch."

"Where were your brothers?"

"I don't know," he said. "They never spent time with her like I did." He picked up her hand and matched the palm to his. "In retrospect she was probably depressed." He was frowning.

She said, "You were too young to pick up on that. You shouldn't feel bad."

He shot her a grateful smile. "I know," he said. "But I do wonder about my dad. Anyway, then Anders wanted to take tae kwon do, so she signed us all up for it, and she turned out to have a gift for that, too. Now she's an instructor."

"Really," Theo said. "That's not where I thought this story was going."

"She's really amazing," he said. "But of course she started too late to compete seriously, and I think she regrets that. At least that was one of the things she started obsessing about when she got really depressed. That, and she was always having these fights with people, or thinking they'd slighted her, and she'd tell you the story and it just sounded like nothing, you know? Like just the crap that everybody bumps into all day long. But it all made her so anxious. She wasn't sleeping. I was a sophomore by the time I realized how bad it was getting, and then that semester when I was in your class was when she checked herself into the hospital."

"How long was she there?"

"About a month." He was just holding her hand now, stroking the back of it with his thumb. "She's in weekly therapy now, and she's medicated, and everything seems okay. But that was a pretty rough time. I really thought for a while she might do it."

"I can't believe you were going through all that while you were in my class."

"Part of it, anyway."

"I had no idea."

He gave her a rueful smile. "Well, good. Why should you have?"

"I mean your work didn't suffer."

"When I focused on work I didn't have to think about things. I'd just really pay attention to the reading. Everything else was just background noise. I was focused on . . . Abraham Lincoln."

She wanted to make a joke, something about Lincoln, but she recognized the impulse as a desire to dodge an emotional moment in which she might say the wrong thing. And then suddenly the thing she wanted to say was *I love you. Let's get married.* She swallowed the words back, as appalled and embarrassed as if she'd uttered them. She didn't touch him, even though she wanted to. "I'm sorry," she said. "I don't know what I would have done, but I wish I'd known."

He leaned over and kissed her. Then he pulled back, looked at her like he couldn't quite believe his luck, kissed her again. Who wouldn't want to be kissed like that?

"So that's my mom," he said. "I'll take you to meet her sometime."

She nodded, although the thought of that filled her with panic, and then she wondered whether the panic came from the story of this brilliant, thwarted, medicated woman or just the thought of what it would mean to meet Wes's mother, and then she wondered whether she should now begin making confessions about her own upbringing. Wes knew, of course, that her parents were dead, but she'd never gone into detail about what that loss had meant, and never wanted to, or maybe she did want to, but if she did she'd probably cry, and then he'd hold her while she cried, and my God at this rate of increasing emotional intimacy she'd end up either fleeing the city to escape him or actually marrying him. So she said, "You know what phrase I hate? Just loathe beyond all reason? *Made love*."

He didn't miss a beat. "So you don't want me to say, *Let's make love*." He lowered his voice seductively. "I just made love to you."

"Ugh." She put her hands over her ears. "Stop it."

"Sweet sweet love," he said. "We made it and made it. Or maybe you prefer *knocking boots*."

She took her hands off her ears and grinned at him. "Bumping uglies."

"Beast with two backs."

"Schtupping."

"Roll in the hay."

"Roll in the sack."

"Doing it."

"Banging."

"Boffing."

"This could go on all day," he said. "Let's do something else."

"Like what?"

"Have you ever been to the design school?"

She shook her head.

"It's really cool," he said. "I'd like to show it to you."

"You wouldn't rather . . . hump?"

"Hump?" he said. "Hump? Really?"

She laughed. "I couldn't think of another one."

"Hump," he said again. He kissed her and rolled out of bed to get dressed. All those synonyms for *sex,* and neither of them had said *fucking*. She found that she was grateful for that.

Wes had been right: the design school was cool, in the way that Mac computers and Volkswagen commercials were cool: sleek, with bright colors on expanses of white creating a wink-wink austerity. She liked the way the hallways split in two, seemed to crisscross on their way up and down. She passed a glass-walled classroom, filled with worktables instead of desks. "We have class here sometimes," Wes said, pointing to an area set off from the hall by dangling wires. Sketches were pinned to the wall, and Theo crossed to look at them, noticing as she did that Wes was hanging back a little, as if suddenly shy. "Is one of these yours?" she asked.

It was indeed—a drawing of a faucet, something it had never before occurred to her needed to exist. But of course! As Wes had told her, someone needed to design everything. Someone always had to be in charge. She asked him questions and he talked and pointed, explaining the way things worked. Watching him Theo was overwhelmed with longing. Why wasn't she studying design? Or architecture? Or urban planning? She wanted to be able to sketch something, then make the something she'd sketched. Why couldn't she do that? Why hadn't she tried?

"I think it's amazing you can do that," she said.

He turned, wearing a look of genuine surprise, and a slow smile spread across his face. "Thanks," he said.

"You're welcome," she said. She felt at once gratified by how touched he seemed, and uneasy. Why was he so touched? Why did he give her such power over his emotions, more power than she wanted to have? To recover from her confusion, she moved away toward a flight of stairs, and Wes followed.

"Look up," he said when they got to the bottom, so she did, and was startled to see a student perched high above her on a ledge, feet dangling carelessly down. He had a laptop in his lap, holes in his jeans that exposed his bony, hairy knees. "How'd you get up there?" she asked. He didn't answer. He didn't move. Maybe he had earphones in. She took another step down to see him from another angle. "Hey," she said, and when he didn't move, "Hey, up there." She looked at Wes, who was watching her with an expectant smile. "Is he doing some kind of performance art?"

Wes shook his head. "He's not real."

"You're kidding."

"Nope." He pointed at a tiny sign on the wall. She moved to read it and saw the name of the piece—*Ethan*—the name of the artist, the fact that the work was given in honor of the students. "Ethan. Huh," she said, turning back to the guy. "He's amazingly lifelike." She studied him again. That knee. How was someone able to make that? When she'd been a dancer what she did was far more ephemeral than a sculpture, but still it was physical, it was the leg extended, the arm raised, the body leaping. When she danced she made something—she made something out of herself. Now her life was all ideas—ideas folded into other ideas, so that sometimes she lost track of her own argument. She took the concrete—the facts, the numbers—and made it abstract. It was probably no coincidence that when she gave up dancing she turned entirely to intellectual pursuits. Her body wasn't good enough, so she'd see what she could do with her mind.

She startled at the feeling of Wes's fingers slipping through hers. Now that's physical, she thought wryly, because at his touch she felt a certain and immediate desire, as if her whole body was a button he could press. What she wanted from Wes was so beautifully clear, and maybe just for today she wouldn't think about her uneasy feeling that he'd been right to worry she was using him. Just for today she wouldn't think about anything. Just for today she'd let things be.

Outside they strolled down the sidewalk, still holding hands, awaiting a destination. "Let's go get coffee," Wes said.

"Metaphorical coffee?"

"I don't think that has caffeine," he said, and she laughed.

"Theo!" somebody said. Startled, she looked up. The sun was in her eyes, and for a moment she saw nothing but the dark outline of a person on the opposite side of the sidewalk, closing in. She made a visor of her hand. "Noah?" she said.

"In the flesh." He was carrying a Starbucks cup, wearing an old T-shirt and shorts with a dramatic tear on one leg. A long thread dangled from the tear.

"What are you doing here?" she asked. She was still holding Wes's hand. She couldn't let go now. It would be awful to let go. Resisting the urge, she tightened her grip.

"Oh, I don't know." Noah lifted his coffee cup, as though to say he'd come for that. "I'm not teaching today, and there are no papers to grade yet. So I'm out wandering." He had a sheepish air, as if she'd caught him doing something embarrassing, when she was the one who'd been caught.

"I'm just surprised to see you," she said.

"Likewise," he said. He looked at Wes, and then back at Theo expectantly. Theo introduced them, and then Wes had to wiggle his fingers free, because it was his right hand she was holding and he needed it to shake Noah's. She put her own hand in her pocket, as if to hide it. The two men said it was nice to meet each other, or she assumed they did. It was hard to hear over the blood thrumming in her ears.

"What are you two up to?" Noah asked.

"We were looking at the design school," Theo said. "Wes was showing me around. I'd never been there—can you believe it? Yeah, it's pretty cool."

Noah nodded. "I'll have to check it out."

"Yeah, you should, you definitely should."

Noah made a move, as if he was going to go on past them, as if he was going to go check it out right now. But then he stopped. "So how do you two know each other?" he asked.

Theo really wished he would stop saying *you two*. "We met in a bar," Wes said, knowing, she supposed, that she wouldn't want to confess the truth, at the exact moment that she suddenly felt compelled to do so. "Wes was my student," she added.

Noah's eyebrows shot up. "Oh."

"Yeah," Theo said, trying to make a joke of it. "He was young and nubile, so . . ." She and Noah both looked at Wes, as if he were on display, and Wes obligingly struck a pose, putting both hands on his hips. She couldn't decide if she was gratified that he played along, or disgusted. "I'm kidding, of course," she said. "We only just . . . I mean, we just met again. He's not my student anymore."

Noah nodded slowly. Theo was in agony to know what he was thinking, but there was no way to find out besides asking directly, which she couldn't do, and which was no guarantee of finding out. "Josh is at my place," he said to Theo. "I don't know if you knew."

"No, I didn't," she said. "Okay. That's good."

"He wondered where you were."

"Okay," she said again, which made no sense as a reply. If Josh wanted to know where she was, he damn well could have called her, so there was no reason for her to feel guilty, no reason for Noah's tone to have that hint of reproof. "Well, I'll call him," she said.

"Great," Noah said. "I'll tell him." He looked Wes in the eye and said, "Nice to meet you, man." Wes said it back, and then Noah raised his coffee cup at Theo and went striding off as though he had some urgent purpose, which they all knew very well he didn't.

Theo started walking in the opposite direction, just to move, and Wes fell in beside her. She didn't notice the silence between them, so deafening was her embarrassment, her conviction that any slim chance she might have had with Noah was now forever and ever blown. "You could have told him you were staying with me," Wes said after a block or so.

"Yeah, but it was already bad enough," Theo said. "Jesus." It took her a moment to notice that he'd stopped moving, standing in the middle of the sidewalk so that two chatting girls had to split to go around him. She went back to him. "What are you doing?" she asked, and only then did she really look at his face and register the anger there.

"That was him, wasn't it," he said.

"Yes," she said. He resumed walking, not looking at her, and she fell into step beside him. She expected him to want to talk about it, to argue or plead. She was braced, her shoulders high and tight. But he didn't say anything, and so neither did she, even as her initial agitation passed and she grew uneasy with his silence. With the grip of her own emotions loosened, she had room to worry about his. He was angry, that much she knew, but what specifically was he angry about? He could be angry at the reminder that Noah existed, or at her for the way she'd acted and the things she'd said, or at himself for the way he'd played along.

She stopped walking and turned to him. "I want to buy you a treat," she said.

"What?"

"Something you loved as a kid. A hot chocolate with whipped cream. Or a hot fudge sundae. A Happy Meal?"

He considered her, his expression serious. Did he see the offer for the apology it was? Did he understand she appreciated the happiness he gave her? "I'd take a hot fudge sundae," he said.

They were the only people inside Graeter's, and he got not just a sundae but an übersundae, complete with a brownie, multiple flavors of ice cream, and a name: the 1803. They sat at one of the little tables, in the old-fashioned ice cream parlor chairs, white, with curlicue backs. "I got this for its historical value," he said.

"I see. I thought maybe it was because you admired the design," she said.

"That, too," he said. "My reasons can be complicated."

"Most reasons are," she said. The words felt overly significant, and after she said them she couldn't meet his eye. She busied herself wiping a drop of chocolate ice cream from the table. When she looked up he was watching her.

"Do you want a bite?" he asked. He held up a spoonful.

She nodded, relieved he hadn't taken the opportunity to delve into her reasons, because she'd have been hard-pressed to explain what they were. As he slipped the spoon inside her mouth she closed her eyes. The ice cream felt good against the roof of her mouth, smooth, cold, sweet. He said, "You like being in love with someone who's not going to love you back."

She opened her eyes. He looked at her. "Why would I like that?" she asked.

He shrugged. "I don't know." He plunged his spoon back into the sundae, put a big bite in his mouth. That mouth had been all over her body, those hands, too. And he was kind, and funny, and smart, and everything she might have said she wanted in a man, if she were inventing one, and what's more he seemed to understand her, and want her anyway. He was a little too young, perhaps, but as he kept saying he was not her student anymore. She wasn't even currently a teacher. Did she not want him more because she already had him? Was that the problem? Was he right about her? How sad to imagine that what she desired most was to live with desire unfulfilled. He swallowed his bite, scooped out another, and offered her the spoon. "Have another," he said. "It's pretty fucking good."

16

Adelaide was finally taking Josh to meet her friends, or in other words, the rest of the company. The party was in an apartment downtown. He was driving, and she was in the passenger seat of his car, sitting upright, wearing a small, inward frown. He knew her well enough now to know what the expression meant. She was debating something, and after a while, when she was sure she knew what she wanted to say, she'd tell him what it was. In the meantime he changed the music on the car stereo, then changed it back again. He couldn't find something to suit his mood, a phenomenon that always left him in a mildly agitated state. Sometimes he'd just barely register the tension in his body and mind, and then realize, with some relief, what was causing it—the wrong music. Tonight he was fully aware of the problem, but couldn't fix it anyway. Maybe he couldn't match his mood because he couldn't decide what his mood was. So many things in his life were unsettling: camping out on the futon in Noah's study, feeling cut off from his family, dating a girl who was still able to make him nervous, nervous enough that when Eloise had exiled them he'd quickly discarded the idea of going to her.

Adelaide turned her head to him. "When I introduce you," she said, "how do I say your job?"

"How do you say my job?" He said it like he was more baffled than he was.

"You know what I mean. Do I say 'Josh works for a company that makes apps,' or 'Josh is in business development,' or 'Josh works with computers'? Or what?"

"How about 'Josh does something so mind-blowingly awesome I can't tell you about it because your mind would be blown'?"

She laughed. "I knew I was setting you up."

"Just keep pitching me those slow, easy ones." He changed the music again. "How about 'Josh is the John Lennon of iPhone software'?"

"I hope not."

"'Josh is a rock star,'" he said, then registered her last response. "Why don't you want me to be John Lennon?"

"He was mean and he died young."

"Mean? I guess he could be kind of mean."

"I saw a documentary," she said. "He was mean to his first wife."

"But not to his second," he said. "That's the important thing. Plus, he was troubled in an interesting way, right?"

"I don't want troubled in an interesting way."

"What do you want?"

"You."

"Is that your way of saying I'm boring?"

"It's my way of saying you're untroubled in an interesting way."

"Ah. I'm Paul McCartney."

"Okay," she said. "So I should say, 'This is Josh. He's Paul Mc-Cartney'?"

"Yes. I knew we'd figure it out eventually."

She stretched elaborately, even her fingers splayed, and yawned. "I'm nervous," she said.

"Afraid they won't like me?"

"No! Afraid you won't like them."

Josh wanted to believe her, but he wondered.

After all that, once they arrived and the introductions began, she made no effort to explain what he did. She just said, "This is Josh." They reacted like they knew what that meant. This was a small kind of fame, but gratifying anyway. The apartment building was very cool—a days-of-yore type of place with wrought iron curling lavishly around the jerky, dignified elevator and great acoustics in the marble stairwells. The apartment belonged to Adelaide's ex, Carlos, a fact which Josh had known all along, and which was, now that he was here, making him unaccountably tense. He did his best to relax. He made dumb jokes, and the dancers laughed at them. They smiled at him in a friendly way.

"He's funny," one of the girls said to Adelaide, and Adelaide said, with a comfortable pleasure, "I know." Even meeting Carlos was not so bad. Josh was taller, so he had that going for him, and Carlos shook his hand without squeezing extra-hard or looking him in the eye too long or any other displays of manly challenge.

"This is a great place," Josh said.

"Thanks," Carlos said.

"It's like an old apartment building in New York. The marble stairwell, and the elevator."

"I know," Carlos said. "It's pretty cool."

After that they ran out of things to talk about, both of them looking away, nodding to some inaudible beat. "Josh . . ." Adelaide began just as Carlos said, "I . . ." They both said, "What?" and "Go ahead." And then finally Carlos said, "I should probably check on the ice," and everyone smiled and made noises of humorous agreement, and he was gone.

"So," Josh said to Adelaide, turning to face her.

"So," she said. She raised her eyebrows.

So that's your ex was what he'd been thinking, but he said, "I think he really likes me."

She laughed. "They all like you."

"Yeah, but he, he really likes me."

"You think so, huh?" She reached up and joined her hands around the back of his neck, like they were at a high school dance.

"It was in his eyes."

She lifted up on her toes—a ballet dancer!—and kissed him. "Aw," someone said, and they broke apart and smiled, as if at applause.

That was the end of their moment in the spotlight, Josh's big debut. That had been the wedding; the rest was the marriage. Everybody went about their business.

They talked about teaching, rehearsals, company class. They talked about performances they'd seen. They gossiped about other dancers. They talked about promotions. They all touched each other, all the time. As Josh watched, one of the women pushed another's mouth up into a smile. Another was grooming her friend's hair. He thought of a book he'd read about bonobos: the grooming, the bisexuality, the peaceful, indiscriminate fucking.

"Teri Metzger's a principal now," a woman named Nicole told Adelaide.

"They did it in midseason?" Adelaide said, surprised. "I wonder why."

Josh didn't wonder why. Josh didn't know what they were talking about. He asked Adelaide if she wanted another drink—she didn't, she'd barely touched the one she had—and slipped off to the kitchen.

Carlos was at the fridge, selecting a beer. He straightened, stood there with a bottle in his hand, frowning at the label, and then, decision made, pivoted and saw Josh.

"Hey, man," he said, in an extra-friendly voice. "You need something?"

"Ballet lessons, I think," Josh said and smiled to show he was joking.

"You want one?"

For a moment Josh thought Carlos meant a lesson. But he meant a beer. "Sure."

Carlos handed him a bottle and looked around for the opener. It was on the counter behind Josh. They reached for it at the same time, pulled their hands back, and reached again—oh, we're dancing now, Josh thought—but Josh got it first, and handed it over. Carlos smiled his thanks. Even the way he pried off the bottle caps was graceful, graceful and authoritative. "Yeah," he said, "it can be tough to hang out with dancers. We try, you know. We say, 'No more ballet talk,' but then we backslide. Everybody's always nervous the first time they bring somebody else around."

"Because you're worried the date won't like the dancers, or the dancers won't like the date?"

He shrugged. "Both. We're a tight-knit group, and also the opposite sex thing can be weird. If you were a regular girl, would you want your boyfriend's friends to be ballerinas?"

Josh shook his head.

"And Addy always says the guy thing is weird, too. Like some guys are weird because they think we're all gay, and some guys are weird because they'd be happier if we were gay, you know, especially once they see where we put our hands." He caught himself. "I mean, you know, it's a weird thing."

Josh made a face of mock confusion. "No idea what you're talking about," he said.

Carlos laughed, and then suddenly wore an earnest expression. "Nice to see Addy happy."

"She's great," Josh said. *Addy*.

"She is, yeah." Carlos winced as if he'd said something inappropriate, as if he'd loaded those words with desire. "Oh, sorry, man," he said. "She told you we went out, right?"

"Yup," Josh said.

"I'm drunk. Just tell me to shut the fuck up."

"No worries," Josh said. He leaned back against the counter, crossed one ankle over the other, and tried, with this relaxed and casual pose, to counteract how he felt, which was like punching the guy in the face. That whole elaborate display of apology had been just a segue into saying this fact aloud, making sure Josh knew. Maybe not because Carlos still wanted Adelaide. Maybe just because he didn't want Josh to think he was special. "I guess you understood each other, both being dancers," Josh said. If they were going to out-nice each other, Josh was going to win.

"That's true," Carlos said. "But sometimes you understand too much, you know?"

Josh didn't. He'd never dated a musician. Why the hell hadn't he? What kind of life would he now be leading if he'd fallen for a girl in a band?

"You spend a lot of time together," Carlos said. "Either that's awesome or it splits you up."

"Have you ever dated someone who wasn't a dancer?"

Carlos thought about it, then nodded. "Not for long, though. My girlfriend now is in the San Francisco Ballet."

"That's far."

"Yeah, too far." He shook his head. "Too close, too far," he said.

"That's love for you."

Carlos laughed, a surprised, appreciative sound. Josh killed it with ballet dancers. He was going to state for the record, based on his limited but profound experience, that ballet dancers were not themselves that funny. Thus their outsize appreciation of his moderate wit. He could make a new life as a stand-up comedian, if ballet dancers could make up the entire crowd.

"We almost broke up a couple months ago," Carlos said. "Over the distance."

Josh was a little surprised to be told this. Not that he wasn't accustomed to unsolicited confidences. Sabrina used to say he should have been a spy or a reporter, the way people told him things. "I don't ask them to," he'd say, because she said this like an accusation. She'd roll her eyes and say, "Everything about you asks them to."

Still, your ex-girlfriend's date seemed an unlikely confidant. "I'm sorry," Josh said.

"Yeah." Carlos looked down at his beer. "I don't know what will happen."

"It's tough," Josh said. They contemplated uncertainty for a melancholy and weirdly intimate moment. To escape it, Josh lied about having to deliver a drink to Adelaide and left the kitchen with a beer and a glass of wine in his hands.

He turned the wrong way out of the kitchen, maybe on purpose, and instead of correcting himself kept going into Carlos's study, where all the coats groped each other in a pile on the futon. He took a breath, gulped back some beer, pretended to be checking out the dance magazines on Carlos's desk. He was about to go back to the party when he heard two voices passing by in the hall. One said, "What will happen if they want you? Will you go?"

The other said, "I don't know. I'd have to think about it. It would be an amazing opportunity. I can't not go because of some guy I just met, right?"

That voice was unmistakably Adelaide's.

He sat on the futon, sinking down into the coats. He took a sip of the beer and then—because why not?—of the wine. It was a weird combination. *Some guy I just met.*

Will you go?

Some guy I just met.

Eloise had always called a melancholy mood the Slough of Despond, and not until he had to read *Pilgrim's Progress* in a British Lit survey did he realize she hadn't made that up. It had always seemed such a perfect description, capturing the sludgy, degrading self-pity of those moods. He could see such a slough up ahead, murky and deep. He'd been telling himself that he was unsure of his feelings for Adelaide, but reviewing the situation from among the coats he feared he was very nearly in love. He loved the way her serious aspect could be disrupted by her happy, goofy smile, as if an early Beach Boys song suddenly started playing in the middle of Mozart's Requiem.

At Adelaide's last performance, he'd finally articulated to himself the quality of movement Claire had described. Where Claire was all precise, exacting elegance, Adelaide had an emotive looseness, a melting quality that was at once moving and seductive. She gave the impression of a wildness barely contained. Her body was an expression of joy. Later he'd be unable to stop thinking about the way she moved. In the moment it brought tears to his eyes. This happened to him on occasion with live music, and from time to time he'd tried to pinpoint why beauty without sadness could summon tears. When Adelaide's piece was over, and he was pressing on his eyelids, pretending he merely had an itch, he imagined asking his sisters why he wanted to cry. Theo would use the word *ephemeral* and probably quote a poet. Claire would say, "You just do."

That kind of beauty—it was desire and desire fulfilled all at once. He'd had no idea how much he could want to see her leap until she did. And then it was all he'd wanted.

But forget all that—this was the first time he'd used the word *love,* and he'd used it right after hearing her call him "some guy I just met." Was that a coincidence? Maybe he thought *love* as soon as he saw a challenge to overcome, or a cause for which to martyr himself.

Adelaide was ambitious and independent. They hadn't been dating that long. Okay, he was hurt, but could he really be surprised? What had she ever done to suggest she needed him, besides falling asleep while he sang? She'd told him—*she'd told him*—that ballet trumped all. Without ballet she wouldn't exist. But he was still surprised at the idea that she might leave him behind. Maybe he was surprised by how surprised he was, since he'd understood exactly what she'd meant by *wouldn't exist* even though he'd pretended not to understand. He'd been telling himself it was only a fact or two about his past he was keeping from her, but sitting there, alternating beer and wine, he had a feeling it was more than that he'd held back. He and she understood each other, but she didn't know that. Maybe she never would know. She'd disappear in pursuit of her *amazing opportunity,* without the slightest glimmer of how completely he understood.

17

"What should we do in here?" Eloise said to Heather, standing with her hands on her hips in Heather's living room. She'd spent the last two weeks at Heather's house, which felt rather like traveling, being in a hotel or more accurately a bed-and-breakfast, carefully cluttered with objects and throw pillows to make it look like home. She might have been happy to live that way indefinitely, pretending she didn't really live anywhere. But that morning, as they were drinking their coffee in the kitchen, Heather had suggested they consider what things of Eloise's they should bring over, how to combine their stuff and their lives, and then she'd quoted George Carlin on the meaning of life being about finding a place to put your stuff. Eloise could see that Heather meant this joke not only as truth but as message: Eloise needed to really, truly, finally move in, so Heather could really, truly, finally be happy. So Eloise had agreed immediately, because hesitation about this project might have suggested hesitation about Heather, and she was not going to suggest that now, not now or ever again.

She looked over the two couches—one large, one small, both extremely poofy—and the blocky coffee table and the enormous painting of overlapping circles made by one of Heather's artist friends. She'd just as soon leave it be. It was hard to see how her stuff was going to mix with this stuff. "Hmmm," she said. She tried to say it enthusiastically.

Heather came up behind her and slipped her hands through the triangles of Eloise's arms. She slid a palm under the front of Eloise's shirt and rested her chin on Eloise's shoulder. "We should get rid of that love seat," she said. "And bring your couch over."

"My couch is orange," Eloise said.

"I know," Heather said, sliding her palm over Eloise's breast.

"Your couch is purple," Eloise said.

"So?"

"We're going to have an orange couch and a purple couch? In the same room?"

Heather put a light kiss on Eloise's jawbone. "Why not?" she said. "We're wild and crazy."

"Are we?"

"Our tastes are really different," Heather said. "It'll be more mix and mix than mix and match."

"We don't have to bring my stuff over," Eloise said.

"No, no! I want to."

"Because this has all been an elaborate plan to get my stuff," Eloise said, smiling. "I can't believe you really want it."

"I really want it," Heather said, with deliberate innuendo, turning Eloise toward her.

Before Eloise left for work, she agreed to meet Heather at her own house that afternoon to consider furniture and kitchenware. She didn't want combining their lives to be such a daunting and lengthy project. She wanted it to be boom, done, but until she moved her stuff in Heather wouldn't consider it official. Heather wouldn't consider it official until Eloise told the kids, but the piping little voice that reminded her of that could just shut the hell up, because there was no need to discuss your personal life with people who weren't going to be part of it. And the voice that said that they *would,* inevitably, be part of it—well, that voice could shut the hell up, too.

The day promised a distractingly annoying series of meetings, and Eloise found herself looking forward to discussing with Marta Bowen for the millionth time why Marta had to take her turn at teaching Monday/Wednesday/Friday, just like the rest of the faculty. At ten of ten, there was a knock on Eloise's office door, and she turned expecting to see Marta's scowling face, and instead saw a man in a suit, a very pale man in a suit, regarding her somberly. "Yes?" she said, with curt politeness, because he had the air of someone who mistook her for someone else.

"Are you Eloise?" he asked, which was strange, because a work-related stranger would have asked whether she was Professor Hempel, or Dr. Hempel, or the department chair.

"I am," she said.

"I'm Gary Paula."

"Gary Paula?" she repeated blankly.

He looked very uncomfortable, the man in his recognizably expensive suit. "I'm Claire's boyfriend."

She stared at him, dumbfounded. He might as well have told her he was the second coming, or an alien. "Claire's *boyfriend*?" she said. That did not seem like the right word.

"I need to talk to you," he said, and when she didn't answer he went on looking uncomfortable, but advanced into the office anyway and took the chair nearest her desk, as though she'd invited him to. He leaned forward and looked at her intently, as if he was considering whether to offer her a job.

"I can't imagine what we have to talk about," she said.

Both his expression and his tone dismissed that assertion. "Claire's unhappy," he said.

"Really." She sat back in her chair and tented her fingers. "What a surprise."

Another dismissive face. He seemed to have been braced for that blow. "I don't think it's about me," he said. "I think it's about you."

"Is that right," Eloise said. "*That* surprises me."

"Well, it shouldn't," he said. "You are her mother."

There was accusation in his voice when he said the word *mother*. Wasn't there? Eloise was sure she heard it, but she wasn't proud of her childish response. "I am not."

"Essentially you are," he said. "So of course it's hard for her to be treated like this by you."

"Treated like what?"

"Like she's nothing to you," he said. "Like you don't want to see her. Like you've disowned her."

At those words Eloise vaulted out of anger into contempt, noting the nervous way his leg began to jiggle, even as he held her gaze. She cocked her head and studied him, enjoying the power of detachment. This was how the world must look from the throne. She spoke slowly, biting her words. "I cannot imagine what kind of self-righteous jackass you must be to come here under these circumstances to tell me how to treat my niece. You left your wife and your three-year-old child for a girl just out of high school. You surely knew that girl, young enough to be your own daughter, had lied not only to her employer but to her family about her whereabouts. You surely knew what kind of opportunity that girl was giving up for the dubious prospect of marriage to you. Let me say again, you allowed her to quit her life for you, while you abandoned your wife and child. That is the kind of person that you are. And yet here you sit, like you have something to say to me."

Now he had the good grace to flush, red splotches appearing on his cheeks and neck. "What kind of person I am," he said, "isn't the question."

"It's the question in my mind," Eloise said.

"I understand why you don't like me," he said.

"Well, ten points for you."

"And I understand why you're angry at Claire."

"Congratulations, again."

"But I can't imagine that you don't still care about her, and that is why I came here to talk to you, because I would imagine it would bother you as much as it does me to see her in pain. She misses her family. She feels like she's lost you. She's been sleeping a lot. She's had little appetite. She cries. She's been like that ever since that dinner at your house."

Eloise nodded. She could feel the anger surging back. "It must be a terrible blow to leave your wife for a teenage girl, only to have that girl turn out to be kind of a drag."

He stood, as though shoved to his feet by righteous indignation. "She needs you," he said.

Eloise looked up at him and said, "She has you, doesn't she?"

He put a hand to his face, as though suddenly weary, and dropped back into the chair. Eloise felt a scientific interest in all his various displays of emotion. What would be next? Would he throw something? Would he weep? "It doesn't have to be a choice between us," he said.

"Really?" she said. "Because that's how it seems to me."

The look he gave her next was almost pleading. "Love just finds you sometimes," he said.

"Oh, spare me," she said, shaking her head. "Spare me, spare me. Save it for your wife."

He flinched. "I don't feel good about any of this. If that's what you want to hear."

"What I want to hear is that she's left you and gone back to dancing. That's the one and only thing I want to hear."

He nodded slowly, and she thought this conversation might finally be over, but he spoke again. "It was her idea to quit dancing," he said. "Not mine."

Eloise frowned. "You didn't want her to quit?"

"God, no. That's a lot of pressure." He gave her a weird, pained smile. "Now I have to be worth it."

"Why would she quit on her own? After all that?"

He lifted a shoulder. "Ask her."

Eloise shook her head furiously and stood to wave him out the door, but he reached up and put his hand on her arm. "I have a daughter, too," he said.

What was that supposed to mean? "Claire's not my daughter," she said.

He ignored this. "I can't imagine I'd want her to be with someone like me, when she's Claire's age."

Eloise shook her arm free. "I don't understand why you're telling me this."

He sighed. "I guess I'm apologizing."

"So why are you doing this? To all of these people? Your wife, your daughter? Claire, Claire's family? What is wrong with you?"

"Love just finds you," he said again, helplessly. "I thought you might understand that."

"What are you talking about?"

"Because of Heather," he said.

Eloise stood still a moment. Then she said, "What do you know about Heather?"

"Just what Claire's told me."

In Eloise's head, she punched him in the face. Or maybe she kicked him in the balls. Either way he dropped to the ground in pain. "And what has Claire told you?" she asked.

"That you're involved with her, but you don't want anyone to know."

She nodded, glancing outside her office to see if the secretary had heard. The secretary wasn't there. Getting coffee, maybe. Taking a bathroom break. Just going about doing the normal things we do, when some asshole isn't in our office trying to fuck up our life. "I'm done talking to you," she said. "You can tell Claire—from me—that if she's unhappy there's a very good solution, and that's getting the hell away from you." She folded her arms. "Now get out of my office," she said.

Eloise was done. She was done, and it was not her responsibility to rescue Claire from her own bad decisions. But that wasn't even what she'd been asked to do! At least there would be sense in attempting a rescue, even if the mission was sure to be ill-fated. No, the man wanted her to withdraw her disapproval. He'd come there to make some kind of back-ass-ward request for her blessing. Oh, poor Claire, made unhappy by the fact that Eloise got mad at her when she fucked up. Poor little dear. Just like when she was three and sobbed like her heart was breaking because Eloise yelled at her for pulling the cat's tail. Well, we certainly don't ever want to hold a child responsible for the bad decisions she makes. That might lower her self-esteem! As though Eloise hadn't spent the last sixteen years admiring the girl from the audience. As though she hadn't expended great quantities of time and money in pursuit of the girl's dream, which was to be admired, and admired, and admired some more. No wonder Claire was depressed—she was used to looking out at a crowd who found her beautiful. Now she was reduced to an audience of one.

This was not usually how Eloise saw her niece—as a narcissist, cold to the needs of others—but it was the vision of Claire that was still in Eloise's mind when she arrived at the house to meet Heather. Even aggravating Marta Bowen hadn't been able to drive away the conversation with Gary Paula, and what Eloise resented most was the guilt he'd made her feel, how he'd planted the idea in her that she should go talk to Claire. Forgive her? Hug her? Hold her hand and promise to be there no matter what? Eloise was not going to do that. She was not required to do that. But it took a lot of anger to drive away the guilty conviction that she should.

Heather's car was in the drive, and since Eloise had given her a key Heather would already be inside. Eloise heartily wished they hadn't planned this for today. She didn't want to sort knickknacks with Heather. She didn't want to do anything with Heather at all. What she wanted was to be alone, where no one could ask how she felt, or what she was thinking, or see any evidence of thoughts or feelings on her face.

Heather was in the kitchen, with some sort of utensil in her hand. She looked up and smiled as Eloise came in. "Hey," she said. She leaned in for a quick kiss. "How was your day?"

"I feel so domestic already," Eloise said.

Heather laughed, more out of happiness than amusement. "I've been separating out things I think you might want to keep." She waved the tool in her hand at the kitchen table, where, Eloise saw, there was a cardboard box, neatly labeled KITCHEN in Heather's handwriting. She held up the tool for Eloise's inspection. For a moment Eloise couldn't retrieve the name of it. It had to do with beating eggs. She could picture it in motion, but what was it called? She knew the word was in there somewhere. She almost had it, and once she did the relief she felt would be enormous. "Do you know where you got this?" Heather asked. "I have a whisk at home, but this one might be better."

Whisk. That was the word. *Which whisk.* "Isn't a whisk a whisk?" She hadn't meant to sound irritated, but she had, and Heather's face, which had been so open and cheerful, went blank. Heather looked at the whisk like it required immense concentration. She had a gift for withdrawal, for silent disapproval, the kind that refused to even look at you, not out of anger but to give you a private moment to consider the error you'd made and choose to rectify it. To Eloise's mind this determined non-anger was the most aggravating thing about Heather, the way it let her claim the higher ground. "You know I don't really care about this crap," Eloise said. The sentence had started out annoyed, but consciously she'd softened it into conciliatory. "Anything you want is fine with me."

Heather dropped the thing back in its drawer. "Aren't you attached to some of your tools? Your pots and pans?"

Eloise shrugged. "I'm not attached to anything." Heather made no comment, though if she were insecure she might have said, *Not even me?* She didn't. She wasn't insecure. This was one of the things to love about her.

"Well, what about the couch? Have you thought about that?"

Eloise sighed. "Could we move it on our own? Could we borrow a big car from someone?"

"I thought maybe we'd want to get movers for whatever you decide to bring over. It's more expensive, but so much easier on the back."

"Movers?" Eloise went over to the kitchen table and looked inside the box. There was a wok, with some salad bowls stacked neatly inside it. Beside the box on the table Heather had lined up the funky vintage glasses Eloise had bought in Yellow Springs the day they went there together a few months back. They were black with pink-orange flowers, and they kept drinks strangely cool—probably, Eloise thought now, because they contained some kind of terrible chemical, every miracle bringing with it the possibility of cancer. "I don't know if I want to deal with movers." She'd never employed movers in her life—and wasn't that exactly what was wrong with her, that she was forty-five and had never employed movers.

"I can deal with the movers," Heather said.

"We'll have to make an informed choice," Eloise said. "It's so much work to get informed."

"It's really not. Have you heard of a little thing called the Internet?"

"Maybe I should just sell everything." She took a silver cheese slicer out of the box and looked at it. Where had this come from? She had absolutely no recollection of it. Truly, she'd be willing to swear she'd never seen it before.

"That's a bit rash," Heather said. "We could use some of this stuff. And what about the kids? Shouldn't you give them a chance to look and see if they want anything?"

"Like what?"

"I don't know. Their childhood beds? Something that belonged to their parents?"

"There's not much of that. I didn't keep much of that."

"I think you understand what I'm saying here."

"Okay, fine. I'll ask the kids to tell me what stuff they want. Okay? Then I'll get rid of everything else." She pulled her phone from her bag and sent a quick email. "Boom. Done." She tossed the phone onto the table. "Happy?"

"What is the matter with you?"

"Nothing's the matter with me."

"Why are you so hostile?"

"I'm not."

"Something's going on," Heather said. "You're definitely hostile. You're in kind of a frenzy."

Eloise looked at her.

"Okay, it's a calm frenzy. But it's still a frenzy, Eloise. It's crazy to get rid of everything you own. I know you're upset about Claire. But a nineteen-year-old making a bad romantic choice is hardly reason for you to throw your whole life away."

"Not my *life*," Eloise said. "My *things*."

"Either way," Heather said. "I know you don't want to hear this, but she's a grown woman now and her choices are her own."

Eloise dropped the slicer back in the box. "You don't get it. You never had kids."

"I hate it when you say that."

"I know you do. But it's true."

"I hate how you say it like I'm a lesser human being."

"You really think that's how I judge people? I didn't ask for these kids! It's not a judgment to say you don't understand. It's a fact. You don't understand. I'm sorry you don't like that. I'm sorry all people without kids don't like that, but it's fucking true."

"I know what it's like to take care of something."

"Oh my God." Eloise held her hand up in the stop position. "Do not start talking about how you always had dogs."

"I meant you."

"I am not a child."

"They're not children either."

"You want to know why I'm upset?"

"Yes, I want to know that, yes."

"Gary Paula came to my office."

Heather made a face. "Who's Gary Paula?"

"Claire's *boyfriend*."

"Oh, honey," Heather said. She moved toward Eloise but didn't quite reach her. "What did he want?"

"He wanted to tell me that she's upset because I'm mad at her."

"And he thinks you should do something about that?"

"Yes," Eloise said. "Exactly."

"That's crazy," Heather said. "I can't believe he came to your office like he had any right to intervene."

"It *is* crazy." Eloise dropped into a chair and rubbed her face. "Like I'm not supposed to be angry at her."

Now Heather did walk all the way to her. She pulled Eloise's head against her stomach and rubbed her back. "He made you feel bad, didn't he."

"He did," Eloise said. "He made me feel really bad."

"I'm sorry, honey. You shouldn't feel guilty about this."

"There was something else," Eloise said into Heather's shirt. "He kept saying I should be more sympathetic to the way love just finds you. That's what he kept saying, love just finds you."

"You should be more sympathetic? Like you in particular?" Heather's hands stilled.

"Right," Eloise said. She pulled away and looked up at Heather.

"Because . . ." Heather looked back. "Because he knows about me?"

Eloise nodded. "Claire figured it out," she said. "She figured it out and she told him."

"Oh," Heather said. "And that upset you, too."

"I can't believe she told him," Eloise said. "I can't believe she figured it out. Why didn't she ask me about it? Why did she just assume? And what if she's told Theo and Josh? I mean, Jesus. Thanks for letting me in on your discussion of my personal life."

"And why can't they know about your personal life?" Heather asked, her tone sharp. She stepped away from Eloise, her hands dropping to her sides. "They're your kids."

Eloise shook her head. "That's just another thing you don't understand."

"I'll tell you what I do understand," Heather said. "I understand that you're ashamed of me."

"Oh, bullshit," Eloise said.

"I'm not saying you think I'm embarrassing. I'm saying you think the fact of me is embarrassing. The fact of our relationship. You're ashamed to be with me."

"I certainly am not."

"You're ashamed to be with a woman. If I were a man you'd have told them who I am to you a long time ago."

"No, I wouldn't have," Eloise said. "They'd probably have guessed."

"I don't believe you," Heather said. "I don't believe it wouldn't be different."

"It's not shame or embarrassment that keeps me from telling them. It's *privacy*. I felt so exposed, like this guy had something on me, like he won."

"If you didn't hide it, it wouldn't feel like that," Heather said. "You spend way too much time confusing silence with strength."

Eloise had all this anger and it wanted to go somewhere. Not at Heather, she reminded herself. Not at her. Heather had every right to be frustrated, not just at this moment but globally. Eloise had known perfectly well, beneath her agitation and her desire to share it, that the very fact that she saw Claire's knowing as a problem would remind Heather of what she feared most in being with Eloise—that Eloise was keeping some wiggle room. And Eloise had dumped it on Heather anyway, as if what she'd desired most in the world was a hurtful fight. "Silence *is* strength," she said. "Haven't you ever heard of John Wayne?"

Heather folded her arms and considered this. "If you're John Wayne," she said finally, "who am I? The schoolmarm? The hooker with a heart of gold?"

"I think you're more schoolmarm than hooker," Eloise said.

"I can't decide whether to be insulted by that." Heather turned away, going back to her task, willing to drop the fight. Why was she willing? Why did she take care of Eloise? Why, after Eloise had been testy and ungrateful and unwilling to talk, would Heather still tell her where she'd put the floss she'd bought only because it was Eloise's brand? "Heather," she said, "why do you put up with me?"

"Well, I love you, don't I," Heather said, opening another drawer. "And I know you love me. I know you want to be with me. I know I'm not just kidding myself."

"I do love you," Eloise said. "I could have a job in Chicago, if I didn't."

Heather went still. After a moment, she closed the drawer and turned to Eloise. "What are you talking about?"

Eloise wished she hadn't said anything. They'd been at the end of the argument, the denouement. Some part of her, some devilish, contrary part, must have wanted to keep it going. "Jason Bamber offered me a job in Chicago."

"Who is Jason Bamber?"

"That guy who came to speak here. Remember?"

Heather made a face that said she remembered. "What kind of job?"

"Editor of a historical journal he's starting."

"When did he offer it to you?"

"That night when I went to see him."

Heather nodded slowly, taking this in. "And when did you say no?"

"Uh." Eloise hesitated. "I didn't."

"I see." Heather stepped away from the counter, looking around at the half-sorted mess as if she'd never seen it before. "So you kept this a secret, which I'd like to think was so you wouldn't upset me but was probably because you were actually thinking about taking it. So you were making that decision without me. Then you finally brought it up so you could get credit for not taking the job, only to reveal that you haven't actually said no to it."

Eloise said, "I—"

"Jesus, Eloise," Heather said. "How much do you expect me to take?"

"It's not like that."

"Okay. Then explain it in a different way."

Eloise took a breath. She puffed out her cheeks, pressing her lips together. Then she shook her head. She couldn't explain it. Heather was right. "I'm sorry," she said.

"Will they give you the job if you want it, just like that?"

"More or less. But I'd still have to go through the process. I'd still have to interview."

"So go do it."

"What?" Eloise had no right to be hurt. She knew that and was hurt anyway. "You want me to move to Chicago? You're breaking up with me?"

"I didn't say that. I said go interview. I'm sick of going around and around with you like this. You want to be here with me or you don't. You go and interview and decide on your own if you want the job."

"What about you?"

"What about me?" Heather said. "You weren't including me in the decision, so go ahead and make it by yourself."

"Would you come? If I took it?"

Heather sighed. "I don't know. Just go. Just take me out of the equation. I'm sick of feeling like your dirty secret, like your all-purpose obstacle." She crossed the kitchen toward Eloise with such angry purpose Eloise flinched. But Heather just reached past her to grab her bag from the table. Then she started for the door.

"Heather—"

"Just go," Heather said again, not stopping. "Consider me officially out of your way."

18

Friday morning Josh packed a bag and left it in the car when he went to work, so that he could go straight to Adelaide's afterward, and not interrupt whatever would be going on with Noah and Marisa at Noah's place. It had taken him a week to ask Adelaide if he could spend the weekend with her when Marisa came. He'd thought about not asking, about finding someplace else to stay. He couldn't help feeling like asking was a test. Like everything was a test. Every moment that he was with her and she didn't tell him about whatever it was that might take her from him, the guy she just met—every one of those moments was a test she failed. Or maybe it was a test he failed. Maybe every moment she wondered whether he was worth telling, and again and again he proved he wasn't. Finally he asked her if he could stay the weekend. Of course, she said, like he should have taken her agreement for granted.

They had a double date planned with Noah and Marisa that night—dinner and maybe a drink afterward. This had been Noah's idea. Josh didn't want to go out with Noah and Marisa, he'd never wanted to. He foresaw little pleasure in combining their tension and unspoken anger with his own. But Noah had asked, and it had never even occurred to Josh to refuse. Why hadn't it occurred to him? Instead Josh had suggested they might want to be alone on Marisa's first night there, and Noah had smiled uncomfortably and said they'd been fighting a lot, so, no, not really. Josh knew they'd been fighting. He'd heard Noah on the phone, saying things like "You keep saying that, but nothing you do suggests that you mean it," and Josh had lain there on the futon in Noah's study and thought bitter thoughts about love.

About what he'd heard Adelaide say, he'd said nothing. After the party he'd been awake half the night replaying the moment—the words she'd used—and abusing himself for saying nothing. He left her place for work the next day without mentioning it and then spent the next several days trying not to think that history was repeating itself. Maybe he hadn't really liked a girl between Sabrina and Adelaide because no one had struck him as likely to provide the necessary amount of emotional abuse.

Claire called midday, while he was at lunch with Ben, and he picked up the phone and frowned at her name on the screen. The phone vibrated insistently in his hand. Ben paused in the consumption of his sandwich to watch him. "Girl trouble?" he asked, when Josh put the phone down without answering it.

"Indeed," Josh said. The other day, Adelaide had asked him if he'd spoken to his sisters lately. "No," he'd snapped, "and I'm not going to." Both of them were so surprised by his sharpness they let a moment of quiet pass, and then started talking about something else as if the exchange had never happened.

"Want to discuss?" Ben asked.

Josh shook his head, and then amended his response. "It was my sister," he said. "I'm pretending I'm an only child."

"Ah," Ben said. He took another bite and spent a moment contemplatively chewing. "How's that going?"

"Great." Josh grinned at him. Ben was an only child. "I just pretend to be really, really self-involved."

"And spoiled," Ben said.

"Super spoiled," Josh said. "Super, super selfish."

Ben stared into his iced tea glass as if dismayed to find it empty. "I've always been a little jealous, honestly. When I was a kid I had imaginary siblings."

"I bet imaginary ones are a lot less trouble."

"No doubt," he said. "But also imaginary."

"I know what's happening here," Josh said. "There's a moral to this story."

Ben shrugged. "No moral. I just always figured, you know, if you had a sibling or two, you'd be a little less alone in the world."

"That's a moral," Josh said. "You're teaching me a lesson."

"All I'm saying is that Katie and I are going to have more than one kid."

"I'll call her back, okay?"

Ben feigned innocence, putting his hands in the air. "What do I care? I'm too busy being oblivious and self-involved."

"I didn't say oblivious."

"It goes along with self-involvement."

"Well, why don't you teach me that, instead?" Josh asked. "I'd like you to teach me that."

He waited to listen to Claire's message until he was back at his desk. "Joshy," she said, "I really need your help with something. Please call me back." The longer he waited to call her back, the less he'd want to. So he went ahead and pressed Send, hoping for voicemail.

But she answered. She answered with happiness in her voice. "There you are!" she said.

He supposed it wasn't fair for this to annoy him, with its suggestion that she'd been trying to reach him for days when in fact she'd made no more effort than he to get in touch. Scratch that—it was fair. "Here I am," he said. "Where are you?"

"I'm at home," she said. "Did you see Eloise's email? I'm thinking of going over to the house."

"What email?" He called up the screen as she spoke.

"The one about seeing if we want anything from the house."

"Oh, yeah." He was scanning it. He'd clearly read it earlier, without having absorbed a word. "I guess I'll need to do that, too."

"I thought maybe we could go together."

He looked at his computer like it might have a response to this suggestion. "I can't go right now, though. I'm at work."

"I thought maybe after work."

"I can't do it today."

"But she said by the end of the week."

"Did she?" Josh looked at the screen again. "Oh yeah. I guess I didn't take her that seriously. She can't sell the house. She doesn't own it yet."

"But she's so pissed at me. I don't want all my stuff thrown out."

"I don't think she'd do that."

"Did you think she'd throw you out of the house?"

"Well," Josh said. "No."

"Please go with me," Claire said. "I can't handle seeing them by myself."

"I don't think they're there. Theo's not, I know that. And I'm pretty sure Eloise is staying with Heather."

"But they might be there. You can't guarantee they won't be."

"You could call first."

"Then I'd have to talk to them."

Josh sighed. "You have to talk to them sometime."

"Please, Joshy. Just go with me. I need you. You're the only one who's on my side."

He wasn't sure this was an apt characterization, but he couldn't say no to her. Who *could* he say no to? He couldn't say no to anyone. He hadn't wanted to stay at Adelaide's place the night of the party. Not even the promise of sex had seemed worth the extra time in the humiliation of her company. But she'd asked, and he'd said yes, because that was what he did.

"Fine," he said to his little sister, this insistent girl. "I'll do it. Fine."

Josh didn't want to look through his own things, let alone all the furniture that belonged to Eloise. He'd come back after the first weekend at Noah's and packed most of his clothes, and now he didn't want to go back into his room. Was there any chance Eloise would throw out his guitars, the band posters, all that memorabilia of his modicum of success? Go ahead, he thought. I dare you.

He paced the downstairs for a while, at one point forcing himself to stop and consider the couch. Did he want this couch? Couches were expensive, so it might be good to take it, if he had someplace to put it, which he didn't but should. What an idiot he was, that he hadn't found his own place yet. He'd been staying with Noah like the arrangement was temporary without making any attempt to plan his next step. Was he awaiting rescue? Had he—this question smacked him upside the head—had he been waiting to see if Adelaide would ask him to move in?

He groaned aloud. He had to get out of this house. He really did. He went upstairs to hurry Claire along.

She was sitting cross-legged on her bed, looking through a bin labeled CLAIRE: 2 TO 11. When he walked in she looked up with a smile. "Are you about ready?" he asked.

"Look at this," she said, holding up a child's drawing of two little girls in pink tutus.

"Did you draw that?"

"No," she said, still smiling, "you did."

He nodded, looking away. "Ballerinas everywhere," he said. "Not a drop to drink."

"That must be one of those references I don't get," Claire said mildly. She bent back over the bin.

"Why don't you just take that?" Josh asked. "Take the whole thing."

Claire looked up at him with her unearthly eyes. "I guess so," she said. "I guess Eloise doesn't want this stuff."

"I don't know why you're mad at Eloise," he said suddenly. "You're the one who left."

"I'm not mad at her," Claire said. "That's not it."

"You're the one who took off," Josh said. "We didn't even know where you were, and then when she finally sees you, you announce that you're going to take her house."

"I know," she said. "I'm sorry." She was sitting frozen, holding a birthday card in her hand. On the front it said, *Because you're 3*.

"She's not behaving well," Josh said. "But you can't really blame her."

"I thought she'd be more . . ."

"More what?"

"More open," Claire said. "More understanding."

"What did you want her to understand?"

Claire lifted one shoulder and dropped it, her eyes fixed on his face and wide. "Love," she said, like it was a question.

"Are you serious? Love? Are you serious?" Josh shook his head. "You're an idiot, Claire."

"What?"

"You're wrecking your life over this, can't you see that? This guy isn't a port, he's an iceberg. You're drowning and you don't even know it."

She was staring at him with her mouth open. The stupid shock on her face provoked him.

"How can this be news to you?" he said. "Can you really not see what's going on here? You've sacrificed yourself. You've given up who you are, and it's not worth it, it's not worth it in any way. He's not worth it. The worst part is on some level you know he's not worth it."

"That's not true," she said. "I love him."

"Maybe you do," he said. "And maybe you just wanted an excuse to give up. You were tired and you were uncertain and you didn't want to be in charge of your own life anymore so you handed it to him. This pale, bald, forty-something developer with a kid. Is this some father thing? Some daddy complex? But, Jesus Christ, Claire, you never had a father. I can't believe you'd want to take somebody else's away."

Her eyes were full, and then spilling over, and this, too, annoyed him. "That's not what I did," she said. "He still sees her."

"That's what you did," he said. "At least be honest."

"Josh," she said, "why are you being so mean to me?"

"I hate what you did," he said. "I hate what you're doing. I just hate it. It makes me sick."

"I thought you understood." She put her face in both hands. She said, her voice muffled, "What do you think I should do?"

"You should fucking leave him, Claire. For your own self-respect." He heard those words come out of his mouth, and the echo of Theo's voice saying them. "I have to go," he said.

"Wait a minute," Claire said, and she was crying hard when she said it, but he didn't wait. He left her in the room where she'd lived, back when they all lived together.

Josh had to knock on Adelaide's door and stand waiting with his bag, because of course he didn't have a key. It didn't take her long to open it, so at least that was something. "Hey," she said with a smile.

He leaned into a quick kiss and they went inside. He thought she might say, *Put your bag in the bedroom*, or *I emptied a drawer*, or something about hangers, but she didn't. He set his bag by the door. "How was your day?" she asked, going into the kitchen to put away dishes.

"It was okay," he said and wondered how she failed to hear the lie. "How was yours?"

"Long," she said, closing a cabinet. "I was worried I'd be too tired for tonight, but I've gotten a second wind."

"That's good," he said. "I'd feel weird about canceling."

"Oh, I wouldn't have made you cancel," she said. There was a clanking as she pulled a handful of silverware from the basket. He really wished she'd stop doing the dishes, but instead she pulled open a drawer and one by one dropped pieces of silverware in it. It was quite the domestic scene.

"I think I should go back and stay at my house for a while," he said. "My aunt's house, I mean. It's ridiculous that no one's living there. It's ridiculous that I'm sleeping on Noah's futon while there's a huge empty house just sitting there."

"I figured you'd want to get your own place."

"But that place is free."

"Sure, but you do have to get your own place eventually."

"What do you care if I get my own place?"

She stopped putting silverware away and turned with two spoons in her hand, cocking her head at him. "I care what you do."

"Well, good," he said. "I guess that's something."

"What is going on with you?"

"Nothing," he said. "I got into it with my sister, that's all."

"Do you want to talk about it?"

"I really don't."

"You don't seem like yourself right now."

She was right; he wasn't himself. He was Theo, as his attack on Claire had proved. Or he was Sabrina, being cruel just because he could, refusing to explain his reasons. "I'm sorry," he said, but the words came out sounding angry. He tried again, with more success. "I'm sorry. I'll try to be myself."

Adelaide nodded, like the problem was solved.

But being himself, being sorry, plunged him back into a morass of guilt over Claire. How cruel he'd been, how he'd left her in tears, his little sister, when of all people he really should have understood. An hour later he walked into the restaurant where they were meeting Noah and Marisa with Claire's weeping face still on his mind. Though he participated in greetings and introductions he was distracted, replaying the things he'd said to her. He'd called her an idiot. He'd said she made him sick. This, from the one person she thought was on her side. Or, at least, the one person besides Gary, who probably now seemed even more necessary than he had before. He'd made the same mistake as Theo after swearing he wouldn't. The guilt he felt at this was followed by a surge of anger—why was it always his job to be the nice one, to hide how he felt in the interest of harmony? He couldn't recall signing a contract that he would never speak his mind. His aversion to anger struck him now as a defect he should root out and destroy. The desire to avoid conflict made him weak. It had made him weak with Sabrina. It was making him weak, now, with Adelaide. If he were an animal, he'd be the type that curled up small and waited for the attack to end.

At the table he tried to deploy his usual charm, he really did. He made introductions and said interesting things about each of the two women to the other one. He made reference to his first conversation with Marisa, and she was obviously pleased at how well he remembered her. But he could feel that his smile was wan, hear that the interest in his voice sounded less interested than usual. His ability to put others at ease so rarely failed him he had nothing to fall back on in its absence. After only a few minutes he subsided, too tired for speech, and left the conversation to the other three.

"So Josh tells me you work for a producer," said Adelaide, who, judging from the puzzled and pleading looks she'd been giving Josh, did not enjoy having to pick up his slack.

"Well, actually"—Marisa shot a glance at Noah, gave Adelaide an uneasy smile—"actually things have kind of fallen apart."

"Oh no," Adelaide said. "What happened?"

"We were on the verge of getting this movie made, mostly because of the talent attached, and then the actor pulled out. The deal fell apart, and the studio isn't renewing my boss's contract."

"So what does that mean?" Adelaide asked.

"It means she's out of a job," Noah said.

"No, it doesn't," Marisa said. "It doesn't mean that. She can't really pay me right now, not without the studio money coming in. But she'll get another deal, I know she will."

"Here's a really sad story," Noah said. He nudged Marisa. "Tell them."

"Oh, no," Marisa said. "They don't want to hear that."

"I'll tell them," Noah said. "Marisa worked two weeks without pay and then when she goes to ask Anita if she's made any progress on a deal Anita starts crying about money."

"No, she wasn't crying about money. She was crying because she felt bad for not paying me."

"That's what she told you, anyway."

"It was true." Marisa appealed to Adelaide and Noah. "She cares about me. I've worked for her a long time. And she knew I wouldn't be able to survive much longer without pay. She was apologizing, and I was saying I understood, but that I couldn't keep on working without pay, because I wouldn't be able to afford to eat. She said she might end up in the same boat, that already she felt like she couldn't go out to lunch anymore. I'd brought a peanut butter and jelly for my lunch, so I gave her half of it."

"The woman lives in a million-dollar house," Noah says, "and she guilts Marisa into giving her half her sandwich."

"It wasn't like that," Marisa said.

"I can't believe this all happened so fast," Adelaide said.

"That's Hollywood," Noah said. "Easy come, easy go. It's hard to make a life there."

"You just have to be determined," Marisa said. "You have to stick it out. I bet it's the same in ballet."

"Sort of," Adelaide said cautiously, flicking Josh an uncertain look. Yes, they're using you to fight with each other, Josh thought. Haven't you ever seen that before? Without help from him, Adelaide went on talking. "Before you get on with a company, yes. But a lot of times once you're hired you stay with the same company. I mean, sometimes contracts aren't renewed, or the company goes under."

"You have to be determined to stick with it, though, right?" Marisa said. "You have to withstand criticism and setbacks."

"Oh, definitely," Adelaide said. "Somebody's always telling you what's wrong with you." She laughed self-consciously. "My thighs have been the bane of my existence."

"Your thighs are about as big as my arms," Marisa said.

"You'd have to see me onstage with the other dancers," Adelaide said. "Then you'd see what I mean. But it's not just your body, it's trying to perfect the dance. Like, the ballet master says you're not holding your pinkie right. You can spend hours trying to hold your pinkie right."

"That's what you do," Marisa said, "because you have to."

"Absolutely," Adelaide said. "I dread the day I have to stop dancing."

Marisa looked at Noah like she'd scored a point. "You have to stick it out," she said again. "I'll find another full-time job, or Anita will get another deal."

"But in the meantime . . ." Noah said.

"In the meantime, I'm getting PA work when I can."

"PA?" Adelaide asked.

"Production assistant. It means I help out with a shoot, like for a commercial or a music video or whatever. I run errands."

"She has to do other work, too, though," Noah said.

"Well, yeah, I have to pay the rent," Marisa said. "My friend got me a job waiting tables at Umami Burger. You know Umami Burger?"

Adelaide and Josh shook their heads.

"It's good. It's supposed to be one of the best burgers in the country."

"Here's to that," Noah said, lifting his martini. Everybody dutifully raised and clinked their glasses, though the toast was clearly ironic, certainly hostile, and under the table Adelaide squeezed Josh's thigh. A gesture of solidarity? A request for rescue? Josh couldn't be sure. By now shouldn't he know her well enough to be sure?

The waiter arrived with their food, and as he put Noah's plate in front of him, Noah said, "This is supposed to be one of the best burgers in Cincinnati."

"It is," the waiter said. "It's pretty awesome."

"Cincinnati's not the whole country, though," Noah said to the waiter.

"I think this burger could compete nationwide," the waiter said. "It's that good, I promise."

Noah lifted his in two hands and took an enormous bite. The waiter set down the rest of the plates and then stood for a moment, awaiting Noah's verdict. "You're right," he said, still chewing. "This is a superdelicious burger."

The waiter smiled triumphantly, asked if they needed anything else, and told them to enjoy. Noah held the burger out to Marisa, who dutifully put down her fork and took a bite. He watched her chew. "Awesome, right?"

"It's good," she said, her tone one of mild agreement.

"But not as good as Umami."

"Well," she said, "Umami's pretty special."

Noah looked at Adelaide and Josh. "Umami's in L.A.," he said.

Josh needed to speak. He'd gone too long without speaking. His silence was becoming conspicuous. He summoned his resources and opened his mouth. "I'll have to go, next time I'm out there. But I don't know when that will be."

"Did you used to get out there a lot?" Marisa asked.

"You know, from time to time," Josh said. Adelaide was looking at him with curiosity. "Not super often."

"For meetings with labels?" Noah asked.

"A couple of times," Josh said. He didn't look at Adelaide, searching for a subject that might end this line of questioning. "Do you like L.A.?" he asked Marisa, even though, given the tension between her and Noah, and its source, that was a really dumb thing to ask.

She nodded, but before she could elaborate, or Josh could think of another topic, Noah said, "I think you should put the band back together. Or start another one."

Adelaide looked at Noah with a game but confused smile.

"Ha ha," Josh said.

"Why is that ha ha? You're only, what, twenty-six? It's not like your music career has to be over."

Adelaide turned her smile to Josh. He could tell she thought maybe Noah was making fun of him, or her, or both of them. "Music career?" she asked.

"I'm serious, man," Noah said. "You're too good to quit for-ever."

Adelaide frowned. "What did you quit?"

Now Noah was the one to look confused. He gave Josh a quizzical look. Josh needed to say something, to signal Noah—what? To stop? To keep going? He had no energy. Couldn't they see that? He had nothing to say. "Blind Robots," Noah said. "Josh's band."

"You had a band?" Adelaide asked.

"You didn't tell her?" Noah sat back in his seat, amazed, then leaned in to give her the rundown. "They were pretty big. They toured with some huge bands, headlined in Europe, put out three albums. You don't know any of this? You might have heard one of their songs—" He sang a line from "Untrue Stories." He shook his head at Josh. "I can't believe you didn't tell her."

Josh looked at Adelaide, whose face was the picture of confusion.

"You had a band?" she said again.

"Yeah. Blind Robots?" Josh tried for jokiness. "You've probably never heard of us."

"Why? You think I don't know about music?"

"No, no, that's not what I meant," Josh said. He was surprised by the hurt in her voice. "That's not what I meant at all. We just had kind of a small following. I mean not *small* small, but not like huge. Our last album sold forty thousand copies, which is good, right, but it's not like . . . yeah."

"He's being modest," Noah said. "They were awesome."

"I didn't even know you played an instrument," Adelaide said.

"Oh, he fucking rocks on guitar," Noah said. "He can shred

like crazy, though he kind of kept that in reserve. And he was the singer. You've never heard him sing? Amazing vocals. Plus, you play, what else, man, keyboards? Bass?"

Josh nodded. "A little drums," he said. "But not that well."

"And mandolin? Didn't you play mandolin on 'Everything but the Sun'?"

"Yeah," he said. "That was me."

Marisa leaned toward Josh. "Noah's probably tried not to seem like a stalker, but he knows all about you." She smiled. "So I know all about you, too."

Noah shrugged. "I'm an enthusiastic guy," he said. "I share my enthusiasms."

"Yes, he does," Marisa said.

"You did sing for me once," Adelaide said.

"That's right." Josh smiled at Noah and Marisa, everybody just joking around here. "She fell asleep."

"You were singing me to sleep," Adelaide said.

"I did a good job," Josh said.

"Wow," Adelaide said. She shook her head. "Wow," she said again. "I had no idea."

"You didn't know you were getting a professional lullaby," Josh said.

Adelaide nodded like she was taking all of this in, but she didn't look at Josh. Oh, that's right, he thought. I'm always in the wrong.

Noah threw his hands out in mock outrage. "How come you never sing me to sleep?"

"I'm sorry, man," Josh said. "I suck as a roommate."

"Aw, Noah likes having you around," Marisa said.

"I get lonely," Noah said. "Some people insist on living in L.A."

"You have to go where the work is," Marisa said. "You came here for a job." She looked at Adelaide. "You came here for a job, too, right?"

Adelaide nodded. "The director recruited me. I was in the training program at the Boston Ballet, and she saw me dance and asked me to come here. So here I am."

"What if you, like, got offered a spot at the ballet in New York? Wouldn't you go there?"

"I don't know," Adelaide said. "Not if it was a spot in the corps. I'm twenty-nine, so I couldn't start over working my way up in a company."

"But still, it would be New York, right? Isn't that the place to be for dancers?"

"We have a good company here, and I'm a principal."

Josh looked at her. "So you'd never leave?"

She met his eyes, then dropped her gaze. "Well, I don't know. It would depend on what else I was offered."

"But my point is, you have to go where your work is," Marisa said. "So that's here for you, and it's here for Noah. It's not here for me."

"I don't see how you do the long-distance thing," Josh said.

"It's hard," Marisa said.

"It fucking sucks," Noah said.

"It seems practically impossible," Josh said. "You have to choose to be together or not. Don't you?"

"Josh," Adelaide said under her breath, putting her hand on his arm.

"Well, don't you?" he asked, looking at her.

Adelaide turned away, smiling what struck Josh as an onstage smile. "So what good movies have I missed lately?" she asked Marisa. "I don't think I've seen one in months."

"That shocks me!" Marisa said.

Adelaide laughed. "When's the last time you went to the ballet?"

"Touché," Marisa said. She began to list movies Adelaide should see, adding commentary on plot and performances. Josh felt alone, encased in a bubble of drunken misery, even though looking at Noah, who was disconsolately dipping a french fry in ketchup, he could see his friend felt the same. Josh wanted to embrace Adelaide, beg her to stay with him, apologize again and again. He wanted to run.

The car ride back to Adelaide's apartment was a silent one. He thought of family trips, before his parents died, and how his father would achieve a few moments of peace by offering rewards for whoever could stay quiet the longest. Josh always won, in his memory at least, and so got to choose the next CD, or the place where they'd stop for unhealthy food and crappy toys. He'd always had a knack for silence. Adelaide might challenge him, but he'd win.

When they got inside, Adelaide went immediately to the bedroom. He went to the kitchen, got a beer he didn't want, and sat on the sofa, drinking it in defiance of himself. She returned in comfortable clothes, her hair pulled back, her feet hidden away in their usual white socks. How many pairs of those socks did she own? She sat far from him on the couch and curled into the arm, tucking her feet under her. He wasn't going to speak. He seemed to be at the point of drinking where alcohol no longer had any effect, and as full as he was the beer hitting his stomach was unpleasant. But he kept drinking it.

Adelaide moved, maybe as a precursor to speech, but, no, she was leaning forward to get her laptop off the coffee table. She opened it and waited a moment for the screen to brighten and then he listened to the clicking of keys. She leaned in close, her long neck bent as her eyes scanned the screen. He pretended not to watch her. She seemed oblivious to him anyway, now typing again, now reading something else. What the hell was she doing? When was she going to speak?

"'Where is Josh Clarke?'" she said finally, her eyes on the screen.

"What?" he said.

She looked up, at last, and pointed at the computer. "People want to know where you are."

"Do they?"

"You never Google yourself?" She raised her eyebrows as though she found this hard to believe. She read aloud again. "'I heard he got a regular job. Is this like Moe Tucker working at Wal-Mart? So, so wrong.'"

"Huh," Josh said. He drank more beer. In fact he didn't Google himself, or at least hadn't for some time, precisely to avoid commentary like that.

"Who's Moe Tucker?" Adelaide asked.

"She was the drummer for the Velvet Underground."

"'What a waste of talent,'" she read. " 'Any chance of a come-back?' So Noah's not the only one waiting."

"Maybe he wrote that," Josh said.

"He can't have written all of them," Adelaide said. "Your name brings up four million hits."

"They're not all me," he said. "It's not an unusual name."

"Blind Robots . . ." She typed, narrowed her eyes at the screen. "That brings up about two million. I've been dating a famous guy, and I'm the only one who doesn't know it."

"I'm not famous," he said.

"You seem pretty famous to me."

"I guess you're mad," he said.

She looked at him now. "I'm embarrassed," she said. "I feel like an idiot. I can't believe I didn't know this huge thing about you. I can't believe you kept that from me."

"I'm sorry. I should have told you," he said, but then, without warning, remorse morphed back into anger. "But what about you? You're not telling me everything."

"What do you mean?"

"You had some audition or something. You're thinking of leaving."

"How do you know that?"

"I heard you at Carlos's party. I heard you saying you couldn't stay here for some guy you just met."

"Oh," she said. She leaned forward to return her laptop to the table, close its screen.

"So that's me," he said. "Some guy you just met."

"That's not true," she said. "Except it is true, isn't it? Isn't that how you're acting?"

"What do you mean?"

"You didn't tell me about the band!"

"The band is over! The band is done! You didn't tell me about something that might take you away from here. Something that's *now*."

"Because I didn't know if it would amount to anything. This choreographer, this guy who came in for New Works a couple years ago and set a piece on me, he asked if I'd audition for a company he's putting together. But I don't know if he'll want me, and I don't even know if I'd want the job. They'll be based in New York, but they're going to travel constantly, and they're all contemporary ballet. I don't know if I want to do that."

"So you haven't auditioned yet?"

"No. It's next month."

"Were you going to tell me?"

"I didn't really know where we stood," she said. "I didn't know how you'd react."

"I don't understand that at all."

"You don't? Then why didn't you tell me about the band?"

"Because I was tired of people liking me because of that! Do you know how many girls have dated me just because I used to be a musician?"

"No, I don't," she said. "And I don't want to. But I'll tell you I can get in the door with almost any guy by telling them I'm a dancer. Isn't that what happened with you?"

"I just liked you," he said.

"Well," she said, "there's no way to prove that."

"There's no way to prove that knowing about my band wouldn't have made you more interested either," he said.

"I didn't need to be more interested."

"Oh, you could have fooled me. You don't tell me about something that might make you move. You don't ever ask me about my job."

"I didn't think you wanted to talk about it."

"Really?"

"Every time I brought it up you made a joke or changed the subject. So I quit asking."

"Oh." Even with the reason clear, the agitation remained. He cast about for something else to feel upset about. "What about your friends? Why did it take so long to introduce me?"

"I told you. Some people are freaked out by us. One guy I dated said we were all too thin. He said just by myself I seemed fine but when he saw me with all the other girls it was too weird, how alike our bodies were. He said it made him feel like ballet was a cult."

"Whatever." Josh stood up, carried his empty bottle to the kitchen, and set it on the counter. She stood, too, waiting with her hands on her hips for him to return. "So," he said, "had you heard of us? Did you recognize any of our songs?"

"Yeah," she said. "If I'd known who you were, you're probably right. I'd have been interested right away. So I guess I don't pass the test."

"Well, neither do I, apparently."

"What should I have said to you about this audition? Should I have asked if you'd date me if I moved? Should I have asked you to go with me? I was afraid to bring it up. You've never even called me your girlfriend."

"Because I couldn't tell if you wanted me to!"

"Why didn't you ask?"

"Why didn't you?"

She pressed her lips together and shook her head.

"If you get that job, are you going?"

"Maybe," she said.

"Then what is the point of this?"

"I guess if you don't know, then I don't know," she said.

"Seems like we understand each other for the first time," Josh said.

"How could I understand you?" she said. "You didn't tell me who you *were*."

"Yes, I did."

"No," she said. "You didn't."

She was right. He didn't want to say so. So he said, "You've never even let me see your feet."

She looked away. He saw that she was standing in fourth position, her posture upright as ever, and found that he could no longer bear to look at her. Her loveliness was an affront. He'd left his bag right by the door. It was a matter of only a few steps to reach it, almost no effort to pick it up, to open the door and step outside. He thought he heard her say his name before the door closed behind him, but he couldn't be sure. She didn't follow him. If she'd really wanted to, she could have followed him, chased him down the hall in her stupid, hateful socks.

He wanted to be alone, he thought, but he realized when he unlocked the door to his house—his old house—that he'd been hoping someone would be there. But all the lights were out, and though he went from floor to floor and room to room turning them on, he couldn't find another person inside.

19

When Theo was small, she'd gone through a phase of being terrified her parents would abandon her, and her parents, in turn, had been alarmed by the unwavering intensity of her fear. She was young enough—five or six—that she probably wouldn't have remembered this later, except that this particular phase had made such an impression on her parents that they'd brought it up several times through the years, the same way they'd often told her how she'd once said, after passing her cold on to baby Josh, "Is that very nice to take away a person's vaporizer and give it to a baby?" and that she'd tormented three-year-old Josh mercilessly by referring to his overalls as "OshJosh."

The story they most often told was about her falling asleep on the stairs. She'd refused to go to bed before her parents did, afraid they'd sneak out of the house when she wasn't awake to stop them. If she came downstairs, or they caught her out of bed, they took away her TV time and her desserts and her bedtime stories, so she took to creeping halfway down the stairs and waiting there, running back up to her room when she heard them coming. One night she fell asleep on the stairs and tumbled down them. Her parents heard a terrible thumping and came running. She lay on her back on the landing looking dazed and hurt, but not making a sound, still trying not to alert them to her misbehavior. They checked her over and made her tell them how many fingers they were holding up, and then they carried her back upstairs, put her in their own bed, and climbed in on either side of her. This part she thought she remembered, her father's arm around her, her mother's hand stroking her hair. "Why would you ever think we'd leave you?" her father asked. Her mother said, "Don't you know that's the last thing we'd ever do?"

Theo didn't want to be alone now any more than she had then, but she feared—she knew—that eventually she would be. Sitting on the stairs—an act of hopeful desperation. Trying to stop what couldn't be stopped. Trying to keep an eye on people, who nevertheless eluded you the moment you dropped your guard. Her parents had left her with Eloise; now Eloise had left her, too, and Claire, and though Josh hadn't technically left her, he held so many things against her that just being around him exhausted her, struggling to keep all that resentment at bay. She was tired of trying not to fight with him. She had friends, of course, but none of her closest ones were still in Cincinnati, and so here she was lying awake at dawn on a Sunday in bed next to this sleeping boy, which maybe was a cosmic kind of sitting on the stairs, neither here nor there, neither up nor down, waiting for somebody to come along and get her.

Could she maybe, possibly, be over Noah? Was it possible she was falling for Wes? She tried to catch herself off guard with these questions, surprise herself into a definitive answer, but this was difficult. Ha! her mind said. I knew you were going to ask that. And then, smugly, said nothing more. She needed a clarifying moment. She awaited epiphany. In the meantime she had to act on what she did know, which was that she shouldn't take indefinite advantage of Wes's generosity.

But this conviction left her with a dilemma. It made little sense to get her own place here when she didn't know how long she'd be staying, and had come here to save money in the first place. And had no money in the second place. It was this dilemma that had woken her early. She reviewed its particulars again and again without arriving at any conclusions.

As the room lightened, she got out of bed without waking Wes, and then, without exactly making a decision, she got dressed, found her bag, and went outside. In fall Cincinnati mornings grew darker, headed toward a winter when it would be pitch-dark from 5:00 P.M. to 8:00 A.M. Pretty soon it would seem strange to see people on the sidewalks in the morning and the evening. Shouldn't we all be in bed? She walked to her car, parked three blocks away, and then she got in and started it. She couldn't think of where to go, so she went home. When you can't think of anywhere to go . . . Had she seen that stitched on a throw pillow somewhere?

The house was still and dark, of course. She let herself in quietly and closed the door as if trying not to wake someone. Though the sky was getting brighter, the rooms were still dim, but she felt a resistance to turning on the lights. She went into the living room and stood in the center of it looking around. She felt like a visitor to a museum of her life. All the framed photos on the surfaces, a pair of her earrings waiting in a decorative dish on the bookshelf. It was like a set designer had planned this place.

She walked up the stairs, trailing her fingers along the banister. How long would she remember what the wood felt like beneath her hand? Maybe she wouldn't remember at all, never having reminded herself to pay attention. Still, she knew. She knew without remembering. But without the banister there to touch, how would she ever know she knew? Sense memory doesn't work without input from the senses. She needed the house. Why couldn't Eloise understand how much she needed it?

She was walking past Josh's room to hers when his door suddenly opened. Theo started back, clapping her hand over a scream. There, in a pair of boxers and his skinny white chest, was her brother. "You scared the shit out of me!" she said. She felt startled awake, jarred out of her melancholy mood.

He looked at her with a zombielike glaze. His hair was tufted out on one side, and he had a pillow crease on his cheek. "I guess I fell asleep," he said. He scrubbed at his face with one hand and looked at her again.

"What do you mean you fell asleep? It's pretty early for you. Weren't you just asleep in the normal way?"

He shook his head, then said around a yawn, "I was up most of the night."

"Doing what?"

He lifted a shoulder, looking away like he didn't want to tell her.

"What are you doing here, anyway?"

"I'm staying here for now. I came back on Friday."

"Did you ask Eloise?"

"No," he said. He ran a hand through his hair, making it wilder, and looking at him she saw the little boy he'd been. His hair a wild explosion of curls because their mother loved it that way, his big eyes, his endless series of T-shirts featuring pictures of guitars, because though their mother bought him other shirts those were the only ones he'd wear. She remembered the intense look of concentration he used to wear in the backseat of the car, trying to learn the words to a song on the stereo, the way he'd mumble his half-understood version of the lyrics, the way she used to tease him about what he got wrong, her parents saying, "Theo, be nice. He's your little brother, be nice," and suddenly she felt a surge of tenderness for him like she hadn't felt in quite some time.

"Are you okay?" she asked.

He seemed to seriously consider the question before offering her a rueful smile. "I don't really know," he said.

"What were you doing all night?"

He sighed. "I feel stupid telling you."

"I won't judge," she said, and he looked so skeptical that she was torn between defensiveness and laughter. "For once," she said.

"I was writing songs." He watched her for her reaction, and she tried to keep her face neutral, afraid if she responded with too much excitement he'd get mad. "I finished a couple that had been in my head awhile, and then I wrote two new ones."

"Wow," she said.

"I know, right? I don't know if they're any good, but they *feel* like they're good."

"I bet they're good," she said, and she grinned at him. "I bet they're really good."

"Well," he said. "I appreciate your faith."

She turned away briskly, because a nice moment should be preserved, and said, "There's still coffee in the house, right?"

"Yup," he said. "I picked up a few things yesterday, so there's half-and-half, too."

"Oh, thank God," she said. She headed for the stairs.

"You're such a baby," he said. He grabbed a T-shirt from inside his room and followed her.

"You put cream in your coffee, too," Theo said.

"Yes, but I can drink it black."

"I can, too. I just have to pretend it's medicine. Nasty, nasty medicine."

"Medicine's not always nasty. Remember how we loved it when we were little?"

"Oh, the pink ear infection stuff. That was my favorite."

"I was always partial to cherry Tylenol," he said.

"That stuff sucks," Theo said, "but to each his own," and then they were in the kitchen, and he wanted to use the French press instead of the coffeepot, and she called him a snob, and he said he just had better taste than she did, and then she made a show of seeking his approval about how well she'd ground the beans, and really, they hadn't gotten along this well, this *easily,* in such a long time that she felt nearly giddy with the relief and pleasure of it. She wouldn't press him on his situation. She wouldn't ask him a single thing.

"So what are you doing here?" he asked, when they were sitting at the kitchen table with their mugs.

"I've been feeling a little homeless," she said. "I can't decide what to do about that. So I came back home."

"You've been staying with that guy?"

"Wes, yes." She took a sip of coffee, burned her tongue, and grimaced.

"That rhymed," Josh said.

"It did indeed."

"Are you making faces because of him?"

She shook her head. "Burned my tongue." He nodded and blew on his own coffee with an air of concentration. She could tell he, too, was trying not to ask too many questions. Sometimes she forgot, in her conviction that their problems were all about his sensitivities, that she, too, had buttons to push. "He's a great guy," Theo said. "But he's a little young for me."

"How young?"

"He's twenty-two." Josh looked so neutral at this news that Theo laughed. "You can react," she said.

"That's not so bad. He's allowed in a bar."

"True," she said. "That *is* what I look for in a man." She sighed. "I don't know. I don't know what I'm doing. I honestly don't really know what I feel about him. Or where I should live. Or what I'm doing here."

"Here at the house? Here in Cincinnati?"

"Here in the world," she said.

Josh tested the coffee and pronounced it cool enough, so Theo drank some, and for a moment they sat there in silence. Then he said, "Why don't you come back to the house, too? It's silly for it to sit here empty while we impose on other people."

"The way Eloise has behaved is just so unfair."

"I don't worry so much about fairness." He grinned at her. "I'm the middle child. I'm more about negotiation."

"You're the good one," she said.

"I'm the good one." He sighed. "Allegedly."

"Truly!" Theo said. "You came to pick me up that night from that bar, and you never asked any questions. I don't even know if I thanked you."

"Was that you thanking me just now?"

"I think it was," she said. She pretended to consider. "Yes, it was."

"I have to tell you, Theo," Josh said, but then it took him a moment to go on. "About Sabrina. You were right. I was an asshole."

Just the day before, Theo would have been thrilled by this admission. Now she resisted it. "Oh, I don't think so."

"I mean I was pathetic."

"I know what you mean." Theo shook her head. "You loved her, you know? What good did I think talking was going to do? I should have kept my mouth shut."

"I don't know," he said. "You were right. Maybe when someone else is making a terrible mistake it's your duty to tell them. Maybe the problem wasn't you talking but me not listening." There was a silence while they both considered that. Josh said, "But then again I was pretty fucking mad at you."

"I noticed," Theo said.

"You did?"

Theo laughed. "I'm astonishingly perceptive," she said.

"And always right?"

"Yes," she said. "I'm always right."

A couple hours later, Theo knocked on Wes's door, even though he'd given her a key. He opened it frowning and stepped back to let her inside. "Where have you been? I thought we were going to brunch."

"I'm sorry," she said. "I went back to the house, and I ran into my brother."

"Oh," Wes said. "I thought nobody was living there now."

"He's been there since Friday," she said. "He's been writing songs."

"Really? That's awesome!"

She'd known this information would distract him. That was why she'd offered it. What a coward she was. "Yeah, I'm really glad," she said. "He doesn't know yet what he'll do with them."

"He should record a solo album is what he should do," Wes said.

Theo made a noise of assent, moving past him into the living room. She felt a premature nostalgia for Wes's indie-rock decor. "I really appreciate you putting me up all this time," she said. "It's been incredibly nice of you."

"Nice of me?" Wes came up behind her and touched her arm. "What's going on?"

She sat down on the couch and waited. He looked at her warily a moment and then sat beside her. "My brother thinks I should come back to the house, too, until some decision is made."

"You don't have to do that," he said. "I like having you here."

"I know, but, Wes, don't you think this happened awfully fast? It's like we're living together."

"We *are* living together."

"But we barely know each other."

He frowned. "Is that really what you think?"

"I mean we haven't known each other long."

"We've known each other nearly three years."

"I'm not counting when you were in my class."

"Why not?"

"Because that was different, obviously. That was a totally different thing."

"We were the same people."

"Look," she said. "I just think we should take a step back."

"You're breaking up with me."

"Breaking up?"

"Yes, Theo. We've been a couple these last few weeks, whether you realized it or not, which clearly you didn't. So if you end things, people call that 'breaking up.'"

"I didn't say I was ending things."

"No," he said. "You said I've been 'incredibly nice.' You're still wearing your jacket."

She looked down at herself as if to confirm this. She hadn't even unbuttoned the jacket. She'd sat down with her bag still on her shoulder. "I don't think I want to end things."

"But you don't know?"

"No, I don't know, and I told you that from the beginning! I've never made a secret of my lack of knowledge."

Wes nodded slowly. "So this is about that guy."

"No. Not really. I don't know. Maybe."

"Did something happen with him?"

She shook her head. "I haven't even seen him since we ran into him. But, Wes, I still don't know whether I'm over him. Don't you want me to figure that out? Otherwise, aren't I being horribly unfair?"

"So you want to figure that out, and then if you decide you're over him, you want me to be waiting for you, and if you decide you're not, you want me to get over you. Or are you hoping even if you decide you're not I'll be waiting for you? Just in case you ever do change your mind?"

She began to protest that no, that wasn't what she was doing, but yes, it was. Wasn't it? "That's awful," she said.

"Yes," Wes said. "Yes, Theo, that's awful. And no, I won't wait." He stood up, walked into the kitchen, then came back, holding his wallet and keys. "I am an actual person, not just the idea of one," he said. "And I love you."

"You do?"

"Are we ever going to get to a point where I tell you how I feel about you and you don't act surprised?"

"I'm sorry," she said.

"I'm tired of you being sorry," he said. "It's time for you to be something else." He picked up his coat from the armchair and thrust his arms into the sleeves. He looked around—for his phone, she knew—but didn't find it. "I'm going out while you pack up. You can slide the key back under the door."

"Don't go," she said.

He said, "Neither of us will like me very much if I don't." He gave up on the phone, heading for the door.

"Wes," she called after him, and he stopped with his hand on the knob, but she had no idea what she wanted to say, just that she wanted to say something. "You're too young for me," she said. She meant it as a kind of apology, but of course he didn't take it like that.

"Oh, Theo," he said, yanking the door open. "Fuck off."

After he left, she found his phone under a book of hers on the coffee table. She spent a long time thinking about where she should put it that he'd be sure to find it, finally choosing the kitchen counter. Then she packed up her things, as he'd instructed, and made his bed with more precision than she'd ever made a bed in her life. It looked like a bed in a showroom. It looked like a bed no one had ever slept in. She sat on it and bounced the mattress like she was thinking of buying it, and then she got up before the urge to lie down could overcome her. She had a lump in her throat, but she wasn't going to cry. You could cry all you wanted when someone left you, but how ridiculous to cry when you left someone. How self-serving and foolish and unfair. She smoothed out the quilt again to erase all signs she'd been there.

She locked the door and then worked his key off her key chain and slid it under the door. A feeling of panic seized her, and she crouched down to peer under the door, but the key was gone. She couldn't even see it. Even if she wanted to, there was no way to get back in. As she turned to go she thought about how happy he'd looked when he asked if she was moving in, the way it had seemed for a moment—for longer than a moment—that she could. But she couldn't have stayed. Something so easy couldn't possibly be right.

20

At dinner in downtown Chicago with Jason Bamber and two of his colleagues, Eloise had three glasses of wine and a wonderful time. Chicago at night! She'd forgotten. After the wine Eloise suggested they all go up to the Sears Tower. "I never did that when I lived here before," she said. "I was too cool."

Jason and his colleagues argued for a while about whether the Sears Tower or the Hancock Tower was best, and Eloise thought they really were going, and was disappointed when the colleagues begged off, saying they had to get home. "So," she said, putting her palms flat on the table and looking at Jason. "Which will it be?"

He grinned. "My place or yours, you mean?"

She laughed, shaking her head. "Sears or Hancock?"

He groaned. "Are we really doing that?"

"Hell, yes," she said. "I'm an out-of-town visitor. I'm a tourist! You're lucky I don't make you take me to the Navy Pier to ride the Ferris wheel."

They went to the Hancock, because it was closer. They clambered into the cab laughing like college kids, and Eloise could have sworn that, glancing at the rearview mirror, she saw the cabbie roll his eyes at them. That just made her laugh harder. Jason put his hand on her thigh. She looked down at it, then back at him, eyebrows raised. He raised his eyebrows back. What was going to happen here? She didn't know, but she couldn't deny that, even if nothing happened, she was enjoying walking up to the edge. She lifted the hand, patted it, and put it back in his lap. "Down, boy," she said.

The elevator ride to the top of the Hancock Tower was shockingly quick, as advertised, and the view was amazing. Eloise felt fully justified in gaping like a yokel. She walked toward the windowed wall like a person hypnotized. Down below she could see the Navy Pier, the lights of the Ferris wheel in all their crass and gorgeous brilliance. Jason joined her at the window and she pointed. "That's where we're going next," she said.

"I love it here," Jason said, with feeling. "I couldn't live anywhere else."

"Shhh," Eloise said, putting her finger to her lips. "Don't jinx yourself." She set off to walk the perimeter of the room, Chicago from all sides. What was it about this city that made it seem so much better than her own? Was it that it was bigger? That it was richer? That it had more buildings? That it just didn't seem so goddamn sad?

On the way back to her hotel, Jason vibrated with anticipation, shooting her looks, and she debated what to do. Right at that moment, still a little tipsy, enjoying his desire, feeling some curiosity about being with a man again, she found herself inclined to sleep with him. But she was sober enough now to hesitate. If she did sleep with him he'd expect something from her when she came here, and she wasn't so sure that if she did end up coming it wouldn't be partly in pursuit of solitude. He might expect something from her whether she slept with him tonight or not, but if she didn't those expectations might be more manageable. Also there'd be terrible guilt about Heather, who, no matter what Heather herself said, still had a claim on her. Eloise had gone on staying with her since their fight in demonstration of that claim. Eloise had apologized and apologized, and then Heather had been her usual warm and endlessly forgiving self. But a couple nights ago, Eloise had woken to find herself alone in bed and after a few moments registered the sound of Heather crying in the bathroom. She hadn't knocked, though she'd hesitated a long time at the door. She didn't know what to say. That the sound of Heather weeping broke her heart. That she loved her like she'd never loved anyone she'd ever been with. That she might leave her anyway.

So when Jason asked if he could come in, Eloise shook her head and said, "Big day tomorrow."

"Ah," he said, sinking back against the seat. "Interviews that aren't really interviews."

"Hey," she said. "It's your department chair *and* the dean."

He made an impatient gesture. "Just a formality," he said. "But I understand."

She felt sorry for disappointing him, and annoyed that she was sorry. She almost said they'd still have tomorrow night, but for God's sake, Eloise, don't promise him anything! She went up to her room feeling she'd made a narrow escape.

The next morning before her interviews, she walked over to her old apartment building and looked at it from the outside. It was a fairly nondescript building, and she found that she'd misremembered many of its details, though she'd gotten the location right. The memory that visited her, as she stared up at the window that used to be hers, was of a party she'd thrown in grad school and then refused to attend. During this particular party, held during her exam year, she'd gone down to the coffee shop on the street and read one of the books from her list. She'd been really into the book and hadn't felt like stopping to exchange chit-chat and idle departmental gossip, which, in the mood of that moment, seemed like a colossal waste of time. She'd hoarded her time back then, refused to spend it on things that did not promise the maximum result, like, for instance, a social event that sounded only okay. She thought, with a benevolent smile at her younger self, that she'd probably come off as self-righteous and haughty. That was the thing, though—back then she hadn't cared. When she watched one of those movies about the selfish painter or musician or scientist who chewed through everyone around him, she identified with him while everyone else cluck-clucked about how sad it was. For God's sake—in high school she'd even identified with Howard Roark, the hero of *The Fountainhead,* at least until that whole weird rape scene. To her the fact that her grad school classmates had teased her about her antisocial behavior and that to shut them up she'd agreed to have a party was a black mark against her as well as them. She remembered taking satisfaction in the exasperation on their faces before she shut her own door on them and went downstairs. It had been similar to the exasperation displayed by the men she'd dated, about whose disappointment and longing she couldn't seem to care very much, maybe because she was unknowingly a lesbian, maybe because she just really didn't care.

When had she begun to take other people's feelings so to heart, to believe that she owed something to everybody she encountered? It was as if she'd been converted from *The Fountain-*

head by *The Giving Tree*. Shut up, you stupid tree, she thought now. I don't want to be a stump.

Her interviews went well. She thought so, and Jason said so, too. "This job is yours if you want it," he said, dropping her at her hotel so she could freshen up before dinner.

She was still repeating that phrase to herself—*mine if I want it*—two hours later, standing in the hotel bathroom brushing her hair. She'd spent most of that time attempting a nap, too abuzz to sleep, turning the words over in her head. Now she had fifteen minutes before Jason would arrive to pick her up, doubtless expecting to hear that she'd take the job. She was looking at her pores in the magnified mirror when she heard her cell phone ringing. She went to answer but couldn't locate the source of the sound. The phone was in her bag, but where was her bag? On the floor, as it turned out, where it had fallen off the bed and spilled some of its contents, though not the phone. By now the phone had stopped ringing, but she stuck her hand in the bag and felt around for it anyway. Hunting among loose change, pens, and scraps of paper, she wondered why she still ran for the phone, in these days of caller ID and voicemail, these days when no call was ever lost. It was a residual habit from childhood, when the phone rang and you didn't know who was calling before you answered, when it could be anyone in the world on the line. She remembered busy signals. She remembered what a miracle call waiting had seemed. She remembered believing that she didn't need a cell phone, which was like remembering an old love. You knew what you had felt but could no longer access that feeling, so that it didn't quite seem to have ever belonged to you at all. Of course she needed a cell phone! She needed to be sitting on a bed in a hotel room in Chicago with it in her hand, frowning at the unknown number on the screen. A mysterious caller—that, too, was a relic of a long-gone age. Calling someone on the phone was now an act of either intimacy or marketing. She waited for the phone to announce a message, but that didn't happen, so she called the number back, because these days every minor mystery could be solved.

The phone rang twice, and then a man said hello, his voice as wary as Eloise felt.

"You called me?" Eloise said.

There was a silence, and the man said, "Eloise?"

"Who is this?" she asked.

"It's Gary. Gary Paula."

Eloise froze. He was persecuting her. "How did you get this number?" she asked.

"It was in my phone, my landline, I mean. Claire must have called you from this number."

"Oh," she said and fell silent, as if all her questions had been answered. She wasn't going to ask what he wanted, especially because she thought she already knew. He wanted her to be a better mother. He wanted her to help her little girl. He'd forgotten again that she wasn't exactly a mother, and the girl wasn't little, and it was his fault Claire needed help at all.

"I'm calling to see if you know where Claire is," he said.

Eloise's heart leapt into her throat. Yes, that was exactly what it did. From a distance, she heard herself say, "What do you mean?"

"I take it that's a no."

"Yes, it's a no," Eloise said. "Could you explain yourself? Last I heard she was with you."

"Well, she's not with me anymore," Gary said. "She's gone."

"What do you mean, gone?" Eloise closed her eyes against her own instinctive alarm.

"She left, and I don't know where she went."

"When was this?"

"Monday. I came home and found a note. Hang on, I'll read it to you." She heard him rustling, and then he read, *"Gary, I think you should go home to your family. I'm sorry. This was wrong. We shouldn't be in touch. Claire."*

"That's it?"

"That's it." He cleared his throat. "That's it."

"And that was four days ago? You lost her four days ago, and you're just now calling me?" She was as angry as if he were a disastrously negligent babysitter, a person to whom she'd foolishly entrusted her child, though of course she hadn't picked him to take charge of Claire and never would have, and hadn't even realized Claire needed to be in somebody's charge.

"I hesitated to call you," he said. "First of all, you told me in no uncertain terms that she wasn't your responsibility anymore. Plus I kept thinking she'd call. Or come back. I did not imagine that she'd really make such a choice so precipitously, without even speaking to me on the phone."

"But she hasn't called."

"No."

"And you don't have any idea where she might have gone?"

There was a pause and then he said, "I don't know anything about her life. Not really. That's become clear to me in the last few days. I haven't even met her friends. So, no, no, I have no idea where she might have gone, or why she left, or what the hell she could possibly be thinking. I've been reduced to waiting for her to update her status on Facebook. Frankly I thought she might have gone to you. I thought maybe you talked her into leaving me."

"No, I didn't," Eloise said. "But I damn sure wish I had." She snapped her phone shut, turned, and lobbed it toward the door to the hallway, where it landed hard and subsided. She turned toward the back of the room like she was headed somewhere, but there were just the windows behind her with their view of Chicago, utterly unhelpful. "Shit," she said, about Claire, but also because she suddenly saw the lack of wisdom in throwing and possibly breaking her phone. She went to pick it up. The screen still glowed and everything looked normal. "Good, good," she said, as if the phone needed soothing. The phone made no response. "What now?" she said to it. The person she imagined answering was Heather. But she could make decisions without Heather, couldn't she? She'd made decisions on her own for years.

Eloise scrolled to Claire's number and pressed Send. One ring. She exhaled a ragged breath into the pause. Two. Three. Four. Then the mechanical click of voicemail answering, and Claire's voice saying, cheerfully, that she couldn't get to the phone. Eloise hesitated a millisecond after the beep and then hung up. She didn't know what to say. She didn't even know how she wanted her voice to sound.

She walked back into the bathroom and observed her own in-decision in the mirror, then remembered texting, and felt a rush of gratitude for the modern age. She wrote: *Can you please tell me you're alive?*

Waiting for an answer, she listed possible actions and inac-tions: Waiting. Calling Claire's friends. Checking with Theo and Josh to see if they knew where Claire had gone. If her impulse was to run after Claire, did that mean chasing her was what she should do, or even what she wanted? Maybe it was just like running for the phone—a residual trait from an earlier time. When your child ran out the door you followed her, unless your child was nineteen, and it wasn't your door she'd run out of, and you had no idea where she'd gone.

Claire might have told Josh where she was, but she wouldn't have told Theo. Theo would judge her, just like she'd judge Eloise if Eloise told her she'd once again let Claire get away. Eloise could picture the look of mingled reproach and worry on Theo's face, and if she talked to her over the phone instead of in person she'd still hear the judgment in her voice. Funny that she wasn't picturing the adult Theo, wearing that very familiar expression, but the girl. It was how she'd looked when Eloise was late to pick her up, or said *shit* in front of Claire, or refused Claire her bedtime book when the child wouldn't pick her up her toys. Eloise could still see four-year-old Claire sprawled facedown on the floor, crying in gulping sobs, saying, "I want a bedtime book." She remembered how it felt to stand over her saying, "I told you what would happen," how she'd had to combat the powerful urge to give in with the frustrated anger of being constantly and stupidly defied. Because a child had to be made to follow the rules, even if your enforcement of those rules caused that child pain. If you never let a child be upset, you might think you were loving her in the purest, most generous way possible, a way that would keep her feeling safe and secure and compassionate in equal measure to the compassion she'd been shown. But in reality you'd be creating a little monster who thought nothing mattered in the world but her feelings. And yet Theo would appear in the doorway of the bedroom—her own bedroom, since Claire insisted on sleeping with Theo—and look at Eloise like she was cruel, like she was incompetent, like she'd failed. After Eloise left, her rule enforced, Theo would hold Claire and comfort her, and tell her a story in defiance of the idea—if not the letter—of the law. Eloise never tried to stop Theo from doing this. In truth she wanted Claire to get what she wanted, too.

Her phone buzzed. Claire had written: *I'm alive.* Eloise wrote back, *Where are you?*

Elsewhere, Claire wrote.

Eloise wrote, *Where is that?* But Claire didn't answer. At the airport that day Eloise had pretended not to remember how she'd answered that question herself when Claire was a child. But she remembered. Of course she remembered! She'd said it over and over, like a prayer, like an incantation: *As far as you can get from here.*

It was time to meet Jason in the lobby, so she headed down, feeling both utterly uncertain and strangely calm. She didn't know what she was going to tell him. She'd have found it difficult to explain why, after everything else—the fights with Heather, the fights with Theo, the interviews—this felt like the moment when she had to decide. Here or there. Then or now. What life would it be?

The elevator doors opened. She stepped out and saw Jason— waiting, full of longing and promises—and she knew for sure she was going back home. She knew it as soon as she spotted him, and the knowledge grew heavier and more certain as she crossed the room to meet his happy, anticipatory smile. "I'm so sorry," she said, "but I have to stay in tonight, and go ahead and drive home tomorrow."

He flinched with surprise, then looked at her speculatively. "Are you joking?" he said. "I don't remember you joking this way."

She shook her head. "I'm so sorry," she said again. She explained, using the words *child* and *disappeared,* against which little argument could be made, though she could see in the mulish look on his face that he was hard-pressed not to make it.

"Do you still want me to keep you in mind for the job?" he asked.

She noticed how his language had changed: from *it's yours if you want it* to *keep you in mind.* She did, she did want him to—oh, the idea of it! But she knew, without wanting to know it, that she was never going to take the job. She couldn't bring herself to do all that would be necessary, and whether that was a failure of nerve or an acknowledgment of what really mattered she couldn't say. That was in the eye of the beholder. "No," she said.

"Eloise," he said, "come on. You're entitled to your own life." On his face was the exasperation she remembered from the night of that grad school party, the inability to understand why she thought some new pursuit, some act of self-indulgent self-discipline, was more important than what they'd had planned.

She didn't try to explain any further. There wasn't any explaining it. She could have made different choices, but all that mattered were the ones she'd made.

She got back to Cincinnati in early afternoon, but then she couldn't decide where to go. She'd cleared her schedule, canceling classes and rescheduling meetings, to accommodate the Chicago trip, so no one was expecting her. Not even Heather—Heather had left for work early on the morning of Eloise's departure, not waking her, not leaving a note. In the days leading up to the trip Heather had made a point of not asking a single question about it, not even when Eloise was coming back. The kids didn't know she'd gone to Chicago. Now, as she drove without purpose along the river, not a single person knew where she was. It didn't take long to leave Cincinnati, to find yourself in the country, or a small town whose old and impressive and empty buildings suggested a long-gone prosperity. She could keep driving and in a little more than an hour she'd be in the land of the Amish, another world, another time, a place where she could never live, because she'd be foreign and useless and wearing all the wrong clothes.

It was funny, when something happened to make you think about it, what a small piece of the world you actually lived in. Eloise would have said she lived in and was from Cincinnati, but really she lived in and was from the neighborhood of Clifton, and hardly ever even went into certain parts of her neighborhood. That street tucked back in the woods she'd seen once, in high school, when she'd gone to a party there—it was a half mile away from her and in thirty years she'd never been back. And on other streets, where the houses were smaller and more run-down and the crime higher than on hers—could she really be said to live in the same place as the people who lived there? There were so many lives to be led in one city, in so many different neighbor-hoods, on so many different streets. Claire could still be here and yet be elsewhere, as the last few months had made clear. She might be living in a split-ranch in the suburbs, or above a tattoo parlor in Northside, or across the river in small-town Kentucky. She could be shacked up with a frat-boy investment banker in Mount Adams, or hanging out at a gay bar on one of the gentri-fied strips of Over-the-Rhine, or staying in one of the many guest rooms of the house of her rich friend in Indian Hill.

Cincinnati. Queen of the West, City of the Seven Hills. Elo-ise had left and she had come back. She turned the car around and drove until she saw the skyline—and wasn't there relief as well as regret in that familiar sight? What would she really lose if she finally admitted that this was her home, if she allowed herself to belong?

She drove through downtown into Over-the-Rhine, letting impulse guide her left and right, and then when she reached the ballet she let that same impulse take her into the parking lot. The woman at the front desk recognized her, and they exchanged pleasantries, then Eloise strolled down the hallway toward the studios like she belonged there. Several of the male dancers were in one studio, and Eloise paused at the glass wall to watch as they leapt and spun in unison. Really, it was easy to believe that they could fly. Across the hall were the female dancers, Adelaide among them. Eloise stood there watching. What they did was even more impressive up close than it was on the stage, because up close they were real, actual human beings making those impossible leaps.

They took a break and Eloise watched Adelaide walk to the back of the room, her hands on her hips. She was breathing hard, but not a single hair had escaped from her bun. They were so severe with their hair. They were so severe with their bodies. They were very, very hard on themselves. Perfection required that. And Adelaide was perfect, she was beautiful, there were tears in Eloise's eyes. What an amazing thing it was to sacrifice your body to bring such beauty to the world. To focus your life so narrowly, to believe with your whole self in a singular importance. Like being a nun. Like being a revolutionary. Like running away from home.

Sometimes Eloise had worried about Claire's devotion to ballet, about what it was doing to her poor little feet, about the early onset of this kind of singular passion. But it was hard to think that Claire working so hard was wrong when it was such a pleasure to watch her dance. Out of the studio she was quiet in a way that sometimes suggested confident reserve, sometimes withdrawn insecurity. But when she moved she embodied certainty. The life she wanted was incredibly difficult to achieve and yet so appealingly simple in its clarity. You didn't strike out on your own to become a ballet dancer. You tried to belong, doing what they asked you to do and hoping for admittance. You took classes and learned steps and auditioned for companies, every stage of the process neatly labeled with a number or a name. Children's Division 1. Academy Level 2. Trainee Program. Now a *pas de bourrée*. Now a *soutenu*. Ballet was a well-laid path marked out through the messiness of life, and it was very easy to want for Claire what Claire wanted for herself. And now what did Claire want? What should Eloise want for her? She had absolutely no idea.

She had a strong desire, now, to talk to Adelaide, so she went back out to the lobby to wait. She sank into a leather love seat and tried not to notice the way the woman at the front desk kept sneaking looks at her. She wondered, if Claire never came back to ballet, what her niece could possibly find to replace it. It was one thing to grow up without faith, the way Eloise had, and so never miss it, and so be baffled by other people's evocations of it, the praying and the weeping and the sincerity. It was another to lose, or even to vanquish, faith, the way Heather had. Once you'd had it, you knew what you were missing. Last Christmas Eve, Heather had cried, not because she believed but because she missed believing. In the absence of God, she'd made a religion of her work, and of her politics, and on those foundations she'd built a faith-based community. Maybe Eloise hadn't been able to sustain her own career because what she'd had was not faith but ambition. Or maybe because inheriting the children had divided her, and faith is not something the divided self can sustain. Was that what had happened to Claire when she fell in love with Gary? Or had she just wanted to quit ballet, and so looked around for something else to believe in? Poor Claire—you can make a religion out of love, but not forever and ever, amen. At least not if you lack the capacity for devotion, for nothing in the world but that person and your belief in that person, like women were once upon a time, and even now, supposed to offer up to men. If Claire had been unable to do that, Eloise was glad, but it was no wonder the girl had panicked. In the absence of devotion, there was nothing but the self.

The dancers began to emerge, and after two or three clumps of them went by, Adelaide appeared, walking with two other girls. She carried a heavy bag on one shoulder. She wore sparkly gold slip-on shoes, like a genie, or a harem girl. The woman was an athlete, doubtless much stronger than Eloise despite her small frame, and yet it was so easy to think of her as a particular kind of incarnation of the female—the yearning, graceful body, the supplicating poses, the fragility and lightness of a woman that a man could lift into the air.

As she neared, Eloise stood to catch her eye, and Adelaide saw her and looked first surprised, then wary. Eloise couldn't blame her for the wariness. She lifted her hand and held the girl's—the *woman's*—gaze so she'd know Eloise wanted to talk to her. Adelaide turned to say a smiling good night to her friends, and then, slowly, she approached.

"Hi," Eloise said.

"Hi," Adelaide said back. She waited. She was probably much

better than Eloise at waiting. She'd spent a lot of years perfecting stillness, as well as its opposite.

"I wondered if I could talk to you about something," Eloise said.

Adelaide looked at the floor. "Is it about Josh?"

"No," Eloise said. "Why? Is something wrong?" Adelaide hesitated, and Eloise asked, "Did you break up?"

"Not exactly. I'm really not sure."

Eloise took a step back and sank down into the couch again. She was surprised by how badly she was taking this news. "I'm sorry to hear that," she said. "Would you mind if I asked what happened?"

Adelaide hesitated, then perched on the edge of the cushion beside Eloise. "We had a fight," she said after a moment. "Because I have an audition I didn't tell him about, and he had a band he didn't tell me about."

Eloise raised her eyebrows. "You didn't know about Blind Robots?"

Adelaide shook her head. "I don't know why he didn't tell me."

"I can guess," Eloise said. "Do you want to hear my guess?"

"Okay."

"He's embarrassed that he quit."

"Really? That's not what he said."

"What did he say?"

"He said he'd had plenty of girls like him just for that, and he wanted me to like him for him."

"Well, there might be truth in that, too. But I think he didn't want to tell you because he didn't want to explain what happened, which is that he quit the band for the woman who was his girlfriend at the time, and every time he thinks about that choice he feels ashamed of himself, and he didn't want you to be ashamed of him."

"Why would I be? I mean, why is he?"

"Oh, because she was awful. Truly awful. She emotionally abused him, if you want to know the truth. She made him feel small and worthless, and he stuck around anyway, and he gave up the other things he cared about in pursuit of affirmation he was never going to get. And I bet he took a look at you, somebody whose whole life is devoted to this incredibly difficult art form, and he just couldn't bring himself to tell you that he'd given his own art form up. He's been trying very, very hard to think of himself as someone who never was a musician, and never wanted to be. He doesn't want you to think he's a quitter, or a loser. He'd rather you assumed he's content with his life as it is."

Adelaide frowned. "And you don't think he is?"

"You know," Eloise said, "I really don't know. Josh is quite good at hiding what he actually feels in the interest of harmony. He's good at hiding what he actually feels even from himself. I think it's a family trait."

Adelaide sank back into the couch now. "I wish he could have told me these things."

"Can I ask—why didn't you tell him about the audition?"

"I don't even know if I'll get the part, and if I do I don't know if I want it."

"And you want to make that decision on your own."

"I guess so." She looked away, across the lobby toward the studios. "I get Josh's point—I've had plenty of guys be interested because I'm a dancer, and then when that interest wears off there's not much left. They figure out what that really means, and they don't want to deal with it. It's a weird life I lead. I can't have kids before I retire, really. I can't be normal. And, you know, I'm twenty-nine. I won't have options much longer—I won't be able to dance much longer. I can see retirement coming and it scares me."

"I can understand that."

"But then, if you postpone everything else for dancing, when you quit dancing you might not have anything else." She gave Eloise a rueful smile. "So I'm afraid of retirement. And I'm also afraid of ending up alone."

Eloise nodded. "I just don't think normal is what Josh wants."

"I don't know what he wants," Adelaide said. "He hasn't told me."

"You could ask."

Now Adelaide grinned, a goofy, broad grin that transformed her face. "You make it sound so easy," she said.

"I do, don't I?" Eloise said. "I make it sound like the easiest thing in the world." She had an urge to touch the girl, pat her shoulder or smooth her hair, though of course it didn't need smoothing. But she didn't, because Adelaide didn't seem the type to welcome unsolicited touch. Although it was hard to tell, wasn't it? Who wanted what, and from whom, and who needed comfort, and who was just afraid to ask for it, and who genuinely wanted to be left alone. "I hope you two work it out," she said.

"Thanks," Adelaide said. "That's really nice. I hope so, too." She hesitated. "I actually had the impression that you didn't like me."

"Oh hell," Eloise said. "I'm sorry about that."

"It's okay. I'm not very good with new people. I do much better with an audience than I do up close."

Eloise laughed. "I feel the same way about myself," she said.

"Josh isn't like that, though," Adelaide said. "Even though he used to be a performer. God! I just can't believe I didn't know that. Do you know what I did, after we fought and he left? I bought all his music."

"You did?"

"I've been listening to it ever since. I can't stop listening to it. It's really good. And also, you know, it's *Josh*."

"I do know," Eloise said. "I know what you mean." Adelaide had said his name with such feeling, Eloise was sure she loved him. Loved him enough to work this out? Loved him enough never to hurt him? Did anybody love anybody enough for that?

"I'm sorry," Adelaide said. "You wanted to ask me something."

"Oh," Eloise said. "Yes. But I don't know exactly what it is." She gave the other woman a weak and sheepish smile. "I guess I want you to explain Claire to me. I guess I thought you might understand."

Adelaide frowned. "You mean her quitting?"

"I guess," Eloise said. "I guess that's what I mean."

Adelaide went on frowning, her gaze on the floor. "I don't know," she said. "I can't imagine quitting. And it's not like she talked to me about it. I'm sure she didn't want to tell me."

"That's probably true. She really admires you."

"But I wouldn't judge her. I know how hard the life is. I mean, I'm sorry about it—it's a loss to ballet, because she's amazing, she's really something special, and when you teach and you see that kind of talent you want it to be put to use."

"I know."

"Yeah, you know what?" Adelaide said abruptly. "I'm lying. I *am* disappointed in her. I don't think she really wanted to quit ballet. I don't think she really found the love of her life. I think she just got scared."

"Really?"

"She was probably freaked out by leaving home. I had to refuse to teach her anymore, you know. That's the only way I could get her to audition for other programs."

"I remember that."

Adelaide glanced at her. "She took it hard, didn't she. I remember when I told her she seemed like she was struggling not to cry."

"She took it hard," Eloise said. There had been crying on the floor, followed by a quiet, doomed resolve. Eloise's heart had ached for her, and yet she'd thought this pain was necessary—thought Claire needed to go. "But I was grateful to you."

"All I wanted when I was her age was to go to New York."

"Me, too. But not Claire. Claire gave that up to stay here, and now she's run off again, left Gary, but I don't know where she's gone. I don't know if I should try to find her, or just leave her alone."

Adelaide shook her head. "She'll turn up," she said. "If she's not still here she's gone somewhere she knows."

"How do you know?"

"I just know. She wouldn't go someplace new. She wouldn't strike out on her own."

"You're so sure."

"I understand her. She puts everything into her dancing. It's almost like she has no resources outside of that. She's spent all her time thinking about how to move onstage. She's got very little idea how to move through the world."

"So there's nothing to her but the dancing?"

"No, no, I didn't mean that. More like, she wishes there was nothing else to life."

"Is that how you feel?" Eloise asked.

"I used to," Adelaide said. She gave Eloise a small, rueful smile. "I'm trying not to anymore."

Giving in to her impulse, Eloise put her hand on the other woman's arm. Her slender, elegant, strong but fragile-looking arm. Eloise looked her in the eye and said, "Josh loves you."

Adelaide's color rose. "Really?" she said.

"I don't want you to lose each other," Eloise said. "Call him. Go see him. Don't let him go."

Adelaide seemed caught by Eloise's intensity. "I won't," she said. "I promise."

So maybe she'd fixed that one, Eloise thought, walking out toward the parking lot. Maybe she'd done something right. Could she manage something else? *Somewhere she knows,* Adelaide had said. Where did Claire know? She knew Cincinnati. She knew New York, but it seemed unlikely she'd have gone there. She knew Sewanee, Tennessee, where her grandmother lived. Sewanee, where Francine had gone to school and then returned, that tiny town on top of a mountain, that remote and quiet hideaway.

Eloise waited until she reached her car to call, and then she took a deep breath and pressed the necessary buttons.

"Oh, thank God," Francine said. "Where have you been? I've been calling the house."

"I was out of town. Plus I've been staying with someone. Why didn't you call my cell?"

"I hate cell phones," Francine said. "Who are you staying with? That woman Heather?"

Eloise froze. "How'd you know?"

"She answered the phone once when I called, and when I asked for you she asked who was calling, and introduced herself like there was some reason for us to know each other."

"But you never said anything."

"No, because you didn't." Eloise could picture her mother's pleased-with-herself expression. "I know more than you give me credit for."

"Clearly."

"I don't know why you wouldn't tell me."

"I don't either," Eloise said. "Obviously there wasn't any point to not telling. So I'm looking for Claire. Is she there?"

"Of course she's here. Why do you think I've been calling you? She took a bus here," Francine said. "She went to Nashville and then came here. She just brought this one little bag so I thought she wasn't staying long."

"But . . ." Eloise prompted.

"But now it seems like she might stay indefinitely! I mean it's already been five days. And she's not really herself, Eloise. I open a bottle of wine and she drinks two-thirds of it. And then she's sleeping it off half the day. She cries. She says she's ruined her life. All she talks about is how everyone hates her and will never forgive her."

"I see," Eloise said.

"She's always been so poised, so graceful," Francine said, clearly wistful for that previous version of her granddaughter. "You never knew what she was thinking."

"Not lately anyway," Eloise said.

Francine sighed. "It's all a bit too much for me, honestly." Something in her voice brought to mind Eloise's first day back in Cincinnati, after Rachel died. Her mother on the bed, a dark sculpture of grief. Her mother asking, "Why did she leave her children with me?" For the first time Eloise imagined that there had been not just petulant anger in that question but genuine sorrow, genuine desperation, genuine regret. She'd held so much against her mother for so long. The way she was never quite there in the room with you, the way she always seemed to be thinking about something else, the way she always had reasons not to do things for you. She was *tired*. She was *overwhelmed*. Life was too *chaotic*. Maybe, for her mother, all of that had been not just an excuse but the truth. Funny that Eloise felt this sympathy—maybe even empathy—for Francine now, at this moment, as her mother made her way to one more exasperating, predictable request.

"Can you come get her?" her mother said.

21

Theo was in the middle of a paragraph that could go two ways. She got up from her desk without paying attention to what she was doing and went down the stairs, her mind still turning over sentences, in an unthinking search for something to eat. She took the back stairs into the kitchen and found an open bag of chips in the pantry. At the counter she stuffed chips in her mouth, staring into space, and then there was a sharp rap at the door, startling her so badly she crumpled the bag in her hand and crunched the chips within. "Dammit," she said, both about the chips and about the person at the door. Because who could it possibly be? It couldn't be anyone. Maybe the mailman, or the UPS guy. She went slowly toward the door, trying to see out the sidelights who it was, and she caught a glimpse of a blurry male figure, not in uniform, and too short to be Josh. The conviction leapt into her mind that it must be Wes, and she felt so horrified at this idea that it was hard to understand her disappointment when she opened the door and the person standing there turned out to be Noah.

"Oh, hey," Noah said. "I didn't know you'd be here."

"Yup," she said. She looked down and saw potato chip crumbs

on her breasts. "Pardon my messiness," she said, brushing them away. "I was just taking a break to do some mindless eating."

"Oh, I'm sorry, were you working?"

"I was, but come in." She moved back, pulling the door the rest of the way open, and after a moment of hesitation he stepped inside. "Were you looking for Josh?" she asked, pushing the door shut behind him.

"I was," he said. "It was an impulse. I was headed to the movies, and then suddenly I didn't want to go to the movies, I wanted a drink, but I didn't want to drink by myself, and I thought I'd stop and see if he was home."

Theo shook her head. "Still at work," she said. She didn't want to look at him, so she turned and headed for the kitchen. "You can have a drink here," she said over her shoulder. "I also have chips."

"I don't want to interrupt your working," he said, following her.

"You already have," she said, and then, surprised at herself, she turned and flashed him her most brilliant smile, so that he'd think she was joking when she clearly hadn't been. Why the impulse toward bitchiness? What had he done to her? "I welcome interruptions," she said.

"Me, too."

"So," she said, opening the fridge. "Beer?"

"Sure," he said.

She handed him one, found the bottle opener, and handed him that. Then she pulled down a big bowl and dumped what was left of the chips into it. Now what? She looked at him, and instead of eating or drinking he was just leaning against the counter looking at her. She gave him a nervous smile and went to get a beer for herself.

"So you're back here, too?" he asked.

"I am," she said.

"How long have you been here?"

"About a week."

"Did something go wrong with, um . . ."

"Wes," she said, though it felt strangely disloyal to tell Noah his name.

"Yeah. Weren't you staying with him?"

"I was, but it just started to seem like all that happened too fast."

Noah nodded. He drank some of his beer. He nodded, again, as if at something he was thinking, his eyes on the floor. "I'm sorry," he said. He looked up at her. "I mean, if I should be sorry."

"I don't really know," she said. "I've been trying not to think about it."

"Here's to that," he said.

"How was your weekend with Marisa? She was here last weekend, right?"

"It was not so good," he said. "We broke up."

"Oh no," she said. "Now I'm sorry."

He shrugged. "She was never coming here. No matter what she was never going to come here. I mean she's *waiting tables* there. *That's* why she has to stay in L.A."

"She lost her job?"

"She's convinced she'll get another one." He sighed. "It was never going to work out. One of us had to see that sooner or later."

"So you broke up with her?"

"No." He laughed, and then to her alarm she saw that his

eyes were filling with tears. He pressed the heel of one hand to one eye, sniffed, gave her an embarrassed, watery smile. "She broke up with me."

"Oh, Noah," she said. When a person is crying, you should go to him, but she couldn't move. She gazed at him from the other side of the room.

"It's okay," he said. He swiped at his eyes, looking around, and she grabbed the paper towel roll behind her and advanced, holding it out. He thanked her, tore a towel off slowly, wiped his eyes. "I'm embarrassed," he said.

"Don't be," she said. She was standing much closer to him now, leaning on the island, very near the bowl of chips. She had a strong, nervous urge to eat more, but you can't cram your mouth with chips in the face of someone's tears.

"I'm an idiot," he said.

"Why?"

"I've been doing this for so long. I've been dating her for seven years. What was all that time for?"

"That happens to everybody. Look at Josh."

"Has it happened to you?"

"No, I've never been with anybody that long. Not even close. But maybe something's wrong with me."

"Nothing's wrong with you," he said.

"Hmmmm," she said. "Depends on who you ask."

"Theo," he said, "I wish . . . that day at the museum . . ."

"Oh," she said. "Speaking of idiocy."

"No, no," he said. "I just wasn't sure, I didn't quite understand . . ."

"It's okay," she said.

"No, listen." He took a step toward her. "I was the idiot then, too."

She dropped her gaze, heat in her cheeks, blood in her ears, her mind a humming blank. What was happening? She couldn't see his face, her eyes on the floor, and so she just waited for him to move or speak. She'd been such a child in his presence, such a silly, yearning child, Jane Eyre with Mr. Rochester, Emma with Mr. Knightley. Theo with Mr. Garcia. She should have guessed that when, finally, he kissed her it would be in this way—him lifting her chin with his hand so that she had to meet his eyes, leaning in to kiss her as if that kiss was a gift he had to bestow. What she had been asking him for, all girlish and beseeching, he gave her at last.

Maybe it was because she'd pictured this moment so often and so long that she was having such trouble actually living it. That she seemed to be an actor in a part rather than herself. What had it been like to live in the days before the movies and TV had shown us every moment we could possibly expect to live? What had it been like when your experience actually seemed to belong to you? Noah's mouth was on her mouth. His hand had slipped from her chin to the side of her neck. Her mind was detached, but her heart was wild. He pulled back and looked at her. She didn't have to open her eyes, not having closed them. "I'm sorry," he said. He dropped his hand. "I'm sorry," he said again.

"Did I not kiss you back?" she asked.

"Um. At first I thought yes. But no, no. I don't think so."

"I'm sorry," she said. "I went out of body there for a second."

"My fault," he said.

"No, it's mine," she said, and then, to put an end to this conversation, she kissed him. Be quiet, mind. Be quiet, guilty un-certainty. Desire has its own morality. What you want you should have. What you've wanted for so long you must have wanted for a reason.

She kissed him, and then she kissed him harder. She pressed her whole body against him, because why not, why not, why not. He lifted her up and put her on the island—my God, this really was a movie, but no, don't think about that, be in the moment, he's kissing you, he's kissing you. She did her best. She wrapped her legs around him. He slid his hands under her shirt, and then he pushed her shirt up, and then he was kissing her breasts where they emerged from her bra, her fingers buried in his hair. This was what was happening.

Did she hear the door? She didn't think so, though how she could have failed to was a question that would puzzle her for quite some time. Maybe she heard it but didn't register it, con-centrating as she was on trying to enjoy kissing and being kissed, on insisting to herself that she didn't want to stop this, there was no reason to stop this, this was what she'd wanted for so god-damn long.

All she could say for sure was that she was half-naked on the kitchen island, Noah's mouth on her breasts, when she registered a sound and looked up to find her aunt staring at them. Theo froze, and then Noah jumped back wearing an almost comic ex-pression of horror. Theo yanked down her shirt.

"I'm going to go back out," Eloise said. "And pretend that didn't happen." She turned on her heel. The front door opened and closed. There was a throbbing silence. Theo didn't know what to say, or how she felt. The only emotion she could register was embarrassment.

"Wow," Noah said. "That was super awkward."

"Super awkward?" Theo repeated. There was nothing to do but laugh, so she laughed. "Did you see the look on her face?"

"Oh my God," Noah said. "I think maybe she wanted to kill me."

"Or me!"

"Now what do we do? Where did she go?"

"I don't ever want to see her again."

"No, me neither." He groaned. "I'm going to have to quit my job."

"I'm going to have to quit my family!"

The front door opened again, and they both froze. "I'm going upstairs," Eloise called, and then they heard her footsteps as she ascended.

"Thank God," Noah said. "I was thinking about running out the back door and abandoning my car."

"Where would you run to?"

"I don't know," he said. "Maybe I'd just keep running forever." He looked at her seriously after he said this, and there was some kind of apology in his expression. "Should I go?" he asked.

"I guess so," she said. "She's *my* aunt."

He nodded as if he understood what she meant by this. He hesitated, and then he leaned in and gave her a quick peck on the cheek. "I'll call you," he said.

Maybe he would call her. She went on sitting on the island after he left, unable to choose her next move. Maybe he'd call her, and he'd ask her on a date. They'd go to the movies. They'd go to Graeter's and get a sundae with two spoons. They'd go back to his place and make out on the couch. At some point she'd be sleeping in his bed, all evidence of Marisa removed from his room, boxed up, sent back, given away. The thought of all this made her very, very tired. It was like reshooting the movie with the lead actor changed. Why was it so hard to tell the difference between what you thought you wanted and what you wanted? Why did people have to be such a danger to themselves?

She had had reasons for her choices. Good reasons. Hadn't she? At this moment she couldn't recall what they had been. What she wanted was Wes. That was finally clear to her, just in time for it to be too late to matter. It seemed bizarre and fantastical that by her own volition she'd made it impossible to go straight to his apartment and climb into his bed, to lie with her head on his chest, listening to his heartbeat, that steady, persistent, essential sound. A week ago she could have done that, and now she couldn't, and that was her very own fault. How had she failed to see what luck it was to have found him, what a blessing it was to be found?

She pushed herself off the island, straightened her clothes, and went upstairs to face the judgment of her aunt.

Upstairs in her bedroom, Eloise was yanking the dirty clothes from her bag so she could replace them with clean ones. Theo appeared in the doorway, looking rather like she had all those years ago when she'd shown up in the middle of the night to confess her drunkenness. "I'm sorry," she said.

"For what?" Eloise asked irritably.

"For the scene downstairs."

"You don't have to apologize," Eloise said. "Though I'd prefer not to have seen that. Someday we'll be able to have memories erased, and I'll go get rid of that one."

"You must think I'm awful."

"Why? Because he has a girlfriend?"

"They broke up last week."

"Then why would I think you're awful? I've known for a while you had a thing for him."

"Really?"

"Sure. I could see it all over your face every time he came around. If he broke up with his girlfriend, why shouldn't you get what you want?"

Theo came into the room, a little timidly, like she thought Eloise might shoo her out again, a bothersome, naughty child. When that didn't happen she sat down on the end of the bed and looked at her hands. "I've been seeing someone. More than that—I've been living with him, up until a week ago."

"Josh told me."

"He did?"

"He sent me an email letting me know where you both were. In case I was worried."

Theo nodded.

"That's not a criticism," Eloise said, sighing, because she could see Theo had taken it as one. "I could've been in touch as easily as you. I was in kind of a state."

"Me, too," Theo said. "Except the state I was in was ignoring my life to hang out with a twenty-two-year-old."

"So you broke it off with him?"

"He said that's what I was doing, when I left his place to come back here."

"But you don't want it to be over?"

Theo sighed. "No. No, I don't. What's wrong with me that I've had such trouble deciding what I feel about someone I've been . . ." She glanced at her aunt and finished, lamely, "seeing."

Eloise shrugged. "Feelings go up and down," she said. "Feelings aren't sitting there like an object, or ticking on forward like a clock."

"I feel like I just cheated on him," Theo said. "Should I tell him? Should I apologize?"

Eloise frowned. "He thinks you broke up with him, so no," she said. "But then I'm perhaps not the person to ask."

"What do you mean?"

Eloise hesitated, but, really, what reason was there at this point not to tell her? "I cheated on Heather just a few weeks ago. Well, I guess it depends on your definition of *cheat*. I made out with this guy. She'd probably define that as cheating, so I guess I have to, too."

"Wait a minute," Theo said. "You cheated on Heather?"

"Yeah, I know, I suck. I have no excuse."

"No, I mean, you cheated on *Heather*?"

"Oh," Eloise said. She laughed. "You actually didn't know?"

Theo stood up. "She's your girlfriend?"

"Yes, she is. Everyone's been announcing that this was in no way the secret I thought it was, so I assumed I'd been equally deluded with you."

"Who's been announcing that?"

"My mother, for one. And Gary told me that Claire knew."

"Claire knew? She never said a word. What about Josh? How long has she been your girlfriend?"

"About three years. I don't know about Josh."

"Three years? I can't believe this."

"You have that in common with Heather. She's been quite put out with me."

"With good reason!"

Downstairs the front door opened and closed. Footsteps crossed the foyer. "Who is that?" Eloise asked.

"It must be Josh," Theo said. "He's been staying here, too."

"Oh," Eloise said. Then she called, "We're up here, Josh," and moments later he appeared in the doorway. He looked at his aunt, then his sister, then back at his aunt, and frowned. "What's going on?"

"She's a lesbian," Theo said.

"Huh." Josh looked at Eloise, who couldn't repress an urge to wave. "Heather?" he asked.

Eloise nodded.

"It turns out I'm not actually that surprised," Josh said.

Theo looked at him in astonishment. "Why not?"

Josh shrugged. "They spend a lot of time together."

"They're friends!"

"Well," Josh said. "There was just something."

"Just something? Why does nobody tell me about this something?"

"Simmer down, Theo," Eloise said.

"Why should I? You've been lying to us for years. You threw us out of our house."

"You're twenty-eight years old."

"It's still my house."

"Not technically. Technically it's your grandmother's house."

"You know, you were always like this," Theo said. "I'd come to you with something and you'd shrug and say, 'Ah, well,' or make some dry aside and that was all I'd get from you. I mean just today, with what happened today, all you say is, 'People screw up, get over it.' How helpful is that, Eloise? Could you have thought of anything else to say to me in the last seventeen years?"

"What happened today?" Josh asked, but they both ignored him.

"What did you want me to say?" Eloise asked.

"I don't know! Something motherly. I wanted you to be comforting. Sometimes I wanted you to tell me I'd done wrong. Or tell me what to do. Just tell me what to do! You always assumed I knew."

"You always seemed to know."

"I was eleven years old!"

"I'm not completely sure what we're talking about here," Josh said.

"I believe she's accusing me of having been an inadequate replacement for your mother."

"That's not fair," Theo said, her voice trembling. "That's totally unfair."

"How so? That's not what you were doing?"

"Guys," Josh said.

"You can't ever let me make a point!" Theo said. "You can't let me have a legitimate reason! If you can't win the argument by logic you just try to make me feel bad."

Eloise yanked open a dresser drawer and grabbed a pair of jeans. "I don't know what you're talking about," she said.

"I'm talking about the house!" Theo said. "I'm talking about the house!"

Eloise turned on her, the jeans still in her hand. "I have a legitimate reason for wanting the house. It's called 'money.' It's called the money I need and all the money I've spent. What's your logic, Theo? I want it so I should have it? I want it even though to get a job I'm going to have to move away?"

"Maybe I'm not going to move away," Theo said.

Eloise's hands were shaking as she put the jeans in her bag.

"You're not, huh. And you're not worried about what you'll have to live on? Okay, I understand you now. You don't understand the need for money, never having needed it yourself. Know why you've never needed it yourself, Theo? Because I gave it to you."

"You wish you'd never taken us," Theo said.

"Theo!" Josh said.

"You wish you'd left us with Francine and gone back to Boston. You think we ruined your life."

Eloise shook her head. She wanted to deny this. She couldn't find the words, choking on her own guilt and grief and Theo's bitterness. "Now who's trying to make the other one feel bad," she managed to say. She zipped her bag, not looking at either of them.

"Where are you going?" Josh said.

Eloise looked at him, but she could still see Theo in her peripheral vision. She could feel her there, accusation personified. "Claire has run off again, this time to your grandmother's, and your grandmother, true to form, can't handle the drama. So I'm going to get Claire. You can come if you want." As soon as she lifted the duffel bag she knew she'd packed it too heavy, but she hefted it anyway, doing her best to carry it out of the room as though it wasn't heavy at all. Her eyes were stinging. It seemed like a long way to the car.

She reached it, though, and sat inside, trying to decide how long to wait to see if either of them would follow. Josh, to come with her. Theo, to say she was sorry, she hadn't meant it, not any of it. Or, even better, wouldn't it be nice if Claire suddenly appeared from nowhere, and announced that the last couple months had been a massive practical joke? Eloise didn't want to go get her. She was afraid of a Claire who couldn't stop crying. She was afraid like she hadn't been in years, not since she'd first encountered tears and tantrums and realized with shock that now she was the one who had to know whether the child needed comfort or firmness, and if comfort, how much and if discipline, what kind and if advice, what was it? She was the one who would wear herself out with trying do the right thing and still make a great many mistakes. What had Rachel been thinking, leaving her children to Eloise?

Still in the bedroom, Josh looked at Theo, who seemed to be struggling against tears. Critical words were on his tongue, but at the sight of her face he couldn't voice them. Poor Theo. She took things so to heart, and spent so much energy trying not to show it. "Let's go with her," he said.

Theo shook her head. "I can't," she said. "I don't want to."

"Come on, Theo," he said. "Things can't go on like this."

She shook her head again. "Nobody wants me," she said, in a child's tremulous voice, and then she put her face in her hands and began to sob. She sat down hard on the bed and cried, curled in on herself. For a moment—just a moment, before he went to her and took her in his arms—Josh saw her clearly, more clearly than he had in a while, or maybe for the first time ever. She was his sister, his older sister, his role model, his judge and jury. She'd known life without him, but he'd never known it without her. She could understand him like no one else or crush him like no one else. She and Claire were the people in the world who came closest to being him. Wasn't that something to marvel at, how little DNA separated them from being each other? And yet she was a person outside all of that. She had her own secrets. She hid her own hurts. She struggled and she failed. She needed him.

He held her until her sobs diminished into sniffs, and then

he got her tissues, and ran after Eloise, who was sitting in her car staring at the house with a blank expression, not yet gone. He told her to wait for them, and then inside he packed his own bag quickly and supervised Theo, now wrung out and moving slowly, while she packed hers. Then he carried both bags to the car and opened the back door for Theo, who climbed inside without a word to Eloise and closed her eyes. It felt good to take care of people, to set his own worries aside. He offered to drive and Eloise took him up on it. "Don't worry," he said to her worried expression. "It'll be okay."

Later, after they'd stopped for dinner, with Theo asleep in the backseat, Eloise asked, "Do you feel like I didn't want you?"

He didn't, but he knew he would have told her, *no, never,* even if he did.

The car slowed for the turn onto the road through Sewanee, and Theo woke to murmuring voices, darkness, movement. Josh was talking. "I thought you just knew the place from when we all visited Francine."

"No, we came a few times when I was a kid," Eloise said. "Francine rented a house in the Assembly a couple of summers. Maybe three. Then she insisted we come visit when your mother was applying to colleges. Rachel was her good girl, you know, so Francine thought she might actually do what she wanted. She didn't even try it with me."

"I always liked coming here," Josh said.

"I liked it, too," Eloise said, "but mostly when we went for walks without Francine. I do like how peaceful it is. How little changes. It's a good place for nostalgia because everything is always the same."

"Kind of like Cincinnati."

Eloise laughed. "More actually changes in Cincinnati," she said. "Unbelievable as that is."

Theo listened with her eyes closed, resisting the urge to combat Eloise's reflexive dismissal of her city. She didn't want them to know she was awake. Why? What was she hoping to hear? Some secret they hadn't let her in on? Some life lesson? Some explanation for everything? Maybe she just liked being transported somewhere, listening to voices in the dark, memories of the sleepy arrivals of childhood.

They were silent a moment and then Josh said, "So you really think she'll call me?"

"I really think she will," Eloise said. "Or that she'd be glad if you called her."

"Thank you," Josh said, his voice heavy with emotion. And then, in a lighter tone, "But will she ever let me see her feet?"

Eloise laughed. Theo felt the pang of exclusion: They sounded so at ease with each other, so familiar, so full of immediate and intuitive understanding. While she pretended sleep in the backseat, afraid of how their tones might alter into wariness if they knew she was listening.

When the car stopped in Francine's drive and Josh turned the engine off, Theo opened her eyes. Josh turned around to see if she was awake. When he saw that she was he gave her an encouraging, reassuring smile. "Should we go in?" he said.

Eloise didn't look at Theo. She had her gaze fixed on her mother's house—small, stone, on an isolated road that curled through woods full of deer. Nothing like Francine's other house. Theo watched as Eloise opened the car door and swung herself out, moving as if against resistance.

Josh got out, and then Theo followed, the last duckling in line. What would happen when they saw Claire? Theo expected drama. She expected a return to earlier arguments, emotions lobbed like grenades. Around them the woods sang with insects. The night was so dark here, no streetlights, no city buildings. The stars were visible and bright. It felt like her sister had gone back to fairyland, and they'd followed, bound and determined to return her to the actual world.

The door to Francine's house opened and Claire stood waiting in a rectangle of light. Her too-short hair was pulled back into an unsuccessful bun, so that an electric halo of hair stuck out around her head. She wore a long, sleeveless top over leggings and as they approached Theo saw her shiver a little in the cool night air, cross her arms over herself. Her eyes were frightened. She looked like what she was, a dumb kid. A dumb kid who had no idea what she was doing.

Everyone looked at Eloise to see what she would say. But Eloise didn't say anything. She held out her arms.

22

Theo woke early to a room bright with morning light. Francine had inadequate curtains and no blinds on the windows in this room, which were small and looked out into the woods. It was the room Theo had always stayed in with Claire when they visited their grandmother, but this time she'd slept in it alone. Claire and Eloise had stayed up late talking, a conversation in which Theo hadn't felt invited or entitled to participate. Claire had been sleeping in the other guest room, and Eloise must have slept there, too.

As soon as Theo opened the door she smelled coffee and knew Francine was up. Francine was an early riser, up at 5:00 A.M. and incredulous of anyone who slept much later than that. She'd already been in bed when they arrived. Theo could smell bacon, too. When they visited, Francine always cooked breakfast as soon as she herself got up, and then left it on the kitchen counter. Soggy bacon, cold eggs, toast a little too moist with butter. Theo and Josh always dutifully heated up these offerings and ate them. Eloise would make noises of disgust, mutter about passive aggression, and leave, taking Claire with her and returning an hour later with a cardboard cup of coffee from the local café.

"I don't know how you can drink that swill she makes," she'd say to Josh and Theo as they grew older. It was true Francine's coffee was awful, and not helped by the addition of skim milk, which was the only dairy in the house. It was the gruel version of coffee. But Theo and Josh never wanted to hurt Francine's feelings, and found it unnerving that Eloise actively wanted to.

Josh was still asleep on the couch, a pillow over his head, when Theo tiptoed past. Sure enough, eggs and bacon were waiting on the counter. Theo was up so early that they were still warm. She fixed herself a plate and, steeling herself, a cup of coffee, and carried plate and mug into the dining room to find Francine. Her grandmother looked up from the paper and smiled as Theo came in. She was fully dressed in a collarless white button-down shirt and bright red pants. She wore purple glasses and dangling silver earrings, her hair in a neat white bob. "Good morning," she said. "Would you like a section?" She pushed the pile of newspaper on the table toward Theo.

"No, thanks," Theo said. She sat down and put her napkin in her lap.

"Did you sleep all right?" Francine asked.

Theo nodded, her mouth full of eggs.

"You must be tired, up this early," Francine said. "You stay up too late."

"We got in late," Theo said.

Francine pulled a face. "You always stay up late."

"I went to bed before the others," Theo said.

Francine raised her eyebrows. "You did? I thought you'd be in the thick of it. Fighting or making up or whatever you've all been doing. Having group therapy."

"No," Theo said. "They seemed to be doing fine without me."

"Hmmm," Francine said. "Is that a problem?"

Theo shrugged. She poked her eggs with her fork. Her grand-mother waited. Theo had always been careful not to let Francine elicit any criticism of Eloise from her, not once she understood what pleasure Francine took in it, and how it would sound com-ing back out of Francine's mouth as soon as Eloise gave her an opening. But it's hard not to voice our complaints about someone to a person so ready and willing to hear them. This morning Theo was unequal to the effort it would take to resist. "I don't know why she had us all come," she said. "She didn't need us at all. She and Claire could have worked it out on their own."

"So they did work it out? Claire's going back with you?"

"I'm guessing," Theo said, "based on all the apologizing she was doing, and all the comforting she was getting in return."

Francine settled back in her seat, lifting her mug from the table and looking at Theo over it. "Are you angry at both of them? Or just Eloise?"

"Both of them."

Francine looked thoughtful. "Claire I know all about. Why Eloise? Is it just about the house?"

"It's about the house. It's about a lot of things."

"Like what?"

Theo shook her head. Her grievances sounded so petty and childish when she had to voice them. She couldn't bring herself to describe how she'd felt seeing Eloise take Claire in her arms, so maternal, so forgiving, exactly the person she wasn't for Theo. "We had a fight yesterday."

"What about?"

"I guess . . . I guess about what kind of parent she was. Or wasn't."

Francine frowned. "And what kind of parent was she? Or wasn't she?"

Surprised by the sharpness in her grandmother's voice, Theo took a bite of toast instead of answering. "Busy," she finally said.

"Busy," Francine repeated. "You mean she wasn't baking you cookies and cooing over your drawings?"

Theo, stung, said, "That's not what I mean."

"You know she had to work," Francine said. "She had to support you. And even if she hadn't needed the money, why would you have wanted to take her work from her? It was what kept her going."

"I didn't—"

"Do you know you're the age she was when she inherited you? She was twenty-eight. Do you ever think about that? She was just starting her career. She was used to being responsible only for herself. You're upset about the house, and whatever else you're upset about, and I'm not saying those things don't matter, but do me a favor and imagine if you suddenly had to take care of three children, by yourself, and you had to pay for them and dress them and feed them and comfort them and encourage them and take on the utterly impossible task of replacing the two parents they've just lost. Imagine that that's what happened, and that you didn't even have your brother or sister anymore. You know what? Everything that mattered to you, just on your own, you'd have to set aside. But it's not like those things would go away. You might never finish your dissertation. That would haunt you. You'd feel like you'd failed." Francine shrugged, like none of this mattered much, despite the emotion in her voice. "You'd feel like you'd failed at a lot of things."

"I never said she failed."

"Sure, you did, or you thought it anyway. You think she failed as a mother. But imagine, right now, you're suddenly responsible for three other people. You have no idea what you're doing. There's no backup." Francine set her coffee on the table, hard, and pushed herself up to standing. "That was Eloise. She was totally alone."

Blindsided, in need of a defense, Theo said the first thing she could think of. "There was you."

Francine uttered a rueful, one-syllable laugh. "There wasn't me," she said. "I wasn't exactly mother of the year. Just ask my daughter." She moved around the table, headed in the direction of her room.

"So I can't hold anything against her?" Theo asked. "She can't ever be in the wrong?"

"I didn't say that, honey," Francine said, still walking away. "I never said that."

In early afternoon Eloise found Theo at Green's View, one of the scenic lookouts from the bluff into the valley below. They'd had a ritual of coming here when the kids were younger. After they'd arrived, before they unpacked their bags or, sometimes, even before they brought them inside, they'd walk here from Francine's, strolling down the middle of the road, spotting deer and picking wildflowers, stepping aside for slow-moving cars and pickup trucks. To look out over the world from this spot was to take a deep breath. All the movement of life was stilled into beauty. They liked it especially at night, because as city dwellers they rarely saw stars like the ones here, because at night the towns below were stars, too, a shimmering pattern of lights, natural and untroubled. When people asked Francine why she was moving back here after so many years, she'd repeatedly said, "For the view." She'd even said that to Eloise. But there were views in Cincinnati! There were views aplenty. She could have said, *Because I felt at home there, and I have never felt quite so at home, quite so much myself, anywhere else.* Eloise would have understood that, and maybe felt somewhat less angry and betrayed. Maybe not. At any rate Francine never said that. Maybe that was what she meant by *For the view.*

Theo was sitting on the grass just above where the bluff began to drop off more steeply. She had her knees up and her arms wrapped around them. As Eloise drew closer, Theo heard her feet on the gravel and turned to see who was coming. It gave Eloise a pang, how quickly Theo turned back around. "We've been looking for you," Eloise said, when she got near enough to be heard. "Everybody's ready to go."

Theo nodded, her gaze still on the valley, or maybe on the sky. "It's so pretty here," she said.

"It is," Eloise said. She sat beside Theo, a foot or so away, and mimicked her pose.

"But you never wanted to live here."

"No." Eloise shook her head. "This was Francine's place. I always thought of myself as a city mouse."

Theo gave her a sidelong glance. "And Francine's a country mouse?"

Eloise laughed. "Sort of. In her way."

"If you had lived here," Theo said, "you don't think you would have been happy?"

"I don't know," Eloise said. "Maybe. I mean, you're yourself in every place, of course, but some places bring out a better version. Or maybe not better. Maybe just the version that feels right."

"Why can't you be happy in Cincinnati?"

Eloise held her breath a moment, then let it out in a rush. "I'm going to try," she said. "Why can't you be happy anywhere else?"

Theo glanced at her again, then turned away without answering. After a moment she said, "I wasn't upset because your girlfriend was a girlfriend."

"Oh," Eloise said. "I know."

"It was because I didn't know."

"I know," Eloise said again. "I'm sorry."

"I'm glad you have somebody."

"I am, too," Eloise said. "Assuming I still do."

Theo nodded. "Assuming," she said. "Always assuming." She looked up at the sky and blew out a long breath. Then she returned her gaze to the valley. "There are a lot of places to live," she said.

"That's true." Eloise wanted to say more but chose not to push it. Theo seemed almost to be talking to herself.

"You can always come back," Theo said.

"I did," Eloise said.

"I won't fight you anymore about the house."

"Oh," Eloise said, surprised. "Thank you."

Theo was silent for what seemed like a long time. Eloise stole glances at her profile, wondering what she was thinking. Maybe that Eloise was making her miserable, wanting to sell the house, pushing her to leave. Maybe that Eloise had failed. But when Theo spoke she said nothing of failure or misery. What she said surprised Eloise so much it took her a moment to register the meaning. "Were we worth it?" Theo asked, and Eloise stared at her without speaking, Theo's long brown hair slipping out from behind her ear, the severe and vulnerable line of her part. "Were we worth all the things you gave up?"

"What do you mean?" Eloise asked.

"Even though we're fuckups?" Theo said. "Even though we're twenty-somethings who still live at home? Even though we make bad romantic choices and wallow in self-pity despite our privileges and fail at our chosen pursuits?"

"Theo," Eloise said. "I love you."

"I know you love me," Theo said. She turned and looked her aunt in the face. "I'm asking if I was worth everything you gave up. If I never finish my dissertation. If I never have a family. If I never succeed. Then you gave up your own successes so that I could fail."

"Nothing I did or didn't do is your fault," Eloise said. "I don't want you to feel like that."

"I'm asking if *you* feel like that. I'm asking if we were worth it."

Were they worth it? All the sleep she'd lost. All the *time*. All the vanished possibilities. The move home. The less prestigious job. Maybe not, if you took out emotion, if you made it a balance sheet. All those old-school feminists who warned against motherhood—they hadn't exactly been wrong. But what about Claire's childish delight in terrible jokes, the way she laughed so hard at them that Eloise laughed, too, though they weren't the least bit funny? Claire's little giggle. Claire's serious expression as she struck an arabesque in recital. The first time Josh played her a song he'd written. The delight on his face when she took him to his first concert. The way he'd call from college, a supposedly selfish teenager, and ask with genuine interest how she was. And Theo. Theo's heartbreaking efforts to always be good. Theo coming to her with a history book she'd read, wanting to discuss it.

The time when Theo, thirteen, had written her a note that said, *Thank you for taking care of us. I know sometimes it's hard.* What about all of that? What about the sublime?

"Yes, you were worth it," Eloise said. "Yes, for God's sake. Yes, you absolutely were. Unless it could bring your parents back, I wouldn't trade my time with you. I promise you. I wouldn't change my life."

It was what she had to say, of course, but she meant it. It was an enormous relief to find that she meant it, and that she could say it aloud.

23

Between Sewanee and Cincinnati there were six hours and three hundred and sixty miles, flat, unvarying interstate punctuated by Murfreesboro and Nashville, Bowling Green and Louisville. Plenty of time to talk, plenty of time to fall silent and let the car fill with the whoosh of rapid driving, or the music Josh approved. Josh pictured his grandmother's solitary figure, waving goodbye, and imagined, rightly or wrongly, that she was lonely, that she sometimes regretted choosing solitude over company. Theo thought of Francine's reproofs and Eloise's reassurances. She'd resolved, sitting on the edge of the mountain, to give up on the house, to pursue a job in earnest, to try to win back Wes, and part of her wished she could have stayed there in that spot, where those actions were just valiant resolutions, beautifully unrealized. Eloise thought of her long and tangled history with her mother, her stored-up resentment, her anger over the house, which they'd left undiscussed. To her surprise, Francine had moved, on parting, from her usual one-armed back-patting hug into a full embrace. She'd said in Eloise's ear, "Come visit me sometime on your own," and their history—that resentment, that anger, that fear of giving in to the child's longing for her mother and then finding that longing betrayed—made Eloise pull from her embrace with a quick and insincere "Sure," even as she battled the urge to cry.

Come visit me, Eloise thought now, shaking her head in bemusement. She glanced in the rearview mirror and saw Claire in the back, looking out the window, twisting a strand of hair around her finger. What would happen to her? They all, off and on, were wondering that. She said she was sorry she'd given up her spot in the company, but would they take her back? Would someone else take her? How much would she have to suffer for her mistake? They didn't ask, no one feeling the need to punish her, now that they had her back.

CINCINNATI, 100 MILES, a green sign said. They had so much to do at home. Apartments to find. Apologies and confessions to make. Jobs to apply for. Songs to write. Arguments to have. Josh would go see Adelaide when he got home, Eloise would go see Heather, and, after three days of screwing up her courage, Theo would go see Wes. But, in the car, they still didn't know what would happen, whether Heather and Wes and Adelaide would take them back, whether, if they did, they'd stay together, who would end up living where and with whom.

CINCINNATI, 7 MILES, and Eloise remembered that she hadn't paid the electric bill. She hoped when they got back the lights would still turn on. She thought of the thousand things to do in the workweek ahead, and how all she wanted was to put her arms around Heather, and how many difficult conversations might be necessary before that wish was granted. Josh, too, was thinking about work now, and Theo about her job applications, and the endless list of tasks and duties thrummed through all their heads as they drew closer and closer, these things that you could forget when you went away but rushed back in when you returned, like a swarm after you, like a normal, difficult life.

Then: The skyline. The turns they always made. The house. The front door swinging wide. Their feet on the creaky stairs. Their toothbrushes returned to their places in the bathrooms. Their own beds. They were home.

Acknowledgments

I'm enormously grateful to the people who took the time to explain their professions to me: Wendy Kline, Isaac Campos-Costero, Sylvia Sellers-Garcia, Jeremy O'Keefe, Nathaniel O'Keefe, and Sarah Hairston. Any errors are wholly mine. My thanks to my editor, Sally Kim, and my agent, Gail Hochman, who always make my books better, and to Allegra Ben-Amotz and the other good people at Touchstone. Thanks also to UC's Taft Research Center for their support and to two of my former students who helped make this book possible: Julianne Lynch, who offered invaluable edits, and Liv Stratman, who provided invaluable child care. My love and gratitude, once again and always, to my husband, Matt O'Keefe, and to the rest of my family, especially my assorted siblings: my brother Gordon Stewart and his wife, Alexis Yee-Garcia; my brothers-in-law Jeremy and Nathaniel O'Keefe; and my sister-friend, Dana O'Keefe.

About the Author

Leah Stewart is the author of the novels *Body of a Girl, The Myth of You and Me,* and *Husband and Wife*. The recipient of an NEA Literature Fellowship, she teaches in the creative writing program at the University of Cincinnati and lives in Cincinnati with her husband and two children.